D1278959

The Open Door

Beryl Matthews was born in London but now lives in Hampshire. She grew up in a family of enthusiastic readers, and books have always been a very important part of her life. As a young girl her ambition was to become a professional singer, but lack of funds drove her into an office, where she worked her way up from tea-girl to credit controller. Her hobbies are writing, reading, swimming and golf. Writing takes priority though, and everything else has to wait.

THE OPEN DOOR

Beryl Matthews

This first hardcover edition published in Great Britain 2004 by
SEVERN HOUSE PUBLISHERS LTD of
9–15 High Street, Sutton, Surrey SM1 1DF,
by arrangement with Penguin Books Ltd.

British Library Cataloguing in Publication Data

Matthews, Beryl
    The open door
    1.   Young women - England - Fiction
    2.   London (England) - Social life and customs - Fiction
    I.   Title
    823.9'2 [F]

    ISBN 0-7278-6081-X

Printed and bound in Great Britain by
MPG Books Ltd., Bodmin, Cornwall.

' . . . behold, I have set before thee an open door, and no man can shut it: . . .'

Revelation 3:8

I

Bermondsey, London. September 1913

The door across the street opened and Rose caught a glimpse inside the house; the walls had colourful paper on them and the furniture gleamed from continual polishing. She let out a ragged sigh. How she longed to be clean! She continued to gaze at the posh houses and felt anger rise inside her. Why did some people live in comfort and ease, and others, like herself, in squalor?

She was a seething mass of questions. Her whole life she'd been asking, Why? Her search for knowledge was like a living thing inside her, never giving her any peace. Everyone kept telling her she was only a child and shouldn't bother with things nobody could understand, and it was useless asking questions at home because all it ever got her was a clip round the ear. School was different, though. She smiled when she thought about it. She might be only eleven but she was clever, her teacher said so. She soaked up knowledge, but was never satisfied – Miss Gardner had to push her out when the bell rang. 'Rose,' she'd say, taking from her whatever book she was reading, 'go home, child.'

'Can I take it with me?' she would plead. 'I'll take good care of it, Miss.'

But the answer was always the same, it was not allowed, so she would try to sneak into a bookshop without anyone seeing. If she was lucky, she could huddle in a corner and read for half an hour or so, but if she was spotted she was thrown out. Today she'd hardly set foot inside the door before she was marched out again.

It made her so cross. Just because she was shabby, they thought she was up to no good – but she wasn't and she'd fight anyone who said she was. All she wanted to do was look at the books: there were rows and rows of them in there and it was like heaven to her.

Her dark, resentful eyes swept over a well-dressed couple. The man waved a hand angrily and shouted at her to go away, but she ignored him. The only difference between her and them was that they had money and she didn't.

She looked down at her worn frock and ground her teeth. One day things would be different.

'What are you up to?' a stern voice asked.

'Nothing,' she replied, looking the policeman straight in the eyes. 'They needn't worry over there, I'm not dangerous,' she said, cheekily, and saw surprise in his eyes: she knew how to speak properly – every day she listened to her teacher and copied her.

'What are you doing round here?'

'Just looking. You can't arrest me for that, can you?' Again her gaze was direct; she had learnt early that it was a weakness to show fear.

'Where do you live?' he persisted.

'Over there.' She pointed across the river. 'Garrett Street.'

He stroked his chin thoughtfully. 'I'd better walk you back.'

Her laugh was scornful. 'You new around here?

Someone should've told you that the coppers have to come down our street in threes.'

'Oh, and why is that?'

'Because our filthy, rat-infested hovels are full of bullies who don't want the police to know what they're up to. They must be a couple of hundred years old and should have been pulled down long ago.'

'Well, you'd better be getting home. Your folks will be worried about you.'

She gave him a pitying look and lapsed back into the London twang. 'What makes you think they care tuppence about me?'

His smile was tinged with sadness. 'What's your name?'

'Emily Rose, but everybody calls me Rose, when they're being polite.'

'And what do they call you when they're being rude?'

'"That black-eyed bitch," among other things.' Her eyes flashed like jet, defying him to laugh.

There was a shout from across the street. 'Constable, send her away. She belongs round the docks with the others of her kind. This is a respectable area.'

The policeman raised his hand in acknowledgement, and turned to the girl beside him. 'You'd better go.'

'What's he talking about?' she demanded.

'He . . . um . . . thinks you're older than you are.'

'Older?' It took a few moments for his meaning to sink in, then she started across the road with a growl, but the policeman caught her and held her back.

'Oh, no, you don't.'

Rose tore herself free and glared at him. 'He's calling me a tart! You should have let me at him – he deserves a thrashing for that.'

'Do your duty, constable,' the man called, from a safe distance.

'It's all right, sir, she's only a child.'

The man laughed. 'Is that what she's telling you?'

Rose swore and started across the road again, but the policeman held on to her.

'Let me go!' she demanded. 'He's calling me a liar now.'

'Well, to be honest, you don't look like a child,' he said, slackening his grip slightly. 'And with your black hair and foreign looks, you're already a pretty girl.'

'Even with the dirt?' she sneered.

'Your clothes have seen better days, but you're clean enough.'

At that Rose felt a little better and smoothed down her frock. At least her efforts to stay clean had not been in vain.

'Off you go, Rose, and don't come here again, will you?'

'I got as much right as anyone else to go where I want. That man might own a big fancy house but he don't own the street.'

'That's true, but you're not welcome in this part of town.'

She glowered. 'Well, some day I'm gonna change that.'

As she turned away she heard him mutter, 'Poor little sod.'

Rose spun back, flushed with anger. 'Keep your pity, Mister, because one day I'm going to be living like them over there – you see if I'm not!' Then, fists clenched in determination, she turned and ran across the bridge.

*

4

'Rose! Where've you been? Come and get the kids their tea.'

She stopped, one foot on the stairs. She had been about to make her getaway to an empty space somewhere. She'd found a whole page of a newspaper today and wanted to read it. It was a rare prize, so her visit to posher parts had been worth while.

'Rose!'

She sighed, folded the paper carefully, then slipped it into her pocket. It would have to wait until later.

In the scullery it was bedlam. 'Quiet!' she yelled.

The noise stopped instantly and six pairs of eyes, ranging from blue to hazel, turned in her direction. She stared at the children, defying them to speak, then said, 'Sit at the table.'

They scrambled on to the chairs, but eight-year-old Bob scowled. He was a bully, just like his father, but he knew better than to try to beat Rose.

Her mother put a large bowl of dripping on the table and a loaf of bread. 'When they've had their tea, put them to bed.'

'Why me?' she protested. 'Why can't Flo take a turn?'

'Because you're the oldest.'

Rose began to cut thick slices of bread and spread them with dripping. It was useless arguing. It never got her anywhere because her mother was too worn out with trying to look after them all. She cast her a worried glance. She was having another baby. Where the blazes were they going to put it? The house was already full to bursting.

A little hand came out and tried to take a slice. She slapped it away and made the mistake of looking at their expectant faces. The scene tugged at her heart – six little urchins with grubby faces and empty bellies. She tried to be hard, she really did, because turning off her emotions was the only way she could stand this hell, but this wasn't right!

Diving down to the bottom of the dripping bowl, she scraped out some of the rich dark jelly and spread a little on each slice of bread, then handed it round and watched the kids eat like wolves – except the youngest, Annie, who was too small to manage the big chunk of bread.

Rose squatted beside her and started to break it into smaller pieces. 'Come on, Annie,' she coaxed, 'eat it.'

'I'll have it if she don't want it.' Bob made a grab for it, but Rose was too quick for him.

'Leave it alone, you greedy pig,' she scolded, then turned back to Annie. She didn't like the look of her: the child's face was so white that her skin looked almost transparent. Annie was the only one of her brothers and sisters Rose worried about: at two, she couldn't talk properly, or walk, and Rose doubted that she would live very long.

'Mum?' Rose went to stand next to her mother, who was at the stove, stirring a pot. 'What you cooking?'

'Scrag-end of beef with dumplings.'

It smelt delicious and Rose's stomach grumbled. 'Can I have some of the gravy for Annie?'

'This is for your dad.'

'I know, but Annie's sick and she needs proper food. It isn't right he gets a dinner at night and everyone else gets next to nothing.'

'I do the best I can, but you know how the old man gets into a rage if he doesn't have his meat and gravy.'

Rose bit back angry words and glanced at her mother's rounded stomach. 'Why do you keep having kids?' she asked, her lip curling with distaste.

'Because that's the way it is. We have to accept our lot in life.'

Why? Rose wanted to shout, but knew she'd be wasting her breath. She took another quick look at Annie, who had eaten a little of her bread. 'What about that gravy, Mum?'

'All right, then, just a little.' Her mother ladled some into a plate. 'Annie does look sick. It's not that I don't care,' she protested, 'but your dad must come first. We'd be in a right pickle without him.'

Rose took the plate and said nothing. As far as she could make out, he never did anything for them. He drank too much and got nasty with a few pints inside him.

She soaked the rest of Annie's bread in the gravy and was relieved when the little girl ate it. Then she swept her sister up in her arms. 'Come on, let's get you into bed. I'll try and get you an apple tomorrow, shall I?' she whispered. 'Our secret, eh?'

Rose spat on the flat iron and watched it sizzle.

'What's she doing that for?'

She kept her head down and concentrated on her ironing. She hated the way he never spoke to her directly.

'Answer your dad,' her mother said sharply.

'It's the school prize-giving tomorrow.' Rose ironed carefully around a patch on the skirt of her frock.

'Ha! Thinks she gonna win somefing, does she?'

'Yes, I do.' She put the iron back on the stove, picked

up another and spat on it. She wasn't ashamed of being clever, and that probably made him madder because he couldn't even write his name.

'How did you ever have a kid like that?' he yelled at her mother now. 'Look at her, she's like a bleeding cuckoo in the nest.'

'She likes learning,' her mother defended Rose weakly. 'There's no shame in that.'

Rose shut out the talk: it was best not to listen to his ranting. She put down the iron, held up the frock and examined it critically. It was too old to do much with, but at least it was clean and pressed.

'Look at her, putting on airs and graces. She thinks she's too good for us.'

I might have to live in this place, Rose declared silently, but inside I'm different. She sighed.

Her father pushed his chair back from the table. 'Where's your purse, Marj? I need some beer money.'

'I haven't got any. I spent the last on your dinner tonight.'

'I don't believe you, woman. Give me your purse.'

Marj pulled it out of the pocket of her pinny. He snatched it and tipped out the contents on to the table. 'A penny!' he bellowed. 'How am I going to have a night out with that?'

'It's all I've got.'

With a snarl, he pocketed the coin and stormed out of the house.

'Oh, Mum,' Rose muttered, 'how you going to get by?'

'I don't let him know everything. I've got a few pennies put aside and I'll get some oxtail tomorrow and give you all a treat for your tea. You're right about Annie, she's looking peaky, but so are you all.' She sat down heavily. 'I haven't being paying much notice just lately – this baby's draining me.'

'I'm not going to get married and have squalling babies when I'm grown-up,' Rose declared.

Her mother gave a rare smile. 'That won't be easy, my girl, because you're going to be quite a beauty. The men are going to chase after you in packs.'

'They'll be wasting their time,' Rose said confidently. Then something occurred to her. 'Mum, why am I so dark?'

'Well . . .' her mother seemed to be searching for words ' . . . you take after my mother's side of the family, I expect. We've got Italian blood and it's come through in you.'

'What were they like?'

'I don't know. I never knew any of them.' Marj hauled herself to her feet. 'I'm going to have a rest.'

As their mother left the scullery Flo wandered in. 'Anything to eat?' she asked.

'Only bread and dripping.' Rose pushed the bowl towards her sister. Let the lazy devil do it herself.

Flo grumbled a bit, then sat down and started to eat.

'Flo?'

'What?'

'Can I wear the good boots tomorrow?'

'No, they're mine.' Flo spread more dripping on her bread.

'Oh, go on,' Rose pleaded. 'It's the school prize-giving and I want to look nice. You can wear mine for a day, can't you?'

'They've got holes in. What if it rains?'

'It won't rain. Anyway, I've put some thick cardboard in them.'

'I dunno.'

'I'll get you an apple tomorrow if you let me have them.' Rose was sure she could bribe her sister.

'Where you gonna get that from?' Flo was suddenly interested.

'That's my secret.'

'How many can you get?'

'Two or three.' She hoped.

Flo considered. 'I'll let you wear them for two apples,' she said.

'Don't be greedy!'

'Oh, all right.'

At nine o'clock that evening Rose crept out of the house and ran across the bridge. As she made her way round to the back of the big houses, she shivered in the fading light. Then she pulled herself together and told herself sternly that she needn't be frightened about taking a few apples from these people because they already had more than they could eat. However, that didn't ease her conscience, which was surprising: you didn't find much honesty in Garrett Street.

She reached the garden where she'd seen the fruit trees; they'd been loaded with apples the other week and she hoped they still were. She took a deep breath, pulled herself to the top of the wall and peered into the deepening gloom but could not see if the fruit was still there. She'd have to go over and take a closer look. Hoping the owners didn't have a dog, she jumped down from the wall and crept towards the tree. The apples were still there.

She grasped a low branch, pulled herself up, careful to keep the trunk between herself and the house, she removed three large apples, hesitated, then took another. They'd never miss it.

She shoved the fruit into the bag she'd brought with her, scrambled down and ran for the wall. She scaled it rapidly and then, her heart beating wildly, she ran back across the bridge and headed for the alley behind the row of shops at the top of her street. It was dark now but she knew how to get to her secret hiding place. The cobbler's yard was full of junk piled up against a wall, and she heaved aside an old mattress to reveal a small, sturdy cupboard. She put the apples inside then replaced the mattress, making sure it covered the cupboard. They would be safe in there from man or rodent until tomorrow. Then Rose ran into Garrett Street and laughed as she remembered the man who had insulted her today: she hoped it had been his apples she'd pinched.

2

Rose wished they'd get on with it.

She tried not to fidget or kick off Flo's boots because she might not be able to get them on again, and she didn't want to go barefoot to collect her prize.

She was going to win, she kept telling herself. She was always top of her class – but was she top of the school? Doubt crept in and she looked down at the floor to hide her expression: she didn't like people to see what she was thinking. Then her head came up again. Of course she was good enough to come first.

Her gaze locked on the prize and her heart nearly burst with yearning. She wanted it so much!

The Head, Mr Spencer, stood up and banged on the table for quiet. A couple of small prizes were presented, but Rose wasn't interested in them; there was only one thing on that table she wanted.

'And now we come to the top award,' the Head said, looking around the room. 'This is a special prize for the pupil who did best in all subjects.'

Rose was almost afraid to breathe. He was droning on about excellence, or some such thing, but her ears were tuned for only one thing: her name.

'And the winner is . . . Emily Rose Webster.'

The long-held breath whooshed out of her lungs.

'Emily,' the Head actually smiled, 'come and receive your prize.'

She was on her feet immediately, the pinching boots forgotten in her excitement.

'Well done, Emily. I want you to come and see me at the close of school today.' He held out the prize.

Her hands closed eagerly around the beautiful Bible. This was the best thing she had ever had in her life, a treasure beyond her wildest dreams. It was black, real leather, she was sure, with gold lettering, and it was just the right size to fit into the large patch pocket on her dress. She could keep it with her all the time.

'I hope you're going to read it,' he said, smiling again.

'Oh, I will, sir. I've already learned quite a lot of it. Miss Gardner lets me read it at break-time.'

'That's right, Mr Spencer,' Miss Gardner told him from her seat on the platform, 'I've never met a girl with such a thirst for knowledge.'

Rose looked at her teacher with affection. Miss Gardner was quite young, around twenty-three, Rose thought. She had grey eyes, shiny brown hair, and always looked so clean and tidy. She was a good teacher and answered Rose's questions patiently.

The Head smiled at Rose again. 'Don't you go and play during the free time?'

'No, sir, I'd rather read.' She had no interest in games; all she needed was between the covers of books.

For the rest of the day the precious Bible was never out of her sight, and at the end of lessons, Miss Gardner gave her a bag to put it in. 'That will keep it clean.'

'Thank you, Miss.'

Miss Gardner looked at the clock. 'You'd better go and see the Head now.'

Rose made her way along the corridor. On reaching

the door marked 'Mr Spencer', she knocked and waited. She was a little worried because you were only called to his office when you'd done something wrong.

'Come,' he called.

She stood in front of the desk, wondering what he could want with her.

'Emily, you've done remarkably well this year and shown a love of learning that is unusual . . .' He hesitated and looked at her closely. 'We have decided to offer you the chance of a free place at the secondary school.'

The big school! Her eyes opened wide. 'Thank you, sir – '

He held up his hand to stop her. 'You must ask your family first, because although they won't have to pay the fees, they will have other expenses. It will mean new clothes, and books.'

Her spirits sank. Then she rallied. This was her chance – she couldn't let it go. 'I'll ask them, sir, but I'm sure everything will be all right.'

He nodded gravely. 'You must let me have your decision by tomorrow morning. The place will be given to someone else if you are unable to take it.'

'You won't have to do that, sir.' She spoke with a confidence she wasn't feeling.

'I hope you're right. Now, off you go, and see me first thing in the morning.'

She hurried away, her mind in turmoil. The chances of her taking up this place at the big school were slim, but she *had* to try.

'Did you win?' her mother asked, as she walked into the scullery.

'Yes.' She held out the book. 'Isn't it lovely? The Head's signed it.'

'Very nice, Rosie.' Her mother put plates on to the scrubbed wooden table. 'Something to be proud of, eh?'

Rose nodded. Today had been the best day of her life. Suddenly she became aware that the room was silent. A quick look told her that the children were already sitting at the table, waiting expectantly for their tea.

'What a lovely book,' Nancy whispered.

'Have you got clean hands?' Rose asked the timid seven-year-old, who was gazing at her with big blue eyes.

Nancy held them out for inspection and Rose placed the book in front of her, knowing it would be quite safe with Nancy. Then she turned back to her mother. 'Something smells good.'

'I got a nice bit of oxtail cheap – the butcher was about to close.'

Rose helped to dish up the food then sat next to Annie and started to feed her. Their mum had done well today – there was even some potato in it. When she saw how much Annie was enjoying it, Rose spooned some potato from her plate on to the little girl's.

'Rose!' her mother scolded. 'You need that just as much as she does.'

'I'm fine, Mum, you know I get the free dinner at school.'

'What did you have today?'

'Bowl of pea soup, chunk of bread, semolina pudding. It's much the same every day.'

Marj looked at her daughter intently. 'Does it shame you that you have to have the dinner provided for the poor kids?'

Rose shook her head. 'I don't care what other people think. If they want to make fun of us because we're poor, it's up to them.'

'You've a strange way of thinking. I can't make head nor tail of you sometimes.'

With a shrug and a grin Rose turned back to Annie. 'You eat that all up,' she coaxed, 'and then you can have our secret.'

Annie giggled and obediently swallowed her food.

Flo rushed in, late as usual, and quickly cleared her plate. Then she looked at Rose. 'You get it?'

'Of course, top prize,' she said, her dark eyes glinting with devilment.

'You know I didn't mean that.' Flo kicked the leg of her chair impatiently.

'Oh, I thought you did,' Rose teased.

'I know all about it, silly! I was in the hall when you got it, wasn't I? We're sick of hearing how clever you are. Our teacher's been bleating about it all day, and I got fed up and told her you was wearing my boots.'

Rose tried to keep a straight face. 'And did you tell her what you were charging me?'

Flo laughed. 'Not likely, 'cos she started to tell the class what an example the Webster girls were, one clever, the other generous and kind, and I wasn't going to do nothing to change her mind.'

'I'll bet you weren't,' Rose muttered.

'So, did you get them?' Flo persisted.

Rose picked up the bag she had collected from its hiding place on her way home from school, took out an apple and gave it to her sister, who disappeared to eat it in peace.

'You got any more?' Bob eyed the bag greedily.

She took out another and carefully cut it into identical pieces, then handed them round.

'Flo got a whole one,' the boy complained.

'She let me wear her boots today and that was her reward, but,' she flashed him a stern look, 'if you don't want your piece I'm sure one of the others will eat it.'

He snatched it up and headed for the door.

She heard her mother sigh. 'That boy doesn't know when to be grateful.'

Because he's the image of his dad, Rose thought. 'All the others are enjoying it, aren't you?' she asked, glancing around the table at the children who nodded, their mouths full of apple. 'And you won't mind if I give Annie a whole one, will you?'

'No,' they all said together.

'She looks poorly,' Will said quietly. He was only six, but he seemed to understand about other people's troubles.

She cut an apple into small pieces for Annie.

'Where did you get them from?' her mother asked.

'I went scrumping.' She held out the last apple. 'This one's for you.'

'Oh, you shouldn't have done that. I wouldn't like to see you get into trouble with the law. We get enough of that with your dad – and, anyway,' she waved aside the apple, 'you should keep it for yourself.'

'No, you need it more than I do, and I can have a bit of Annie's. I don't think she'll eat it all.'

Her mother nodded. 'She don't look good, does she?'

'Can't we get a doctor to look at her?'

'I wish we could, but where are we going to get the money from? Doctors don't come cheap.'

Neither do posh schools, Rose thought, with a sinking heart. She turned back to Annie, and was pleased to see she'd eaten more than half of her apple. 'Was it nice?' she asked, wiping the sticky fingers with a rag.

Annie pushed the rest of the fruit towards Rose. 'You,' she said, quite clearly.

'Sure you've had enough?'

''Nough.' Her pale face was showing a bit of colour.

'Goodness,' Marj said, surprised, 'she's trying to talk.'

Rose popped the remains of the apple into her mouth and picked up Annie. 'And at her age she should be running around.'

'Some kids are more forward than others. She's like you, a thinker.'

'Hmm, don't know how you can tell that,' Rose said, as Annie laid her head on her shoulder.

'She's the same as you when you were born. You didn't say much at first, but your eyes were always alert and following what was going on, taking everything in.'

Rose laughed loudly. 'I can't imagine me being quiet.'

'Well,' her mother grinned, 'it didn't last long. As soon as you could talk you never stopped asking questions.'

'I have a job getting answers, though, don't I?' Rose couldn't help pointing out.

'That's because you're asking the wrong people. We don't know nothing around here,' her mother said, resignedly.

'I must have got my brains from someone and they didn't come from Dad.'

Her mother looked at the apple in her hand and said nothing.

'You make sure you eat that,' Rose said sternly. 'Don't go giving it to the old man.'

'I won't. He wouldn't appreciate it anyway – it hasn't got hops in it.' She pulled a comical face, and Rose laughed. It was good to see her mother relax.

Rose stood up and brushed back her hair. He must have finished his dinner by now. She braced herself and walked into the scullery.

'Rosie came top of the school today,' her mother said, unable to hide her pride.

'Humph!' was the only response from the man sitting at the table.

'Yes,' Marj continued undeterred, 'and they've given her a Bible.'

That caught his attention. 'Where is it? Might be able to get a few pennies for it.'

Rose's heart leaped in alarm. Thank goodness she'd hidden it.

'Who do we know who'd pay good money for a Bible or any other book? Not many around here can even read,' her mother pointed out.

'Why couldn't they have given her something we could flog?' Without waiting for an answer, he got to his feet. 'I'm off down the pub.'

'But you haven't got any money,' her mother said.

'Yes, I have.'

'Then you'd better give me some for food.'

He counted out a few pennies, careful not to let them see just how much he had.

A glimmer of hope grew inside Rose. Where he'd got the money from she didn't know or care, but he was in a better mood tonight. This was her chance.

'I've been offered a free place in the big school,' she blurted out. 'I'll be able to learn to type and get a job in an office afterwards.'

'No!' The refusal was instant.

'But, Dad – '

'I said no.' He turned to her mother. 'Her and her high and mighty ideas! How does she think we're going to pay for her to go to a posh school?'

'We might be – '

'Don't be daft, woman,' he cut in. 'You won't get a farthing from me. I don't even have to have her under my roof, you know that, Marj.'

He stormed out and her mother sat down with a stricken look on her face.

Rose felt her dreams tumble like the walls of Jericho. 'Why does he hate me?'

'He doesn't – '

'Come on, Mum, you know he does, and what did he mean about not having to keep me?'

'Don't take any notice of that. You know he talks a lot of rubbish when he's had a few pints.'

Rose eyed her mother. She was hiding something. 'He was dead sober when he said it, Mum.'

Her mother fiddled with the teapot.

Rose didn't like this. She could usually talk openly with her mother and she'd never considered her secretive. What was this all about? 'Tell me why he said he didn't have to keep me, Mum.'

'Well . . .' Marj lowered her head, then drew in a shaky

breath and looked up at her daughter. 'I suppose you're old enough to know, and it's better I tell you than someone else. You're not his child. I was expecting when I met him and he took me in.' She looked at Rose imploringly. 'I didn't have no choice. It was that or the workhouse.'

So she was a bastard. Shame and fury raged through Rose. 'Who is my father?' she asked, after a long pause.

'I can't tell you.' A tear trickled down her mother's cheek. 'I'm so sorry, Rosie.'

'Don't upset yourself, Mum, I'm strong enough to survive anything,' Rose said gently.

'I know you are, but I hate to hurt you.'

'It's not your fault.' Rose couldn't believe she was talking so calmly when she was boiling with rage inside, but she didn't want to distress her mother any further.

'I was taken advantage of, then turned out. I was innocent and too trusting.' Marj wiped her eyes on her pinny.

'Tell me who he is,' Rose said, 'and I'll go and teach him a lesson.'

'That's what I'm afraid of. You've got his quick temper.'

'And his looks?' Now she understood why she was so different.

Marj Webster nodded.

'I see. Was he tall?'

'A giant of a man.' Her mother clasped and unclasped her hands. 'More than six foot.'

'Does he still live in London?' Rose asked, even though she knew her mother didn't want to say any more.

'How do you know he comes from London?'

'Because you've never been anywhere else, have you?'

'You've got a mind like a razor.' Her mother sighed.

'A bit like him?' Rose asked, but that was all the information she was going to get because her mother had closed her mouth tightly. Still, she'd found out quite a lot.

'About that school . . .' Her mother blew her nose.

'I know – it's impossible.' That admission nearly tore Rose apart.

'If I had any money I'd see you went, but I can't do it on my own, not even if I took in more washing.'

'You're not to do that! You're working yourself to death as it is, Mum.'

'But you've worked so hard for this chance.' Her mother was on the verge of tears.

'There'll be other chances.'

But inside Rose was screaming at the injustice of it all. No one was going to know that, though.

3

'Come.'

Rose turned the door handle, stepped into Mr Spencer's office and waited for him to finish what he was doing.

'What did your family say?' he asked.

'Can't take it, sir.' She spoke clearly, but it was an effort to keep her voice steady.

'Is there no way?' he asked kindly.

'Only if I don't have to have new clothes.'

'I'm afraid you have to be dressed the same as the other pupils. It's a rule of the school.'

'Would they give me time?' Rose was grasping at any straw. 'I might be able to get a weekend job and buy the things bit by bit.'

'No, Emily. You wouldn't be allowed to do that.'

'No, of course not, sir.' She had already known it wouldn't be possible, but she'd had to try, hadn't she? Had to make one last effort not to let this chance slip away, but it was hopeless and she felt bereaved.

'I'm sorry you can't take the place because you deserved this opportunity.' He stood up, turned his back to her and gazed out of the window.

When he didn't say anything for some time, Rose began to fidget: she didn't want to miss her lessons. Should she go? But he hadn't dismissed her. 'Can I go, sir? Class will have started.'

He turned back to her. 'I'm afraid you'll have to leave, Emily.'

'Begging your pardon, sir?'

'You will have to leave,' he repeated.

'Leave?' The word came out in a strangled squeak.

Mr Spencer nodded. 'I'm sorry. I know how much you like school.'

Like it? It was her whole world. 'But why?'

'We can't teach you any more here.'

'Yes, you can! I've got lots to learn. I don't know nearly enough . . .' She ground to a halt as her voice wavered.

'Emily.' He came and sat on the edge of the desk in front of her. 'You're always the first with your hand up, you know all the answers and you're way ahead of the others.'

'It doesn't matter. Don't make me leave, sir. I'll sit at the back of the class. I won't answer any questions. I don't mind doing the same lessons again.' She stopped to take a breath. 'Don't make me leave,' she whispered, her voice breaking. 'I'm only eleven.'

He straightened up and said briskly, 'The decision has been taken.'

Rose struggled to pull herself together. She had been making an exhibition of herself, she saw. She would never lower herself to behave like that again. Whatever disappointments she had to face in the future, she would *never* beg for anything again.

'When do you want me to go?'

'At once.'

The two words sliced through her like a knife and she opened her mouth to ask if she could stay until the end of term, but closed it again. No more pleading.

24

'You might as well have your dinner before you leave.'

Semolina pudding would choke her today, she thought, and her stomach heaved. What was she going to do? No more books, no more learning.

'You may go now.'

'Goodbye, sir.'

'Rose!' Miss Gardner was hurrying towards her. 'What are you doing in here? I've been looking for you everywhere.'

Rose was in a small classroom where they taught the six-year-olds, huddled on one of the tiny seats, her knees sticking up above the desk. It had been the first quiet place she had seen after leaving Mr Spencer's office, and she had slunk in to lick her wounds like an injured animal.

'Have you had your dinner?'

Rose looked up blankly and shook her head.

'Well, don't bother. We'll go into the park and you can share my sandwiches. I want to talk to you.'

Rose unwound herself from the small bench and stood up.

'Come along. Let's find a seat in the sun.'

It was a lovely day. Rose turned her face to the sun's warmth and closed her eyes, feeling bewildered and numb. Then she opened them and watched her teacher spread out a cloth on the seat. 'There we are, plenty for both of us.'

The food looked delicious, but Rose wasn't sure she could eat anything today. It was the worst kind of nightmare and something she had not thought to face for two or three years.

She knew some children left at twelve or thirteen, but

she had always hoped she would be able to find a way to stay on.

'Try to eat, Rose,' Miss Gardner said. 'I know you've had a shock, but there might be something we can do about it.'

'I don't see how. My dad won't hear of it.'

'I guessed this might happen. What are you going to do, Rose?'

She shrugged and bit into a sandwich. She had decided she was hungry after all. She made sure she swallowed before she spoke. 'Suppose I'll get a job.'

'Hmm. Children as young as you shouldn't have to work.'

'I don't have no choice.'

'You do not have a choice,' her teacher corrected, 'no double negatives, remember?'

'Sorry, Miss Gardner, I forgot.' Rose's eyes filled with tears, and she fought for control. 'I'm going to forget everything, aren't I?'

'Not if I can help it.' She handed Rose a banana. 'My intended is a teacher at the secondary school – '

'You getting married?' Rose interrupted, looking at her teacher with fresh eyes. She'd thought she had more sense than that.

Miss Gardner nodded. 'Some time, but we haven't decided when. Now, as I was saying, he would be willing to take you for lessons on a Sunday afternoon.'

'Oh.' Rose didn't know what else to say – she was having a job taking all this in. Why would a stranger want to teach her?

'So, what do you think, Rose? Would you like Mr Trenchard to help you?'

She nodded wordlessly, and tears welled in her eyes again. Lessons!

'Could you get away from your family for a couple of hours, or do you have to look after the children?'

'Sunday's all right,' Rose told her, excited now that the offer had finally sunk in. Then her expression clouded. 'But I can't afford to pay anything.'

'He doesn't want payment. I've told him all about you and he'll teach you for nothing, as long as you're willing to work hard.'

'Oh, I will, I will!' she cried, leaping to her feet. 'He won't be sorry, you'll see.'

Miss Gardner laughed at her joy. 'That's what I told him. Would you be able to start this Sunday at three o'clock?'

'Yes, please. Where?'

'At my house.' Miss Gardner took out a piece of paper and wrote down her address. 'That's where I live. Do you know the street?'

'I think so. It's on the other side of the park, isn't it?'

'That's right. You'll need to take the number five bus and it will drop you right at my door.'

'I can walk.' It was less than ten minutes on the bus and she was used to walking everywhere.

'No, Rose, it's a long way. Here.' Miss Gardner opened her purse and gave her a penny. 'Take that for your fare.'

'I couldn't, not after everything you're doing for me.'

'Of course you can.' Miss Gardner tucked the coin into Rose's pocket. 'Mr Trenchard will be waiting for you on Sunday. Try not to be late.'

'I won't.' Nothing in this world was going to keep her away from her lessons.

'There's one more sandwich left and you'd better take it with you.'

Rose accepted the packet and slipped it into her pocket with the banana – an unheard-of luxury. After that exciting news she was hungry enough now to eat it all herself, but she would save it for Annie.

As wonderful as the thought of the Sunday lessons was, it still hurt to know that she couldn't go to school any more. Still, she had been given a chance to carry on learning and that was something to be grateful for. A couple of hours a week was better than nothing, and Mr Trenchard must be good if he taught at the big school. She pushed away her gloom and began to wonder what exciting things he was going to show her.

She wandered along for a while, deep in thought, until she found herself in front of a church, its door wide open. She didn't want to go home so she decided to go in and read her Bible, which she had kept with her since she'd been given it. She settled on one of the pews, gazed around for some moments, then opened it.

'Are you lost?' A man in a flowing black coat came and sat beside her.

'No.' She smiled. 'I saw the door open and thought I'd come in and read for a while.'

He glanced at the book in her hands. 'Where did you get that?'

'It's mine,' she told him, wondering why everyone jumped to the conclusion that she was dishonest. Being poor didn't mean you were a thief. 'Look, it's got my name in it, see? I won it for coming top of the school.'

'And why aren't you at school today?'

'Because they've made me leave. I had the chance of

a free place at the secondary school, but I couldn't take it because we're too poor. The Head said they couldn't teach me any more and I had to go.'

'How old are you?' the man asked.

'Eleven.' Rose looked at him carefully. Perhaps he could answer some of her questions? 'Why do some people have so much and others, like me, can't even afford a few new clothes to go to another school? It doesn't seem right,' she said.

'There have always been the poor and the rich.' He pointed to the Bible she was clutching. 'If you read that you'll see it's so.'

'I have read it,' she told him indignantly.

He gave a smile of disbelief. 'Right through?'

'Yes, every single word, and I've started on it for the second time, but it only makes me want to ask more questions. I still can't understand why some people are rich and others poor.'

'It's just the way things are. We have to accept our lot in life.'

Rose snorted. She was sick and tired of hearing that. She held out the Bible. 'Show me where it says that in here. I've never seen it, and look at this.' She flicked over the pages until she found the place she wanted. '"God is love." If that's true, it doesn't make sense that some people don't know where the next meal is coming from, does it? If you love someone you don't try to hurt them, do you?'

He patted her hand. 'You're too young to understand these things yet. You'll know more when you get older.'

'Well, you're older,' she said rudely, 'so why can't you tell me?'

'We're not here to question the wisdom of God.'

'Why not?' She turned the pages again, looking for a well-known passage. When she'd found it she held it out. 'It says here, "Come now, and let us reason together, saith the Lord." I know what "reason" means – I looked it up in the dictionary at school. Why can't I ask questions?'

He stood up, clearly having had enough of her. 'You don't know what you're saying, child. God has His own purpose for each of us and we must be satisfied with that.'

She looked at him suspiciously. He didn't seem to have the answer to anything. 'Are you a priest?'

'No, I'm the verger.'

'What's that?'

'I take care of the church and assist at services.' Before she could ask anything else, he turned and hurried back to his duties.

She watched him walk away, disappointed that he hadn't been able to answer her questions. But that was nothing new, was it?

On the way home she decided not to tell anyone about the Sunday lessons, and that she would wait until her mother was alone before she told her that the school had turned her out.

Annie held out her arms as Rose walked into the scullery. She stooped down to her, ignoring the others sitting at the table. 'Hello, Toots, you're looking better today.' She dived into her pocket and brought out the sandwich. 'Want a bit of cheese?' She was rewarded with a smile, and started to break off small pieces to pop them into the little girl's mouth. When that was finished, she took out the banana and peeled it.

'Where'd you get that?' Bob demanded.

'My teacher gave it to me, and it's for Annie.'

'She had the cheese so why can't we have the banana?'

'Because there isn't enough to go round and she needs it more than you.'

'You're mean,' he whined.

Suddenly there was a thump on the table. Rose turned to see Annie pulling herself upright on her chair, gripping the table for support. Her face was red with fury and she was looking at her brother with loathing. 'Not mean,' she said clearly, lifting an accusing finger at Bob. 'Wosie good. You mean.'

Everyone burst out laughing, except Bob, who stood up so suddenly that his chair went flying.

'Who taught *her* to talk? Haven't we got enough to put up with with one bossy girl?' Then he stormed out of the room.

'Ugh.' Annie screwed up her face and plonked down on to her chair. 'Bad boy.'

'There! I told you she was like you, Rose.' Her mother wiped tears of laughter from her eyes. 'That put the boy in his place.'

'At last I've got someone to stick up for me,' Rose joked.

Then there was a tug at her sleeve and she looked down at Annie. 'Bed.' She held up her arms. 'Tired, Wosie.'

Rose picked her up, the little girl laid her head on her shoulder and was instantly asleep. 'All that talk has tired her out, but it's good to see her showing some sign of life.'

'It is, and if she gets her strength, I think she's going to be a force to be reckoned with.' Her mother was clearly delighted at this turn of events.

Rose hoisted the sleeping child higher on to her shoulder. 'I'd better put her to bed, or else she might tell *me* off.'

She left the scullery with the welcome sound of her mother's laughter in her ears.

Right, that was the last of the little ones in bed. Now she'd go down and see if there was any tea left in the pot.

Flo was there with her mother and the old man – she refused to think of him as her father now. Her sister smirked when Rose walked into the scullery. 'Rose has been kicked out of school,' she said with relish.

'What?' Her mother was shocked.

'I was going to tell you later.' Rose looked at her sister accusingly. 'Can't keep your mouth shut, can you?'

'Didn't know it was a secret,' Flo protested.

'What's going on?' the old man demanded.

Rose sighed. 'They said that as I couldn't take the free place at the big school, I'd have to leave because they couldn't teach me any more.'

'Oh, Rosie,' her mother moaned. 'What a terrible thing to happen to you.'

'What's terrible about it, woman? She can get a job now and pay for her keep. It's time she did something useful. Tell her to go down the Labour tomorrow.'

'That's what I'm going to do.' And why don't *you* try it? Rose thought.

He grunted and stood up. 'About time.' Then he left for the pub.

'Why didn't you tell me?' her mother said.

'I was going to when you were alone, but Big Mouth here' – she glared at her sister – 'had to blurt it out, didn't she?'

'I don't know what all the fuss is about. You've only been turned out because you're too clever for us,' her sister muttered, then stormed out of the scullery.

'Don't go into service, Rose,' her mother said.

'I might not have any choice. There can't be much else for me to do.'

'You mustn't!' Marj's mouth had set in a straight line.

Rose was taken aback. 'I'll try not to.'

'I won't have you being a skivvy for someone else, and I need you here anyway. You've got a brain, you deserve better.'

'I'll see what they've got at the Exchange tomorrow.'

Rose couldn't help wondering why her mother was so agitated. She'd been in service when she'd been young, hadn't she? Was that where she'd got into trouble? Yes, that was probably it, she thought angrily. Some man had got her pregnant and her employers had dismissed her.

Injustice made Rose angry, but she controlled herself. Her mother must have suffered so much and she didn't want to add to her burdens by exploding in rage. But she would not let anything like that happen to her.

4

'Next!' The man looked up briefly as Rose came and stood before him. 'Sit.'

She boiled. Who did he think she was? A dog?

'Name.'

'Emily Rose Webster.' She had to hold her temper in check as she needed a job. If she got cheeky he would throw her out, because there were plenty of others he could choose from. The Labour Exchange was packed.

'Age?'

'Fourteen,' she lied, without a blink.

'Can you read and write?'

She looked him straight in the eyes. 'Of course I can, and I'm good at numbers too.'

He scribbled on a form, then handed it to her. 'Go there.'

'When?'

'Now.'

'What is it?'

'Factory. They make metal cans and things.'

Her mouth was open to ask another question when he shouted, 'Next!'

She pushed her way out through the heaving mass of people, stood on the pavement and grinned reluctantly. What a daft conversation that had been. Still, he hadn't doubted her when she'd said she was fourteen. Being tall had its advantages.

★

The factory was as crowded as the Labour Exchange had been.

A boy took her form and showed her into a long corridor lined with chairs, filled with hopefuls looking for work. 'Wait here.'

Damn. She groaned under her breath. That man must be sending everyone down here. What a waste of time. She had waited three hours at the Labour and it looked like she'd have another two or three hours of hanging around. If only she could be at school. A sensation of something between despair and anger swept through her, but she pushed it away.

She leaned against the wall and studied the others. They were all young – boys and girls – and some evidently didn't know what a wash flannel looked like. Poverty hung around every one of them, as if they had labels around their necks, while desperation and need were imprinted on each forlorn face. Again, the words *This isn't right* filled her mind.

Nearly two hours later she was still there but several chairs were empty now. So was her stomach, which rumbled in protest. She was going to miss her school dinner – even the semolina. Try as she might, she couldn't keep the picture of her beloved classroom out of her mind, and her vision blurred.

'That's her, Mr Baker, sir.'

Rose looked up to see the boy standing in front of her with a man of about forty, she reckoned.

'Miss Webster, come with me.'

He turned immediately and strode along the corridor, leaving her to trot after him. He opened a door at the end of the passage and as they stepped through it the noise

35

stopped her dead. Rows and rows of machines were thumping away, men were hammering, and down at the end she could see benches filled with youngsters who were packing huge boxes. And by the look of them she needn't have lied about her age – if they were fourteen she'd eat her boots.

She covered her ears.

The man in front of her didn't slacken his pace and was soon disappearing through another door. Finally he stopped in a small office. The quiet was a blessed relief.

'What are they making in there?' she gasped.

'Tin cans.' Mr Baker sat behind a desk and looked her over critically. 'Sit down, please.'

She did as ordered.

'Your form says you can read and write?'

'Yes, sir.' She added the 'sir' because he looked as if he expected it.

'And you know how to add?'

'Yes, sir.'

'Six twelves?' he threw at her.

'Seventy-two, sir.'

He raised his eyebrows at her quick response. 'You know your tables?'

'All of them.' Her dark eyes shone with pride. 'Would you like me to recite them for you?'

'I don't think that will be necessary.' His expression remained the same but his lips twitched at the corners. 'I need someone who can add correctly.'

'Oh, I can do that.' Rose smiled, showing a row of perfect teeth. This sounded promising.

'And you are fourteen?'

'Yes, sir.' It was getting easier all the time.

'Very well . . . er . . .' He looked at the form again. 'Emily.'

'Rose. Everybody calls me Rose.'

He nodded. 'You can start tomorrow at seven o'clock.'

'Do I have to work in that racket?' she asked boldly.

'Yes, but you'll soon get used to it, and if you prove yourself good at figures, I might consider moving you on to something else.'

'Fair enough. I'll bring something to stuff in my ears.'

He seemed to be having real trouble with trying not to smile. 'You'll work from seven to six, Monday to Friday, and seven to one on Saturday. The pay is six shillings a week.'

'Thank you, sir.' It wasn't much, but at least she'd got a job.

He stood up. 'Come with me, and I'll show you the way out.'

When they went back through the factory, she stuck her fingers in her ears and rushed through the workshop as quickly as she could.

By way of celebration she decided to walk home and spend her fare money on a nice piece of cod in batter for Annie.

'How'd you get on?' her mother asked, as Rose walked into the scullery.

'I got a job and I start tomorrow.'

'What kind of a job?'

'It's in a factory and the noise is awful, but the boss said he'd move me later if I can add up well.'

Her mother smiled in relief. 'That sounds fine. Did you tell them you were only eleven?'

'No.' She grinned. 'I said I was fourteen, but I'm not sure he believed me. He probably didn't care. He just wanted someone who could add up.'

'Well, you won't have any trouble with that. I've never known anyone so quick at reckoning.'

Rose looked around. 'Where's Annie?'

'Still in bed. Hasn't been too bright today.'

'Oh?' Rose tore up the stairs and rushed to Annie's bed. 'What's up, Toots?' she asked.

'Tired, Wosie.' She yawned and held out her arms.

Back in the scullery a few minutes later, with Annie, Rose asked, 'How long's she been like this?'

'Most of the day. She won't eat anything.'

Rose sat down, holding the child firmly on her lap. Then she opened the bag and put the fish on to a plate. 'You got something I can give her with this, Mum? I couldn't afford the chips as well.'

Her mother dished up a spoonful of mashed potato. 'How's that?'

'Fine, thanks.' Then she fed Annie, coaxing her to take every mouthful, until the plate was empty.

'Well, I'll be blowed,' her mother exclaimed. 'You can get her to do anything.'

'Not me.' She grinned at the little girl. 'It was the fish, wasn't it?'

'Yum, yum,' was the little girl's reply.

'Why wouldn't you eat your dinner today?' Rose asked her.

Annie screwed up her little face. 'Ugh, bread.'

'The little minx,' her mother murmured, 'I think she'd rather starve than eat something she doesn't want.'

'She's got a stubborn streak, all right, but I think she's ill.' Rose brushed Annie's hair away from her face, which was alarmingly white. 'We're all sick of bread, Annie, but we have to eat it.' She tickled the little girl's tummy. 'It fills us up in there.'

Annie giggled and struggled to get down. Once on the floor she grabbed a chair, pulled herself upright and took a couple of wobbly steps. Then she sat down and beamed at Rose. 'Walk now, showed you.'

'There's a clever girl,' Rose and her mother said, encouragingly.

'Clever, like Wosie.'

'Don't you turn out too clever or you'll get thrown out of school, like me.' Rose heard the bitterness in her voice.

'How much they going to pay you?' her mother asked, changing the subject.

'Six shillings a week.'

'Don't tell the old man how much, will you?'

'No fear. I'm going to keep a shilling for myself and give the rest to you.'

'I'll see it all goes on food and clothes. I'm sorry you've had to go out to work, but a bit of extra money'll be a big help,' her mother admitted.

Rose knew that, and was glad, but she wished the knot of resentment inside her would go away.

When she came into the scullery after putting the kids to bed, the old man said, 'Has she got a job, then?'

'Yes, and she starts tomorrow,' Marj told him.

'How much they paying her?'

'Five shillings a week.' Marj didn't hesitate.

Rose hid a smile. Her mother was almost as good a liar as she was.

'What? That's robbery.'

'I was lucky to get anything.' Rose glared at the man, who was clutching his knife and fork, waiting for his dinner. 'It was like a madhouse down at the Labour Exchange, and I only got this because I'm good at adding up.'

'She can give me her pay packet at the end of each week.' He started to eat the dinner Marj had put in front of him.

Oh, no, she wouldn't! She wasn't going to work like a slave and give him the money to drink. 'I'm giving it to Mum for my keep. You said it was time I paid my way.' She spoke boldly, expecting to receive the back of his hand, but to her surprise he didn't move.

He scraped his plate clean, stood up, reached for her mother's purse and tipped it upside down. It was empty. 'You've never got any money, woman,' he complained.

'I've got eight kids and you to feed, not forgetting the rent.'

'Well.' He looked smug. 'We'll soon have a bit more when she gets her money.'

'And all of it will go on decent food and warm clothes for the children. Winter's on the way, you know,' his wife told him.

He scowled and went out without another word.

Rose left the house and walked until she had calmed down. The very idea that that man might get his hands on her wages! As she wandered along the riverbank, she picked up a stone and threw it into the water, then watched the ripples as they spread outwards. Everyone kept telling her she was just a child, but she didn't feel like one. In fact, she knew she'd never been like the other children – all she'd ever wanted was to learn.

Something deep inside was telling her that knowledge was the only way to improve her lot. She didn't know why she felt like that, but something drove her all the time, and one day she would find the answers she was looking for.

5

Rose shoved the wadding into her ears, picked up a pencil and started counting, writing the tally neatly in the book. She gritted her teeth in concentration. It was like being in the depths of hell, but the boss had said he'd find her something else to do if she proved her adding was good, so she was determined not to make any mistakes.

The time passed at snail's pace and the noise made her feel sick. To have been wrenched out of the classroom into this was almost more than she could bear.

She continued writing. The only way to get through it was to shut everything out and concentrate on what she was being paid to do. So, using every bit of stubbornness she possessed – which was a considerable amount – she blocked out her surroundings. When someone tapped her on the shoulder she jumped. It was the foreman who had shown her what to do when she'd arrived and his mouth was moving, but she was so dazed she didn't understand what he was saying.

He grinned and pulled the stuffing out of her ears. 'Time for dinner.'

She looked around and saw that a lot of the men had already stopped work. As the last of the noisy machines was turned off, she rolled her eyes in relief.

'Give me your book and go to the canteen, Rose.' He handed her back the wadding. 'You'll need that this afternoon.'

'How do you stand this every day?' she asked, rubbing her temple.

'You'll get used to it.'

'Never!'

He opened the book. 'It's unusual for Mr Baker to give this job to someone so young, but you've got a neat hand. Let's hope the figures are right.'

'They are,' she said stoutly. 'You won't find one mistake, and you can show it to the boss because I don't want to do this job any longer than I have to.' Then a horrible thought struck her. She had been thrown out of school because she was too good, so if she was too good at this job would the boss refuse to move her to something better?

The foreman put the book into his pocket. 'Off you go now or there won't be anything left for you.'

Rose queued up for her dinner. It was only broth and a chunk of bread, but it was free for the youngsters. She found herself a seat in the corner, away from everyone else. She needed a few quiet moments, and was surprised everyone else didn't feel the same after working in that awful noise all morning.

A crushing feeling of despair swamped her, but she fought it with all her might. It wouldn't help her. She tried to replace despair with gratitude, but it was difficult. The only beacon of hope was her Sunday lessons.

The rest of the day was agony as the metal was pounded into tin cans, and Rose had just about reached screaming point when it was time to knock off. As soon as she was outside the building, she headed for the park and ran and ran, putting as much distance as possible between her and the hated factory.

When she got home the scullery was empty, except for her mother.

'I've saved your tea,' she said. 'Sit down and tell me what your first day was like.'

At the mention of the factory, Rose froze, unable to move or speak as the horror of the day surfaced. Misery swamped her, and tears poured down her cheeks.

'Oh, Rosie!' Her mother reached out to comfort her, but Rose stepped back. Sympathy would only make things worse – and it had. She sobbed uncontrollably.

Suddenly there was a cry of anguish and someone grabbed her leg. 'Don't cwy, Wosie, don't cwy.'

Rose brushed away the tears and saw Annie wrapped around her leg, her little face contorted with distress. Forgetting her own unhappiness, she picked the child up. 'It's all right, Toots.'

'Not all wight. Wosie *never* cwy.'

'I'm silly today.'

Annie gave her a disbelieving look. 'You not silly.'

Rose sighed. What she had told Annie was true – she had been acting like a baby, and she would make sure she never did it again. 'Don't you believe it. And what are you doing still up? I never saw you when I came in.'

'Under table.'

'Hiding, were you?'

Annie nodded and ran her small hand over Rose's face. 'Not cwy no more?'

'Never, I promise.' And that was one promise she would do her best to keep. 'Why aren't you in bed like all the others?'

'Wait for you.'

'Oh?' Rose gave her mother a questioning look.

'She'd only let Will near her and he's too young to put her to bed.'

'What about Flo?'

'Annie screamed the place down when she tried to pick her up.'

'You mustn't do that, Toots,' she scolded gently. 'You must let Flo put you to bed at night because I'm going to be coming in too late to do it.'

'Why you late?'

'I have to go to work now.'

Annie seemed to chew that over for a while, then she nodded. 'You come see me when you get home?'

'I promise.' Then Rose glanced at her mother. 'That was a long sentence, even if it did take a lot of thought and effort.'

'Yes, she's coming on. Must be all those treats you bring her.'

'Oh, I almost forgot. I didn't catch the bus home so I got this.' She produced a small orange and Annie shrieked with delight.

'What that?'

'Shush.' Rose put her finger to her lips. 'Don't want to wake the others up, do we?'

Annie shook her head vigorously. 'Not Bob, he eat it all.'

The orange was split between Annie, Rose and her mother, but the little girl had the lion's share.

As Rose had only worked for half of the week, she received three shillings in wages. She handed it all over to her mother but was given sixpence back.

'I'm not taking everything. You must have something for yourself,' Marj said.

Rose returned twopence. 'This will be enough for me, but when I've worked a full week I'll keep a shilling.'

Her mother took it reluctantly. 'What are you going to do with your pocket money?'

She lifted up her foot to show the holes in her boots. 'I'm going to save up for a pair of shoes.'

At last it was Sunday, and she could go for her lesson.

Rose got on the bus and fidgeted all the way, anxious not to miss her stop. They were there in no time. She made sure her frock wasn't too crumpled and smoothed her thick mop of black hair with a lick on her hands, then opened the gate and walked up the path.

'Hello, Rose.' Miss Gardner greeted her with a smile. 'Come in.'

She stepped inside the house. Everything was lovely and clean, and she was glad she'd had a good wash before she came. It was not grand, like the big houses across the river, but it was a whole lot better than the place she lived in, and it looked positively empty.

'I like your house, Miss.'

Miss Gardner looked pleased. 'Thank you. I inherited it from my father and I've worked hard to make it pleasant and comfortable.'

'It's certainly that,' Rose remarked, with genuine admiration. Fancy owning your own house. If she ever lived in a place like this, she'd be happy.

'Mr Trenchard's waiting for you.'

Rose fished in the pocket of her frock. She pulled out the penny Miss Gardner had given her and handed it to her. 'I didn't need this. I've got a job now, but thank you very much for lending it to me.'

The teacher looked doubtful. 'Are you sure you have enough for your fare home?'

Rose showed her the coins she had left after paying for her bus ride. 'I've still got this.'

'All right.' Miss Gardner took back the penny and studied Rose thoughtfully. 'You didn't have to return it. You could have kept it.'

'Oh, no!' Rose was horrified. 'I couldn't have done that when I had enough to pay for myself. It wouldn't have been right.'

'Ah, so this is Rose.'

A tall man with spectacles propped on the end of his nose came out of another room. Rose liked the look of him.

'Are you ready to start the lesson?'

'Yes, please, sir.' She followed him into the front room.

A large table over by the window was covered with books and Rose gasped with delight, then ran over to it. Oh, they were beautiful. Her hands ran over them lovingly and she turned to Mr Trenchard. 'These all yours?'

He nodded. 'Sit down, and we'll have a look at them, shall we?'

Still smiling, she sat, then turned her large dark eyes on him expectantly.

'What I want to do this afternoon is find out what you know, and then I'll be able to plan a course of study for you. If you're as bright as Miss Gardner says, I'll teach the same subjects you would have taken at the secondary school, and after a while I'll set you some exams.' He paused, took off his spectacles and polished them. 'Would you like that?'

She nodded eagerly. 'Yes, please, sir. I'll work very hard and I learn quick.'

He poured them a cup of tea from a pot standing on a small table, and handed the plate of biscuits to her. They were whole ones, she saw with pleasure, not the broken ones they had to buy because they were cheap. Then he opened one of the books.

For the next two hours Rose answered questions, did exercises and read aloud for Mr Trenchard. She also subjected him to a constant flow of questions, and was overjoyed when he answered all of them in a way she could understand. He was indeed a good teacher.

Finally he closed the books, and smiled at her. 'Well, Rose, I can see you're eager to learn and have an inquiring mind.'

She pulled a face. Oh dear, had she overdone the questions? 'Everyone gets fed up with me, but I can't help it because I've always been like this. It's a bit of a nuisance at times.'

'You mustn't think like that. You have a thirst for knowledge and it's a rare gift.'

'Do you think so?' Rose had never heard her questions referred to as a gift before: where she came from she was looked upon as an oddity.

'Yes, it is, and I'll see if I can assuage your need for knowledge.'

'Assuage?' she repeated. 'What does that mean?'

He opened a large dictionary, found the right place and pushed it towards her. 'What does that say?'

She read it carefully. 'To satisfy,' she told him, then grinned. 'It's a good word. I'd not heard it before.' She fingered the large book. 'Will you teach me lots of new words?'

'If you keep coming I'll try to teach you everything I know.'

Her eyes opened wide. 'You will?'

He nodded again. 'I think you should learn Latin.'

'Latin!' Rose sat bolt upright. 'Only those in the posh schools learn that.'

'Rose,' he leaned forward earnestly, 'I believe you have a lot of potential, and Latin could be useful to you in later years.'

'Then I'll learn it,' she told him confidently. She had met Mr Trenchard this afternoon for the first time, but already she trusted his judgement.

'Good, we'll start next week.' He took a watch out of his waistcoat pocket, flicked it open, then closed it and slipped it back. 'That's enough for today. Come at the same time next Sunday.'

'Has two hours gone already?' she asked, sorry the lesson was at an end.

'I'm afraid so.'

'I wish they went that quick at the factory.'

'How are you getting on there?' he asked kindly.

Her bottom lip trembled, but she remembered her promise to Annie and herself, and banished the tears. 'I hate it. They shouldn't have made me leave school. I wouldn't have minded doing all the lessons again.'

'It's a great shame, Rose, but we'll see that you still get a good education. However, as you will only be having two hours a week tuition, it will take longer and you will need determination.'

He used long words, but she knew what that one meant. 'I got plenty of that. You'll see.'

He looked at her thoughtfully. 'Yes, I do believe you have. I've written out some exercises for you to do during the week.'

Rose took the paper from him and started to read it eagerly. 'I can do this.'

'I'm sure you can.' He handed her a little notebook, a pencil and a rubber. 'I want you to write the answers in this book – in your best handwriting – and bring it back next week.'

'How much is the book and stuff?'

'Nothing, you may take them,' Mr Trenchard told her.

'Oh, no,' Rose said, scandalized at the suggestion. 'I can pay, look.' She pulled the coins out of her pocket. 'Is there enough here?'

'More than enough, child, but you need not.'

'I want to,' she told him firmly. 'You're being very kind by giving me these lessons, and I wouldn't be happy letting you spend any of your own money on me. It wouldn't be right.' She pushed a penny towards him.

He pushed it back. 'That's too much.'

'You take what's right then.' She laid out the money for him to see.

He slid a farthing from among the coins on the table, but Rose was not having that, and gave him another. 'These things cost more than a farthing – I know because I've seen them in the shops. You mustn't spend your money on me, Mr Trenchard, it isn't right.'

'You use that word a lot,' he said, sitting back, folding his arms and looking at her intently.

'What word?' Rose frowned.

'"Right". Tell me what you mean.'

She reached for the dictionary. 'Shall we look it up?'

'No.' He took the book from her and closed it. 'I want you to explain what the word means to you, what you are thinking when you use it.'

Rose clasped her hands in her lap and stared into space. 'Well . . . when something isn't right, then it shouldn't be happening.' She fidgeted and gave him an appealing glance.

'Go on.'

'I'm not used to being asked what I think.'

'I don't suppose you are.'

Rose arranged the books in a neat row on the table while she sorted out in her mind what she wanted to say. Then she sat back. 'It isn't right when some people have so much and others have to live in the dirt. It shouldn't be like that and something ought to be done about it. It isn't right for me to take money from you or Miss Gardner when I have some of my own . . .' She tailed off, hoping that was enough explaining.

'And why do you feel like that?' he coaxed.

'Well, you and Miss live a whole lot better than me, but you work hard for your pay and you're not as rich as those who live across the river.'

'And would you take money from them?' he probed.

'No, I would not,' Rose exclaimed indignantly. 'I don't want charity from the likes of them.'

'But you wanted the free place at school.'

'That was different. I'd worked hard for it.' She could not understand why he was asking all these questions.

'So you think you have to earn the good things in life?'

'How else am I going to get them?' She leaned forward, and spoke with passion: 'But I'm not just talking about me, sir. I think I've got enough brains to make a difference to my life if I work at it hard enough, but what about those who don't know how to escape? That's what I mean by something being not right. There should be some help for them, but there's nothing.' She ground to a halt and glanced at him anxiously.

'So, what are you going to do about it?'

'Me?' she squeaked. 'What can I do? I'm nobody.'

Mr Trenchard's face was alight with pleasure, and she couldn't help wondering what he found so interesting about this talk. She was babbling away like an ignorant kid.

'Don't think one person can't make a difference because they can. One voice raised against injustice can have a dramatic effect.'

Rose pulled a face, not quite believing him. 'It would be a bit like a "voice crying in the wilderness",' she quoted.

He nodded. 'I agree, but think about the difference that single voice made.'

She remembered when she had tossed a stone into the river, and smiled broadly. She was beginning to understand where his questions were leading. 'When I threw a stone into the water it sent out ripples that kept going in ever-widening circles.'

'Exactly!' He leaned forward. 'One small pebble, but the splash it made kept reaching out and changing the surface of the water.'

Now she'd got it.

'Each one of us can make a difference in this world. It

might be in just a small way, but it could open the path for bigger things. Take Miss Gardner, for instance. There are very few women teachers, but she persevered until she was given her post. Her actions might make it easier for other women to go into the profession.'

'She's a good teacher,' Rose said, with affection, 'got ever so much patience. Without her help I wouldn't have won the Bible.'

'Do you like reading the Bible?'

'Oh, yes, it's my favourite book.' She pulled it out of her pocket. 'I keep it with me all the time. It's safer than leaving it at home.'

'And do you understand it?'

She laughed. 'No. But that doesn't matter because I love trying to work out what it all means.'

At that moment the door opened and Miss Gardner came into the room. 'John, we will be late for the service if we don't leave soon.'

Rose leaped to her feet. 'Oh, I'm so sorry. I've kept you talking way past time.'

'Don't worry about it,' Mr Trenchard assured her. 'It's been a very enlightening discussion.'

'Enlightening?'

'Hmm. Revealing. You have opened the door of your mind just a crack for me, and now I have an idea of the way you think and feel. It will help me to prepare lessons that you will find interesting and helpful for your mission in life.'

'I don't have a mission in life – except to get out of the slums, of course,' she told him, feeling rather self-conscious. He was saying some strange things.

'I think you do, but you just don't know what it is yet.

Now, off you go, and come at the same time next week.'

'I will, sir, and I'll have all my exercises done.'

Rose ran across the road to wait for her bus, her head buzzing with all the things they'd talked about.

Two pairs of eyes watched her as she waited at the bus stop, already reading the exercise paper.

'What do you think, John?'

He slipped his arm around Grace's shoulder. 'She's everything you said and more. She has a remarkable mind and it would be criminal for her to stay where she is. She couldn't have had a worse start in life, but she doesn't belong in Garrett Street.'

'I agree with you, but I think she already knows that, and believes education is the way forward for her.'

'And she's right. She has a wisdom far beyond her years, but that hasn't come as a result of education. It's something she was born with.' He removed his spectacles and frowned.

'What is it?' Grace asked him.

'I don't know, really. It's just that there's something familiar about her.'

'Such as?'

He studied the girl across the road. 'The directness of her gaze, the way she carries herself, the pride and determination in those great dark eyes . . .' He tailed off, then shrugged. 'I can't pin it down, but I feel sure I've met someone like her before.'

6

At the end of another dreadful week, Rose walked into the scullery and found the place almost as noisy as the factory. 'What's going on?' she bellowed.

Flo was nowhere to be seen. Bob was tormenting a screaming Annie. Nancy was cowering in the corner, frightened of her own shadow. Will was trying to pull Bob off Annie. Bert and Charlie were on all fours, pretending to be dogs and 'barking'.

Rose grabbed Bob's collar and pulled him away from Annie, which added to the racket as he yelled at the top of his voice. 'Quiet!' she thundered. 'Where's Flo?'

'Up-up stairs,' Nancy whispered.

'Mum's having another kid.' Bob lashed out at Rose in an effort to get away from her.

'So you all thought you'd run riot, did you?'

'We weren't doing no 'arm,' Bob argued.

Rose glared at him. 'And hurting a little girl isn't doing any harm?'

'Wosie . . . fwightened,' Annie wailed. 'Nasty boy.'

'All right, Toots, I'm here now.' Rose picked her up and turned to the rest of them. 'Nancy, stop whimpering.'

'Sorry, Rosie,' the seven-year-old whispered, 'but I'm scared of all that shouting.'

'I know, but you've got to be brave because Mum's going to need your help with the new baby.'

'Oh.' Nancy's face lit up. Nancy loved babies, though

what she saw in them was a mystery to Rose. 'And you' – she peered under the table at Bert and Charlie, aged four and three respectively – 'what do you think you were playing at?'

'Dogs,' they answered, and scuttled out of her reach.

'Well, pick something quieter next time,' she told them briskly.

'Rose!' Flo rushed into the scullery. 'Thank goodness you're home. Mum's having a bad time and the baby won't come.'

'Who's with her?'

'Mrs Jenks and Mrs Peters.'

Rose handed Annie to her sister and went up the stairs. Her mother's hair was spread across the pillow in soaking wet strands, and she was gasping in pain. 'Is there anything I can do?' Rose asked Mrs Jenks.

'No, love, we just have to wait. The kid's in no hurry to come into this world.'

And who could blame it? Rose thought bitterly. There wasn't much waiting for it. 'How much longer do you think it will be?'

'Another hour or so.' Mrs Jenks seemed unconcerned.

Rose winced visibly as another spasm caught her mother, then went back downstairs where, mercifully it was now quiet.

'Is it going to be long?' Flo was close to tears.

'Mrs Jenks thinks another hour or so.'

'It's awful, isn't it? I don't want any kids.' Flo was shaking.

'I'm sure I don't! Where's the old man?' Rose asked.

'Dad? He poked his nose in, but when he knew the baby was coming, he disappeared quick.'

Rose wasn't surprised.

Two hours later they heard the squalling of a new baby, and Rose sighed with relief. It sounded healthy enough and she only hoped her mother was all right. Although she hated the thought of another mouth to feed, she was glad it was all over.

Mrs Jenks came into the scullery. 'That's done then. You have another brother.'

No one looked enthusiastic about that.

'How's Mum?' Rose asked.

'Tired, and she's going to need a lot of rest, but she's come through it pretty well.'

'We'd better go and see her. Come on, Flo.' Rose stopped at the door and glared menacingly at the other children. 'I don't want to hear a peep out of any of you.'

When they came into the room their mother looked exhausted but managed a weak smile.

'I'm going to need your help,' she told both of them, 'because I'll be laid up for a while.'

They nodded.

'Do you want to see the baby?'

Without a word they walked over to a drawer that had been turned into a cot and gazed at the tiny bundle. Rose was overcome with guilt: it was wrong to resent this little thing – he hadn't asked to be born. But the thought of another child in the house was almost too much for her. They were already sleeping three to a bed.

'He's so tiny,' Flo said in awe.

'Yes, but he's got a good pair of lungs on him. He'll be all right. I'm going to call him David.' Their mother struggled to sit up. 'Flo, you look after the others while

Rose goes shopping. There isn't much food in the house. Rose, there's some money in the top drawer over there. The rent collector's coming tonight and there's enough to pay off what's owing. The rest I want you to spend on food.'

Rose rummaged through the drawer and came up blank. 'There's nothing here.'

'But there must be.' Her mother became agitated. 'Have another look. I put it right at the back so your father wouldn't find it.'

After another thorough search, she turned to her mother. 'I'm sorry, but it isn't here.'

'He's found it,' her mother cried. 'What are we going to do? I promised the rent man the money tonight.'

Rose was furious and dismayed at the same time. Of all the thoughtless, selfish men in this world, the old man must take the biscuit. 'At least I got paid today.'

'That'll be enough for some food, but what about the rent?'

'I'll get the money.' Rose lifted her head in determination, but inside she was trembling with fear. She knew what she had to do.

Her mother lay back. 'Oh, Rosie, what would I do without you?'

'Find a better hiding place?' Rose joked.

Once the shopping was done, Rose started to cook a meal for them all. The old man wouldn't get any favours tonight. He'd have to eat the same as everyone else. She had managed to get a large ham bone and some vegetables from the market. It would make a nourishing soup, which would last a couple of days, with luck. A suet pudding was boiling away too – that would fill them up.

'Rose?' Flo's bottom lip trembled. 'Are we going to get chucked out?'

'Not if we can get the money back.'

'How are we going to do that? I don't think I'd have the nerve to ask him.'

'I don't fancy it either, but we'll have to.' Rose squared her shoulders, trying to give the impression that it was nothing to her, but she'd seen the old man in a rage many times and it wasn't something to look forward to.

'He'll flatten you!' Bob said, with relish.

'Well, if he does you'll be sleeping in the gutter tonight.' She was pleased to see he didn't like *that* idea.

'Wosie!' Annie crawled out from under the table, pulled herself upright and tottered towards her sister. 'Eat.'

'I don't know how you understand her. She talks so funny,' Nancy said, helping the little girl on to her chair.

'You have to listen carefully.' Rose sliced the bread and put a large piece in front of Annie. 'Dinner won't be long, Toots.'

As if that was a signal, the rest of the kids sat down. They ate the ham soup with enthusiasm and wiped the bowls clean with chunks of bread. While they were tucking into the suet pudding, Rose took a plate of soup up to her mother, and was pleased when she ate everything, and then had a helping of pudding.

They were just finishing their meal when the old man arrived, smelling of booze. 'What's for dinner?' he demanded, pulling Will out of his chair and sitting in it, holding a knife and fork at the ready.

'Dad, don't you want to see the new baby?' Flo asked hesitantly.

'They all look the same.' And without looking up, he dived into the food.

'Mum's had a bad time.' Rose was going to make sure he knew.

'Rubbish, she's strong as an 'orse. Got any more of that puddin'?' He scraped his plate clean and held it out.

'It's all gone.' He grunted and stood up, ready to walk out. Rose took a deep breath and positioned herself in the doorway. 'I need the money you took out of Mum's drawer.'

'You got paid today,' he snarled.

'That's all gone on food. You took the rent and the week's food money.'

His face turned purple with rage and he lashed out, catching her a stinging blow on the side of her head. 'Don't you give me no lip! It's none of your bloody business. Out of my way!'

She straightened to her full height, pleased to see she was now eye to eye with him, and stood her ground. 'We'll end up in the workhouse if you don't stop drinking and gambling – '

She saw the blow coming and didn't flinch, although the force of it made her head swim and her vision go cloudy. 'They'll turn us out for sure if we don't pay today.'

With a growl of rage he tried to push her out of the way but she was too strong for him, and the blows he rained on her were futile. He had done his worst and she would not budge.

'Wosie!' Annie screamed, clambering over to grab her father's ankle. 'Don't hurt Wosie!'

He lifted his foot and tried to shake her off.

'Flo! Take Annie away,' Rose ordered her sister, not taking her eyes off the old man – she mustn't show a sign of weakness or fear.

When the little girl was safely out of the way she held out her hand. 'The money.' Her dark gaze was unwavering.

He hit her again.

'Leave her alone!'

Through the haze of pain she recognized Bob's voice with a jolt of astonishment. Why was he defending her?

The old man pushed him roughly away and tried to get past Rose, but she wouldn't move. He was not in a strong position now because even the kids were ganging up on him. They were all lined up beside Rose.

He took a shilling out of his pocket and placed it in her outstretched hand. She snorted. 'And the rest.'

'I ain't got no more.'

'Dig deeper. I want every penny you took.'

He licked his lips, but then, with a snarl of fury, he took out more coins and thrust them at her. Rose did a quick calculation. It wouldn't be enough to clear all of the outstanding debt, but it would satisfy the rent man for another week. Anyway, it was no use trying to squeeze any more out of him because he'd probably spent it.

'Now get out of my house,' he shouted. 'Go and sleep in the gutter where you belong.'

Her fingers closed around the money and she stepped aside. He rushed out past her, uttering a stream of abuse, but she didn't care. She had won.

Only then did she allow herself to shake and feel the pain.

'Oh, Rose.' Flo rushed over and started to dab the blood off her lip. 'Sit down and let me clean your poor face.'

'Don't fuss.' Nevertheless she allowed Flo to tend her because it gave her a chance to calm down. Her action had been born of desperation and, although she hadn't shown it, she had been frightened and very aware that she was still only a child. But she couldn't have seen them evicted, not when they had a newborn baby and her mother was weak.

Annie held on to her skirt and looked up at her with frightened eyes. 'Hurt?' she asked tremulously.

Rose stroked her hair. 'I'm all right.'

'There, that's stopped bleeding now,' Flo muttered, 'but you're going to have a black eye.'

'It'll heal – and we got the money, didn't we?' She tried to smile at her sister. 'Ouch!'

'Yes, Rose, but you took a beating getting it.'

'He won't touch me again,' she vowed. Then she saw that she was surrounded by all of the youngsters. She had never known them to be so quiet, except Annie, who had begun to sob. She lifted her up and cradled her on her lap. 'Shush, Toots, it's all over now.'

'You're hurt bad.' Will's eyes brimmed over with tears, and Bob edged closer for a better look.

'Thanks for standing up for me, Bob,' she said. 'It was brave of you.'

He studied her carefully, then his usual surly expression came back. 'I still don't like you, but you was tryin' to help us.'

'Rosie!' Her mother was calling from upstairs.

'Oh, dear, she heard the row.' Flo wrung her hands.

'She could hardly miss it. I'd better go up.' Rose touched her face carefully. 'How do I look?'

'Terrible.'

With a helpless shrug, she went up the stairs.

'What was going – ' Her mother stopped when she saw her. 'Oh, Rosie, your poor face.'

'I made him give me the money back – or, at least, as much as he still had.'

'Is there enough for the rent man?' her mother asked anxiously.

'Almost. We'll be a bit short, but I think it's enough to keep him quiet for the time being.'

Her mother closed her eyes. 'Thank God!' Then she opened them and studied her daughter with new respect. 'You're having to grow up fast, aren't you?'

Flo poked her head around the door. 'You should have seen Rosie stand up to Dad,' she said in awe. 'When he hit her she didn't move, she just stood there, refusing to let him go until he'd handed over the money. He's – he's told her to get out.'

'Flo, don't bother Mum with that now,' Rose told her sharply.

Their mother, weakened by the long, painful birth, began to cry silently, then made an effort to pull herself together. 'You're not to take any notice of that. I won't have you turned out on the street.'

They left her to rest and went back downstairs.

'You're not going to leave us, are you?' Nancy asked, her face as white as a sheet.

'No fear.' Rose tried to smile, but her lip was too badly swollen, and the split opened again.

Flo handed her a cloth to wipe away the trickle of blood.

The rent collector came on time. 'Your ma in?'

'She's in bed. Had another baby today.'

'She promised to pay me tonight.'

Rose held out the money. 'I got most of it.'

'Hmm.' He checked his book. 'This'll still leave you a bit behind.'

'How much?'

'Four and sixpence.'

'You'll have it all next week.' Rose spoke with confidence, and hoped he believed her.

He studied her battered face. 'You look as if you've had a beating.'

'I'm all right.' She lifted her chin proudly. 'You'll get your money next week and that's a promise.'

'Same time next week, then.'

It was impossible to sleep. Rose held the damp cloth over her swollen left eye, and her lip hurt too.

She heard the door open and looked up to see the old man standing there. 'You still here? Thought I told you to get out.' His speech was slurred.

'You did, but I'm not going.' The expected cuff around the ear never came.

'You're a nasty piece of work,' he snarled. 'I should have made Marj get rid of you when you was born. I knew you was nothing but trouble.'

She watched him lurch out of the door and breathed

a shuddering sigh of relief. Alone again, hopelessness and anger overwhelmed her.

There *had* to be more to life than dirt, hunger and beatings.

7

'Are you going out, Rose?' Flo put the last of the plates away.

'Yes.' She slipped the exercise book into her pocket. Thank heavens it was Sunday – she couldn't wait for her lesson. 'Why?'

'Would you take Annie with you?'

'Oh, I don't know that I can.'

'Oh, please,' her sister begged. 'I've not had time to go and see my friends for ages.'

Rose knew this was true because since she'd had to go out to work Flo had been good about helping with the little ones. 'I suppose I could.' She looked around the scullery. 'Where are the others?'

'Bob's out, Nancy and Will are with Mum and the baby, Bert and Charlie are next door, so that just leaves Annie.'

The little girl was sitting on her chair and looking expectantly from one to the other. 'Be good, Wosie,' she promised.

Rose sighed inwardly. There was nothing for it: if Miss Gardner didn't want her little sister there, she'd have to miss her lesson this week. It was a crushing thought.

'All right, you go and meet your friends.'

'Hooray! Thanks.' Flo was out of the house like a shot.

'Want a ride on a bus?' she asked the little girl.

Miss Gardner gasped when she opened the door.

'I've come to tell you I can't have my lesson today,' Rose said quickly. She hadn't realized how horrified her teacher would be to see Annie with her.

Miss Gardner pulled her in and closed the door. 'What's this all about, Rose?'

'I've got to look after my sister because Mum's just had another baby, and – '

'That's not what I meant. I'll be happy to look after the little girl while you have your lesson. I'm distressed about the condition of your face.'

'Oh, that.' Rose hadn't given her bruises and cut lip a thought.

'Wosie hurt,' Annie told the woman, her little face serious.

'I can see that, sweetheart.'

'Dad hit.'

'It's nothing.' Rose was glad Annie couldn't say much yet or she'd be spilling out the whole story to Miss Gardner.

Miss Gardner turned Rose's face towards the light.

'Do you feel well enough to have your lesson?'

'Oh, yes. It's just I thought you might not like me bringing Annie.'

The little girl looked worried. 'Me good.'

'I'm sure you are.' Miss Gardner reached out and took her from Rose, then stood her on the floor.

Annie tottered and grabbed hold of the nearest skirt.

'Her walking isn't too good,' Rose said.

At that remark, Annie's face puckered with outrage. She reached up and took Miss Gardner's hand. 'I walk.'

Rose smiled, or as much as her sore lip would allow. 'She's stubborn too.'

'Like Wosie,' Annie said, looking up at the tall lady with something like a touch of pride.

Miss Gardner laughed and led her away, careful to let her go at her own pace. 'Would you like a lesson, too?' she asked her.

Annie nodded so hard she nearly fell over.

'Rose?' She turned and saw Mr Trenchard studying her intently. 'Are you ready to start?'

'Yes, please.' She followed him into the front room and sat down, eager to study. She was glad she hadn't had to give up her lesson: the thought of it had kept her going all through the long, noisy week.

'May I see your homework?'

She handed it over and watched as he checked everything carefully. 'Excellent,' he told her, after a while. 'I've set you more difficult exercises this time.'

'I'll enjoy that, sir. I like something to puzzle over.'

'Good.'

The time flew by, as it always did when Rose was surrounded by books and had someone with her to answer her questions. She was sure she was going to learn much more like this than she would in a classroom with other children. And Mr Trenchard was starting her on Latin today. It was all so exciting.

When the door opened and Miss Gardner came in carrying a tray, with Annie holding on to her skirt, Rose looked at the clock in surprise.

Miss Gardner put down the tray, sat Annie on a chair and gave her a cup of milk. 'John, this is Annie.'

Then she said something so quietly that Rose couldn't hear it.

Mr Trenchard nodded and stooped down to the little girl. 'Hello, Annie.'

The little girl cast Rose a glance to see if it was all right for her to speak to him. When her sister nodded, she smiled at him, milk all around her mouth.

He watched as she drained the cup and put it carefully back on to the table. Then he wiped away the milk with a napkin and asked, 'Will you let me have a look inside your mouth, Annie?'

Rose started in alarm.

However, Annie didn't seem at all put out by the strange request and opened it.

Mr Trenchard slipped his finger under her tongue and peered inside. Then he smiled, ruffled her hair and stood up. 'I think you're right, Grace,' he said. 'I'll go and see if Edward's in.'

As he walked out, Rose asked, agitated, 'What's the matter? Where's he going?'

'We think there's something wrong with Annie's mouth and that's why she has difficulty speaking. I don't believe she's backward, Rose, it's just that it's an effort for her to form the words so she doesn't bother.'

'Oh.' Rose was relieved. 'I'm so pleased you don't think she's short of brains, but what about her walking?'

'That's probably due to lack of nourishing food,' Miss Gardner told her gently.

'We do our best,' Rose said. 'All the other kids are strong enough, but Annie's always been a bit sickly. Why do you think she can't talk properly?'

'We're not sure, but Mr Trenchard's brother is a doctor and he only lives next door. He'll be able to tell us.'

At the word 'doctor' Rose's heartbeat accelerated. 'We can't afford doctors.'

'Don't worry,' Miss Gardner soothed her. 'This won't cost you anything.'

The door opened and a man strode in carrying a small black bag. He was older than Mr Trenchard, but they were obviously brothers.

'Hello, little one,' he said kindly, as he pulled up a chair and sat beside the wide-eyed Annie. Then he opened the bag and took out a flat thing. 'Will you let me have a look in your mouth?'

Clearly Annie was not too sure about this. She shot Rose a frightened look. 'Wosie?'

'It's all right, Toots.' She sat beside her little sister and took her hand. 'He's a doctor and he wants to see why you can't talk properly.'

Annie cast the big man beside her a quick glance, her eyes lingering on the implement he held in his hand, then turned back to Rose. 'Hurt?'

'No.'

Annie gave a little sigh, faced the doctor and opened her mouth.

The examination didn't take long. When the doctor had finished, Annie muttered, 'Ugh,' picked up her cup and looked into it hopefully. Finding it empty, she put it back on the table. Miss Gardner hurried to pour some more milk and was rewarded with a sweet smile. Rose noticed how the grown-ups in the room looked at the little girl with affection, and began to understand why she herself took so much trouble with her sister. She was a little charmer.

'How old is she?' the doctor asked.

'Two and a half.'

He looked across at his brother. 'You were right, and it's time it was dealt with.'

'What's wrong with her?' Rose couldn't hide her anxiety.

'It isn't serious but it should be put right, or it will be an impediment in her life and that would be a shame.' He smiled at Annie. 'She's a lovely child but she's tongue-tied.'

'What's that mean?'

'It's a restricted mobility of the tongue because of an abnormality of tissue connecting it to the floor of the mouth.' He rattled off the medical explanation.

Rose had to let that sink in for a few moments. 'You mean she can't move her tongue enough to get the words out?'

'Yes.'

Annie couldn't go through life like that – it wouldn't be right. 'Can anything be done about it?'

'It's a simple operation and if you'd like to bring her to the hospital next Wednesday at ten I'll put it right for her.'

'Hospital?' Rose fingered the few coins in her pocket. 'How much will it cost?'

'I take a few charity cases and I'm prepared to make Annie one of them.'

'Charity', of course, was a dirty word to Rose, but pride wouldn't get Annie's trouble sorted out. 'Give me the address.'

He handed her a card.

'Thank you. We'll be there. How long will it take?'

'Not long, but as she's rather frail I'll want to keep her overnight. I'll make special arrangements for you to stay with her, if you would like to?'

'Thank you.' Her insides knotted in apprehension as she realized she'd have to take time off from the factory. She hadn't been there long – would the boss let her miss work, or would he sack her on the spot? She hated the job, but work was hard to come by, and the money made a difference to her mother.

She stooped down in front of Annie. 'Next week the doctor's going to put your tongue right so you'll be able to talk properly.'

Annie looked doubtful.

'But you mustn't be afraid because I'm going to stay with you all the time.'

The little girl looked at the tall doctor. 'Hurt?'

'No,' he laughed, 'you won't feel a thing.'

Annie seemed satisfied with that, but as he turned away, she caught hold of his coat. 'Wosie hurt.'

'I know. I'm just going to have a look at her too.'

'Tank you.'

'Who hit you?' he asked, as he examined Rose's face.

'Dad. Ugh, nasty,' Annie informed him.

'Annie!' Rose scolded.

'Did,' the little one protested.

'I know, but you don't have to tell everyone.' Rose raised her eyebrows at the doctor. 'You sure it's a good idea to free her tongue?'

Everyone laughed, including Annie.

The doctor smoothed some ointment on to her lip. 'Why did he do this?'

'Took lent.'

'Annie!'

'You took the rent?' he asked, puzzled.

'No, of course not.' Rose knew she'd have to explain now that her blabbermouth sister had aroused their interest. 'He took the money Mum had put aside for the rent collector. I had to get it back,' she added simply.

'Did you succeed?'

'Yes, but he didn't like it.'

'Hmm. I can see that.' He patted something on to her bruised eye, then handed her a small jar. 'Put some of that on night and morning. It'll help to reduce the swelling.'

'How much?'

'Nothing.'

'You don't have to treat *me* like a charity case,' Rose told him indignantly. 'I can afford to pay for a bit of salve.'

'Such pride.' The doctor looked at his brother, who nodded in agreement. Then he sat beside her. 'I realize you have a tough life, Rose, and you need to be strong, but don't be too proud to accept help when it's offered. Some of us do care what happens to you, you know.'

Rose felt ashamed of her outburst. 'I'm sorry.'

He gave an understanding smile. 'You must learn to take as well as give. The two go hand in hand.'

Rose knew that he was right: she loved to give, but pride reared its head when her role was reversed. 'I'll try.'

Annie, clearly fed up with being left out, wriggled across the chairs until she was sitting on the doctor's lap.

Rose couldn't believe her eyes. She'd never seen her sister behave like that – and to have the nerve to sit on the man's lap . . . Good Lord, he must be furious. She reached out for her and the little girl came willingly.

'Wosie cwy, no cool, 'ate din,' she informed everyone.

The doctor frowned at Rose. 'I'm afraid I didn't understand that.'

'She means I was upset because I had to leave school, and I hate the noisy factory, and . . .' she glared down at her sister ' . . . I think she's not having that operation.'

Dr Trenchard stood up, chuckling. 'She's got character.'

'A bit too much of it,' Rose muttered darkly. Here she was, trying to keep her life and feelings to herself, and this bundle of mischief had told everyone their business. And she couldn't even talk properly! What on earth was she going to be like when she could get her tongue round the words?

Rose knocked on the boss's door and sent up a silent prayer that she wasn't about to lose her job.

'Come.'

She went in, feeling rather like Daniel entering the lion's den.

'Yes?' Mr Baker asked abruptly, then stared. 'What happened to your face?'

'Ran into a door,' she lied.

He snorted in disbelief. 'More like somebody's fist, by the look of it.'

Rose saw little point in trying to deny it. He knew where she came from. He didn't seem to be in a very good mood. Oh, hell, she thought, but pitched in anyway. 'I need Wednesday and Thursday off, please, sir.'

'Why?'

'My sister – she's only two and a half – has to have an operation and she'll be scared if I don't stay with her.'

'What's the matter with her?' he asked sharply.

'She's tongue-tied, sir, can't speak properly. They've got to – '

'I know what it means.' He sat back and looked her up and down. 'Operations are expensive, how are you going to pay for it?'

'I'm not, sir. The doctor's doing it as a charity case.'

'Who is he?'

'Dr Trenchard.'

'I know him. He's a good man. How did you come to know him?'

Rose bit back the retort that it was none of his business, but after a moment's hesitation, she decided to tell him the truth – after all, her job might depend upon this interview. 'His brother is giving me lessons every Sunday afternoon. He's a teacher at the secondary school.'

Mr Baker looked interested. 'And why is he doing that?'

'I won a scholarship but couldn't take up the place because we couldn't afford the new clothes. My school made me leave because they couldn't teach me any more.'

'How old are you really?'

That had torn it. Now she was definitely going to lose her job. 'Well, I'm not fourteen,' she hedged.

'I've been aware of that from the beginning.' He sat up straight. 'How old are you?'

'Nearly twelve, sir.' That sounded a bit better than eleven, she comforted herself.

'Good grief!' He was startled. 'And they made you leave school?'

Rose nodded. It still hurt. 'Are you going to sack me?'

He shook his head and she breathed a sigh of relief.

'If you can't go to school, then someone must employ you. Your work is good and you appear to be very bright,' he told her.

'Top of the school, I was,' she said, with pride.

'And what is Mr Trenchard teaching you?'

'Reading, writing, arithmetic, history and Latin.'

'Latin!' Now he was astonished. 'What good is that going to do you?'

'Don't know, sir, but it's fun and he said it might be useful later on.'

Mr Baker's gaze ran over her again, thoughtfully this time. Then he nodded. 'Very well. You may have leave this week, but don't make a habit of it.'

'I won't, sir, and thank you.' She couldn't believe it. He'd given her the time off, he knew her real age *and* he hadn't sacked her.

8

August 1914

It was too hot to sleep. Rose slid carefully out of the bed she shared with Flo, picked up her books and made her way downstairs. The scullery was a little cooler, but not much. The night was humid and stifling, and the heat only made their living conditions even more unbearable. It encouraged vermin, she thought, with a shudder, as she put her books on the old wooden table. At least that was clean – it was scrubbed every day.

After the bank holiday, Mr Trenchard was going to set her an exam, so as she couldn't sleep, she might as well study. First, though, she would read a bit more of her Bible. She had reached the Book of Revelation, and found it most puzzling of all.

She lit a candle rather than the smelly oil lamp, and settled down to read.

Some time later, she picked up her pencil and underlined a sentence, then sat back, deep in thought.

What did that mean? ' . . . behold, I have set before thee an open door, and no man can shut it: . . .' The thought of an open door was exciting, but there didn't seem to be an open door anywhere in her life. Every turn she made seemed to lead to a dead end and there was no escape. She had a job she hated, she was still locked in poverty, and as far as she could see only her mind was free. No one could cage that. She could weave wonderful dreams and wander where she pleased, was free to explore others' thoughts and ideas through their writings.

She chewed the end of her pencil. Was that what the passage meant? When all other doors appeared closed, was the door of your mind the one that 'no man can shut'?

But if she believed that, it would surely be like accepting that things like poverty couldn't be changed? She rejected that idea. There must be a way of opening those closed doors and stepping through into a better life. And she wasn't talking about dying – oh, no, the improvement in life had to take place here, or what was the struggle for?

She threw down the pencil and stood up to get herself a cup of water. Even that was warm.

'Can I have a drink, Rosie?'

She spun round. 'Annie, I didn't hear you come down.'

Annie grinned. 'I haven't got any shoes on.'

Rose poured her some water and handed it to her. 'Can't you sleep?'

'Too hot.' Annie drank the water and put the empty cup on the table. 'What you doing?' she asked.

'I couldn't sleep either so I thought I'd do some reading.'

Annie nodded, yawned and trotted back to bed.

Rose watched her go. What a difference in less than a year. After the operation she'd begun to speak properly and now she could talk the hind legs off a donkey. Her health and confidence had improved and she was like any normal three-year-old, under everyone's feet.

Rose rinsed the cups and decided she'd better get down to some serious studying, but before she could sit down, the old man lurched in.

Drunk again, she saw, and turned away in disgust. Since their run-in over the rent, he'd stayed out of her way as much as possible.

She jumped when she felt a hand slip round her waist. She turned quickly, sending the old man staggering across the scullery.

'What do you think you're up to?' she demanded, hands on hips.

'Don't be like that, Rosie.' He held on to the table to steady himself. 'I was just trying to be friendly.'

'Friendly?' she blazed. 'When have you ever been friendly to me?'

He came towards her, a crafty look on his face. 'If you give me a chance, I'll show you how nice I can be.'

'You're disgusting!'

'What's disgusting about it?' He leered. 'Come on, Rosie, I'll teach you things you can't learn from no books. You're turning into quite a beauty, and someone's going to get you before long.'

He reached out, clearly intending to run his hands over her again, but she slapped them off her. 'Get away from me.' She had her back to the sink and he'd blocked her only escape route. She was frightened.

'Come on.' He got within touching distance again. 'You're not my flesh and blood, so there's no harm in it.'

This was unbelievable. He'd hit and insulted her all her life, and all of a sudden he wanted to touch her.

'You think you're better than us, don't you?' He swayed drunkenly. 'But let me tell you, girl, you're in the dirt and some day you'll see there's no way out. We takes what little pleasure there is in this life – '

'Not with me, you don't!'

'You was born a bastard and yer only fit for one thing,' he shouted.

Rose felt like strangling him.

He smirked, and then, with surprising agility, made a lunge for her.

She sidestepped and he fell against the stove.

'Stand still, you slippery bitch.'

She clenched her fists and lifted them. 'You take one more step towards me and I'll knock your teeth down your throat.'

He saw evidently that she meant what she said, and stepped back. He forced a laugh. 'You're too serious for a young'un, girl. I was playing a joke on you.'

'I didn't see the funny side of it.'

Thank heaven it was Sunday. That set-to with the old man last night had unsettled her, but she could forget it for a couple of hours while she had her lesson. Rose sighed as she looked around Miss Gardner's pleasant front room, a haven of peace. She picked up a newspaper and sat in one of the comfortable chairs, at once absorbed in what she was reading.

'Don't frown like that, Rose.' Mr Trenchard walked into the room.

Rose looked up from the paper. 'Hello, sir.'

'What's making you scowl so?'

'Do you think there's going to be a war?'

'It looks very likely. But tell me what you've gleaned from the paper.'

'Well.' Rose leaned forward. 'There was a short report last month about some Archduke and his wife being killed in a place called Bosnia – '

'And what do you think that has to do with us?'

'It's complicated, but it seems that Austria is about to declare war on Serbia, with Germany's support, and if Germany threatens France, we will go to war with them.' She watched Mr Trenchard polish his spectacles. 'Have I got that right?'

'Yes. That's exactly the situation.'

Rose frowned at the newspaper again. 'I find it hard to understand why we should have to fight. I hope it never happens.'

A week later that was still Rose's hope when she took some of the children out for a treat. It was a scorching August bank holiday and she wanted to get out of their cramped little house. She sat under a huge tree and watched them. Annie was chattering happily to another little girl she'd just met, Will and Charlie were chasing pigeons and Nancy was sitting quietly beside her on the grass.

'This is a nice place,' Nancy said. 'Thank you for bringing us, Rosie.'

She turned and smiled. 'Better than Garrett Street, isn't it?'

'Oh, yes. What's this place called?'

'Green Park,' Rose told her. 'As it's so hot I thought it would be nice to come somewhere with lots of nice shady trees.'

'Feels cooler here,' Nancy agreed.

'Rosie!' Charlie and Will skidded to a halt in front of

her. 'There's a shop across the road selling lemonade.'

'And you'd like some, I suppose?' She stood up.

They nodded eagerly, then looked doubtful. 'Only if you've got enough money.'

'I think I can manage that, and we'll see if they've got some buns too.'

'Wow!' said Charlie. 'This is the best day we've ever had.'

Rose was glad she'd thought of this treat. She'd tried to get all the kids to come with her, but Flo was with her friends, Bob had vanished, as usual, and Bert wasn't feeling well. Still, she'd take the other three a bun too. After buying herself some new shoes, she'd been saving up for a winter coat, but in this heat winter seemed a long way off and it wouldn't do any harm to spend a little of the money.

When they'd enjoyed the lemonade and buns, they went back into the park for another hour and then, reluctantly, made their way to the bus stop for the homeward journey.

There was a lot of noise, with people talking excitedly, so Rose looked towards the newspaper seller. Her heart raced with alarm.

'What does that say?' Will asked.

The news placard read, 'WAR INEVITABLE.'

For four months the recruitment campaign raged, using any means to get the young men into the army. They flocked to join up. There were many reasons why the boys and men enlisted – excitement, patriotism, fear of what others might say if they didn't, and many because they couldn't get any other work.

The children found it all very interesting as one man after another from their street joined up.

'You going in the army?' Bob asked his father, jumping up and down with excitement. 'Jack's dad's just come home for Christmas and he looks smashing in his uniform.'

'That's all right for your mate's dad but I'm not fit enough to fight.'

Bob eyed him suspiciously. 'What's wrong with you?'

'I got a bad back.' He gave his son a sharp clip round the ear. 'Anyway, it's none of your bloody business. You're too young to understand.'

Bob ran out of the scullery, straight into Flo.

'Have you heard?' Flo cried. 'The Germans have shelled Hartlepool, Scarborough and Whitby. There's loads of people dead.'

There was silence around the table as they all tried to take in this piece of distressing news.

'Oh, my.' Their mother sighed. 'It'll be our turn next, you see if I'm not right.'

'Don't be daft, woman,' her husband told her scathingly. 'Their guns can't reach London.'

'No, but they've got Zeppelins.'

Nancy whimpered. 'What will we do if they drop bombs on us?'

'It might not come to that,' Rose said soothingly. 'We don't know what's going to happen, do we?'

Nancy gave a tremulous smile, clearly trying to be brave.

The old man's chair scraped back and he stood up. 'You're all talking a lot of nonsense. The war won't last long.'

Marj Webster shook her head sadly. 'Everyone said it would all be over by Christmas, but it isn't, is it?'

'I'm off down the pub, then. I'm not staying here to listen to your doom and gloom.' With that, he stormed out of the house.

'Things could get rough, couldn't they?' Rose said to her mother quietly.

'Yes, though you probably know more about it than I do, Rosie, with all your reading. What does Mr Trenchard think?'

'Well, he says it won't be the quick war everyone was expecting, and now the Germans have started to attack the ordinary people . . .' She tailed off.

Her mother looked out at the crowded back-to-back houses and frowned. 'If they drops bombs on a place like this it'll be terrible.'

Rose gave a humourless laugh. 'If it wasn't for the people living here I'd tell the Germans to come and destroy it. It would be one way of getting rid of this slum.'

'You really do hate living like this, don't you, Rosie?'

'I've never made a secret of it, Mum.'

'I know, and perhaps one day you'll get out of here, but for the moment we must get through this war as best we can.'

Rose nodded. The months or years ahead were going to be a hard struggle for everyone.

9

June 1916

Mr Trenchard removed his spectacles, polished them, then laid them on the table. 'I'm afraid this will be our last session, Rose.'

'Last?' She tried to hide her shock. It was a terrible blow to hear that he was going to stop her Sunday visits. However, she couldn't expect him to bother with her for ever, and he had been teaching her for almost three years now. 'I'm sorry about that, Mr Trenchard, but I do understand. It's been good of you to keep up the lessons for so long, and I've enjoyed every minute of them,' she assured him. 'You've opened up a whole new world to me.'

'Rose, you're only fourteen and I'd be happy to teach you for many years to come, but I'm afraid I have received my conscription papers.'

She was horrified. They'd been at war for nearly two years and she was aware that there was now compulsory conscription, but she had never thought that he would be called upon. 'But you're a teacher and needed at home,' she blurted out.

'Women are taking on men's work now, as you know.' He sighed. 'It's ironic that it's taken this dreadful war for a woman's worth to be recognized.'

That was true enough, Rose thought. She herself had

been promoted, and the factory was working continual shifts to turn out all that was needed for the war effort. 'Isn't there an age limit, sir?' she asked, looking frantically for a reason to keep him from getting killed.

'Forty-five.'

'Oh.' Mr Trenchard was nowhere near that old. 'Are you going into the army?'

'The navy.'

That was a relief. It was dangerous in the navy, of course, as the sinking of the *Lusitania* last year had shown, but at least he wouldn't be going into the trenches. The losses there had been horrific.

'Grace and I will be getting married next Saturday, Rose, and we'd like you to come to the wedding.'

'Oh, thank you, sir, I'd like that.'

'I think it's time you called me John, don't you?'

'I don't think – '

He smiled at the look of doubt on her face. 'This war is changing many old attitudes, Rose, and I would like to think we have become friends.'

She realized that what he'd said was true, they had become friends, but more than that: he had been her teacher, guide and someone she had been able to confide in. She was going to miss him dreadfully. She had talked to him openly and honestly, telling him things she would normally have kept to herself.

He understood her volatile nature, and she respected his intelligence and genuine kindness – but now she was going to lose him. It had had to come, of course, she knew that, but not like this.

She would pray for him every day, and if there *was* a God He would not let this good man die.

'I want you to do something for me while I'm away, Rose.'

'Anything,' she answered immediately.

'Will you visit Grace regularly?'

'Of course I will.' She swallowed hard, trying to keep tears at bay, although she felt as if her foundations had been torn away.

John patted her hand. 'That will be a great comfort to us, and I shall be able to picture you both sitting here, surrounded by books.'

Oh, Lord, she was going to cry.

'Don't grieve for me, Rose,' he told her gently. 'I've set out a programme of reading and study for you, and when I return I shall expect you to have completed it.'

She took the books and sniffed loudly, as a tear ran down her cheek.

He waited while she composed herself. 'I don't want you to neglect your studies,' he told her sternly. 'You have a fine mind, but you will never reach your full potential unless you continue to work. I was in the process of preparing some examinations for you to tackle, but they will have to wait for a while.'

'What kind of examinations?' she asked wistfully.

'Secondary standard.'

'What?' Her eyes opened wide in surprise. 'Do you think I'd be good enough?'

'With a bit of extra coaching, I think you might be. That's why I don't want you to stop studying.'

Rose sat up straight 'When the war's over will you still teach me?'

'Of course. I shall look forward to taking up where

we've left off, and discovering how much you've learned while I've been away.'

She smiled. 'I'll see if I can surprise you, then.'

He tipped back his head and laughed. 'You have continually surprised me, Rose, from the moment we met.'

They were both laughing when the door opened and Grace came in with Annie – the little girl was a frequent visitor now.

'How lovely to see two such happy faces.' Grace beamed.

It was only when Rose looked into her eyes that she saw how worried Grace was about John going into the navy, and she vowed to help them as much as she could. She would never be able to repay them for what they had done for her. John had become the pivot of her life, opening doors in her mind and giving her a wider view of the world.

'I was so happy to hear about your marriage,' she said brightly to Grace.

'Thank you.' Grace put the tray of tea and biscuits on the table. 'I hope you're coming to the wedding?'

'You couldn't keep me away. I'll buy a new frock, so you won't be ashamed of me.'

'We'd never be ashamed of you,' Grace and John said together.

Annie clambered on to a chair and slid across until she was sitting on John's lap. Then she turned her large eyes to him. 'Can I come to your wedding, please?'

'We shall be very upset if you don't,' he told her seriously.

'Can I have a new frock too?' she squeaked excitedly.

'Hmm. I think you should have new shoes, too. You've

got holes in the bottom of those.' Rose could see them plainly as her sister waved her feet about in excitement.

Annie lifted up a foot and showed it to John. 'They've got holes and they're too small.'

He tutted. 'Then you must definitely have new ones.'

Annie glanced uncertainly at Rose. 'Don't worry, Toots, I think I can manage it.' There went her winter coat again, she thought philosophically. She had never been able to get one as something else was always more pressing.

Grace stooped down in front of Annie, who had got off John's lap now and was sitting on a chair waiting patiently for her milk. 'Will you be my flower-girl, Annie?'

'What's that?'

'Well, you stand behind me during the wedding and hold my flowers for me.'

Annie thought about it for a few moments, then nodded. 'I can do that.'

'Good. That's settled, then.'

Rose studied John and Grace. They had been walking out for a long time and she wondered why it had taken them so long to decide to get married. After all, John was a kind person, not a bit like their old man. 'Is it because of the war that you're getting married?' she asked, knowing it was a cheeky question, but she'd come to know them so well.

'We've always intended to wed,' John told her, not seeming to mind the question, 'but it was frowned upon for married women to work, and Grace had had such a struggle to get a job as a teacher that she didn't want to give it up.'

'But things are changing, aren't they?' Rose asked. 'Lots of married women are working for the war effort now.'

'Yes.' Grace poured Annie some more milk. 'Women are going to have a lot more freedom now, and that's a good thing, don't you think?'

Rose nodded. 'Yes, that's one door open, but we are still restricted.' She thought of herself now as a woman. She turned to John. 'Do you think we will ever get the vote?'

'After the war, the pressure on the government to extend the franchise to women will be immense, and I don't think they will be able to evade the issue much longer.'

'The Suffragettes won't let them, will they?' Rose grinned at the thought.

'Don't get involved with the suffrage movement, Rose,' John told her, as if he had read her mind. 'You wait your time. There will be many things for you to do when you've finished your education.'

'Such as?'

'I'm not sure yet, but one day you will see exactly where your destiny lies.'

Another week done, thank goodness. Rose slumped into a chair and rubbed her temple.

'Headache?' her mother asked.

'Hmm, a bit, but it'll soon go.' She emptied her pay packet on to the table, counted out eighteen shillings and gave them to her mother.

'Rose, you must keep more for yourself. You're working like a slave at that factory.'

'Everyone is, but you need it more than I do.'

Her mother gave her back two shillings. 'You must think of yourself more.'

'But I do,' she protested.

'No, you don't, my girl. I know how badly you need a winter coat, but each time you've saved enough together, you spend it on me or the children, and it isn't right.'

Rose grinned when she heard her mother use that phrase, remembering the first Sunday lesson she'd had. John had asked her what she was going to do about injustice and had pointed out that one person could make a difference.

'Why don't you get yourself a coat from the tallyman?'

That brought Rose out of her reverie. 'You know I won't have anything unless I can afford to pay for it,' she reminded her mother. The old man's theft of the rent money had made a deep impression on her. Now she had an aversion to debt of any kind.

'Jobs are secure now,' her mother pointed out. 'You'd be able to afford it all right.'

'No,' she said, emphatically. 'I'll wait until I can pay for it.'

'But that could take some time, and you're going to need it soon.'

Rose dismissed the idea with a shrug.

'There.' Her mother gave up and poured her a cup of tea. 'You drink that, it will soon clear the headache.'

'The cure-all brew.' Rose laughed.

'Don't mock it. There's a lot of truth in some of these old wives' remedies.'

Rose didn't argue. Her mother was a great believer in that kind of thing.

'Better?' Marj asked.

She nodded, and it was true: the niggling pain had almost gone.

'Rosie.' Annie ran into the scullery. 'Is it time to get ready yet?'

'We've got plenty of time,' she told the impatient child. 'The wedding isn't until four.'

'Oh.' Annie stood on tiptoe to look at the clock on the shelf. It took her some time to work out where the big and little hands were. 'It's one o'clock now?' she asked hesitantly.

'Very good,' her mother praised her.

Although Annie was now five, she was small for her age, and still lagged a little behind the others, but she was improving all the time, and Rose hoped she would soon catch up.

'We're going out soon, Toots, and I want you to put your clean knickers in a bag.'

'Why?' Annie looked puzzled.

'Because we're going to the public baths,' she told her. 'What for?'

'To have a bath, silly. We can't wear our new frocks without being clean, can we?'

As she reached out to pick up her empty cup, Rose noticed a letter on the table. 'What's that?' she asked, her heart beginning to thump uncomfortably. The only other time they'd had a letter delivered to them was when they'd been up to their eyes in debt.

Before her mother could answer, the old man came in. Since the start of the war, he'd been forced to take work in a munitions factory and he'd never stopped complaining about it. Rose, however, had been glad to see him do something useful for a change.

'There's a letter for you.' Marj held it out to him.

'Well, read it for me,' he said irritably.

Marj opened the envelope.

'What does it say?'

'It's your conscription papers. You're to report for the army next Wednesday.'

'What?' He snatched it out of her hands and thrust it at Rose. 'She read it wrong.'

After a quick glance, Rose handed it back. 'That's what it says.'

'But I can't!' he bellowed. 'I'm not fit enough. I told them – my back – '

'They don't agree,' Rose told him. 'They've passed you fit for duty.'

He turned pale and, for the first time in her life, Rose felt a stirring of pity for him. She'd never like him, of course, but what chance had he ever had in life? He'd been born in the slums and hadn't had enough education to better himself, so was it any wonder he'd accepted that this kind of life was all he was ever going to get? Now he was about to be dragged out of the only environment he'd ever known into heaven knows what.

'Mr Trenchard has got his papers as well.' Rose needed to offer some comfort – she wouldn't wish the trenches on her worst enemy.

'Is it him what's been learning you all this time?'

'Yes.'

'Knows what's what, does he?'

'Yes, he's very clever.'

'And they've called him up?'

Rose nodded sadly.

He stared gloomily out of the window at the grimy street. 'They must be desperate 'cos they're scraping the bottom of the barrel if they want the likes of me.'

'You mustn't think like that, Tom,' Marj admonished. 'You'll make as good a soldier as anyone else.'

His usual cockiness was restored. 'You're right, Marj, and it's no use grousing about it. I'll go down the boozer and see if any of the others are going, as well.'

They watched him head across the street. It was a wonder there wasn't a permanent groove in the road between their house and the pub, Rose thought.

She looked at her mother. Since she'd had David, she hadn't become pregnant again and looked years younger. She was an attractive woman again.

'I'm thinking of getting a job. Mrs Jenks down the road has offered to look after the kids.' Marj looked at Rose. 'What do you think?'

'With the old man away and the children growing up, it will give you a real change – and extra cash.' Rose was delighted at the idea.

'Yes, and I'll get twenty-five shillings a week from the army, paid straight to me.' Marj frowned at the letter sitting on the table. 'I don't know how he'll cope with it.'

'It's tough for everyone.' Rose paused. She'd never told her mother about the time the old man had tried to mess with her. Some things in life were best left unsaid. 'It's funny, you know, I always call him "the old man", but he can't be forty-five yet or he wouldn't have been called-up.'

'He's only thirty-nine,' her mother told her, 'but the kind of life we lead ages you.'

Rose knew this was true – and another thing that

wasn't right. No one's life should be blighted like this. But the politicians were paying more attention to the working classes now – if only because they needed them, Rose thought cynically.

10

'Hello, Rose.' The woman behind the counter handed her a towel and a bar of soap. 'You can have your usual room.'

'Can my sister come in with me?'

'Of course.' The attendant leaned over the counter to look at the child. 'And what's your name?'

'Annie.' She beamed. 'We're going to a wedding and I'm going to hold the flowers, so we've got to be clean.' She held up the bag she was clutching. 'I've got my clean knickers with me.'

Rose dragged her away before she could tell the woman their entire family history.

'You been here before, Rosie?' Annie asked, trotting along the corridor, trying to peer into the rooms as they went past.

'I come every week.' Her sister's curiosity was insatiable, Rose marvelled. Not like hers, of course – she was only interested in books and learning: Annie wanted to know what was going on around her, what other people were doing. Rose couldn't care less what other people thought and did.

They reached the allotted room and she opened the door. Annie rushed in and peered over the edge of the bath. 'Oooh, it's big.' Her eyes were wide.

Rose couldn't help laughing at the expression on her little face. 'You can come in with me, then you'll be safe.'

It turned out to be more of a playtime than a bath, with Annie squealing in delight, but Rose finally managed to give them both a good scrub and wash their hair. They came out of the baths pink and glowing.

Grace didn't wear the traditional white dress, but Rose thought she looked beautiful. Her frock was of the palest blue, with a heart-shaped neckline and long sleeves. The material was so flimsy that it swirled around her ankles as she walked. Her hat's small brim was surrounded with white flowers and her shoes were also white. To add to the charming picture, Grace was clearly delighted to be marrying the man she loved. John looked distinguished and proud in his new dark grey suit. His brother, Dr Edward Trenchard, was the best man, and because Grace's father was dead, another friend of theirs, Harold, they called him, was giving the bride away. Rose had not met him before, but he looked a kindly man.

Annie took her duty very seriously, looking at her big sister from time to time for a nod of approval. After the ceremony they all went back to Grace's house. It was a small gathering of only ten people, and Rose made herself useful by handing round the sandwiches and tea. It was a happy occasion, for John and Grace were well liked, but she couldn't help feeling sad because John had to report to the navy in a few days.

Rose had just come back from the kitchen with another plate of sandwiches when she heard Annie giggle, and spun round to see what the little rascal was doing. 'Oh, no,' she groaned, 'I can't trust her for one minute at a time.'

Grace laughed and stopped her from dashing across

the room to retrieve the little girl. 'Leave her – Edward won't mind. He's become fond of her since he did the operation on her tongue.'

Rose fidgeted. 'I'm not sure it was such a good idea,' she muttered. 'You ought to hear the things she tells people! And look at her now! She's getting too big to sit on anyone's lap, and why is it always the men?'

'Perhaps she doesn't get the chance at home,' Grace said softly.

'You're right. I've never seen her dad playing with any of them, let alone cuddling them.'

Grace gave her a strange look, then glanced at Annie. 'She's an affectionate child, and I suspect you might be the only one to show her any love – she adores you.'

'Mum loves all of us, I'm sure, but she's just too busy trying to make ends meet to be able to spend any time on us. It's not her fault,' Rose said stoutly.

'Of course it isn't. It must be hard bringing up nine children.' Grace looked across at Annie again and started to chuckle. 'Look at her, the poor little thing's fallen asleep on Edward's lap. She's tired out after all the excitement.'

'I'd better take her home.'

It was an hour later when they finally left the party. Rose had to carry Annie from the bus stop because she was too exhausted to walk. It had been difficult not to cry when she'd said goodbye to John. She was going to miss him so much, and he would be in her prayers every night. She hoped that God would be listening to her.

'You awake, darling?' John kissed his new wife gently.

'Hmm.' Grace wrapped her arms around him and

yawned sleepily. 'It was a lovely wedding, wasn't it?'

'Yes, it went very well.' He paused. 'We should have done this a long time ago, Grace.'

She pulled herself upright, now wide awake. 'I'm sorry I've made you wait so long, but there never seemed to be any hurry. Now we have such a short time together.'

He stroked her hair. 'You make it sound as if I'm not coming back,' he chided. 'You never know, they might give me an office job.'

'Oh, do you think they would?' she asked eagerly.

'Well, of course my eyesight's not perfect, and they seemed very interested in my qualifications.'

'Oh, John! That would be wonderful.'

'We'll have to wait and see, but whatever happens, you mustn't worry about me.' He grinned down at her. 'I'm going to be perfectly safe because Rose has promised to pray for me, and I don't think even the Almighty would ignore her.'

Laughter shook Grace. 'At fourteen she's turning into quite a formidable young woman, isn't she?'

'She certainly is. On the outside she appears distant, unemotional and controlled, and that is the way she wants the world to see her, but you've only to watch her with Annie to see she has a softer side.'

'She's had a hard life and believes she'll only survive by being tough.' Grace laid her head on his chest. 'I hope she doesn't have to take too many knocks and disappointments or that loving spark might he buried beneath anger and resentment.'

'She has a strong will and plenty of determination, and I think she'll be all right. Don't let her stop studying, will you?'

'I won't, but I don't think anything in this world would stop her. She has a voracious appetite for knowledge.'

'I still can't believe she comes from Garrett Street.'

'She must be a real misfit there.' Then Grace started to laugh. 'Didn't Annie looked a picture today in her pink dress?'

John chuckled. 'She told me and Edward that Rose had taken her to the public baths, and described it all in great detail. Rose would have been horrified.'

'It's lovely the affection between them, but have you noticed how different they are? Annie's fair and delicate, and Rose is dark and strong.' Grace frowned. 'You'd never believe they came from the same family.'

'I noticed that especially today when Annie was sleeping on Edward's lap. The little girl is loving, outgoing and trusting, but Rose is quite the opposite. She keeps a tight hold on herself and does not give her trust easily.'

'She trusts you.' Grace smiled affectionately at her husband.

John nodded. 'I do believe she does, and I'm honoured.' Then he slid Grace down in the bed, and they abandoned all talk.

Later, as he was drifting into sleep he awoke with a start. 'Oh, good Lord!' He shook Grace. 'Wake up, darling.'

'What is it?' she said, alarmed.

'I've just remembered who Rose reminds me of.'

'Who?' she asked, puzzled.

'I must be imagining it.' He spoke almost to himself. 'Grace, I've never heard her speak about her father, have you?'

'Now you mention it, I don't think so. But just today

she talked about Annie's father, as if the man had nothing to do with her.'

'She's the eldest, isn't she?'

'Yes.'

'Then perhaps the man her mother married isn't Rose's father?'

Grace shrugged. 'I suppose so, but what are you getting at? Who does she remind you of?'

'Well, I might be mistaken, but she's the image of him.'

'In what way?'

'The dark eyes, for a start, but that isn't all, she has the same blue-black hair.'

'That isn't much to go on.'

'Agreed, but all his characteristics are there – the proud way she holds her head, the directness of her gaze, even the way she moves, and her intelligence. There are too many similarities to dismiss.'

'Who is it?' Grace asked excitedly.

He bent his head and whispered in her ear.

'But – but – ' she stuttered. 'Good heavens! I've met him and you're right, she's the image of him, especially now she's older. But we must be mistaken, he's – ' She came to an abrupt halt.

'I know what you're thinking, but I'm convinced I'm right. When I first met her I felt as if I'd seen her before, but she came from Garrett Street, and that clouded my judgement. Now she's older the resemblance is evident. She must have something to do with that family.' He rolled over and groaned into the pillow. 'Damn it! I *wish* I wasn't going away. I'd love to look into this further.'

Rose stood on the platform with her mother and watched

the men boarding the train. It was a sad scene. Some were already in uniform, but the majority were conscripts trying to put a brave face on things in an effort to comfort their weeping women.

She could see Grace hugging John, and wondered if she should go over to them, but quickly decided against it. She had said goodbye and this moment was for husband and wife. Swallowing a lump in her throat, she looked away, but it seemed as if everyone else on the platform was crying. Even her mother was wiping away a tear as she watched the old man get on to the train. However, he was with a group of his drinking friends and seemed happy enough, which was hardly surprising as they had been drinking since breakfast.

Rose shook her head sadly: they were in for a shock when they sobered up and found themselves in an army camp with the sergeant shouting orders at them.

As the train pulled out of the station, everyone was waving and calling, but Rose watched in silence, wondering how many of the men would come back. She cast a quick glance at her mother and saw that although she wasn't crying her expression was grim.

'He'll be all right, Mum. If anyone can dodge trouble, it'll be him,' she joked. 'After all, he's had plenty of practice.'

'I expect you're right.' Marj sighed and looked around the platform at the silent women now making their way back to their homes.

Rose edged her towards the exit. She had to get back to work.

'Thank you for coming. I couldn't have faced it without you,' Marj said.

Rose pulled a face. 'I don't think he knew we were here.'

'But someone from the family had to see him off to war. He's frightened, you see, and drinking was the only way he could get over it. I just hope the army has a good supply of beer.'

As they walked out of the station, Grace was waiting for them. Her eyes were red but she managed a smile. 'Hello, Rose.'

Rose turned to her mother. 'This is Mrs Trenchard, Mum.'

Grace held out her hand. 'I'm pleased to meet you, Mrs Webster.'

'I'm ever so grateful to you and your husband for helping Rose carry on with her lessons,' her mother said. 'It near broke her heart when she had to leave school.'

'Oh, John has loved teaching her.' Grace smiled. 'You have a remarkable daughter, Mrs Webster.'

Marj nodded. 'Yes, she's always been bright.'

Rose shuffled uncomfortably from foot to foot. She wished they wouldn't talk about her. 'Annie hasn't stopped going on about the wedding,' she blurted out.

'A real chatter-box she is now.' Marj laughed.

'She's a delightful little girl,' Grace told her.

At that moment a woman walked past them sobbing loudly, and Grace gave her a compassionate glance. 'Such a terrible war, isn't it? I expect all your children will miss their father.'

'I suppose so, though they never saw much of him.'

'How many children do you and your husband have, Mrs Webster?'

'Eight,' Marj answered automatically. 'Oh, and Rose, of course, that makes nine.'

'My goodness, you have your hands full.'

'You can say that, all right.'

Grace turned to Rose. 'Will you visit me this Sunday? I expect I shall be feeling rather lonely.'

'Of course. I'll come at the usual time.'

'That would be lovely, thank you. And now perhaps you would both like to come to the tea-room with me. I don't feel like going home just yet.'

'I've got to get back to work,' Rose told her, looking anxiously at the clock above the station entrance.

'What a shame. Would you join me, Mrs Webster?'

'Er . . .'

'Go on, Mum,' Rose urged. 'It'll do you good.'

'That's settled, then,' Grace said, not giving Marj Webster a chance to refuse.

Rose said goodbye and hurried away. Her mother had looked a bit doubtful, but Grace would soon put her at her ease, and if Marj was thinking of going out to work, then she'd have to get used to mixing with other people again.

Rose had had more than her allotted time off work, and broke into a trot, thinking about the conversation they'd had outside the station. Her mother had nearly told Grace that she was not one of the old man's kids, but she didn't think Grace had noticed the slip.

II

December 1916

Rose shivered and pulled her coat around her. She'd go through the park tonight: there were some nice little shops on the other side, and she wanted to find something to give the children this Christmas. She opened the rickety old gate, and smiled to herself. To call this a park was giving it a grandeur it didn't deserve, but it was a bit of green space and everyone used it. There were trees and rough areas of tangled bushes and gorse, but the middle had been cleared. In the winter the youngsters played football and in the summer people walked about or sat in the sun.

Rose shivered again as a gust of biting wind whipped at her. She'd never get a new coat at this rate, she thought, stuffing her hands into her pockets. This one was too small and threadbare, but she couldn't see the kids with nothing to look forward to this festive season. She remembered her own disappointment when she'd been told repeatedly that Father Christmas had had his sleigh stolen and hadn't been able to deliver the presents.

She paused briefly by a group of carol singers. There were about ten of them swinging lanterns and singing at the top of their voices, and another four blowing trumpets. They had collected quite a crowd around them who were also joining in.

Her spirits were high and she was looking forward to Christmas. The old man wouldn't be home – they didn't have the faintest idea where he was, and as he couldn't write there hadn't been any letters from him. Her mum was working so they had more money coming in and, best of all, she'd just heard that John had been given a job at headquarters and would not be going to sea. She couldn't remember when she had felt so happy.

She threw a farthing into the collection tin and hurried on, eager to get her shopping done and out of the bitter wind.

The shops were in view when someone grabbed her from behind and dragged her across the grass into a clump of bushes.

Rose was stunned by the suddenness of the attack. The park was full of people and it had not entered her head that it might be unsafe.

He was pulling her further into the shrubbery. She could feel the branches scratching her face and legs. Terrified, she began to lash out at her assailant and shout as loudly as she could, but all that got her was a slap round the head that nearly knocked her out. Then a large hand was clamped across her mouth.

'Quiet, bitch,' he growled, 'or I'll kill you.'

There was something about his voice that turned her blood to ice. He sounded frenzied, excited and out of control.

She kicked, and heard him grunt as she made contact with his shins. Feeling his grip slacken, she wrenched herself free and started to run, but she hadn't taken more than a couple of steps before he caught her by the hair. She squealed in pain.

When he hit her this time, her head reeled. As she staggered, he threw her to the ground with force, knocking the breath out of her body. She could hear her clothes being torn, but she was incapable of defending herself. Then, with a demented laugh, he was on her.

She didn't know how long she lay there after he'd gone. She was oblivious to the cold; all she could feel was pain.

After a while she became conscious of her surroundings, and the sheer horror of what had happened galvanized her into action, but as she sat up dizziness and sickness overwhelmed her. Amid her distress one thing was clear – she was hurt and needed help.

With a tremendous effort, she pulled herself upright, and wrapped the coat around her torn clothes. She wasn't going to let strangers see her shame. The first few steps were excruciatingly painful, but she held her head high and walked out of the bushes towards the gate.

There were no tears, she was beyond that, just an empty void inside her. She had to find somewhere to clean herself up. But where could she go?

She was nowhere near the public baths, and she couldn't get on a bus in this state. Home was on the other side of the park and, anyway, she couldn't go in like this. The disgusting things that maniac had done to her made her feel dirty and ashamed.

She reached the street and held on to a fence for support. It was an effort to focus on anything so she took a few deep breaths of the cold air and her head cleared a little. That was better. Now, where was she?

Of course, there were the shops she'd been making

for – at the top of Miss Gardner's road. She'd be safe there.

Ten minutes later she was knocking at the door.

'Rose, what a lovely surpr—' A look of horror crossed Grace's face. 'Oh, my dear.'

It was only when she was inside, and felt the warmth and safety of the house, that Rose began to shake. She looked down at the floor and, in a detached way, noticed the blood on her legs and shoes.

'Come with me.' Grace gently led her upstairs and sat her on a stool while she filled the bath with water.

When Grace tried to remove her coat Rose shook her head, stood up and stepped away. 'I understand, Rose,' she told her. 'I'll leave you to see to yourself. Just call me if you need anything.' Then she turned and left, closing the door behind her.

Rose eased herself into the warm water, laid her head back and gave a ragged sigh of relief as her mind shut down. She was vaguely aware that Grace came in, picked up her clothes, and left again.

The water was lovely, she didn't ever want to get out . . .

'Rose?' There was a quick knock on the door and Grace came in again. 'You must get out now, the water will be cold.' She held a large towel.

Obediently Rose stepped out and wrapped the towel around her. It didn't seem as if she'd been in the bath more than a few seconds.

'Edward's here. Will you let him have a look at you?'

She shrugged. She felt detached from reality, but a glimmer of common sense made itself heard. She needed the help of a doctor.

'Come in, Edward,' Grace called, and when he appeared, she said anxiously, 'She hasn't spoken since she arrived.'

'Will you let me have a look at you?' Dr Trenchard brushed the wet hair away from Rose's face, and when she didn't protest, he gently removed the towel.

Rose turned her head and began to study the bathroom. Not only did it have a bath, but a toilet and washbasin as well. Such luxury! The wallpaper was pretty, with little flowers scattered over it. She began to count them, one, two, three . . .

'Where did this happen?' Dr Trenchard asked, as he wrapped her in the towel again.

'Hmm?'

He repeated the question.

'In the park.'

'I'll call the police.' He looked furious.

That catapulted Rose out of her stupor. 'No!' Her voice rang out with force. 'I came to you because I didn't know what else to do, but I won't have anyone else knowing my shame.'

'*Your* shame?' The doctor made her sit on the stool, then he squatted in front of her and took her limp hands in his. 'You haven't done anything to be ashamed of, Rose. This wasn't your fault.'

She wanted to believe him, she really did, but she couldn't. 'I *feel* ashamed.'

'The man who assaulted you should feel shame, not you.'

When she didn't speak, he continued, 'Can you describe him?'

'A soldier.'

'You saw him clearly?'

'No, I felt his uniform.' Rose remembered the rough material under her hands as she'd tried to get away from him.

'Didn't anyone come to help you? There must have been other people about?'

'There were lots, but no one heard me because of the carol singers.'

He squeezed her hands. 'You must let me tell the police. This man is vicious.'

'No!' Rose was adamant.

'She's right, Edward,' Grace interrupted. 'She can't identify him. All she knows is that he was a soldier, and there are hundreds of them around. If you call in the police it will only cause Rose more pain.'

Dr Trenchard sighed wearily. 'You're right, but I don't like to think of him getting away with such a violent attack.'

Rose remembered something the soldier had said, then shook her head. 'I don't think he will get away with anything because he said he was being sent back to the trenches and was going to have some fun before he died.'

Edward Trenchard looked ready to explode. 'Fun! If I could get my hands on him he'd never be able to do this again. I'd see to that!'

'Calm down, Edward,' Grace urged. 'Getting angry will not help Rose.'

He shook his head, then turned back to the girl. 'You know that what's happened to you could have serious consequences?' he asked gently.

She looked at him blankly.

'When is your monthly cycle due?'

'In a few days, I think.'

'At least that might eliminate the danger of pregnancy.' He stood up. 'Grace, will you give her some towels to use?'

'Of course.'

'Now, Rose, I want you to come and see me in two days' time, but if the bleeding doesn't stop within the next few hours, I want you to contact me at once. Is that clear?' he added sternly.

She nodded, deciding that she would never speak of this again, or let a man touch her like that *ever*.

'I've cleaned your clothes as best I could, and mended them.' Grace put them on the edge of the bath. 'I've also given you some of my underclothes.' Then she left the room with the doctor.

Rose retched as she put on her clothes. Then she put on the coat and pulled it tightly around her. The money in the pocket jingled and she was surprised it was still there – but, of course, he hadn't wanted money.

The full horror of what he *had* wanted rushed into her mind, and she retched again. If he hadn't caught hold of her hair she would have escaped. Her hands probed her tender scalp and, with a moan, she started to search the room. In a small cupboard she found a pair of scissors and hacked away at her hair, arranging the black tresses in a neat pile. Then she left the bathroom.

Grace and Dr Trenchard were in deep conversation when she came downstairs. They stopped talking when she appeared, and although they must have noticed her mutilated hair, they said nothing.

'Thank you very much for your help,' she said politely,

her voice devoid of expression. 'I'm sorry to have caused you this trouble, but I didn't know what else to do.'

'You did the right thing, Rose.' Grace reached out and took her hand. 'We're relieved you came to us.'

She pulled away and turned towards the door.

'Where are you going?' the doctor asked.

'I came to buy presents for the family, and if I don't hurry the shops will be closed.'

'Leave it for another day,' he said firmly. 'I'll take you home now.'

The only emotion Rose felt was anger, and now it erupted. 'I don't need you to fuss over me! I'm not a child. I'm quite capable of doing a bit of shopping.'

Edward Trenchard sighed. 'You have just been subjected to a vicious attack.'

Rose looked at him, remembering all he'd done for Annie, and felt ashamed of her outburst. 'You're right,' she said quietly, 'it is going to be hard, but you must let me do it in my own way and in my own time. I'm grateful for your kindness, but you can't help me come to terms with this horror. It isn't only my body that has been violated, something deep inside me has been badly injured . . .' She paused. 'But I'm buggered if I'm going to let it crush me!'

'If anyone can make a complete recovery, it's you.' Grace gave her an encouraging smile. 'You're not a weakling, physically or mentally, and we have great faith in you.'

Rose was glad someone had, because at that moment she felt as if her life was ruined and all her dreams for the future counted for nothing.

'Let me come shopping with you,' Grace said, 'I need

a few things myself, and then I'll see you safely on to the bus.'

Rose considered this for a moment, then nodded, and heard the doctor sigh in relief.

Later that night, Rose sat in the scullery surrounded by her beloved books, but this time they did not give her the comfort she needed. When she'd arrived home she'd told her mother that she had fallen over and hit her head on a lamp-post, and Dr Trenchard had cut her hair so he could examine her head properly. Much to her relief, this explanation had been accepted without question, and her mother had made a neater job of her hair, levelling off the ragged edges. Grace had done well with mending and cleaning her clothes, so apart from some cuts and bruises on her face and legs, nothing else was visible. The tearing hurt inside her was evident only to Rose.

She opened the Bible and read some favourite passages, but at this moment, it was almost impossible to believe in God. Then she found a passage that said, 'God is of purer eyes than to behold evil.' She concentrated hard, trying to get some sense into her befuddled brain. What had happened to her was evil, of that there was no doubt, and the passage seemed to imply that evil did not come from God and, therefore, must come only from mankind. That was an interesting idea, but it didn't ease her distress.

She got up and made herself a cup of tea, wincing at the pain and stiffness in her body, then sat down again. Thank goodness the bleeding had almost stopped. It had worried her.

She closed her books and stood up. She must try to get some rest.

★

Rose watched the children opening their presents and smiled at the cries of pleasure. With Grace's help she had done well with the shopping. David, the youngest, had a stuffed bear, Annie a pretty doll in a pink frock, Charlie and Bert had identical trains, Will was looking at a picture book, Nancy had a sewing kit, Bob a model of one of the latest cars, Flo a warm pair of gloves, and she'd found a pretty scarf for her mother.

Annie came running over, all excited. 'Thank you for my dolly, Rosie. She's got a pink dress, just like the one I had for the wedding. Where's your present?'

Rose laughed. 'I didn't buy myself anything, Toots.'

The little girl frowned, laid her doll carefully in Rose's lap, and ran up the stairs. She was soon back and held out a drawing. 'I made this at Sunday School. I was going to put it on the wall by my bed, but you must have it. It isn't right you've got nothing,' she told her, very seriously.

'Thank you.' Rose took the picture and looked at it carefully. It was a rather good attempt at a Christmas scene of shepherds on a hill with the sheep. 'That's lovely, Annie,' she said. 'It'll be the first thing I see when I wake up in the mornings.'

Annie glowed with pride, picked up her doll and hurried off to show it to her friends.

When the children had all disappeared, Rose and her mother sat and had a quiet cup of tea.

'You're looking better,' her mother remarked. 'You were quite shaken up by that fall you had.'

'I'm fine, now,' was all she said, then changed the subject. 'Have you any idea where the old man is?'

'I think he's in France, but I don't know for sure. I thought he might get leave for Christmas – there seem to be plenty of soldiers who have. I wish he'd get someone else to write a letter for him.'

Rose flinched inwardly at the mention of soldiers.

'Hey, guess what?' Bob erupted into the scullery. 'That Amy from number nineteen has just joined the army!'

'Don't be daft,' Rose reprimanded. 'Girls can't do that.'

'Yes, they can. Jim, her brother, told me. She joined up this week.'

'Bob's right,' her mother interrupted. 'They've formed the Women's Army Auxiliary Corps – WAAC, for short. They started taking recruits this month.'

Rose was immediately interested. 'How do you know, Mum?'

'The posters are everywhere – haven't you seen them? They're plastered all over the Labour Exchange. You have a look after Christmas.'

Rose nodded thoughtfully.

Rose stood in front of the poster, chewing her lip. She'd been looking at it for the last two months, ever since she'd heard about it at Christmas. Should she chance it? She was sick and tired of the factory job, and the desire to do something different was overwhelming. Her body had healed after the attack, but her mind was a different matter: some days and nights were dark when despair flooded her. With a shudder of revulsion, she made up her mind. Since John had gone she'd felt as if she'd been drifting helplessly, which made it difficult to study. Even worse, ever since the attack, she'd felt as if she had a banner hanging over her with the words 'I've been raped' written on it in large red letters. If she didn't do something to pull herself together she would never finish the work

John had left for her. She would be letting him down, and herself, and she could not allow that to happen.

Bad as this experience was, she would get over it in time. Just as the anger and disappointment of being told to leave school at eleven had faded, so would the horror of the rape. This, too, will pass, she thought. It could only ruin her life if she let it. It was up to her.

She pushed aside the lethargy that had weighed her down lately and turned her attention back to the poster. There was no need to read it again, she knew it by heart, but she looked at it anyway.

'Women Urgently Wanted for the WAAC – Women's Army Auxiliary Corps. Work at home and abroad with the forces. Good Wages, Quarters, Uniform, Rations.'

'You thinking of joining?'

Rose looked at the young girl standing next to her. 'Yes. Are you?'

'I'm in service and anything must be better than that.' She looked up at Rose and smiled. 'What about you?'

'I'm in a factory.'

'Ugh, not much better, then?' She held out her hand. 'I'm Hilda.'

'Rose.'

'Let's go in together,' Hilda said excitedly, taking her arm. 'You're very pretty, Rose, you'd look lovely in the uniform.'

That remark gave her confidence: Hilda hadn't questioned her age, so she might get away with it.

An hour later Rose was hurrying back to the factory, feeling more alive than she had since the attack. She and Hilda had been accepted and, much to her relief, there hadn't been any problem with her age. She had stood tall and lied convincingly, and they'd accepted her explanation that she didn't have a birth certificate. The question of a reference was trickier and she'd assured them that she would get one. She would have to write it herself, of course. And if the thought of deceiving them like that worried her, Rose wasn't going to let it stop her. This was her chance to do something different, and she was determined to make the most of it.

Rose broke into a trot. She'd been sent out on an errand for the boss and had taken much longer than she should have done. He wasn't going to be happy when she told him she was leaving. And that posed another problem. She couldn't tell him she had joined the WAAC, because he knew she was too young. She sped through the door and along to his office. Time to lie again.

Luckily he was on his own and she took a deep breath. 'I'm leaving, Mr Baker.'

He didn't look surprised, but he didn't look pleased, either. 'Where are you going?'

'Nowhere, sir, I'm needed at home.' Her gaze was direct. She mustn't appear ill at ease because that might raise his suspicions.

He threw down his pencil and stood up. 'Can't your mother get someone else to help? I don't want to lose you, Rose, especially when we're so busy.'

'It can't be helped. She's having a job to cope with nine children and go out to work.'

'She could give up *her* job,' he suggested hopefully.

'Wouldn't make sense for her to do that because she earns more than me.'

'Hmm, I could give you a rise, I suppose.'

This was getting difficult. Rose didn't want him looking into things too far: he'd soon find out she was telling a pack of lies. 'I must leave, sir, it's all arranged.'

'Very well,' he said, scowling. 'You may go at the end of the week.'

'Thank you.' She turned to make a hasty exit, wondering why lying made her uncomfortable when others thought nothing of it. It must be her conscience, she decided. At times it could be a blasted nuisance.

Later that night, Rose sat in the scullery, elbows on the table, chin propped in her hands. Her mother couldn't understand why she was joining the WAAC. Perhaps I should have told her about the rape, Rose thought fleetingly, but it was too late now. Anyway, she was still ashamed that it had happened to her, and believed that somehow it had been her fault.

'Rose? Can't you sleep again?' Annie trotted into the scullery, a look of concern on her face.

'I'm not tired, Toots,' she replied, with a smile. 'What are you doing up?'

'Can't sleep either. It's cold up there.'

'Come and sit over here.' Rose put a chair in front of the black-leaded range. 'Are you feeling all right?' Although the little girl had improved, she was still delicate and Rose couldn't help worrying about her.

Annie gazed at her big sister, her eyes sad. 'Are you going away, Rosie?'

She nodded. 'How did you know?'

'I heard you talking to Mum, and she was sad.'

'I'm joining the WAAC, but you mustn't tell anyone.'

Annie's bottom lip trembled. 'You will come back, won't you?'

Rose reached out and pulled the child towards her. 'You mustn't be upset. I'll have leave sometimes, and I'll come straight home, I promise.'

'Is that tea I can smell?' Their mother came into the room.

'Can't you sleep, either?' Rose asked.

'No. I've been thinking over what you told me earlier, and I've got over the shock now. It'll give you a chance to see a bit more of life. We'll miss you, but you have my blessing, and we won't tell a soul where you've gone. The WAAC won't find out you're under age from us.'

12

September 1917

The last seven months had been heaven. Rose walked along the country lane with a smile of contentment on her face as she took in the beautiful scenery and breathed the fresh air. How clean and vibrant everything was on this lovely warm September day, and how far away Bermondsey and its squalor seemed. She wouldn't care if she never saw the place again. A shudder rippled through her as she remembered the small, overcrowded house. The bedrooms were the worst and, no matter how careful she and her mother were, the bugs soon returned. It made her feel sick to see them crawling up the walls, and the whole street was alive with rats and mice.

She stopped and gazed at a large oak tree. It was just beginning to show the golden shades of autumn as a gentle breeze rustled its leaves. Life had changed for her beyond her wildest dreams. From the moment she'd arrived at the camp, she had loved the life, and when she'd first seen the sparkling polished floors and pristine sheets, she had felt as if she'd stepped into another world. And as for the food, well, she'd never had so much in her life.

Rose spotted a blackberry bush and leaned across the hedge to pick a couple of berries. She popped them into her mouth and sighed with pleasure as the sharp juice trickled over her tongue. How Annie would love to taste these.

The thought of the little girl still living in those squalid conditions made her feel guilty, but she sent most of her pay home to help her mother and knew that things were a bit easier for them now. With so many mouths to feed, though, money was still in short supply.

She sampled a few more berries, then resumed her walk. She did this at every spare moment, no matter what the weather, because she loved the green, open spaces. There were parks in London, of course, but they were nothing like the fields of corn and rolling hills of the Sussex countryside.

Hilda, the girl she'd met in the recruitment office, had come down here with her, and she'd found herself a boyfriend. But Rose didn't want that: she was happy to wander around on her own, and she had brought her books with her so she could keep up with her studies.

Hilda had been put into the stores to work, but Rose had been learning to type and yesterday she had passed all of the tests. That meant she would get twenty-three shillings a week. The WAAC were teaching her skills that would be useful in the future. She sighed and lifted her face to the sun. For the first time in her life, she was content. She would stay here until the war ended, then decide what to do with her life. This was a time to enjoy.

'Hello, Rose.' Two soldiers fell into step beside her.

She smiled at them. Jim and Fred were harmless enough, and over the last few months she'd realized that not all men in uniform were rapists. In fact, the vast majority were gentlemen and took 'No' with good grace.

'Coming to the dance tonight?' Jim asked.

'I might.'

'Oh, you must,' Fred pleaded. 'We're going back to France in two days' time.'

Suddenly Jim dashed into a field, picked a handful of flowers and hurried back. Then he sank on to one knee in front of her. 'Rosie, will you marry me?'

'Get up, you fool,' she told him, laughing at his antics. 'You want to be careful who you say that to because some girl might accept you, and where would you be then?'

'In France.' He grinned, got to his feet and tucked a flower into her buttonhole. 'But if you won't marry me, at least come to the dance.'

'All right, but you two must promise to behave yourselves.' Jim and Fred had been joking, but Rose hadn't missed the anxiety in their eyes. Returning to France was not something to look forward to.

'We always do,' they protested together, scandalized. Then they broke into broad grins and chuckled.

'We behave ourselves with you,' Jim told her, 'because you're strong enough to flatten us if we didn't.'

Rose said nothing, but was pleased by that remark. During the last few months, she had filled out, due to the regular food and exercise, and although she was always surrounded by eager men, not one took liberties with her.

She waved them goodbye, promised to be at the dance and went towards her quarters.

'Rose!' Hilda was running towards her, and skidded to a sudden halt. 'Have you heard?'

'What?'

'We're being sent to France next week.' The girl hopped from foot to foot. 'Isn't it exciting?'

'France? You sure?' Rose couldn't believe she was hearing this.

'Positive! There have been recruits arriving from other parts of the country all day.'

Rose wanted to shout for joy. This was what she had been praying for. The WAAC had started sending women overseas a few months ago, and she desperately wanted to go.

'We've got three days' leave, starting from tomorrow, then we come back and sail for France almost immediately. We've really got something to celebrate at the dance tonight, Rose.' Hilda grinned.

'Webster!'

Rose watched the officer striding towards her.

'You're wanted in the office, immediately.'

It was an order, and she had learned early on that it was wise to respond smartly, so she saluted and sped off. It was probably something to do with the posting to France, she thought, and was eager to hear more.

One look at the Commander's face told Rose it was serious. She stood to attention and waited, her heart hammering, wondering what she had done.

'It has come to my attention that you have only just turned fifteen.'

As Rose heard that, her hopes and dreams crumbled into dust at her feet.

'Is this true?'

What was the point of lying? 'Yes, ma'am.'

'Why do you girls think you can get away with it?

We're bound to find out in the end, you know.' The officer shook her head in disgust.

Yes, Rose thought, seething with fury, but how did they find out?

'You are dismissed with immediate effect. Hand in your uniform. You will be given your train fare home.'

Once again she was standing in front of someone, being dismissed. The pain was as intense as it had been the first time.

'You may go, Webster.'

Rose turned smartly and left. With a growl of fury, she erupted out of the main doors.

'What was that all about?' Hilda wanted to know, looking anxiously at her.

'I've been dismissed.' Rose spoke through clenched teeth, trying to control her rage. 'I'm under age and someone's told them.'

'I had no idea,' Hilda gasped. 'You look more than twenty.'

'Well, I'm not. I'm only fifteen. And when I find out who did this, I'll tear them apart with my bare hands.' She had to leave all this behind, and her chance to go to another country had gone. That thought nearly brought tears to her eyes. Bermondsey had been bad enough before this, but now she knew that there was something different – something better – it would be unbearable.

'Who do you think told on you?'

'I don't know.' Then Rose looked up and saw her. Amy, from Garrett Street, with a satisfied smirk on her face. Rose went cold with loathing.

Amy came over to her, flanked by two of her friends. 'Not so high-and-mighty now, are you?' she sneered.

Rose gave the three a contemptuous glance. 'I might have guessed it was you,' she said to Amy. 'Are you too afraid to face me on your own?'

'I'm not daft, Rose Webster. Your family's got a violent streak running through it. I've seen you after your old man's had a go at you, and I'm sure you're all the same.'

'Really?' Rose's fingers itched to wrap themselves around the girl's neck, so she clamped them to her hips, and stood with her feet apart.

'I know you want to hit me,' Amy taunted, 'so why don't you try it? We'd love to give you a beating.'

Rose stared at each girl in turn. 'It'll be a pleasure! I can take on the three of you and win.' She was considerably taller than them and had the satisfaction of seeing Amy's friends take a step back. Then she moved forward.

'Rose, don't!' Hilda placed a hand on her arm. 'It's not worth it.'

'Oh, I don't know. If they're caught in a fight, I might be able to get them dismissed as well.'

All three girls went a sickly colour. 'You'd like that, wouldn't you?' Amy said. 'You're a bully, Rose Webster!'

'Of course I am. Look where I came from.' Then she dropped her aggressive stance. The trio of cowards had lost the urge to fight, and the battle was won.

She turned and strode away.

Rose looked out of the train window with unseeing eyes. Just a few short hours ago she had been so happy and now she was devastated.

The rhythmic clatter of the train began to have a soothing effect upon her, and the bitter anger inside her eased. The last few months had been wonderful, but she had lied to get what she wanted, and that never paid. This disappointment was of her own making: she was bound to have been found out sooner or later. Oh, how she wished it had been later! The train pulled into the station, she picked up her bag, opened the door and stepped on to the platform. The noise, smoke and grime of Bermondsey hit her and it was only with extreme determination that she held back the tears.

The sight that met Rose when she walked into the scullery at home made her heart miss a beat. Her mother was sitting at the table, her face grim, and all the children were clustered around her. 'Mum, what's the matter?'

'Oh, Rosie, thank God you're home.' Marj pushed a telegram towards her.

'Missing presumed dead,' the telegram said. Rose thought she should feel something, but she couldn't pretend she had any affection for the old man. What a selfish, hard-hearted bitch she was turning into! However, her mother was upset, and she cared about her, so she sat down and gave a faint smile. 'It only says missing – that doesn't mean he's dead.'

'Well, why would they frighten us by sending a telegram like that?' her mother asked. 'What do they mean by missing?'

'That they can't find him.'

Marj mulled this over for a few moments. 'Do you mean he might have buggered off?'

'It's possible, but he might just have got separated from his company.'

'I never thought of that. But if he's done a runner and they catch him, they'll shoot him.'

'I doubt he's done that, Mum, he wouldn't risk a firing

squad. Don't believe anything until you get a notice from the army. He'll quite likely turn up like the bad penny – as usual.'

'You're right.' Her mother looked at the children. 'We won't believe he's been killed until we hear something definite. It's no good trying to cross our bridges before we get to them.'

They all nodded and drifted away to whatever they'd been doing before the telegram had arrived.

'Rosie.' Annie sat on the chair next to her and put her arms as far round her sister as they would go. 'I didn't know you were coming home today.'

'Neither did I, Toots. They've thrown me out of the WAAC.'

Her mother looked appalled. 'Why did they do that?'

'Bit of bad luck, Mum. That Amy turned up and told them I was only fifteen.'

The stream of bad language that came from her mother's lips made Rose clap her hands over Annie's ears. Then she started to laugh. 'That's just what I thought, but I didn't say it.'

'Well, I hope you gave her a good hiding.'

Rose took her hands away from the little girl's ears. 'No, but I felt like it.'

'What stopped you?' her mother asked.

'I suppose I knew I was in the wrong because I *had* lied about my age.'

For the first time since it had happened, Rose could see the funny side of it. 'She brought two friends with her.'

'I'm sorry this has happened,' her mother told her. 'You were so happy.'

'I know, but I've had a smashing time over the last few months, and I'll always be grateful for that.'

'What a sad day.' Marj poured them a cup of tea. 'The old man reported missing, and you dismissed.'

Rose sipped her tea and said nothing.

'What you going to do now?' Annie asked. 'Are you going back to the factory?'

'I don't think so. I lied to Mr Baker when I left.' She sat the child on her lap. 'So you see, Annie, it never pays to tell fibs because they come back to haunt you.'

'Like ghosts?' Annie giggled.

'Nasty ones!' Rose pulled a fierce face and tickled her sister, who jumped off her lap, squealing.

'What are you going to do?' her mother asked, changing the subject.

'I don't know. It's all come as a shock and I haven't had time to think about it.' Sadness swept through Rose. 'We were going to France,' she said quietly.

Her mother patted her hand. 'Never mind, when this war's over you'll be able to go over there yourself. Things will be different, you'll see.'

Rose's gaze swept around the scullery and she shuddered. She certainly hoped her mother was right, because nothing much had changed here while she'd been away. The oilcloth on the floor had even more holes in it, there was still the nauseating smell of too many people crowded into a small space, and an added feature was a piece of brown paper stuck over a broken window. Rose was dreading what she might find upstairs.

'Rosie?' Annie sat on the bed and pulled her hand.

'What?'

'Will you take me to see Auntie Grace? I haven't seen her since you went away, and I've got a lot to tell her.'

'Isn't she still at your school, then?' Rose asked in surprise.

'No. She's been moved to the big school. They haven't got enough teachers,' Annie said. 'But the new teacher is nice.'

'Good.' Four years ago the secondary school would never have considered taking on Grace.

'Rosie?' Annie tugged her arm. 'When can we go?'

'This afternoon.' And for that she received a tight hug and a wet kiss.

'Uncle John!' Annie squealed, and threw herself at the sailor.

'Rose,' Grace kissed her cheek, 'are you on leave?'

'No, they dismissed me when they found out I was only fifteen.' She tried to sound amused.

'How did that happen?' Grace took Rose's coat and hung it over the banister.

'They were shipping in a lot of new people because we were going to France, but one of them knew me and told them.' Rose shrugged. 'It was my own fault. I took a chance joining up and got caught.'

'Did you enjoy yourself?' John asked.

'I had a lovely time. It was a glimpse of another world. Everything was spotless, the food was regular and it was a treat to wear decent clothes.'

'And how did you get on with the discipline?' he asked perceptively.

'Ah, now, that was hard,' Rose admitted. 'I don't like

people bossing me around, but I thought it was worth putting up with it.'

He smiled in amusement. 'I can't imagine you taking orders meekly.'

'It wasn't easy.' She looked at him thoughtfully: the uniform suited him. 'When did you get home?'

'This morning.'

'Oh, we wouldn't have come if we'd known. You'll want to have a quiet time with Grace.' She took Annie's hand. 'Come on, Toots, we'll come back another time.'

'No, don't go.' John sat Annie at the table. 'Join us for tea, and you can tell me how you're getting on with your studying.'

'You sure?'

'We're both pleased to see you.' John handed round the bread and butter. 'What are you going to do now?'

'I'll have to get a job, but I don't want to go back into a factory. I learned to type in the WAAC.'

'Did you? That might be useful.' John drank his tea and gazed into space, then he smiled. 'Grace, would you look after Annie for an hour or so?'

'What are we doing here?' Rose asked in awe, as they walked along a corridor of Grove School in Southwark.

'I want to see someone.' John stopped outside a room and grasped the doorknob.

'But it's Sunday. No one will be here.'

'He'll be here,' John answered confidently, as he knocked on the door and opened it.

It was the most untidy place Rose had ever seen, and that was saying something. Papers and files were piled on the desk, stacked on the floor and spilling off every chair in the room, and in the middle of the chaos was an elderly man. He looked up distractedly when they came in, then hauled himself to his feet. His untidy hair was grey and thinning at the front. He had removed his jacket and rolled up the sleeves of a creased white shirt. Rose smiled inside. This was the man who'd given Grace away, but that day he'd been tidy and wearing a suit. Then he smiled and his face lit up, the clear grey eyes sparkling.

'John! How good to see you.'

'Hello, Harold.' John eyed the room with amusement. 'How did you end up in a place like this?'

'Damned war. Just because I'm too old to join up they expect me to run this place single-handed *and* teach a class.' He dropped a pile of papers into the wastepaper basket. 'I wanted to retire, you know, but they wouldn't let me. I should have stayed at the University of London, but I thought this might be easier for the duration of the war.'

'That was naïve of you, Harold,' John observed.

'I know that now, but it's a good school, John. There are two hundred boys and a few are bright enough to go on to university.' Harold waved a hand impatiently at the piles of paperwork. 'But I can't keep up with it all.'

'Why don't you get some help?'

'Do you think I haven't bloody well tried – ' He stopped suddenly and looked at Rose. 'I beg your pardon, miss.'

She grinned. 'I've heard a lot worse.'

'This is Rose,' John introduced. 'You saw her at our wedding. Rose, this is Professor Harold Steadman.'

'Pleased to meet you again, Professor.'

Harold Steadman studied her briefly, then turned to John. 'You've brought her here for a reason?'

'She needs a job and doesn't want to go back into a factory.'

Rose started. Was John trying to get her a job? Excitement rushed through her. She cleared two chairs of papers so that they could all sit down. This might take some time, and she wasn't going to budge until it was settled.

John told Harold the whole story then sat back, waiting for his response.

The silence was long and unnerving for Rose, and she couldn't hold her tongue any longer. If there was a chance of working here, she wanted it. 'I can type as well,' she said.

'You'll have to work any hours I say and I'll pay you one pound ten shillings a week.' He gave her another searching look. 'You can start tomorrow.'

'Thank you, sir. What will I have to do?' Rose always liked to know what was expected of her.

'Type letters, lecture notes, run around after me, and get this office into some kind of order.' He screwed up another piece of paper and tossed it into the basket, which was now overflowing. 'Do you think you can do that?'

'Yes, sir.'

John got to his feet. 'Good. Now can I show Rose the library?'

'Of course.' The Professor was already at work again.

As soon as they'd closed the door, she let out a squeal of delight. 'I can't believe he's given me a job! Oh, thank you, John, I'm so excited.' Tears of joy filled her eyes. 'I'm glad they threw me out of the WAAC now.'

He laughed. 'Don't get too excited. That cussed old

man will work you like a slave, but it'll be worth it because' – he opened another door – 'you'll have access to all of this.'

Rose rushed into the middle of the room and turned slowly. She had never seen so many books before. 'Will I be able to come in here?'

'Yes, when the pupils aren't using it.'

'Oh, it's like paradise.'

'Darling, I'm so happy for Rose, but I'm also a little worried.'

'Why?' John took Grace into his arms and settled back on the pillow with a sigh of contentment.

'Isn't the man you think might have something to do with Rose connected to the school?'

'Yes, he's on the Board of Education, but it's unlikely she'll come across him. I don't think he ever goes there.' He started to chuckle. 'He's in for a shock if he does see her – she's grown even more like him over the last few months. From the way Harold was looking at her today, I think he noticed it, too, but he didn't say anything.'

Grace snuggled down. 'I hope she'll be all right. If he does see her and she turns out to be related to him, he could make things difficult for her. He's not a very nice man.'

'We needn't worry about Rose. She can look after herself.'

13

March 1918

Rose had been in her new job six months, and although John had been right about the professor working her hard, she didn't mind. It had taken her a couple of months to wade through all his papers and get them into some kind of order, but he needed watching constantly. He was the most disorganized man she had ever come across. As soon as he went to take a class, she set to and filed everything he had left lying about. He could never find anything and was always calling, 'Rose!' It was hard work but how could she feel anything but joy when she had access to all those books?

She bent down to put the heavy volume back on to the lower shelf, and nearly dropped it when a voice behind her said, 'What have you been reading?'

'Plato.'

'How did you get on with him?' Harold Steadman asked.

'Hard going,' she admitted.

A slight smile tugged at the corners of his mouth. 'Why don't you try something easier?'

'What's the point of that? I won't learn anything that way.'

'I've been watching you carefully over the last six months, Rose, and John is right, you have a fine mind.

However, I believe your reading is too eclectic, you need to make a choice now and study a specific subject.'

She chewed her lip thoughtfully. 'Such as?'

'What are you most interested in?' Harold Steadman leaned against the bookcase and folded his arms.

'I've been considering politics – you know, social reform and things like that.'

He shook his head. 'I can't see you as a politician, you're far too quick-tempered. You'd be rolling up your sleeves and fighting with them.'

Rose burst out laughing. 'I'm not that bad.'

'Perhaps not,' he grinned, 'but you're a determined young woman with firm opinions.'

'Is that a bad thing?' she asked.

'Not at all, but you need to channel your thoughts and decide what you're going to do with your life.'

'I miss John,' she told him, running her hand lovingly over a row of books. 'I've read everything he told me to and now I'm not sure what to do.'

Harold reached out and patted her shoulder. 'Would you let me help you until he comes home?'

Rose nodded eagerly. She'd been tempted to ask his advice on quite a few occasions, but he was always so busy.

'All right. You know I specialize in law, so what do you think about making that your goal in life? It would give you a sound platform to help bring about some of those reforms you were talking about.'

'Law!' she exclaimed in surprise. 'I never thought about that. Could a woman go into that profession?'

'I believe so. Things are opening up. However, if you decide to take this on, you must be aware that you will have to fight hard to be recognized as worthy of it.'

'I don't mind that.' She straightened up. 'I like a good fight.'

He tipped his head back and roared with laughter. 'The first time you get into court, I want to be there.'

'Are you sure I can do this, sir?' She looked at him doubtfully.

He nodded, then took two books from the shelves. 'I want you to start with these. They'll give you an idea of the different branches of the law and help you choose one you would like to study. I will then give you the same lessons the boys here receive.'

Rose looked at the books in her hand and trembled with anticipation. She must write to John and tell him.

The next few weeks passed in a blur for Rose, and it didn't take her long to make her choice. She would become a solicitor. In that job she would be well placed to help ordinary people. Now when she wasn't working, she was studying hard, absorbed in her subject. The more she learned about the law, the more she saw that it would be the right thing for her to do. She remembered the stone thrown into water sending out ripples. Perhaps now she might be able to make a few ripples of her own.

She was hurrying back from the library after finishing her work for the day, when she turned a corner and ran full pelt into someone. Rose gasped as the breath was knocked out of her. 'I'm so sorry.'

'Well, what have we here?'

His accent was posh, and she looked up. The young man standing in front of her was about twenty, she reckoned, and she took an instant dislike to him. He was tall, reasonably good-looking, but his light brown eyes held a sly look. He was not someone to be trusted.

As she tried to walk past him he caught hold of her arm. His grip was painful. 'Let go of me!'

'Oh, she has a temper.' He smirked. 'I like a bit of fire in a woman.' Then he dragged her into a room, kicked the door shut and leaned against it, holding her in an intimate embrace.

Visions of the last time she had been attacked like this came vividly to mind, and her knee came up hard. He let out a yelp of pain and released her. With a mighty push she shoved him away from the door and ran into the corridor.

'You bitch!'

She ignored him and began to walk away. A hand touched her shoulder and she spun round, eyes flashing.

'Are you all right?' Harold asked.

'You should be asking *me* that.' The young man came out of the room, his face contorted with pain. 'She nearly crippled me.'

'Up to your old tricks again, Andrew?' Harold Steadman snapped.

'She threw herself at me.' The boy ran an insolent gaze over Rose. 'A man would have to be half dead to resist such a beauty.'

Rose couldn't ignore that. She thrust her books at the professor and started to roll up her sleeves. 'I can soon see to that.' She stepped forward. When he backed away she sneered, 'Coward!'

'Who is she?' Andrew asked, putting the professor between them for safety.

'Rose Webster. She works for me.'

'Well you can sack her for attacking me.'

'I was defending myself!' Rose exploded. Who did he think he was, giving orders like that? 'Women need protecting from lechers like you.'

'I was only having a bit of fun,' he complained.

'Really? Well, I wasn't enjoying it,' she said scornfully.

'You're not supposed to,' he said smartly. 'Women are supposed to submit to a man's will.'

That did it! She stepped forward menacingly.

'Stop her, Steadman,' the boy yelled in fear. 'She's mad and violent.'

'Then I suggest you get out of here, Andrew, while you still can,' Harold told him softly, 'because I would love to see her give you the thrashing you deserve.'

Andrew went red with fury. 'You forget who you're talking to. You'll both be sacked when I tell my father about this.' He turned on his heel and hurried away.

Harold Steadman watched him silently, a frown puckering his brow, then he turned and stared at Rose, tipping his head to one side as he examined her intently.

She shuffled uncomfortably. 'Will you lose your job?' She was appalled at the idea.

'No. The boy is all bluster.'

Rose faced him, hands on her hips. 'Tell me the truth. Can he have you dismissed?'

'He might try, but his father would not be able to replace me at the moment. I am only here because they couldn't find anyone else, and I would never have taken the job if they hadn't been desperate.'

'He would be able to dismiss you when the men come back.'

'Rose,' he laughed, 'I retire next year, anyway.'

Rose sighed with relief. She would have hated to cause him trouble. 'I'm sorry to have lost my temper, but I wasn't going to let him get away with treating me like that.'

'You were quite right to defend yourself, and it's about time someone put that young man in his place.'

'Who is he, anyway?' she asked, falling into step beside the professor.

'Sir George Gresham's son.'

'Is he the Gresham the library's named after?'

'No, that was his father.' Harold Steadman stopped and looked at her intently. 'Do you know Sir George?'

'Me!' She grinned. 'What would a girl from Garrett Street be doing knowing the nobility?'

He stroked his chin thoughtfully. 'Keep out of his way, Rose.'

'Huh! If he's anything like his son, I don't want to know him.'

'Is there any news about the old man?' Rose asked her mother later that evening as they cleared up after giving the children their supper.

'I've asked, but all they say is he's missing.'

'I expect there are thousands like that,' Rose said sadly. 'It's going to take a lot of sorting out when the war ends.'

'I wonder how much longer it's going on? When it started everyone said it would be over in a few months, but it's almost four years now.'

Could it be that long? Rose had been so caught up in her studies that she hadn't taken much notice of the news.

'Are you still enjoying it at the school?' her mother asked, taking some cups out of the cupboard.

'Yes, it's wonderful . . .' she hesitated ' . . . except I nearly got the professor the sack today.'

'Why was that?' Her mother filled the teapot.

'Some boy tried to assault me and Professor Steadman stuck up for me.'

'I hope you gave the lad what for.' Her mother frowned. 'Who was he, one of the pupils?'

'No. He was the son of one of the school's benefactors – ' A cup crashed to the floor, interrupting her.

'What was his name?'

Rose was startled by the note of panic in her mother's voice. 'Andrew Gresham.'

'He didn't touch you, did he?' her mother demanded.

'No, Mum. Don't take on so.'

Her mother let out a ragged sigh, and sat down. 'You mustn't have anything to do with him.'

'I don't intend to – but why are you in such a state?'

Before her mother could answer, the door burst open and Bob tore into the scullery. He was twelve now and not quite as surly, but Rose still found him the least likeable of her brothers and sisters.

'Have you heard?' Bob hopped from foot to foot in excitement. 'Amy's been thrown out of the WAAC for stealing.'

'How do you know?' Rose asked.

'Her brother's just told me. He said she was in real trouble.'

'Stop jumping about, Bob, and tell me about it quick.' Rose grabbed a chair and made him sit in it.

'She was in France and she kept sneaking into the

140

men's camp. I always knew she were a tart,' he stated gleefully.

'Get on with the story, and keep your opinions to yourself,' Rose scolded.

He pouted. 'Well, she stayed at night with the men, and when they was asleep she picked their pockets. She was stealing food, too, and selling it.'

'Silly girl.' Marj looked at her silent daughter.

'I didn't think she'd be so daft.' Rose shook her head in disbelief. 'She had a good life in the WAAC. Why go and throw it all away?'

'There's no accounting for folks. They do foolish things sometimes,' her mother opined.

Bob jumped up and tore out again.

Her mother bent down and started to pick up the broken pieces of cup, and Rose helped her. 'You were going to tell me why I should stay away from Andrew Gresham,' she reminded her mother.

'Just stay away from him.'

'That won't do, Mum. You know I always have to know why. How do you know him?'

Marj Webster poured them both a cup of tea. She was silent for a moment, then looked up with troubled eyes. 'Andrew Gresham is your half-brother.'

Rose was about to take a sip of tea but the cup clattered back into the saucer. 'That means – that means – ' She couldn't get the words out.

'That means Sir George Gresham is your father.'

'Bloody hell, Mum,' she exclaimed. 'Are you sure?'

'Of course I'm sure!' her mother exclaimed. 'Do you think I had so many men that I wouldn't know who'd fathered you?'

'Oh, I didn't mean that,' she said hastily, 'but it's a bit of a shock.'

'I know that, and I think it's time I told you the whole story.'

They took a gulp of tea to calm their nerves, then Marj Webster began.

'I was in service for Sir George and his wife. I was only sixteen and as innocent as a newborn babe. Lady Gresham was a spiteful creature – '

'Her son must take after her, then,' Rose muttered.

'Don't interrupt, Rose,' her mother reproved her. 'It's going to be hard enough for me to tell this story.'

'I won't say another word.'

'As I was saying, it wasn't a happy household and we were all pleased when her ladyship went away for a few weeks to the country.' Marj fiddled with the empty cup. 'It was then the master took notice of me. He was tall and handsome, and I felt sorry for him. We could all hear the rows they had. Well, one night I had to take him up a drink and he kept me talking for quite a while. He was lonely, you see, and I didn't see no harm in it.'

So the crafty old devil had waited until his wife was out of the way, Rose thought.

'Then he kissed me, just on the cheek, but things got out of hand, and I didn't know what to do.' Marj took a deep breath. 'He was the master, you see, and I'd never been one to disobey.'

Rose clenched her fists.

'When I found out I was pregnant, I went to the master and told him, but he said it was useless to accuse him of being the father because he would deny it, and everyone would believe him, not some servant, out for what she could get.' Her mother poured herself another cup of tea with shaking hands.

'What happened then?' Rose asked gently.

'They turned me out. I had nowhere to go and I was afraid I'd end up in the workhouse. It was then I met the old man. He was working in a shop and I'd seen him a few times.' She looked at her daughter. 'He wasn't a bad man, then, the drink hadn't got to him. Well, he saw how distressed I was and I told him I was in trouble. He'd just rented this house and said he'd take me in. I was that relieved, Rose. We got on well enough and I married him before you was born.'

'Did you ever tell him who my father was?'

Marj shook her head vigorously. 'No fear. He'd have tried to make some gain out of it, and I didn't want anything to do with the Greshams again.'

'When did he start to drink?'

'Oh, he'd always liked a pint, but he started drinking seriously just after Flo was born. He was impossible after that.'

'You stayed with him, though, Mum.'

She shrugged helplessly. 'What else could I do? There was nowhere to go. If I'd walked out, I'd have lost my kids, and I do love you all.'

'I know,' Rose told her. 'You've always done your best for us.'

'I've tried.' Marj sat back and sighed wearily. 'I'm glad I've told you at last. It's a weight off my mind, but you can understand why I want you to stay away from the Greshams. If Sir George sees you, he'll recognize you because you're the image of him.'

'His son can't take after him, then, because we don't look like brother and sister.'

'No, he's like his mother.' She looked at her daughter pleadingly. 'If you do run across Sir George at the school, I'd like you to keep quiet about me.'

'You don't want me to admit to being his daughter?'

'You must make up your own mind. But I don't want that man stepping back into our lives. He treated me without a thought for what would happen to me, and I've never forgiven him for that.'

'I won't say anything.'

'Thanks, Rose. I wish I'd had as much sense as you have. Then I wouldn't have got into such trouble.'

'And I wouldn't have been born.'

The worry left her mother's face and she smiled. 'That's one thing I've never regretted – having you. Now I'm exhausted, so I think I'll go and have a nap.'

Rose watched her mother walk out of the scullery and ground her teeth. If she did come face to face with him, she'd break his neck!

14

Rose was busy typing lecture notes the next day when a man stormed into the professor's office.

'Steadman, what's all this I hear about my son being attacked, and you taking the other's part?'

Rose looked up from her typing. The man was well over six feet tall, his black hair was sprinkled with grey and his dark eyes were blazing. The arrogance of rank and privilege was evident in his stance. There was no mistaking who he was.

The professor was silent. He didn't stand up, but sat back and folded his arms.

Rose was getting used to Harold Steadman, and he was showing this man that he did not consider him worthy of respect.

'Send for this person,' Sir George raised his voice, 'and I'll have him expelled. I will have you removed too if you show me any more insolence, sir.'

'You cannot do that to either of us,' Harold informed him calmly. 'You cannot run the school without me, and the young woman isn't a pupil here.'

'Woman! What are you talking about? Are you telling me a female attacked my son?' Sir George looked incredulous.

'Your son was making unwelcome advances and she defended herself. If she hadn't been able to fend him off, I should have had to thrash him myself.'

'How dare you?' Sir George was incandescent with rage. 'And tell me what you mean by "unwelcome advances".' ·

Rose's mouth curled in disgust. Unwelcome advances?

'He was trying to rape her,' Harold Steadman told him plainly.

'Rubbish! Where is this female?' he bellowed.

Rose was on her feet. 'Here.'

Sir George spun round. 'Well? What have you to say for yourself.'

Rose stepped forward until she was standing within two feet of him. 'Your son dragged me into another room and tried to molest me. I made sure he couldn't,' she told him succinctly, and then turned back to her desk. When he grabbed hold of her arm, she gave him a contemptuous glance. 'Let go of me or I'll do the same to you.'

'Why you insolent . . .' He raised his hand, but she stared at him defiantly, looking into eyes identical to hers.

'You don't frighten me. I've been thrashed before.' She shook herself free of his grip. 'It's the sign of a weak man.'

He let her go, but couldn't tear his eyes off her face. Suddenly he was disconcerted. 'Who are you?'

'None of your business!'

'Don't be too sure!' he bellowed. 'You've got the likeness of a Gresham. What's your mother's name?'

'You wouldn't remember it. You took advantage of an innocent girl, then abandoned her.'

'Why are you so sure it was me? I had a younger brother.'

Rose had moved closer to him. The anger she felt for what her mother had suffered at his hands would not be denied. This was one confrontation that was long overdue and she was eager to let the man know what she thought of him. 'It was you, all right. My mother doesn't lie.'

'You forget who I am,' he growled, his face dark with fury.

'I know exactly who you are. You are an arrogant, selfish bastard.'

'*You* are the bastard here,' he snarled.

'And whose fault is that?' She raised her eyebrows.

'I don't have to explain myself to the likes of you.'

'Oh, dear me, I forgot!' she smiled. 'You're the great Sir George Gresham, and as such can do whatever you like to people without having to answer for your crimes.'

At her tone he took a step back. The fury left his face, to be replaced with something akin to respect. 'You've a sharp tongue, girl.'

'Really? I must have inherited it from somewhere.'

The corners of his mouth twitched. 'I can see now why my son was frightened.'

'Your son is a spoilt coward, who thinks he has the right to harass any female he comes across. But I don't suppose he's had a very good example to follow.'

'Hmm.' Sir George didn't seem to hear the insult, but reached out and took hold of her chin, then turned her face to the light so he could see it better. 'You are certainly no coward. Perhaps I should have kept you – *if* you're mine.'

She wrenched herself free.

'What's your name?' His tone was coaxing now.

'Rose. That's all you need to know.'

'Don't be so quick to dismiss me, girl. I could help you.'

That was too much for Rose. 'If you try to come anywhere near us, you'll regret the day you were born.'

'You can't stop me, girl,' he told her, with absolute confidence.

'Oh, yes I can.' Rose held his gaze unwaveringly. 'If you dismiss the professor or me, or try to interfere in my mother's life, then I will blacken your name and ruin your son.'

'And how do you propose to do that?' he asked with irony.

'You will see headlines in all the papers.' Her hand swept across an imaginary newspaper. '"Gresham's Son molests Sister."'

'I will deny you are anything to do with me, and I will be the one they believe. I will denounce you as a fraud who is trying to blackmail me.'

'Not when I explain that I wouldn't touch you or your money.'

'Don't be ridiculous.' He roared with laughter. 'No one would believe that!'

'Don't be too sure, *Father*.' She grimaced. 'One photograph of me will wipe away any doubt. No one could mistake whose child I am. Take a good look.' She turned him so that they were both looking into a mirror on the wall.

'Coincidence. Unless you tell me who your mother is, I cannot verify your claim.'

'I'm not making any claim.' Her eyes swept over him in contempt.

'I don't believe you. No one in your position could resist making money from such a situation.'

Rose heard the slap and saw his head jerk back before she realized what she had done. Expecting him to retaliate, she stood her ground, head up, but he just stared at her in disbelief. His eyes bored into hers as if he was trying to get inside her mind, then he stepped back.

'I have misjudged you.' He spoke softly, as if he couldn't believe it.

'You have! I wouldn't touch a penny of your money. I will never forgive you for the way you treated my mother, and I don't want to see you again.'

He was silent for a while, then nodded. 'As you wish.' He turned and strode out of the room.

Rose took a couple of deep breaths as the door closed. Thank God that was over.

Then she heard a muffled sound and turned towards the professor's table – she had forgotten he was still in the room. He was sitting in his chair, shaking with suppressed laughter, and his eyes were running with the effort of keeping quiet. Someone else was there too. John Trenchard was leaning against the wall, polishing his spectacles and grinning.

'John! I didn't hear you come in.'

The professor roared with laughter. 'I don't suppose you did, Rose. Your whole attention was focused on Sir George.'

She pulled a face, and John chuckled.

'I came in at just the right time. I'd have hated to have missed that.' John put on his spectacles and leaned forward to whisper in her ear: 'I knew you'd put him in his place when you met him.'

She frowned. 'You knew who my real father was?'

'I guessed, Rose. There was always something about you that seemed familiar, but it was only as you got older that I recognized the connection.'

Harold Steadman got to his feet and took her hands. 'Rose, I'm proud of you. That was the first time I've ever seen anyone get the better of Sir George.'

'Oh, I'm not so sure I did.' She felt uncertain.

'You did. I know him well and that's the first time I've ever seen him back away from a fight.' Harold Steadman smiled warmly. 'I think you impressed him.'

'Good Lord, I hope not!' she exclaimed in alarm. 'I don't want him taking any interest in me.'

'That might be a forlorn hope. I don't think you've seen the last of him,' John told her gently.

'But I hit him!'

'That wouldn't have worried him – quite the reverse, in fact.' The professor sat on the edge of his table. 'He likes someone with spirit.'

She groaned. 'I wish I'd known that. I'd have stayed icy calm.'

The two men roared with laughter.

They spent the next hour discussing her decision to study law. John approved the choice of career, and in the tea-room across the street, the two men mapped out a course for her.

'Rose must become a full-time student.' John stirred his tea thoughtfully. 'How can that be arranged, Harold?'

She listened to them scheming, and would have laughed if she hadn't ached with longing to do what they were suggesting. They were talking about the impossible, though.

'We've got some general exams in September,' Harold said eagerly. 'Rose is more than capable of passing them, so I'll sit her at the back of the class and let her take them too.'

'That won't be allowed.' She couldn't stay silent any longer. 'Wouldn't it be better if I stayed in your office, Professor, and did them there?'

'No, no.' Harold Steadman waved dismissively. 'You must be with everyone else, under supervision.'

'I won't cheat!' she told them indignantly.

'Of course you won't,' John said.

She listened for another ten minutes, then sighed wearily. 'You're wasting your time. I'll not be allowed to take the exams.'

The men looked at her as if they had forgotten she was there. 'Yes, you will,' they said together, then returned to the discussion.

Harold Steadman continued, 'Then when I've got the results, I'll put in an application for her to go to the London University – '

'Just a minute!' Rose thumped the table, making the cups rattle. 'If I can pass those exams, where is this leading?'

'I'll get you enrolled at the university, so you can study law.'

'It's the only way,' John told her. 'If you try to do it on your own, it will take you a lifetime to qualify, but only about another three years if you do it full-time.'

'But – but –' she stuttered. 'You're weaving fairy stories.' She started to count on her fingers. 'One, there will be objections if I take the same exams as the real pupils at the school. Two, the university will never agree to let me enrol. Three, I'm never going to be able to afford the money.' She sighed sadly. 'I can't be out of work for three years.'

The professor mimicked her actions and started to count on his own fingers. 'One, I will say that you are my private student and I want you to take these exams. Two, the university will accept you when they see your excellent results. Three, you can work for me at the weekends,' he told her. 'That should give you enough to survive on.'

'But you'll be retiring at the end of the war,' she reminded him.

'That's true, but I intend to write a book, and I'll need a lot of help with that. You're nimble on the typewriter,' he added.

'I'd be happy to help you, but I couldn't take any money from you.'

'Stop letting your heart rule your head, Rose.' He patted her hand affectionately. 'I need a typist, you need money, and I can afford to pay you.'

'But – '

Harold Steadman held up his hand. 'No more buts. Do you want this chance or not?'

Rose screwed her napkin up in excitement. What a daft question. 'You know I do.'

The men winked at each other. 'You leave everything to us,' Harold told her.

Rose looked at them and slowly shook her head. She knew they wanted to help her, but she mustn't get her hopes up too much. What they were suggesting just couldn't come true. She stood up. If she listened to this much longer she might begin to believe it. 'I'm going back to work.'

They hardly seemed to notice her leaving.

The next week passed without another mention of the exams, and she tried to dismiss the idea from her mind as another lost opportunity – another closed door. However, her determination to succeed made her intensify her studying. It was a heavy load. Working all day for the professor and reading long into the night was taking its toll. Not to mention the travelling between Bermondsey and Southwark every day.

'Rose.' Harold Steadman looked over her shoulder. 'I want you to study here for two hours every afternoon, and then go to bed at a reasonable hour. If you carry on like this, then by the time you sit the exams you'll be too tired to think clearly.'

She gaped at him in astonishment.

'Close your mouth and study. I've sung your praises to everyone and I expect you to pass with high marks. Once I've got proof of your academic excellence, I'll go to the university and give you a glowing reference.' He looked smug. 'I should be able to convince them to let you enrol as a student.'

'I still think you're dreaming, Professor.' She didn't dare believe it was possible.

'Have a little faith in me,' he joked. 'There's a dearth of students at the moment, but when the war ends it might be more difficult to have you admitted. There will be young men coming back to continue their studies.'

But there would also be many who would not, she thought sadly.

Some time later that afternoon, absorbed in study, she didn't hear the door open.

'Will you leave us alone, Professor Steadman.' It wasn't a question, it was a demand, but spoken kindly.

Rose looked up and the breath caught in her throat. The lady was a good age, and leaning heavily on an ebony stick with an ivory lion's head handle. She was an imposing figure. Her hair was white, her eyes were dark, and shone with intelligence and alertness. Rose got to her feet and was subjected to a thorough scrutiny. Then the lady nodded, as if satisfied.

'Get me a chair. I'm too old to be standing like this.'

Rose hurried to obey, and waited until she was settled. She didn't have to ask who she was.

'Sit down, or I'll get a crick in my neck.'

The lady spoke with such authority that it seemed natural to obey without question, but that put Rose on her guard. She was not going to be intimidated by any member of the Gresham family. And this was undoubtedly a Gresham.

The lady did not prevaricate. 'You attacked my grandson.'

Rose braced herself. 'Yes.'

'Good for you. About time somebody put him in his place.'

That wasn't what she'd expected.

'Don't look so surprised. I hear you also took on my son.' Her eyes crinkled at the corners.

'It was time somebody put *him* in his place,' Rose said,

and nearly fell off her chair when the old lady chuckled.

'You are certainly my granddaughter. George told me you are the image of me when I was young, and he's right.'

'He told you about me?'

'When he came home with a clear handprint across his face, I demanded to know what he'd been doing. Had to threaten to cut him out of my will before he told me.'

'Bet that frightened him.' Rose tried to smother a grin.

'Indeed.' She put her head to one side. 'This is quite incredible. It is like looking at myself as a young girl.'

'If I'm so like you, then why didn't your grandson notice it?' Rose asked.

'Because he takes after his mother, not the Gresham side of the family. All he thinks about is gambling and chasing girls. You're a beauty and that's all he would have noticed. Did your mother work for us?'

The change of tactic took Rose by surprise. 'Yes.'

'What happened?'

'Your son seduced her and when she became pregnant he threw her out.' Rose gave her the plain facts.

Lady Gresham gazed into space as if trying to bring something to mind. 'Was her name Potter?'

What a memory this lady had. Rose kept her mouth shut.

'I can see by your silence that I am right. I remember the incident well. I questioned my son and he denied having interfered with Miss Potter. Knowing my son as I do, I was doubtful that he was telling the truth, and I told him she was not to be dismissed. I went away for a few months and when I returned I was told that Potter had left of her own accord.'

155

'That's a lie!' Rose leaped to her feet. 'She was turned out with nowhere to go but the workhouse.'

'I know now that that is what happened. I would like to see your mother.'

'No!'

'You have inherited my pride,' Lady Gresham told her, with a wry smile, 'but be careful, it can be uncomfortable to live with.'

'I manage.'

'What are you studying?' Lady Gresham reached out for the book on Rose's desk. 'Law?'

'Is there something wrong with that?' she asked defensively.

'Not at all. My father was a barrister.' She put the book down. 'Which branch of the law are you intending to pursue?'

'I'm going to be a solicitor.'

The lady nodded. 'I'll make you a monthly advance – '

'I won't take anything from the Greshams.' Rose stood in front of the lady, feet apart, hands on hips, her gaze unflinching.

After what seemed an age, Lady Gresham sighed, then nodded. 'I would like to know how you are getting along, though. Will you keep in touch with me?'

'No.'

Lady Gresham appeared to age in front of her as she grasped her stick and stood up. 'If you change your mind – '

'I won't!'

Without another word, Lady Gresham left the room.

15

'How did you get on with the exams?' her mother asked, as soon as Rose walked into the house.

Rose sat down and rubbed her temple. 'All right, I think, but it was hard.'

Her mother placed the cure-all cup of tea in front of her. 'Will you have to take them again if you don't do well enough?'

'No, this is the only chance I'll get. How the professor got away with it this time, I'll never know.'

'From what you've told me, it seems as if he's running the school single handed until the war ends. I expect he can do much as he pleases.'

Rose nodded. 'That's why he's been rushing me, I expect. Once things are back to normal, he won't be able to bend the rules.'

'Don't look so worried.' Her mother patted her hand. 'What happens next?'

'When my results come through, and if they're good enough, the professor will go to the university and try to persuade them to let me enrol.' Rose fidgeted with her cup, then looked up. 'I don't believe he can do this for me, Mum. I'm going to have to be very, *very* good.'

'The professor wouldn't have put you through all this and raised your hopes if he had any doubts.'

'I suppose you're right.' Rose drank her tea. 'Anyway, it's done now, and all we have to do is wait and hope for the best. Even if nothing comes of it, I'll still have learned a lot by trying.'

'Er . . . have you seen any more of the Greshams?' her mother asked hesitantly.

'Not a sign. I don't think they'll come near me again.' She hesitated for a moment. 'But I couldn't help liking the old lady. When I refused to take her money, she asked me to keep in touch.'

'And will you?'

'No.' Rose didn't miss the look of relief on her mother's face.

Annie burst into the room. 'A boy on a bike just gave me this.' She held out a telegram.

'Shall I open it, Mum?' Rose asked gently, knowing what it was. Marj Webster shook her head, opened the message, read it in silence, then folded it again and placed it behind the clock on the mantelpiece. She blew her nose and turned to face them. 'It's been confirmed. Your dad's dead.'

Although she had known what the telegram would say, Rose was still shocked. It had been happening to thousands of families, of course, but this was someone close to them and it felt different. She thought back over the last four years. A generation of young men slaughtered. What a waste.

Annie tugged at her arm. 'Shall I go and tell Mrs Jenks?'

'Good idea, Toots.' Rose watched her little sister run out and realized that she didn't seem upset but, then, why should she? Her father had never given her so much as a passing glance. She searched her mind for something to say, but everything she thought of sounded hollow and insincere.

'Mum . . .'

'You don't have to say anything. I'll be all right when I've got over the shock. I can't believe he won't be coming back, shouting and stinking of beer.'

'No, it'll be strange,' Rose admitted. And a surge of pity rippled through her. 'He never had much of a life, did he?'

Tears ran down Marj's face. 'He was a swine at times, Rose, but he was good to me till the drink got to him. But what else did he have?'

His family, Rose thought, but didn't say it. It had probably been the constant struggle to feed a growing family that had driven him to the pub every night.

'He didn't deserve to die like that,' her mother added softly.

'None of them did, Mum.' Rose sighed. The futility of war filled her mind. Would the sacrifice of all those men help those who had survived, or would everything go back to the way it had been? And if it did, what had it all been about?

Annie returned with their next-door neighbour, who was staggering under the weight of David. Mrs Jenks handed him to Rose. 'Put him to bed. He's sick.'

He was wrapped in an old blanket. Rose pulled it aside. 'What's wrong with him?' Her voice wavered.

'I think he's got the influenza,' Mrs Jenks said, matter-of-factly. 'This epidemic's bad.'

'Should I take him to a doctor?'

'Waste of time and money. They're all rushed off their feet, and there's nothing they can do.'

'I'll help you.' Annie peered at her brother in concern.

'No – and don't you come too close. I don't want you catching it.' Rose stepped away from her sister.

While she was making David as comfortable as possible, she heard someone come up the stairs, coughing. Bert came into the room, crawled on to his bed and scrambled under the blanket with all his clothes on.

'Not you too?' Rose exclaimed, hurrying over to him.

'I feel rotten,' he rasped.

'Get undressed, Bert. You'll be more comfortable.' But her words were ignored – he was already asleep. She removed his boots and left him in peace; she could undress him later.

Rose's mother hurried into the room. 'Oh, dear God. I was praying this would miss us.'

'Not much chance of that,' Rose told her. 'We're crammed together in these houses and any epidemic's going to sweep through here.'

The next three days were agony as Rose watched her two young brothers suffer. She felt so helpless, as influenza raged through the slum dwellings and news of deaths filtered through to them all the time. She was trying to change Bert's soiled bed without disturbing him when she heard her mother give an anguished cry.

'What is it?' She rushed to her mother, who was staring down at the child in the bed.

'David's dead,' Marj cried, and fell into Rose's arms.

'I only went to get him a drink of water. I wasn't away for more than a minute . . .'

Rose closed the little boy's eyes and pulled a blanket over his face, fighting to keep her own tears at bay. Only five years old, and what kind of a life had he had?

She led her distraught mother to a chair and made her sit down. 'I'll go and get the undertaker.'

'No!' Marj clutched at her daughter's arm and looked anxiously at Bert. 'You send Flo. I need you here.'

'All right, Mum.' Rose hurried downstairs, sent her sister on the errand, and told eleven-year-old Will to make their mother a cup of tea. Then she went back upstairs.

The undertaker was so busy that it was around nine o'clock that evening before he managed to come. Then, with that distressing business dealt with, Rose ordered her mother to get some rest. She was too upset and weary to argue, and once Rose knew she was asleep, she settled herself in a chair beside Bert to watch him through the night. The signs weren't good, and she felt sure that he wouldn't live much longer.

She was right: at about five o'clock the next morning Bert died. It was only then, in the quiet hours before anyone else was awake, that she allowed herself to weep.

For the next two days Rose and her mother scrubbed the place out with carbolic, praying that this was the end of the sickness in their house. They had just finished when Nancy and Will developed colds.

'Oh, Rosie,' her mother moaned, 'I don't think I can bear to lose any more of them.'

Rose had hardly slept for days and was exhausted, but

her mother was distraught with grief. She reached out to her in an effort to comfort her. 'Nancy and Will aren't as bad, Mum. They'll be all right. Why don't you lie down? I'll watch them.'

Her mother left the cramped bedroom and Rose could hear her sobbing all the way down the stairs. She felt herself start to crumble inside, but she shook herself and straightened up. This was no time to fall apart. At least Annie hadn't caught it. Although her little sister's health and strength had improved markedly over the years, she still looked fragile. The mortality rate was high in Garrett Street: the epidemic was taking a terrible toll.

Rose went to look at Nancy, gave her a drink, wiped her face, then sat on the edge of the bed and gazed around the room. It was dingy and crowded with beds, but it was clean. Lord, how she hated this street. She got up and walked over to the window to look out at the crowded back-to-back houses, the piles of rubbish everywhere.

'Rosie?' someone croaked.

Rose spun round and saw Flo holding on to the door. 'I don't feel well and Mum said I was to sleep in here.'

'Get into this bed.' Rose rushed to her sister and helped her undress. Flo was no sooner under the blanket than she was asleep.

Rose dropped her head into her hands. How many more?

'Rosie.' Annie was standing by the door. 'Auntie Grace is downstairs. She wants to see you.'

'Don't come in here, Annie,' she said. 'And Grace shouldn't be here.' She ran down the stairs, her heart thudding. Suppose something had happened to

John. She erupted into the scullery. 'Is John all right?'

Grace stopped her conversation with Marj. 'Of course, Rose.'

'Thank God for that!' She sank on to a chair. 'You should have sent a message, not come here. We've already lost two of the children.' She cast a quick glance at her mother and was frightened to see that she was coming down with a cold too. She suspected that her mother was still on her feet only because of her worry about her children.

'That's why I'm here.' Grace turned back to Marj. 'Have you enough money for the funerals?'

A tear trickled down Marj's face, but she pulled herself together. 'I've got a penny insurance on all of them. I take it out as soon as they're born. It isn't much, but it pays for a funeral.' She blew her nose. 'Thank you for asking.'

'What about your husband?' Grace asked gently.

'Oh, the army took care of that. He's been buried somewhere in France.'

Grace nodded, then smiled at Annie. 'And how are you, little one?'

'I'm not little now, I'm seven years old,' Annie said importantly.

'That old!' Grace raised her hands in mock-surprise. 'I remember you when you were no bigger than a doll.'

Annie giggled.

It was lovely to hear laughter again, Rose thought. Since the sickness had struck them, the house had been hushed, shrouded in grief.

'I wondered if you'd like Annie to come and stay with me until everyone's well again.'

'What a kind thought,' Rose exclaimed. With Annie

away from the house, at least she wouldn't have to worry about her.

'No!' Annie's lips set in a firm line. 'I'd like to stay with Auntie Grace, but I'm not going to leave you and Mum. The funerals are tomorrow and you'll need me. I can make the tea and do all sorts of other things.'

'Of course, she must stay here then.' Grace smiled at the little girl. 'You can visit me some other time.'

Who would believe it was early October? Rose pulled up her coat collar, then put her hand through her mother's arm. David and Bert were being buried together, and it couldn't be a worse day for the funeral. It was dark and grey, with a thick mist of rain drenching everyone standing at the graveside. It was a sparse gathering, with only herself, her mother and Bob. Most of the others were ill and she had flatly refused to let Annie come in this dreadful weather. She had got round her by saying that they would all need a hot drink when they got back, and Annie had reluctantly agreed to stay behind and see to it.

Rose felt her mother shiver and squeezed her arm, as the vicar droned on, mouthing the beautiful words of the Bible without an ounce of feeling . . .

'Such a poor send-off,' Marj Webster murmured.

'I know, Mum. But the neighbours would have come if they hadn't been nursing their own families.'

'As if we haven't had enough to put up with over the last four years. God must think we're very wicked to send this disaster on us.'

'It's got nothing to do with Him,' Rose stated with conviction.

The vicar came to the end of the service, and Rose

breathed a sigh of relief. Her mother needed to be home by the fire, not standing around this bleak muddy hole in the ground. Rose had never believed that you were born, lived, died, and that was all there was to it. There had to be something else, and she hoped her brothers had gone to a better place.

'Where does all the trouble come from then?' her mother asked, as they walked out of the churchyard.

'I don't know, Mum. I'm still looking for the answers to about a million questions.'

'Only a million?' Her mother gave a faint smile, the first Rose had seen for some time.

'Yes. I've managed to whittle them down a bit,' she joked.

It was a month before Rose was back at work. Will, Nancy and Flo recovered from the influenza and no one else caught it, thank goodness.

Rose paced the office, waiting anxiously for Professor Steadman to come and tell her the result of her exam. There hadn't been time to wonder about it, but now she wanted desperately to know.

She walked over to the window. The pupils were hurrying along, books clutched in their hands, and the longing that filled her was almost more than she could bear. Her hand shook as she pushed the thick hair away from her face. Her life had been a series of disappointments, and the dream she had had last night was a vivid illustration of how she felt. She had been running down a long passage, but the door in front of her seemed to get further and further away, no matter how fast she ran. She had gritted her teeth and finally reached it, but when she'd turned the handle, the door had been locked.

She pressed her forehead against the cold window. What a dreadful few weeks it had been.

'Rose.'

She turned at the sound of the professor's voice. She had been lost in thought and had not heard him come into the room. She waited for him to speak.

'I've had your results.' A broad smile of pleasure lit his face. 'And you have received higher marks than any of the other candidates.'

She gasped and held on to the desk.

'I've just been to the university and shown them the results. They were impressed, especially when I explained that you have studied in your spare time – under my guidance, of course.'

She took a deep breath. If he didn't tell her soon, she'd scream.

'However . . .'

Please just tell me!

' . . . as you are a female, they took a lot of convincing, but I have won them round. You start next October.'

Her head came up sharply and her black eyes locked on to his. 'Would you repeat that, please?' The voice didn't sound like hers.

'You can study law there full-time.'

She groped for a chair and sank on to it. 'I can't believe it! How did you persuade them to agree?'

'I prodded their political aspirations by reminding them how much women have done in this war, and that it was almost certain the government would soon give them the vote.'

'I bet they weren't too keen on that idea.' She was beginning to come out of her shock, and realize what a gift she had been given.

The professor smiled broadly. 'No, but I swayed them with the argument that it would not harm their reputations if they took in more women students. It would show them as progressive thinkers.'

Then Rose laughed. 'Good heavens, you're a crafty old devil, aren't you?'

'Have you only just found out?' He rubbed his hands together gleefully. 'I'm proud of you, Rose.'

She felt like shouting for joy. 'I don't know how to thank you, Professor.'

'You work hard and pass all the exams. That's all the thanks I need. And I think it's time you called me Harold, don't you?'

In a rare show of affection, she went up to him and kissed his leathery cheek. 'Thanks, Harold. I won't let you down.'

'Don't let yourself down. It isn't going to be easy. You'll have to face many challenges. You might encounter hostility from other students and some of the lecturers.' Harold studied her intently. 'But the only way they can get rid of you is to find a reason to expel you, so hold on to your temper and your tongue.'

'I'll try.'

'You'll have to do better than that. You will have to learn not to rise to provocation, however infuriating.'

She lifted her head and grinned. 'I'll be as docile as a sleeping kitten.'

'That I would like to see!'

'Now, now, Harold, where's your faith?' Rose chided.

'I want this so badly that you can be sure I won't do anything to jeopardize my chances.'

Suddenly the door burst open and three boys tumbled into the room, shouting, 'It's over! *The war's over!*'

16

April 1919

'Uncle John! Uncle John!'

Rose watched Annie hurl herself into John's arms. He staggered back with the impact of her exuberant greeting.

'He's home for good,' Grace said, her face glowing with excitement as she hung Rose's coat over the banisters.

'Oh, I'm so pleased!' Rose turned to greet him, but found that her sister had dragged him into the front room.

'Ooooh, aren't you tall?' Annie's voice was full of admiration.

'Now what's she up to?' Rose wondered.

'She's just met Bill, by the sound of things,' Grace told her.

'Who's Bill?'

'Someone John met while he was in the navy.' Grace lowered her voice. 'He's had a terrible time. His ship was sunk and he spent four days in a small boat. Only two of the men were alive when they were finally rescued.'

Rose shuddered. So many young men had seen and experienced things they would never forget.

'He doesn't get on with his father, poor boy, so we've given him the back bedroom until he can find somewhere of his own.'

Rose opened her mouth to speak, when she heard Annie again.

'How tall are you?'

An educated, soft voice answered, 'Six feet four.'

'Cor! My sister's nearly as tall as you.'

Rose groaned. But Grace looked up at her. 'You *are* taller than the average woman and you're only sixteen.'

'Nearly seventeen, and I hope I stop growing soon,' she muttered, as they walked into the front room.

'Rose!' John hurried to her side and kissed her cheek. 'Congratulations. When do you start at the university?'

'Six months' time.' She grinned. 'Did Grace tell you how Harold forced them to let me enrol?'

John's face was alight with amusement. 'He's a crafty old devil.'

'That's what I told him!' Rose chuckled.

'John,' Grace interrupted, 'introduce Rose to Bill.'

'Oh, I'm sorry. I was so pleased to see my *protégée* again that I've quite forgotten my manners.' He drew her forward. 'Rose, this is Bill . . . Bill, this is Rose.'

She found herself looking into the kindest, gentlest eyes she had ever seen. He was also rather handsome, but deep lines of strain were etched into his face, making it difficult to assess his age. If you disregarded the lines, she reckoned he couldn't be more than in his late twenties.

'Hello, Rose.' He shook her hand politely. 'I've heard a great deal about you.'

'Has my sister been blabbing again?' She glared at Annie accusingly.

'I haven't said anything, honest.' Annie tipped her head back to look up at Bill, giggled, then sidled up to her sister. 'He's tall enough for you too.'

'Annie! I wish you'd watch your tongue. I've a good mind to ask Edward to stitch it down again.'

Annie laughed, then rushed out to the kitchen to help Grace with the tea.

Bill looked puzzled, so John started to explain about how Annie had been born tongue-tied, but he hadn't got far with the story when the child came back with a plate of bread and butter. She put it carefully on to the table, knelt on the chair beside Bill and delighted in telling him the whole story.

'What a good thing you had the operation,' Bill told her.

This sent Annie off into peals of giggles. 'Rosie doesn't think so.'

When Bill laughed, the strain left his face, and Rose caught a glimpse of just how good-looking he really was. He had dark brown hair, perfectly proportioned features, and his mouth was full and gentle, as were his grey-green eyes. If they hadn't held such a tortured look, they would have been beautiful, she thought, as she studied him from beneath lowered lashes. He had a strange effect upon her, which she had not experienced before, and she didn't like it. It frightened her.

Tea was lively and she didn't have time to dwell on imaginary fears – for that was all they were. Her over-active imagination was playing tricks with her again. Not all men were brutes, and this one was no threat to her.

Rose helped Grace clear up afterwards. When she went back into the front room, she stood stock still in horror. Annie was sitting next to Bill, leaning on his arm, and eyeing his knees with a 'dare I?' look on her face. Rose knew what her sister was thinking: he looked big and strong enough for her to sit on. Rose couldn't understand it: Annie was like a kitten, always looking for warmth and comfort.

'Annie!' she said sharply.

The child sighed, slipped off her chair and came to Rose. 'I don't think he'd mind,' she said, quietly this time. 'He's a nice man.'

'You're too big, Annie. And why do you always want to sit on a man's lap?'

'I like men.'

Oh, my God! Rose thought. We could be in for trouble when she grows up. She stooped and straightened her sister's dress. 'Well, you mustn't do it any more, Toots. It was all right when you were a baby, but you're getting to be a big girl now.'

'I am so,' Annie agreed reluctantly.

'Who wants to go to the pictures?' John asked.

'Me! Me!' Annie rushed over to John and grabbed his hand. 'What's on?'

'Buster Keaton.'

'Rosie? Can we go, please?' she pleaded.

'All right, but you be good now, Annie.'

'I'm always good,' she declared with conviction, and let Grace help her with her coat.

There was still a chilly wind blowing as they made their way to the local fleapit, as it was affectionately known, but Annie seemed oblivious to the weather. She was chattering nineteen to the dozen to John and Bill.

'What a difference in her,' Grace remarked, as they walked along behind them.

'Yes. When she was two I didn't think she'd see her third birthday, but she's surprised us all.'

'She doesn't miss much that's going on around her,' Grace observed.

'I know that to my cost.' Rose pulled a face. 'I have to be careful what I say and do.'

Grace laughed quietly. 'She's very perceptive – especially where you're concerned. She loves you so much.'

A lot of people were waiting to see the film, so they had to queue for a while. A young man limped along the line playing a violin and Rose's heart ached for him. Once out of the forces, so many were reduced to begging, especially if they were injured, as this one clearly was.

As the man approached them, Rose dipped into her pocket and found a shilling. When she gave it to him he bowed. 'Thank you, miss, and God bless you.'

Bill and John gave him something too. Then the queue started to move and they were soon inside.

'Where's the music coming from?' Annie knelt on her seat to get a better view.

'Down the front.' Rose pointed to the man playing the piano.

'Oh . . .' She stood up then, wobbling alarmingly, to see past the large woman in front of her.

Before Rose could steady her, Bill caught Annie and held her securely.

Annie grinned at Rose. 'I like that music.'

With one smooth movement, Bill lifted Annie off her seat and put her into his. 'She'll be able to see better there.' He sat down next to Rose and eased his long legs into the tiny space. He was a giant, she thought uncomfortably, and leaned as far away from him as she could.

It was a funny film and even Rose forgot her reserve,

laughing until the tears streamed down her face. When it was over, they went back to Grace and John's for a hot drink.

'Are you going to live at the university,' John wanted to know, 'or will you travel there each day?'

'It's difficult to study in our house, so they've given me a room in the staff quarters. I'll go home at the weekends.'

'Why can't you live with the other students?' Annie piped up.

'Because they're all boys,' Rose explained. 'I can't stay in the same place as them.'

'What? Like at home? We have all the boys in one room, and us girls in another.'

'That's right.' Annie seemed satisfied with that explanation, so Rose turned back to John. The thought of him being home again made her yearn for their Sunday talks once more, but it was asking a lot of him when he probably only wanted to rest and be with his wife again.

She hesitated, then drew a deep breath. 'Now you're home for good, would you be able to spare an hour or two for me? I wouldn't expect our usual Sunday lessons, but I'd love to talk to you.' She added hastily, 'You don't have to agree if you don't want to.'

'I'd like that very much, but I didn't think you'd want to now you're going to study full-time.'

'My Latin's not as good as it should be, and there are other things I'd like to learn.'

'Such as?'

'I've been reading about some of the old philosophers, and I'd like to discuss them with you.'

John leaned forward eagerly. 'How did you get on with them?'

Rose pulled a face. 'Blooming hard going. Some of their ideas take a bit of understanding.'

'Would next Sunday be all right for you? We could make it a regular thing, if you like.'

'Oh, John, I'll look forward to it.' Rose could have hugged him, but she didn't, of course. At times like this she wished she was more like Annie – outgoing and demonstrative. Then she noticed Annie stifling a yawn and stood up. 'We'd better be getting back. Thanks for a lovely afternoon.'

Bill unwound himself from the chair. 'I'll see you home.'

'You don't have to do that. We'll be all right on our own.' The last thing she wanted was this disturbing man with her. 'It's cold out there. You stay in the warm.'

'I've known it colder,' he said simply, then picked up her coat to help her on with it.

Grace had buttoned up Annie and the little girl was already holding Bill's hand, looking up at him trustingly. Rose felt backed into a corner: if she protested too much she would seem childish. Anyway, she had Annie with her, so he was unlikely to try anything. Then she looked into his kind eyes. She really must stop believing that all men were the same.

As soon as they crossed the road the bus came and Bill carried Annie upstairs. Rose couldn't help being amused, because as soon as he sat down Annie curled up on his lap and fell asleep. She had finally got her wish.

The conductor came for the fares and she fished in her pocket, but Bill was already paying. She held out the money to him, but he gave it a contemptuous glance, settled Annie more comfortably and ignored her. She fumed: if he thought she was going to let him pay for them, he had another think coming.

Knowing he had his hands full with the sleeping Annie, she slipped the money into his pocket. This produced a resigned sigh. 'I'm not going to let you pay our fare,' she told him firmly.

He spoke then. 'Why not? Do you think it will make you beholden to me?'

'I can afford to pay.' She felt put out by the edge of sarcasm in his voice. 'And, anyway, I don't know you. You might be broke, for all I know.'

'I'm not.' He turned his head and stared at her intently.

His direct gaze made her uncomfortable, and she wished fervently that the journey was over. It wasn't like her to allow anyone to get under her skin in the way this tall man had. She was experiencing emotions she didn't understand, and hoped she would never see him again.

The bus started to slow for their stop and she shook Annie. 'Wake up! Here we are.'

When they were on the pavement, Rose pointed across the road. 'You can get the bus back from there.'

'I'll see you to your door,' he said, taking Annie's hand and starting to walk along the road.

'There's no need for that.' She grabbed his arm to stop him. 'We'll be all right from here, but thank you for coming with us.'

This little speech produced another deep sigh from him.

'Rosie's right.' Annie stood on tiptoe and looked up

at him. 'It isn't safe to come down our street. You look like a toff and they might rob you.'

He stooped down to her. 'What about you and your sister? Will you be safe?'

'Oh, yes. They'd never touch one of their own.'

'I'd kill them if they did,' Rose muttered.

A twitch of his lips showed her that Bill was amused. 'I think I'll still come with you,' he said.

It was her turn to sigh.

'Oh, well.' Annie took hold of his hand again, and gave him an admiring smile. 'I expect they'll think twice before they jump on you. It would take six of them to hold you down.'

'Oh, at least.' There was a hint of laughter in his voice.

Rose saw little point in arguing. She had the strong feeling that this quiet man was made of steel.

When they reached the house, Bill said a polite goodnight, turned and walked away, whistling a lively tune. He was halfway up the road before Rose tore her gaze away from him. Infuriating man!

Bill strode up the dreadful street, feeling as if he was being watched, but the dark shadows and threatening atmosphere didn't frighten him. This he could handle. It was the sea with its inky depths that made his blood run cold. The sight of his shipmates dying before his eyes still tortured him, disturbing his nights, until he was almost afraid to sleep. When he did drift off, the memory of that terrible time played over and over in his dreams. It was like a demented picture running non-stop, making him experience all over again the rage and helplessness he had felt. He didn't know why he had survived, but for the first time he was glad that he had.

He launched into another popular song, whistling easily and in perfect tune. He had felt happy today. The little girl was a delight – so open and loving – and her untainted affection had soothed his wounded soul. As he'd sat in that small boat, watching each man die, the true values in life had become crystal clear. Annie had got it right, but her sister was another matter. He had sensed anger in her when they had walked down Garrett Street. She hadn't wanted him there, hadn't wanted him to see the squalor.

The bus arrived and he hopped on. When he reached into his pocket for a penny to pay his fare, his fingers closed around the money Rose had insisted on giving him. There had been a fierce pride shining in her dark eyes.

Rose Webster was an intriguing mystery, and he didn't know what to make of her. She was breathtakingly beautiful, and her intelligence was obvious, but she gave away little of her feelings. However, he had seen tonight that she loved to laugh and she had enjoyed the film. Yet when he'd seen her home, she had been prickly and guarded.

She lived in a horrible area and obviously hated it, but there was more to it than that, he was sure. He'd love to know what kind of a life she'd had to make her so defensive.

17

October 1919

'You all right, Mum?' Rose could see she had been crying.

Marj took a letter from behind the clock and handed it to Rose. 'This was waiting for me when I got up this morning. Bob's run away to sea.'

Rose read the note. 'The idiot – he's only fourteen. Why'd he do a stupid thing like that?'

'Wants to get out of this dump, he says.' Her mother wiped away a tear. 'When I lay my hands on him he won't sit down for a week.'

Rose sighed. 'Well, there's no point me going after him. He says here he was sailing at first light, so he'll be long gone by now.'

Her mother started to lay the table for the children's breakfast.

'Shall I do that while you get ready for work?' Rose took a plate out of her mother's hand then noticed it was shaking.

'I haven't got a job any more. We've all been dismissed,' said her mother.

'But that isn't right!' Rose exploded. 'The women are still needed. There are so few men around now that they're not going to be able to fill the jobs. A lot of those coming home aren't even out of the forces yet.'

Marj shrugged. 'But that's what they've done. They don't want us any more.'

'It didn't take them long to forget what the women have done during the war, did it?' Rose muttered bitterly. 'Less than a year into the peace and they want them out of the way.'

Marj gave her daughter a wan smile. 'We were needed for a while, but now the men want everything back the way it was.'

'I know, and a lot of women are going to find it hard to go back to the old ways.'

Her mother nodded. 'If it hadn't been for the women, we wouldn't have survived. No one at the factory wanted to leave. We all enjoyed the friendship and the extra cash.'

At the mention of money, Rose frowned. 'What are you going to do, Mum? Prices have almost doubled recently.'

'Oh, I'll manage. Don't you fret.' Marj looked shifty and shoved a piece of paper out of sight.

Rose guessed what it was and whipped it out from under a plate. As she looked at it, her heart nearly broke. It was a reckoning of income and expenses, and the two didn't come close. Visions of their existence before the war came to her with awful clarity. The struggle to pay the rent, the constant hunger . . .

Her mother took the paper from her. 'We'll be all right. You never know, I might get another job.'

Rose knew the chances of that were slim. 'Don't you get a war widow's pension?'

'Yes, but it's only a few shillings.' A look of sadness crossed her face. 'Flo's got a good job in the shop, though, and she might be able to give me a bit.'

Rose thought about her sister, and knew that she had always been selfish. Although she was only sixteen, she was already walking out, and had started saving to get married. 'You still won't have enough.'

Rose could have wept. Her dreams were crumbling again. She took a deep breath, knowing what she had to do. 'I won't go to the university. I'll get a job instead.' Her voice was husky with distress.

'No! I can't have you doing that. I'd never forgive myself if I held you back.' She gave her daughter a proud smile. 'You're going to make something of yourself. You've got the brains and guts to get out of the slums, and I want to see you do it.'

'But, Mum – '

Marj held up her hand. 'I won't hear a word about you giving it all up. You've worked hard for it.'

'I've got a bit put by. You can have that.'

Her mother shook her head again. 'You'll need it.'

'Well, then, I'll be working for Harold on Saturdays so you can have that money. It won't be much, but it'll help.'

'I won't take it, my girl.' Her mother was adamant. 'You've got three years of study in front of you, and you're going to need every penny you can find. How are you going to be a success if you don't eat?'

Rose couldn't argue with that.

'I'll take in a lodger,' her mother declared.

'What?' Rose was startled. 'Where are you going to put him?'

'With Bob gone and you living at the university during the week, that only leaves six of us. Seven when you come home at weekends. I could use the top two rooms

for us and turn the downstairs room into a nice little
let.'

'Do you think you'll be able to get a lodger?' Rose
looked around and pulled a face.

'It's cleaner than most, and there'll be a lot of men
about with nowhere to live.'

The thought of her mother taking a stranger into the
house made Rose feel uneasy. 'You be careful who you
choose, won't you?'

'I'm not daft, Rosie.'

By the time Rose left to start her first term, the room
was ready. They had scrubbed, polished, then put into it
the best bits of furniture. It didn't look too bad, she had
to admit, and her mother was hopeful of finding a lodger.

She arrived at the university feeling somewhat apprehensive. This was a big step for her and the problems at
home had made her wonder yet again if she was doing
the right thing. And was she good enough to take on
such a challenge?

'How are you feeling, Rose?' Harold asked, when he
met her in the corridor.

'Excited, and nervous. What are you doing here?'

'I've come to wish you luck – and you needn't worry,
there will be two other girls as well. They've put you all
together.' He chuckled. 'If the boys cause you any trouble,
you'll be able to support each other.'

'What are they like, these other girls?'

'Middle class, but that needn't bother you.' A grin
spread across his face. 'You're brighter than they are.'

'I hope you're right.'

'Don't go thinking this is a mistake, because it isn't,'

he told her. 'I've every faith in you. You've earned the right to become a student here.'

The word *student* brought on a surge of excitement and the doubts dropped away. She could do this.

'Who are you?'

Rose continued to put away her few belongings, and ignored the strident voice behind her.

'Answer me! Are you the maid?'

The insult made her turn slowly, her dark eyes flashing, but she was outwardly icy calm. She found herself looking down at a short, dumpy blonde with a petulant expression.

'Well?'

'If you're starting here today, then we're sharing a room.' Rose enjoyed telling her that, and fought to stop herself laughing at the look of horror on the other girl's face.

'It's insulting enough being put in this inferior accommodation, but I'm not sharing a room with *you*.'

'We're here because they haven't got any proper facilities for women yet, and they certainly can't put us in with the men. You'd better go and see if they can make other arrangements for you, because I'm staying.' Rose had known she would come across some rudeness and prejudice, so she had started as she meant to go on. No one was going to get the better of her.

As the blonde stormed out, she pushed aside another girl who was just coming into the room. Rose caught her as she stumbled. She was about five feet two, with ordinary brown hair but very nice clear blue eyes. They went a long way towards making her attractive.

She looked at Rose nervously. 'Who was that?'

'A disagreeable girl who doesn't like the idea of sharing a room.'

'Oh dear.' The newcomer glanced around the room and grimaced. 'Bit cramped, isn't it?'

Was it? It looked positively luxurious to Rose. 'I understand that, as we're the only females, they didn't know where to put us. Do you mind sharing?'

'Oh, no. I wouldn't like to be on my own, not with the place full of boys.' She eyed Rose up and down. 'Would you mind if I stayed close to you?'

'Of course not.' Rose was pleased. She had been chosen as a protector already, and she had only just arrived. 'You needn't be nervous of the boys.'

'Oh, I'm always nervous. People frighten me, you see, and I don't know what I'm doing here.' There was an edge of panic in her voice.

'Why are you then?'

'My mother's a sympathizer of the suffrage movement, and has insisted I train for a career. She chose law for me.'

'And how do you feel about that?' Rose was interested in the girl, especially as her mother was involved with the suffrage movement. That indicated a family keen on social reform.

'I like the idea, but I'm not sure I can do it.' She fiddled with her dress.

'I'm sure you can. We'll do it together.' She held out her hand. 'I'm Rose.'

'Harriet.' She gave Rose a rather damp handshake. 'I'm so glad you're here. Can we be friends?'

'Of course. Now, why don't you claim the bed next to

mine and leave the one by the draughty window for her ladyship?'

Harriet giggled. 'Do you think she'll mind?'

'She will, but I'll sort her out if she causes trouble.'

They were both laughing when the blonde came back. 'It seems we're stuck with each other! This is all that's available at the moment.' She threw her case on to Harriet's bed.

'That's taken,' Rose informed her.

'I can have this one, if I want it.' She turned up her nose and sniffed.

Rose resisted the temptation to wipe the haughty look from her face. 'No, you can't. First to come gets the pick.'

'But I was here before her.' She pointed rudely at Harriet.

Harriet started to edge towards the other bed, but Rose put a hand on her shoulder and stopped her. 'But you left again. You didn't want to share a room, you said.'

'It seems I have no choice, unless I want to stay in the same building as the boys.' She snatched up her bag and stormed over to the window.

It was silly to fight, Rose thought. They were going to have to get on with each other. 'We're going to be seeing a lot of each other, so I suggest we try to be civil. I'm Rose, and this is Harriet. What's your name?'

'I'm Miss Bretton.'

'I'm not going to call you Miss Bretton,' Rose told her firmly. 'Haven't you got a Christian name?'

'Angelina, but everyone calls me Angel.'

Rose smothered a laugh. She had never met anyone

less like an angel. 'What are you going to study, *Angelina?*'

'Law, of course. My father's a barrister.'

And mine's a Sir, Rose thought, with a degree of amusement.

'Where do you live?' Harriet asked Angelina shyly.

'Park Lane. What about you?'

'Kensington.' Harriet glanced at Rose.

'I come from Bermondsey.'

'*Bermondsey?*' Angelina looked appalled. 'How did you manage to get a place here?'

'Professor Steadman helped me. He and another teacher have been coaching me.'

Angelina's expression told Rose that she doubted she could read or write, but Rose didn't care. Let people think what they wanted to – she'd show them all in the end.

Rose rubbed her temple and closed her eyes. She was so very weary, but nothing would keep her away from her regular Sunday visit to Grace and John. She had so much to discuss with John and he was giving her the much-needed tuition in Latin. Anyway, Annie would be upset if she couldn't come here once a week. Rose knew that her little sister missed her and looked forward to her coming home every Friday night.

'Do you feel up to this today?' John came in and sat beside her.

Rose opened her eyes and smiled. 'I've been looking forward to it all week.'

The time flew by, as it always did when she was with John. He was the only person with whom she felt she could let down her guard, and she poured out her hopes, fears and the difficulties she had encountered in the first week at the university. They spent the first hour catching up on what she had been reading, and then discussing any subject that came to mind. She soon forgot her tiredness.

They were in the middle of one of their usual arguments when Annie came in with a plate of biscuits for their break. Then Grace joined them and asked how she had got on at the university.

Rose told them about Harriet and the snobbish Angelina, and they were all in fits of laughter when the door opened and Bill came in. She hadn't realized he was still staying with Grace and John.

'I'll be off, now,' he told John and Grace. 'Thank you for your hospitality. I've enjoyed my time with you. Good company, regular food and rest were just what I needed.'

John shook his hand, and Grace hugged him. 'There's a room here for you whenever you want it, Bill,' Grace told him.

Rose gaped. He was in uniform, but it wasn't an ordinary seaman's outfit. She was mesmerized by the decoration on his lapels and the hat tucked beneath his arm.

Annie got off her chair and gazed up at him in wonder. 'Ooh, don't you look lovely?'

With a chuckle, he stooped and kissed the top of her head. 'Thank you, Annie. So do you.'

'Are you going away?' she asked.

'Yes, sweetheart, I am, but I'll come and see you when I'm on leave.'

'You promise?'

He held his hand over his heart. 'I promise.'

'Are you going on a boat?' Annie persisted, holding his hand tightly.

Bill nodded again, his expression tightening. Then he turned to Rose. 'John told me about your brother. I'll see if I can find out where he is.'

Her mouth was still open and she hadn't heard what he had said. 'What kind of a uniform is that?' she blurted out.

'He's a captain,' John told her.

Now Rose understood why he had felt responsible for all those men when his ship had been sunk. And he was going back to sea again. That took guts. She was sorry she had been so sharp with him.

With a genuine smile, she held out her hand. 'Good luck.'

He ignored her hand, leaned forward and kissed her cheek. 'I hope your dreams come true.' He turned on his heel and left.

18

Bill stood on the dock at Portsmouth, his mood as bleak as the weather. He didn't want to go back to sea, but knew that this was something he had to do. His gaze swept over the ship in front of him, but he couldn't appreciate the trim lines, the gleaming paintwork, the impressive array of guns. Thank God they would only be used for practice now. HMS *Grenadier* was the most recent battleship to come into service, and the navy had paid him a great honour by giving him command of her, but he felt no affection for her. How could he? She was a stranger to him. Not like his other command – a battered old cruiser that had felt like a living entity . . .

'Sir!'

Bill snapped back to the present.

'I'm Able Seaman Smithy, sir, your steward.' The sailor picked up Bill's bag. 'She's a fine ship, sir.'

'Yes, very impressive.' He tried to dredge up some enthusiasm, but there was nothing inside him except fear at facing the sea again.

'The crew's all ready and waiting, sir.'

Bill lifted his head and straightened his shoulders. It was time to lay a few ghosts.

As he stepped on to the deck, the welcoming party saluted smartly, and just for a moment – a brief flash – the faces of the men changed. Instead of the fresh-faced eager recruits, he was seeing the other crew, whom he had watched die. Many had been his friends, and in the long sleepless nights, he could still hear their cries as he had searched for them in the inky dark as their ship had disappeared beneath the sea. Gradually all sounds had ceased and the silence had been worse than the noise and confusion. He remembered looking over the side of the little boat into the churning depths. The deathly quiet and vast emptiness of the ocean had nearly unmanned him, but he had held on to his composure by telling himself that this couldn't be the only lifeboat to have been launched successfully. He had jumped overboard at the last moment, and if it hadn't been for the willing hands pulling him into the boat, he would now be with his friends at the bottom of the ocean.

Sweat broke out on his upper lip as the pictures played over and over in his mind.

'Welcome aboard, sir. I'm Petty Officer Stevens.'

'Are you familiar with the ship?' he asked, once more in control, and ready to face the task ahead of him.

'Yes, sir. I've been here a week.'

Bill nodded. 'Come with me. I'll inspect my cabin and then you can give me a guided tour.'

'We're all proud to have a hero of Jutland as our captain, sir.' Stevens nearly bowed.

'There aren't any heroes,' he told the young man, rather sharply, 'just ordinary men who did the best they could.'

'Yes, sir. I'm sure you're right, sir. I was too young to join in the fighting, sir.'

'Be grateful you were.' Bill smiled to soften his rejection of the boy's praise. 'It was damned dangerous.'

Stevens relaxed a little, then smiled back. 'So I've heard.'

His tour of the ship was thorough and Bill was impressed, but the vessel still seemed soulless to him.

The time for sailing came and Bill stood on the bridge, his attention focused on getting the ship safely out of harbour and on to the high seas, where she belonged. As she was new, they were going to spend two weeks cruising and testing all the equipment. Then they would be given their sailing orders. He was already aware it was to be an exercise in diplomacy, showing the flag, but he didn't know the countries they would visit.

Once they were well away from land, Bill stood with his feet apart, felt the ship roll beneath him, and was surprised to find himself enjoying the sensation.

He began to relax, and his mind drifted back to when the petty officer had called him a hero. What a joke! But he wasn't laughing. He had survived Jutland, and put it out of his mind, as horrendous as the battle had been. The thing that haunted him was when they had been steaming to catch up with a convoy and escort it home. They had never reached it. That day the North Atlantic had claimed many lives and blighted many more. However, Bill was determined not to be one of the damaged ones, like some of the poor devils he had seen who had returned from the trenches, mutilated in body and mind.

He left the bridge and walked to the stern of the ship, watching the churning sea as they sped through the dark waters. Then he made himself gaze down into the depths, as he had done in the lifeboat, and he remembered the friends who had sunk beneath the waves, never to return.

Gradually the burden of guilt lifted. He had done everything he could to save his men. It hadn't been his fault that the enemy had been waiting for them, or that rescue had been so long in arriving. He saw at last that he wasn't responsible for their deaths. It had been the bloody war.

He knew then that he had done the right thing in coming back to sea. Only by facing his fears and guilt would he be able to exorcize them. When he returned home this time he would be a whole man. And maybe he would see Rose again.

A slight smile touched his lips as he thought of the dark-eyed beauty. She was touchy, defensive and proud, and she would be difficult to handle. The grin spread. His calm approach to life infuriated her but she had a lot of growing up to do and he had patience. He already knew he wanted to be part of her life, but he wasn't sure how he would achieve that. At times she appeared completely self-contained, not needing anyone, but he knew that was only the image she presented to others. Her love for her family and her friendship with John and Grace told another story. But it would be a challenge to find the girl beneath the carapace she showed the world.

When Rose arrived home the following Friday evening, her mother was sitting in the scullery talking to a stranger. 'This is Mr Pearce, Rose. He's come about the room.'

Rose studied the man, who was scrambling to his feet. He was in his forties, she guessed, though it was hard to tell: so many boys had gone to war and come back old men. He was of average height and stocky build, but he looked clean and respectable. 'Have you seen the room, Mr Pearce?' she asked politely.

'Yes, and it would suit very well.' He paused, looking slightly uncomfortable. 'That's if you'd take me, of course.'

Rose sat down, and saw that Mr Pearce didn't take his seat until both she and her mother had done so. He was polite, which was another thing in his favour.

'Were you in the army?' She handed him the sugar for his tea.

'Yes, I was just under the conscription age limit.'

'That was a pity.'

He smiled, but not with his eyes. 'That's what I thought when I found myself up to my knees in mud.'

Rose's answering smile was sympathetic. 'And why do you need lodgings?'

'My home is in Kent, but I've managed to find a clerical post at the commercial docks.'

Rose's suspicious nature showed itself. 'If you've got such a good position, why do you want to live here?' she asked. 'Garrett Street's a rough place.'

'Oh, I'm not worried about that.' This time his eyes shone with amusement. 'I grew up in Lambeth, so I'll feel quite at home.'

'Maybe so,' she persisted, 'but you could surely afford something better.'

'I'll be earning a respectable wage, but I need to send money home each week. My old mother is living with my sister in Kent and I have to help support them. My sister lost her young man in the war and she won't marry now.'

That explained why he had come to them for a room.

He seemed to be a man who cared for his family, and what he said about his sister remaining unwed rang true. There were many more women than men now, and a lot would remain single. That meant women would need careers.

Rose caught her mother's questioning look, and gave a slight nod. He would do.

On Monday Rose returned to the university. Mr Pearce had moved in immediately, seeming delighted with the arrangement. He had paid her mother two weeks in advance.

'Ah, you're back,' Angelina said, as she came into their room. There was a strange look on her face, as if she was bursting with curiosity. 'Someone's been asking for you.'

'Oh?'

'Sir George Gresham.' Angelina delivered the name as if she was talking about the Archangel Gabriel.

Rose almost laughed. If only she knew. 'Really?'

'Yes.' Angelina looked at her speculatively. 'What would he want with you?'

Rose shrugged. 'Who knows?'

'He's waiting for you in the library.'

Rose continued to collect her papers for the first class of the day.

'Did you hear me?' Angelina persisted. 'He wants to see you.'

'Well, he'll have to wait. I'm not going to be late for my class.'

'Wait?' Angelina squeaked. 'You don't keep someone like Sir George waiting!'

'Why not?'

'Because – because you don't,' the girl stuttered.

'Then it will be a new experience for him, won't it?' Rose gave a grim smile and left the room.

Angelina fell into step beside her. 'Are you frightened of *anyone*?'

'I don't think so. Should I be?'

'Most people are careful around Sir George Gresham. He's a powerful man.'

Rose came to a sudden halt. 'Rank doesn't impress me. He was born the same way as us, and it's what a person is that brings respect, or otherwise. From what I've seen of Sir George, there's little to respect about him.'

'You're a strange one, Rose.' There was a note of grudging admiration in Angelina's voice. 'You come from the slums, but you don't seem ashamed of it, and you have strong views about life and justice and equality.'

'Not all the people who live in squalor and poverty are idiots.' Rose glared at her. 'They have feelings, hopes, fears and dreams, just like anyone else, but most of them drift into apathy because of their constant struggle to stay alive. They're exploited as cheap labour, and considered only half human by the affluent classes. They're locked in a cage, and there doesn't seem to be a way of escape.' She started to walk again.

'But you're going to get out, aren't you?'

'I'm picking at the bars, and education will free me.' Rose reached the room, opened the door, and walked in to take her seat.

Harriet was already there, tucked into a corner at the back of the lecture room. Rose walked up to her, took her arm and towed her further down. They were now about six rows from the front. The seats were arranged in a semicircle and it was rather like a theatre.

'I was all right there,' Harriet whispered.

'No, you weren't.' Rose smiled encouragingly. 'You'll hear better down here. This is going to be interesting. It's about famous court cases.'

The lecturer walked in, stopped and looked at the students. His eyes rested on the three girls. 'You can't sit there. Move to the back,' he ordered.

Rose stood up at once, caught hold of Harriet and Angelina's arms and pulled them to the front row. She made them sit down, then smiled sweetly at the lecturer. She'd never seen this one before and was determined not to let him get the better of her. Just because they were women, she was not going to let them be pushed out of sight.

'I said the *back*.'

Rose smiled again. 'We can't sit there, sir. We're so excited about hearing your lecture that we don't want to miss a word.'

Angelina stifled a laugh, Harriet gasped and Rose kept smiling. She knew she'd hit the right note when he said, albeit grudgingly, 'Very well, you may stay there.'

As it turned out, he was very good and Rose enjoyed every minute of his talk.

They had finished classes for the day and Rose was making her way to the library when she met Sir George. She saw at once that he was furious.

'Where have you been?' he snapped. 'I sent a message for you to come and see me this morning, and I waited an hour. Didn't the girl tell you?'

'Yes, but I couldn't spare the time.'

He caught her arm and pulled her into an empty room, then kicked the door shut behind them. 'Don't be insolent, my girl! I'll have you expelled if I have any trouble with you.'

'And if *I* have any trouble with *you*, I'll go to the Board of Education and tell them what an unprincipled, immoral and thoroughly untrustworthy man you are.' She glanced at his hand around her arm, then gave him a withering look. 'Let go of me, or I'll scream the place down.'

He released her and stepped away. 'My God!' he muttered. 'You really do hate me, don't you?'

'Why does that surprise you? My mother was disgraced by you and took the only option available to her, which was to marry the first man who offered her help and shelter.'

'What happened between your mother and me was a long time ago. I'm sorry now that I was so unfeeling at the time, but you would be astounded at what the staff, especially the young girls, get up to to try and improve their position in life.'

Rose snorted inelegantly. 'So you seduce them then throw them on the streets. Oh, I feel so sorry for you.'

'Don't be sarcastic, girl.'

'Stop calling me girl,' she said tartly. 'My name is Rose.'

'You're going to have to learn to control that temper.'

He had a nerve to say that! 'Like you do, you mean?'

Amusement replaced anger. 'It doesn't matter with me. I'm a man.'

'Really?' She looked him up and down. 'Are you sure? I'd never have guessed it.'

A hint of a smile curled his lips. 'Oh, yes. And I was man enough to father a fiery child like you.'

Rose didn't like the way this encounter was going. The last thing she wanted was for him to think he had any claim on her. 'It's a shame you didn't think of that when you condemned my mother to a life of poverty in a place like Garrett Street.'

He looked shocked. 'Is that where you live?'

'Yes.' She cursed herself for giving away that piece of information – but he would never come across the river, she told herself. 'When you turned her out, my mother had the choice between that or the workhouse.'

'I'm sorry.'

He actually looked it, and that made her even angrier. 'Save your pity. We don't need it.' She looked at the clock in the corner of the room. 'I've got studying to do. What do you want, anyway?'

'My mother wants to see you.'

'What on earth for?' She was astonished.

'She likes you.'

Rose looked away. She had to admit that she had taken to the elderly lady, but she had made it clear that she didn't want anything to do with the Gresham family. She looked back at Sir George. 'No.'

'She hasn't been well,' he went on, 'and your company would cheer her.'

'I'm sorry she's been ill – '

'Then come and see her, it would make her happy.' He gave her a searching look. 'You are so like her – in fact, you're the kind of grandchild she's always wanted.'

Rose bristled. 'I will not be thought of as her grandchild.'

Sir George held his hands up. 'I know you don't want to have anything to do with us, and I understand that, Rose, but my mother is old and she wants to see you.'

She chewed her bottom lip. Would it do any harm to humour an old lady?

'Just this once,' he persisted.

'I won't come to your house,' she told him firmly.

'My mother has a house in Bloomsbury. I'll take you there.'

'No, you won't, I'll go on my own. Give me the address.' She watched while he wrote it down, then took the piece of paper and slipped it into her pocket. 'Tell her I'll be there tomorrow evening after lectures.'

'Thank you.' He gave a brief smile, then opened the door and walked away.

Rose watched him go, angry with herself for giving in. She must be mad.

19

'Come in, miss. Her ladyship is expecting you.'

Rose followed the footman, and gasped as she saw the hall. It was bigger than her whole house. It had electric light and the huge chandelier was breathtaking, sparkling with a rainbow of colours. The walls were covered with red and gold wallpaper. She had never seen anything so beautiful.

'Miss Webster,' the footman announced, then stepped aside to let her enter the drawing room.

If she had thought the entrance elegant, there was only one word to describe the room she had just stepped into: sumptuous. It was like entering another world, and for Rose, of course, it was. She had known the ruling classes lived in comfort but she was dumbstruck by the colour and beauty of her surroundings.

'Thank you for coming, Rose.' Lady Gresham beckoned to her from her chair by the fireplace. 'Sit here, next to me.'

Rose eyed the chair doubtfully. It was covered in gold satin – or was it silk? It hadn't been made to sit on, surely?

Lady Gresham patted the seat. 'Come, my dear, let me look at you.'

Rose gave the chair another uncertain look, then sat down. It was remarkably comfortable. When she looked up the elderly lady was studying her. Then she remembered why she was there and became defensive again. 'I'm not going to make a habit of this!' she declared.

'Of course not,' Lady Gresham said mildly, 'but thank you for coming this evening.' She watched Rose run her hand lightly over the arm of the chair. 'Do you resent the fact that we have so much?' she asked intuitively.

'I don't think that's the right word. When I think of the differences in the way we live, I feel angry. It isn't right, and I find it hard to understand how a society like ours can allow such deep divisions to exist.'

'You think everyone should be equal?'

'I'm not that naïve, Lady Gresham. I know there have always been the upper and lower classes, and I expect in my lifetime there always will be, but everyone's entitled to a decent standard of living, surely.' She straightened and held Lady Gresham's gaze. 'I don't mean we want riches like this. The wealth of the ruling classes has been handed down over generations, and we don't expect to own anything like it.'

'What *do* you expect?' Lady Gresham quizzed gently.

'Clean living conditions, jobs that pay a decent wage so that we can feed our families, and not have to live in constant fear of being turned out on to the streets because we can't pay the rent.'

'Is that all?'

'All?' Rose was indignant. 'Only someone who's never had to worry where the next meal was coming from would ask a daft question like that!' She was getting into her stride now, her surroundings forgotten. 'We don't expect jam on our bread every day, or to be surrounded by silks and satins, but we do have the right to live with dignity.'

'I agree with you. So, what are you going to do about it?'

Rose was startled. John had asked her the same question the first time she had met him, and she still didn't know the answer. She sighed. 'I don't know.'

'But you are going to try?'

'Yes.' She looked into Lady Gresham's shrewd eyes and asked boldly, 'What are *you* going to do about it?'

'I do charity work for the poor – '

Rose cut her off with a sound of disgust. 'The people trapped in the slums don't want charity. They need to be educated, shown how to improve themselves.'

'You're very passionate about education, aren't you?'

'Yes! It's the key that opens some closed doors.'

'Will that answer all the problems?'

'No, of course not,' Rose said sadly. 'But I feel it's very important for everyone to have a good education.' She leaned forward, the fervour of her speech showing how much she cared. 'Do you know what dirt, hunger and violence do to you?'

Lady Gresham shook her head.

'They grind you down until nothing seems worth bothering about. What's the use of applying for a better job when no one will employ you because you can't read or write?' She thumped the arm of the chair. 'They were good enough to die in the war, for heaven's sake!'

Rose stood up and started to prowl around the room, not seeing the expensive furniture, the exquisite pieces of porcelain, or the luxurious rugs. The bright light from the electric lamps was spilling out of the window, piercing the darkness with fingers of yellow, and she glimpsed well-tended gardens that stretched away into the distance.

'Have you seen those poor mutilated men standing on nearly every street corner begging?' Lady Gresham asked quietly.

'How could I miss them? They fought for their country and now they've been abandoned. Someone ought to help them.'

'I've set up a refuge in Mile End for them.'

'Oh?' Rose spun round, suddenly alert again. 'How many can you help?'

'About twenty-five.'

'It isn't enough. There are hundreds.'

'I know and I'm looking for a larger property, but in the meantime we can house twenty-five and feed about fifty a day.' Lady Gresham paused. 'Some of us do care, Rose.'

Rose turned to look out of the window again. She had misjudged this elegant, softly spoken lady. 'Is your son helping?' she asked.

'He's humouring me by trying to find another building for us,' she sighed, 'but I'm afraid he thinks it isn't any of our business, and that the authorities should deal with the problem.'

'But they don't, do they? They live in another world and haven't the slightest notion of what needs doing.' Rose came back and sat down again. 'How old are you?'

'Seventy.'

'That's a good age, but most people who live across the river never see fifty-five.'

'I know, my dear, but things must improve. The first step has already been taken by giving women the vote.'

'Thirty and over!' Rose grimaced in disgust.

'It's a start, and Lady Astor has taken her seat in Parliament. Change won't come overnight, you know.'

'I know.' Rose had given vent to her frustrations and felt better for it, but hearing what Lady Gresham was trying to do for the war wounded had burst her bubble of self-righteous indignation. 'I'm impatient,' she said, with a wry smile.

Lady Gresham laughed. 'It's a family trait.'

Rose grinned. She was feeling a little uncomfortable about her outburst. Who was she to lecture this wise woman on the injustices of society? 'I'm sorry. You didn't ask me here to listen to me rant on about the downtrodden masses.'

'You're wrong. That's exactly why I asked you to visit me. I now have some idea what kind of a person you have grown into.'

'An intolerant, angry one.' Rose gave a self-deprecating laugh. 'Do you know what they call me in Garrett Street?'

'No.'

'That black-eyed bitch. Pardon my language.'

Lady Gresham laughed, her eyes crinkling at the corners. 'I've been called worse in my time.' Then she became serious again. 'You admit you're angry, and that is obvious to anyone who talks with you for a while, but anger, when controlled and used properly, is a useful tool. However, you must be careful not to let it overwhelm you so that it clouds your judgement. You must be its master, and never let it run unchecked.'

Rose recognized some of her own passion glinting in Lady Gresham's dark eyes, and regarded her with new respect. 'Are you speaking from experience?'

'Yes. I caused a lot of upset and grief until I learned that lesson, but eventually I managed to turn my volatile temperament into useful channels.'

At that moment the door opened and Sir George strode in. 'Ah, she came.'

Rose was instantly on her feet, but Lady Gresham caught hold of her arm. 'What are you doing here, George? I don't remember inviting you.'

'I just came to see if she'd kept her word.'

'Her name is Rose, in case you've forgotten,' his mother reprimanded him, 'and of course she kept her word.'

He smiled, not a bit put out by his mother's sharp tongue. 'Good. I'll stay for dinner.'

'No, you won't, George. Rose and I are going to have a quiet meal together. We have a lot to discuss.'

He looked at them suspiciously. 'What are you up to?'

'We are merely getting to know each other. By your callous action all those years ago, you have deprived me of watching my granddaughter grow into a fine young woman, and I find that hard to forgive.'

He shrugged and walked towards the door. Then he stopped. 'Oh, by the way, I've found you the ideal property for your charitable scheme. It's down by the docks.'

When he'd gone Lady Gresham stood up. 'My son is an astute businessman, and it's only because of his careful management that I am able to help a few of these unfortunate men. Now, Rose, will you keep an old lady company over dinner?'

What could she say? It would have been churlish to refuse – and, anyway, much to her surprise, she was enjoying herself.

★

Rose surveyed the array of silver cutlery before her with a flutter of panic. What was it Grace had said? You start from the outside . . . or . . . was it the inside? She had thought at the time that it was useless information she would never need, but now she wished she had paid more attention.

'Sit down, Rose.' Lady Gresham took her place at the head of the table and a servant held out a chair for her, next to his mistress.

As each dish was served, Rose watched carefully to see what Lady Gresham did, then copied her. She quickly cottoned on that you started from the outside and worked your way in, and it was easy enough until she was faced with a strange-looking knife. If it was a knife. When the next dish was placed in front of her, she didn't know what it was. She gave a little sniff and decided it must be fish, but it was nothing like the fish she was used to – it didn't have batter on it.

'Try it. I think you'll like it.'

Lady Gresham hadn't picked up her cutlery for this dish, so she decided it must be the funny-shaped things because they were next in line. She held up the knife. 'Is it this one?'

'Yes.'

When she took the first bite a host of new flavours burst in her mouth. 'Oh, I've never tasted anything like this.'

'I knew you'd like it.'

Rose pushed away her quickly cleared plate. When the next dish arrived, she couldn't take her eyes off it. 'What's that?' she whispered.

'You'll see.' Lady Gresham looked as if she was enjoying the experience as much as her guest was.

A servant in splendid dark green livery started to carve, and she saw that it was a huge joint of beef covered with pastry. The smell and look of the succulent meat made Rose's mouth water. She watched as a large slice was put on to a plate, but before he served it to her, the man looked up. 'Would you like another slice, miss?'

'Yes, please.'

The whole meal was a revelation, and by the time they arrived at the pudding, she was glad she had only had small portions of the previous courses. She had lost count of how many different dishes they'd had. They finished with coffee in the drawing room, and that was a treat too – they only ever had tea at home.

'Did you enjoy the meal?' Lady Gresham asked.

'Oh, yes, Lady Gresham.' She grinned. 'I didn't know what some of it was, though.'

'There is no need to be so formal. You can call me Grandmother.'

Rose put her cup down with a clatter. 'I can't do that! I've only just met you and, anyway, it would cause a scandal.'

'I have survived worse,' Lady Gresham told her.

'No.' Rose shook her head vigorously.

'Why not?' Lady Gresham was unable to hide her disappointment.

'Because my mother will be upset. You might not mind the scandal, but she will. She's always kept this a secret and I won't have her shamed.'

'Of course, it was selfish of me not to think of that.'

She sighed. 'I'm afraid I speak my mind without thinking of the consequences.'

Rose drained her cup and stood up, alarmed now. 'I shouldn't have come tonight.'

'Please don't leave. Trust me, my dear, I will never do anything to harm you or your mother. If you don't want your connection with us to be known, I won't say a word to anyone.'

Strangely, Rose believed her and, with her suspicious nature, that was quite something. But she knew instinctively she could trust Lady Gresham.

'Are you ashamed of your parentage, Rose? You may speak frankly, my dear.'

Rose took a deep breath. 'Of course I am.'

'Even though you are connected to a noble family?'

'That doesn't make any difference. That your son is of high rank only makes things worse. If he had seduced one of his own, that would have been different, but he took advantage of an innocent servant girl.' Rose paused briefly. 'In my eyes that makes him lower than the tramp in the gutter.'

Rose saw Lady Gresham flinch, but carried on. She had asked for frankness, and she was going to get it. 'The fact that I'm a bastard doesn't worry me.' She gave a resigned shrug. 'That's just the way things are, but I'm ashamed to be your son's daughter. As far as I'm concerned, he's a cruel, selfish, unfeeling man, and no matter how high he is in society, I could never like or respect him.'

'And do you hate me, child?' Lady Gresham's voice cracked.

'You're a nice person, and I don't hold you responsible

for your son's behaviour . . .' Rose hesitated, hating to hurt her, but she couldn't let this family think they might interfere in her or her mother's life. 'But I don't think we should meet again.'

Lady Gresham nodded sadly, reached across to a small table, picked up something and handed it to Rose. 'I would like you to have this.'

It was a delicate miniature painting, set in a gold mount studded with gems. The picture was of a young girl with blue-black hair and large dark eyes. The resemblance to herself was remarkable. 'I can't take this,' Rose gasped. 'It must be worth a fortune!'

'I want you to have it.' There was a pleading note in Lady Gresham's voice.

'Is it you?'

'Yes, and if you won't do me the honour of letting me acknowledge you as my granddaughter, then at least take that so you won't forget me.'

Do her the honour? What was she talking about? Where was the honour of having a granddaughter born on the wrong side of the blanket?

Rose handed it back. 'I'm sorry, but this is far too valuable for me to accept. I'd worry about losing it – and it belongs to the Gresham family, not me.'

There was silence for a moment, then Lady Gresham took the miniature and placed it on the table again. 'I'll keep it in trust for you.'

Rose didn't know what that meant, but she was relieved she'd had the sense to refuse the gift. Just think what Sir George would have thought if he had seen her with it – he'd have jumped to the conclusion that she'd stolen it.

Lady Gresham picked up a silver frame, removed a

photograph from it, then handed the picture to her. 'If you won't accept anything of value from me, will you take this photograph? It would make me happy for you to have it,' she added gently.

The picture made Rose smile. It was of a young, carefree Lady Gresham, standing in a cornfield. 'Thank you, I'd like to have this.'

The old woman stood up and kissed her cheek. 'You have made me very happy by coming here tonight, and I have enjoyed our talk. I'm proud to have found such an intelligent, lively member of the Gresham family.'

'I'm not a member of your family,' Rose said firmly, 'and I will not accept your son as my father. He's a stranger to me.' She held out her hand. 'Goodbye, Lady Gresham.'

As she left the room she heard the old lady whisper, 'You may deny it all you like, Rose Webster, but you are a Gresham.'

20

'It's bloody freezing out there.' Angelina tumbled into the small room clutching several packages. 'And it's not much warmer in here. You'd think the university could provide us with a fire, or something. Thank goodness I'm going home for the Christmas holidays.'

Rose looked up from her packing in amazement. Angelina had sworn. After one term the girl had changed a lot; the haughtiness had almost disappeared, and the three now got on well together.

Then Harriet appeared and collapsed on to her bed with a groan. 'I'm worn out, but I think I've managed to find all the presents.'

'What on earth have you two been buying?' Rose asked.

Angelina pulled a garment out of a box and held it up for the others to see. It was dark blue velvet with gold embroidery around the low neck, obviously the latest fashion.

'That's beautiful,' Rose told her, without a trace of envy. 'Let's see what it looks like on you.'

'Yes, do put it on.' Harriet had jumped off the bed to get a better look. 'Where are you going to wear that?'

'Daddy has to go to a big party and he wants me to accompany him.' Angelina undressed hastily in the cold room and slipped the dress over her head.

'He'll be proud of you in that,' Rose told her, then

turned to Harriet, who was no longer so frightened of other people. She still harboured the opinion that she was not as clever as everyone else, but Rose intended to change that. 'Have you bought yourself a new frock too?'

'Yes, but not as grand as Angel's.' She showed them a pale green dress with a delicate lace insert at the neck and more lace around the short sleeves.

Rose took hold of it and held it up against Harriet. 'That will suit you beautifully. You've made an excellent choice.'

Angelina agreed.

Harriet smiled at the compliments, but then she became serious. 'I'm not sure I'm coming back next term. I don't think I'm good enough.'

'Of course you are.' Rose folded her one decent frock carefully and put it into her bag. 'You'll feel better when you've had a holiday.'

'No, I won't. I'm just not clever enough.'

'Don't be daft, Harriet.' Rose laughed. 'It isn't that difficult.'

'You might not think so – you're cleverer than most of the boys – but I'm finding it a struggle to keep up.'

'You're doing all right.' Angelina tossed some books on to a shelf. 'That lot can stay until we come back. I'm going to make sure this is the best Christmas I've ever had. I've earned it. And we shall expect to see you again, Harriet. You're as clever as anyone else.'

Angelina had changed too, Rose thought. Without the snooty veneer, she was a nice girl.

'Isn't that right, Rose?'

'You're brighter than some of the boys,' Rose agreed.

'Ooh, don't let them hear you say that.' Harriet

giggled. 'They don't like us being here and you've made them hopping mad, Rose.'

'Have I?' Rose feigned surprise.

The girls roared with laughter. 'She doesn't even know!' Angelina gasped.

Rose put her hands on her hips and grinned. 'What should I know?'

'Well . . .' Harriet tried to compose herself. 'You've got more brains than them, you're stronger and you don't take any notice of their nasty remarks – '

'Or their amorous advances,' Angelina interrupted. 'Though, come to think of it, not many of them are brave enough to tangle with Rose.'

'You make me sound like an ogre.'

The girls broke into another fit of the giggles.

Rose held up her hands. 'All right, I admit I'm difficult.'

Angelina began to roll around on her bed, thumping the pillow in glee. '*Difficult* is hardly the word I'd use. I'll never forget the look on Bradshaw's face when you threatened to flatten him if he didn't stop following you around. I've never seen anyone scuttle for safety as quickly as he did.'

'Yes, well, he asked for that.' Rose joined in the laughter. Once some of the boys had accepted their presence at the university, they had become quite friendly. Too friendly in some cases.

'And what about that time old Harrison refused to let us into his lecture.' Angelina turned to Harriet. 'Do you remember?'

'I do. What's that expression you use, Rose?'

Rose shrugged, warmed by the camaraderie that existed between them now.

'I remember.' Harriet had another fit of the giggles. 'You were "madder than a wet hen".'

'Oh, yes, I must remember to tell my family that one.' Angelina held her aching sides.

'By the time you'd finished with him, he looked as if he'd just gone five rounds with a prize-fighter.' Harriet looked at her admiringly. 'I don't know how we'd have got through the last few months without you.'

'Rubbish! You must both be pretty strong or you'd never have got this far.'

Harriet squared her shoulders. 'You're right. Perhaps I will come back next year.'

'You'd better,' Rose and Angelina chorused.

'Are you spending Christmas with your family?' Harriet asked Rose.

'Yes, Christmas Day and Boxing Day certainly, but the rest of the time I'll be working.'

'Working!'

'Don't look so horrified, Angelina. I'm nearly broke and I've got to earn enough to get me through next term.'

'It must be hard for you,' Harriet said gently.

'I'm used to it.' Rose gave them a bright smile to show them it didn't bother her, but in truth, it had been a nightmare trying to survive. If it hadn't been for Harold, she would never have been able to stay at university.

Angelina started to pack her bag. 'Who are you going to work for, Rose?'

'Professor Steadman's writing a book and I'm helping him with it. I've also managed to get a job in the grocer's where my sister works for a couple of days before Christmas.'

'Two jobs? But you need a rest as much as we do.'

'I'm all right, Harriet. I'm no stranger to hard work.'

'Good job you're strong.' Harriet picked up her bag. 'Well, I'm off. I'll see you next year.'

'Me too.' Angelina followed Harriet out.

Rose sighed. They were both looking forward to the holiday, but she couldn't say she was. She did feel as if she needed a rest, but she had to work.

Deep in thought she walked along the corridor and cannoned into a solid object. It was Sir George. 'What are you doing here?' she demanded.

'As gracious as ever, I see.'

Since her visit to Lady Gresham, she hadn't seen or heard anything from them, and that was the way she wanted it. She started to walk away.

'Wait!' he ordered.

She turned her head. 'Whatever you want, you're wasting your time.'

In a couple of quick strides he was in front of her, blocking her path. 'I want to ask a favour of you.'

'The answer's no.'

'Now, now, girl, don't be too hasty.'

'How many more times do I – '

He held his hand up in surrender. 'I'm sorry, Rose.'

She gave a grunt of satisfaction, then tried to elbow him aside, but he wouldn't budge. 'Will you please go away?'

'Not until I've asked the favour.'

Since she couldn't go on until he decided to let her, she growled, 'Make it quick, then.'

'Don't they teach you manners here?' he asked, raising an eyebrow in amusement.

'What do you want?' she snapped. 'I've got a bus to catch.'

'Will you visit my mother?'

Her hesitation was for the briefest of moments. 'No!'

'Rose, she likes you. Have a little compassion.'

'I haven't much time,' she told him, trying to ignore a prickle of conscience. 'I'm working all over the holiday.'

'Why?'

'Because I need the money,' she said, in a tone she might have used with an idiot.

'Why don't you let us help you?'

'I don't want your money,' she told him, with a sigh. 'I can manage without your help.'

'My God, you've got more pride than all the aristocracy put together.'

His words made her feel uncomfortable. What was it his mother had said? Ah, yes. 'Be the master of your anger.' Well, she certainly hadn't learned that lesson – *yet*.

'Try to find an hour or two to visit my mother,' he coaxed.

'Oh, all right – but I'm not promising anything.'

'Thank you. Just to know you're considering it will make her happy.'

She was shocked when he bent and kissed her cheek. 'Happy Christmas, Rose. We would have liked to give you a present, but we didn't think you would accept it.'

'You were right,' she said.

On the Saturday morning, Annie came up to Rose, a pleading look in her eyes. 'Can I come to the professor's with you, Rosie?'

'I don't know if he'd like that, Toots, and we'll be working on his book all day.'

'I know that, but I'll be very good, and I can make the tea.' She pulled a notebook from behind her back. 'You can work on his book and I can work on mine.'

'What are you writing?'

'It's a secret until I've finished it, but the professor can have a look, if he likes.' She looked up coyly from under long lashes.

Rose still couldn't deny Annie anything. And she was looking rather pale, so perhaps an outing would do her good.

'And who is this?'

'I'm Annie and Rose is my sister,' Annie told Harold Steadman proudly, 'and I won't be any trouble. Rosie takes me everywhere with her 'cos I'm good.'

The little devil, Rose thought, trying to keep a straight face. Perhaps she herself should take a leaf out of her sister's book: Annie was an expert at getting her own way.

'I see.' Harold stepped aside. 'In that case you had better come in out of the cold wind.'

The library he worked in was a mess, just as the office at the school had been when Rose had first met him. There were books overflowing from the shelves, and papers in great heaps all over the floor, chairs and windowsills – in fact anywhere there was a flat surface.

'Where shall I sit?' Annie whispered.

Rose noticed she was shivering with the cold, so she cleared a chair by the fire and put a small table in front of her so she could put her book and pencil on it. 'You all right, Annie?' she asked, frowning in concern.

'It was cold on the bus.'

Harold's housekeeper bustled in and smiled at Annie. Everyone smiled when they saw her, Rose thought.

'Would you like a nice hot drink?' the housekeeper asked, taking one of Annie's hands and chafing it gently.

'Yes, please.'

'A nice pot of tea for you and Rose, Professor?'

'Thank you, Mrs Stubbs, and some of your excellent fruit cake, if you please.'

'Certainly, sir.'

'Now, let's get down to work,' he said eagerly.

The time passed quickly and Rose was deep in concentration when Harold touched her arm. 'What is she doing?' He nodded towards Annie.

'Writing a story.'

'What's it about?'

'I don't know, she won't tell me.' She looked at Harold and raised her eyebrows. 'But I think she'd let you have a look.'

He winked. 'Very well. I'll read it at lunchtime.'

Rose had been working for about another hour when she heard a rasping sound. One look at her sister had her leaping to her feet. 'Annie!'

'What's wrong?' Harold looked concerned.

Rose picked Annie up, sat on the settee and cradled her in her arms. 'What's wrong, Toots?'

'I'm not feeling well, Rosie,' she croaked.

'Why didn't you tell me? I wouldn't have brought you out if I'd known.'

'I didn't feel too bad when we left home.' Annie closed her eyes and settled against her big sister. 'I'm sorry – I'm a nuisance.'

'You can't help being ill.' She smoothed the hair away from Annie's flushed face. 'I'll have to take her home.'

'Of course.' Harold felt Annie's brow and rang the bell for his housekeeper. 'She's burning up.'

'Whatever is the matter?' Mrs Stubbs rushed over to them.

'She has a fever,' Harold informed her. 'Will you get a blanket to put round her?'

'Want to go home, Rosie,' Annie moaned.

'You can both stay here. It's a long journey for Annie in that condition.'

'Home,' Annie said again.

'Thank you, but we'd better do as she wants.' Rose wrapped the child in the blanket the housekeeper had produced.

'All right, but I'm coming with you.' Harold started to put on his coat.

The journey was a nightmare and Rose had to admit that it was comforting to have Harold's help, but once she was on the last bus, she made him go back. He was not a young man and she didn't want to make him ill too. When they reached their stop, she carried Annie the rest of the way. She was not a baby any more and at eight was a heavy burden, but Rose didn't notice the strain: her concern for her precious sister overrode all other considerations.

With a sigh of relief she reached their house and took Annie straight up to her bed. By this time the child was almost delirious with the fever.

'What's the matter?' Their mother rushed into the room and gave a moan of despair. 'Oh, no! Is it influenza?'

'It looks like it.'

'But she never even got a sniffle when the house was full of it,' her mother said, wringing out a damp cloth to mop her daughter's face. 'Let's pray this isn't as bad as the last epidemic.'

Rose looked at Annie and worry gnawed at her. Even if this wasn't as bad, was Annie strong enough to survive? 'Where's Flo?' she asked.

'I'm here.' Flo came up to the bed and looked at Annie with a frown.

'I want you to go and fetch Dr Trenchard, Flo. You know where he lives.'

'I'll need the bus fare.'

Rose hadn't taken off her coat yet so she searched it, hoping she had enough money left to give her sister. When she found ten shillings, she realized that Harold must have slipped it into her pocket during the journey home and her heart went out to him: there would be enough to pay the doctor. It was much more than she had earned today, but she would make up the time as soon as she could.

She thrust twopence into Flo's hand, and pushed her out of the door. 'Hurry.'

It seemed an age before Rose heard heavy footsteps coming up the stairs, but in fact it was only about half an hour.

With a brief acknowledgement, Edward went straight to Annie. 'Hello, little one,' he said gently. 'What have you been up to?'

Annie didn't answer.

'Get me a bowl of cold water, Rose,' he ordered, 'and a large cloth. We must get this fever down quickly.'

They all worked on Annie until, finally, Edward stood

up. 'That's all we can do at the moment, Mrs Webster. Give her plenty to drink and sponge her down if she starts getting too hot again.' He took a vial out of his bag. 'Give her two drops of this every four hours until the fever breaks and I'll be back tomorrow to see how she is.'

'Thank you, Doctor. What's wrong with her?'

'It's influenza, I'm afraid, Mrs Webster.'

Marj's eyes filled with tears. 'I've lost two children already.'

He patted her shoulder kindly. 'You're not going to lose Annie. She's stronger than she looks.'

Rose knew he was trying to ease their fear, but she was terrified Annie would die.

She followed him downstairs. 'Thank you for coming, Edward. How much do I owe you?'

'Nothing,' he said firmly.

'But you must be paid.'

'Rose,' he said, 'I love that little girl as if she were my own and I won't take money from you. Do you remember what I said about learning to take as well as give?'

Rose nodded. 'All I seem to be doing lately is taking.'

'Good. You'll need all the help you can get until you graduate, and your friends are more than willing to support you.' He looked at her thoughtfully. 'Accept it graciously, Rose, because your day for giving will come.'

He was right, of course, but it was difficult – her pride kept getting in the way.

What a dreadful Christmas it had been. A tear trickled down Rose's face. The house had been hushed and they hadn't known if Annie was going to live or die – they still didn't. And, to add to their worries, they hadn't received any word from Bob since he had run away to sea. The little devil might at least have sent a note to say he was all right. Mr Pearce had gone home to his sister's for a few days, and her mother seemed to miss him.

A little hand touched her face. 'Don't cry, Rosie.'

'Annie!' It was the first time she had spoken since they'd come home from Harold's. 'Are you feeling better?'

She nodded. 'I've been a nuisance, haven't I?'

'No, Toots, never that,' Rose reassured her. 'Are you hungry?'

'Yes. Did I miss Christmas dinner?'

'I'm afraid so, but we've got some chicken stew. Would you like that?'

'Yes, please.'

Rose hurtled down the stairs and into the scullery. 'Annie's awake and she's hungry!'

'Oh, thank God.' Marj Webster wiped her eyes. 'I really thought we were going to lose her this time.'

Rose started to get the food ready. 'She's nice and cool now, and the dreadful cough has almost gone.'

'Is this good news I'm hearing?' Edward Trenchard had walked into the scullery.

'You go and have a look at her,' Rose said happily.

When she took the stew up, Edward was sitting on Annie's bed and the child was giggling.

'Is it all over?' Rose asked him, hardly able to believe her eyes. One minute her sister had looked like death, and now she was sitting up, smiling.

'The worst has passed, but you'll need to feed her well and keep her warm. In a few days you can let her get up for a couple of hours. But,' he gave Annie a stern look, 'you mustn't try to do too much, and you must listen to your sister.' He took the tray from Rose and picked up a spoon. 'And I'm not leaving until I see you eat all this.'

'I will,' Annie promised, and let him spoon the stew into her.

When the plate was empty, Edward turned his attention to Rose. 'You must get some rest now, you look worn out.'

Annie moved over in the bed. 'Rosie can sleep next to me.'

'Well? What are you waiting for?' Edward asked her.

With a yawn, she lay down beside her sister, and was instantly asleep.

21

'Happy New Year!'

It was good to hear laughter in the house. Rose sipped her beer and looked at the smiling faces. With Annie's recovery, 1920 had arrived on a tide of relief. Mr Pearce, or Wally, as her mother now called him, had arrived back from Kent yesterday, and had been determined that they should see the New Year in with music and laughter. He had pushed the furniture back in his room and produced an accordion, which he played with more enthusiasm than skill.

Good Lord, Rose thought as she watched the scene, I've had my nose stuck in books, and haven't noticed how they're all growing up. She studied each one in turn: Flo was sixteen, quite pretty and very sure of herself, Nancy at thirteen had not outgrown her timidity, and Will was twelve, growing into a handsome young man. There was a gap where Bert should have been. For a moment Rose's mind strayed back to the epidemic – what a dreadful time that had been. Nine-year-old Charlie laughed and she glanced at him with affection but then her gaze rested on Annie, who had always been her favourite, and at eight she was showing signs of becoming a real beauty. David would have been nearly six, had he lived.

How things had changed for them over the last few years. They were still living in this deplorable house, of course, but it was cleaner now and not quite so crowded. Her mother had more time and energy to look after the house and the children. Her mind drifted back to those awful times before the war – how had they survived?

A burst of singing brought Rose out of her reverie, and she slid down the wall until she was sitting on the floor and closed her eyes to listen. She wished she could forget the world outside for a while and relax, but however hard she tried, her brain would not let her rest. At such times she wondered if it was a blessing or a *curse* to have a mind like hers; there was always something churning through it.

The year ahead was going to be tough. Annie's illness had stopped Rose working and she had needed money to get through the next term. She couldn't ask her mother to help because despite Mr Pearce's presence in the house she had still had trouble in making ends meet.

More than a year after the Armistice, all the talk about a better life had come to nothing. After fighting and winning the war, everyone had expected improved pay and conditions, but things had slipped back into the old ways.

'You sing, Rosie.' Will jumped on her and tried to pull her to her feet.

'What?' she exclaimed in mock horror. 'You know I'm tone deaf.'

'That's right.' Flo giggled. 'We had a choir at school and the teacher always told her to stop singing. It was nice to know there was something she couldn't do.'

Rose remembered how much she'd wanted to be in the choir, but it was no use, she couldn't stay in tune. At least, that's what everyone told her, but her voice sounded all right to her.

'Oh, well, in that case, don't bother,' Will said, with a grimace.

'I think it's time for bed, anyway,' Marj Webster put in, 'but let's help Mr Pearce get his room straight first.'

The children had all been allowed to stay up as a special treat, but they were tired now and didn't make any bones about packing up. Annie was sleepy, but flushed with pleasure at being allowed to see in the New Year.

When the tidying was done and the children were in bed, Rose wandered into the scullery, too wound up to sleep. Wally stood up as soon as she came in, drained his cup and went out, leaving mother and daughter alone.

'Want a cup of tea?'

'Thanks, Mum.' She sat down. 'Wally didn't have to run away like that.'

'He was tired I expect. It was good to see everyone happy, wasn't it?'

Rose nodded, but didn't reply.

'Nancy leaves school in the spring, and she's already got a job,' Marj went on.

'Oh?'

'She's going to work in an orphanage. She's always liked children,' her mother added, stirring her tea thoughtfully. 'She's going to live in too, so that will be another flown the nest.'

Rose couldn't think of anything worse than looking after dozens of children. Still, her mother was right, it would suit Nancy.

'Er . . . Rose? Do you like Wally?'

'He seems to be a good sort, and he's turned out a respectable and reliable lodger.'

'Yes, he's a good man. We've been walking out, Rose.'
Her mother hesitated. 'Do you mind?'

'Of course I don't. It's none of my business, and if you're happy, that's all that matters.'

'When Wally got back after Christmas he told me his sister has found herself a young man and is getting married, and her husband-to-be is willing to help support their mother, so that will take the worry away from him.'

'That must be a relief for him.' Rose waited, feeling that there was more to come.

'He's asked me to marry him.'

'And are you going to?'

Her mother nodded. 'I never had much of a life with the old man, as you know, but Wally's just the opposite, and I think we could be happy together.'

Rose looked at her mother in a new light. When she had been growing up, she had been disgusted by her mother's endless pregnancies, and by the way they lived. She had assumed Marj had been too weak to fight for something better, but she didn't believe that now: her mother had been trapped in a situation she tolerated only for the sake of her children. It had been this or the workhouse, and as horrible as this was, it was certainly better than that institution. For the first time Rose saw that her mother had done the best she could for her children in impossible circumstances, and was sorry she'd misjudged her.

She smiled. 'I hope you'll be happy, Mum, it's about time.' But it was a mystery to Rose why any woman would want to become a man's property. 'When are you going to wed?'

'In the summer. Nancy will have left by then and I

don't think Flo will stay much longer. That will only leave Annie, Charlie and Will, and they all like Wally.'

'The kids are nearly all off your hands.'

Her mother sighed. 'The house seems quiet when everyone's out.'

To Rose, marriage meant only one thing: squalling babies. 'You might have some more,' she remarked.

'No, my childbearing days are over, thank goodness.'

'I'll congratulate Wally in the morning.' Rose smiled, then asked, 'Does he know about me?'

'I've told him, but he doesn't know who your real father is. That's our secret, Rosie.'

The word 'secret' reminded her of something she hadn't told her mother. She took a deep breath. 'Mum, I've had dinner with Lady Gresham.'

'When was this?' Her mother frowned.

'Not long after I started at the university. She sent for me.'

'I hope they're not making trouble for you.'

'No, we just talked and I liked her,' Rose admitted.

'From what I remember of her, she was fierce but fair. Have you seen her again?' her mother asked.

'No.'

'What about your . . . Sir George?'

'I've had several arguments with him.' Rose pulled a face. 'What a self-opinionated ba– rogue he is!'

'Does that mean you've had a fight?'

Rose started to laugh. 'He said I've got an acid tongue, but it's no worse than his.'

'Do you like him?' her mother asked softly.

'Certainly not,' Rose said scornfully. 'And I'd never forgive myself if I used my connection with him to get ahead. I want to be able to look back in years to come and know I did it all on my own.'

'You've got the pride of the Greshams.'

'Maybe – but I'm not one of them and never will be!'

The next morning, Rose caught Wally before he left the house. 'Congratulations.' She held out her hand and he clasped it. 'Mum told me.'

He beamed. 'Thank you. I know how lucky I am and I'll do my best to make her happy.'

'I'm sure you will.'

'She's very proud of you, and says you're going to do great things in your life. I'm inclined to agree with her.'

'I don't know about that.' Rose laughed. 'Just because I can read Latin she thinks I'm a genius, but I hope to make a difference in some way.' She grew serious again. 'The country's in such a mess and I doubt one person can make any impact.'

'Maybe not, but if people band together they might be able to change things,' Wally said.

'Like the unions, you mean?'

'And the borough councils.'

'Hmm, they don't seem to do much except talk.'

'Don't be impatient, Rose. Even the working man resists change if it comes too rapidly.'

She grinned. 'I've already been told I'm too impatient, but sometimes I just want to shake some sense into people.' He glanced at his pocket watch. 'I'm sorry, I'm making you late.'

She watched him hurry up the street, relieved that her mother had someone to look after her now – and that

Annie was fit again. Heaven knows, Rose wasn't going to be much use to her family for a while.

She chewed her bottom lip. Could she survive on buns for a year?

She was making her way along the corridor to her room when Sir George caught up with her. 'You didn't go to see her!'

'See who?' Rose was a few yards from her room and could hear Harriet and Angelina talking inside. The door was ajar so she stopped.

'My mother, of course.' He was blazing mad. 'She was looking out for you all over the holiday.'

Rose's hand flew to her mouth. She had forgotten Lady Gresham.

'You never intended to go, did you?' he accused.

'Don't you shout at me!' she told him indignantly. 'I forgot because my sister's been ill. We thought she was going to die.'

'Oh.' The fury drained from his face. 'I'm sorry. Is she all right now?'

'Yes, thank heavens.'

'I'll explain why you didn't come. She'll understand.' He put his head on one side and studied her carefully. 'You look tired.'

'I am. Now,' she tried to dodge past him but he didn't move, 'I've only got an hour before my first class and I want to unpack my bag first.'

'Shall I tell my mother you'll call during the next few days?'

'No. I didn't make any promises before Christmas, and I'm not making them now.'

'The weekend, then,' he persisted. 'Would that suit you better?'

'Will you please go away?'

He ignored her. 'Why don't you bring your sister to see Mother? She loves children.'

Rose could have screamed in frustration. Would nothing shift him? 'Nobody knows about you, except me and my mother, and that's the way we want it to stay.'

'Ah, I see. We're a secret, are we?'

'Yes, you bloody well are, and if you don't stop coming here the whole university will soon work out who you are.'

'We're not ashamed of it, Rose. Are you?' he asked mildly.

'I'm your bastard child,' she hissed, through clenched teeth.

He shrugged his huge shoulders. 'That isn't so terrible.'

That did it! 'It is to me!'

She stormed away, leaving a trail of bad language. Just as she reached her room Sir George called, 'Dear me, Rose, even I don't know some of those.'

She wrenched open the door, swept inside and kicked it shut.

'Rose!' someone squeaked.

When she looked across the room, Harriet was sitting on her bed with her hands over her ears, her eyes wide with shock. Angelina was grinning.

Harriet lowered her hands. 'Have you finished?'

Rose nodded.

'Thank goodness for that. Where did you learn such appalling language?'

'Garrett Street. You ought to come there with me

some time, it would broaden your education,' she teased, her anger disappearing.

'I'd rather not.' Harriet gave her a speculative look. 'Who were you swearing at, anyway?'

'Someone who made me angry.'

Rose threw down her bag and started to unpack. Thank the Lord she hadn't been seen with Sir George.

Then it was time for their class. The three girls grabbed whatever books were within reach and hurtled out of the door.

22

Winter turned to spring, and spring to summer, before Rose could think of anything except studying and surviving. She felt drained. The grind of studying day and night during the week, working for Harold on Saturdays, then trying to improve her Latin with John on Sundays had taken its toll. Harold lived in Holborn, only a short bus ride from the university, but Rose went home on Friday nights, and although it wasn't more than twenty minutes from there, it still took up her time: the buses didn't always arrive when they should. Her weekends at home should have been for relaxing, but they were anything but. It was no good grousing, though, she'd known what she was letting herself in for – but it was taking more out of her than she'd expected.

She enjoyed the lectures at the university, and was pleased with what she had achieved so far. Her results had been good, but it wasn't easy. The male undergraduates had finally accepted her and the other girls and, on the whole, they were a nice lot. Angelina and Harriet enjoyed mixing with them now and often went out with a crowd to the pictures, but Rose didn't feel she could spare the time. She liked to spend any free moments in the huge library, or wandering around the beautiful building. The university had been established around 1836, and Rose especially liked the spacious entrance hall. The whole place was impressive and seemed to smell of books, and to Rose, nothing could have been nicer than that.

She sighed, rubbed her tired eyes and tried to concen-, trate on the typing Harold had given her today. Her fatigue had crept up on her, increasing gradually over the weeks, and she realized now that she should have gone out with Angelina and Harriet. With her punishing workload, it would have been sensible to spend an evening away from studying. It was a blessing that the summer term had finished, because her temper was even more volatile than usual. Most sensible people had learned to give her a wide berth.

Harold had been busy over the last week, if the amount of work he'd put in front her was anything to go by, and she typed until she could hardly see. She was relieved when she could go home.

She had to wait ages for the bus, and by the time she reached home she was exhausted and ill-tempered. So when she walked into the scullery and saw Bill sitting there, resplendent in his naval uniform, her composure deserted her.

Her bag hit the floor with a thud. 'What are you doing here?'

'Rose!' her mother said sharply. 'If you can't keep a civil tongue in your head, you can go back where you came from.'

Marj had never spoken to her like that before, but Rose was too tired to care. Without a word, she picked up her bag and started to walk out.

'*Nooo!*' Annie left Bill's side, caught Rose's arm and glared at her mother. 'Don't you shout at my Rosie, like that!' She stamped her foot and tears welled in her eyes.

'It's all right, Annie,' Rose told her wearily. 'I'll go back to my digs. I'm not fit company for anyone at the moment.'

'No, no! Mum, don't let her go! She won't ever come back again,' Annie cried in panic.

Tension made Rose feel as if she would snap in half and, much as she loved her sister, a fuss was the last thing she wanted. Through the haze of exhaustion, she realized she couldn't carry on like this.

Annie tugged again, but she ignored her and kept walking. She had to be alone.

Before she had reached the door, someone much stronger than Annie stopped her, and the bag was taken from her. 'There's no need for this,' Bill said gently. 'Come and sit down. You're worn out.'

Rose didn't protest. The fight had gone out of her, leaving her bewildered and disoriented. She allowed him to lead her back to the table and sit her down. A sigh escaped her.

Annie rushed to get her a cup of tea, but she never drank it. She rested her arms on the table, laid her head on them, and fell asleep.

Bill looked at the dark head and frowned. What the devil had happened to her? The girl he had last seen had been lively, bursting with enthusiasm, and eager to learn; he could hardly believe the change in her.

'I'm sorry she was rude,' Marj Webster apologized. 'She's often short-tempered, but I've never seen her like this.'

'She's tired.' Annie stroked her sister's hair. 'And she's broke too.'

'But she can't be, she gives me money each week,' said Marj.

'That's why she's broke, and hungry too.'

Marj Webster's eyes turned to her eldest daughter. 'I never knew,' she muttered, anguished.

Annie started to cry in heartbroken sobs. 'My Rosie's ill.'

'Shush, sweetheart,' Bill said, soothingly. 'You'll make yourself sick if you carry on like this.'

'Wally should look after Mum,' she sobbed. 'They're going to get married next week.'

'He can't, Annie, he's lost his job,' her mother said. 'That's why I had to take the money Rosie offered me. She said she could spare it.'

'Tell me what's been going on, Annie.' Bill listened to the little girl's disjointed story and was appalled. If it was all true, no one could manage such a punishing workload.

'I don't believe it!' Marj said. 'She told me she had some money saved up.'

'So you see,' Annie continued, ignoring her mother's outburst, 'she's all grown-up now, and if Mum turns her out she won't come back.' She hiccuped and tears streamed down her face. 'And I'll never see her again!'

Ah, that's the trouble, Bill realized. Annie was afraid of losing her beloved sister.

'Don't be silly, Annie,' her mother said.

'I'm not being silly!' She slipped off Bill's lap and sat on a chair beside Rose, who was still fast asleep, oblivious to the row raging around her. Annie laid her head on her arms in an exact copy of Rose's posture.

As he looked at the sisters, Bill swallowed the lump in his throat. 'How did things get so bad?'

Marj bristled. 'Begging your pardon, Captain Freeman, but I don't think this is any of your business.'

'All she cares about is Wally,' Annie muttered.

'Quiet, Annie!' her mother ordered. 'You don't know what you're talking about.'

'Don't shout! You'll wake Rosie up.'

'I'm sorry my girls have been so rude,' Marj Webster said abruptly. 'Thank you for bringing me news of my son. It was kind of you to take the trouble.'

Bill knew he had been dismissed, but he hesitated. Then he asked bluntly, 'Do you have enough money to feed your family, Mrs Webster?'

'I can look after my own, thank you.'

'Humph!' That was Annie again.

Bill's heart ached. He stooped and touched Annie's hand. Her fingers closed around his.

'Was Mrs Webster pleased with the news of her son?' Grace asked, when Bill arrived back.

'What?' He glanced at her, distracted.

'What's the matter, Bill?'

'I'm not sure, Grace.' He rubbed the back of his neck. 'Is John at home?'

'He's in the sitting room.' She followed him.

'Hello, Bill.' John folded his newspaper and put it on the table. 'You look troubled.'

'Have you seen Rose?' Bill sat down and stretched his long legs in front of him.

John nodded. 'She still comes every Sunday. Why?'

'How does she seem?'

'Oh, the same as usual, preoccupied with her studies.'

He looked at his friend thoughtfully. 'Why all the questions?'

Bill told them what had happened.

'Is she all right?' Grace asked, alarmed.

'I think so, but she's obviously at the end of her strength.' He sighed. 'She looked so vulnerable.'

'*Vulnerable?*' John exclaimed. 'I'd never use that word to describe Rose.'

'You would if you'd seen her today.' He told them what Annie had said.

'Well, Rose is used to managing on very little.' John looked doubtful. 'I wouldn't put too much faith in Annie's story, Bill. She adores Rose and isn't used to her being anything but strong and in control. To see her like that must have frightened her badly.'

'Anyway,' Grace put in, 'Harold pays her more than he should. It's his way of helping her through university because she won't take money from anyone without working for it.'

'That's right,' John said sadly. He removed his spectacles, polished them, then slid them back on to his nose. 'She'll let us teach and guide her, but that's all.'

This conversation was not easing Bill's worry. 'You say Harold pays her well, but what if she's giving most of the money to her mother?'

'She wouldn't need to do that,' Grace said. 'Her mother has a lodger and she's going to marry him next week.'

'He's lost his job.'

'What?' John was on his feet. 'Why didn't Rose tell us?'

'Too proud?' Bill asked wryly.

'When she comes tomorrow, you must make her tell you what's going on,' Grace told her husband.

'I'm not sure she'll come,' Bill told them.

'Oh, she'll come,' Grace and John said together. 'Nothing has ever kept her away.'

Rose surfaced sluggishly. Every limb ached and her mind was fuzzy as she hovered between sleep and waking. A candle was flickering, making patterns on the table, and she watched it, marvelling at the multitude of colours, red, orange, yellow . . .

'Rosie?' Her sister's voice penetrated through the mist, and she felt Annie's hand grasp hers.

'Rosie! Are you awake?' Her mother's voice now. She sat up and took a couple of deep breaths in an effort to clear her head. 'About time, too,' her mother scolded. 'You've been asleep for three hours. What have you been doing to get into this state?'

'Leave her alone, Mum. She isn't properly awake yet.'

Suddenly, the addle-headed feeling disappeared and Rose snapped back to full awareness. She had been looking after Annie ever since she'd been born, but now the roles were reversed. 'I'm awake, Toots.'

'Are you hungry?' Annie asked.

'Starving.'

Annie glared accusingly at her mother. She jumped off her chair, took a plate off the top of a saucepan of boiling water and put it in front of Rose. 'We've kept it hot for you,' Annie told her, 'and you must eat it all up.'

Rose looked at the mound of sausage and mash with amusement, remembering the many times she had sat beside Annie, coaxing her to eat.

Her sister watched every mouthful disappear until the plate was empty, then whipped it away and put a cup of tea in front of her. Rose drank it slowly and obediently.

'Now,' demanded her mother, 'tell me what's the matter.'

'Oh, Lord!' The memory rushed in. 'I was rude to Bill.'

'Yes, you were, and I was ashamed. Captain Freeman had kindly come to tell me that he'd met Bob in Australia.'

'Australia?'

Marj Webster nodded and Rose saw tears in her eyes. 'It seems Bob likes it so much there he's going to stay. We won't be seeing him again.'

'I'm glad he's happy,' Rose said.

'Bill said he looks fit and well. He's working on a sheep farm.'

'Bit different from here,' Rose remarked drily.

'Yes, and he was never happy in these crowded streets, was he?' Marj mused.

That was true enough, Rose thought, and was probably why he had been such a difficult child. She had rebelled by reading; he'd got into trouble all the time.

'And where did you think you were going when you started to walk out of here?' Her mother changed the subject. 'You frightened the life out of Annie.'

'I was feeling awful and you told me to go.'

'I didn't mean it – I was just putting you in your place because you'd been downright rude.'

'I'm sorry, Mum, I wasn't thinking straight. I'd wanted to get home so I could rest and when I saw him sitting there I was furious.' She grimaced. 'There's something about him that brings out the worst in me.'

'So I saw.'

'You're not going to leave us, are you, Rosie?' Annie appealed.

'No, of course not, Toots. I was so tired I didn't know what I was doing.' She smiled. 'And what are you doing still up?'

'She was terrified you were going to leave us and wouldn't let you out of her sight, so I thought it best to let her stay with you,' Marj said.

'I thought you might wake up and go away,' Annie gulped, 'and I'd never see you again.'

'Oh, Annie!' Rosie hugged her. 'I'd never leave you.'

'Annie said you'd been giving me money and going hungry yourself. Is that true?' Marj asked.

Rose looked at her young sister in astonishment. 'Where did you get that idea from?'

'Well, you only work one day a week, so you can't be getting much money, and I know you've been giving Mum some of it since Wally lost his job.'

Good heavens, Rose thought. Annie's eagle eyes missed nothing. She'd better explain.

'It's true I've been helping over the last two months, but I haven't been going hungry.' She stood up. 'Have I got any thinner?'

Annie examined her carefully, then shook her head.

'I've had to be careful,' she continued, 'but I've managed all right.'

'But you didn't look well when you came in,' Annie said, unconvinced. 'And you're never sick.'

'So you decided I was starving myself?'

Annie nodded.

Understandable, Rose thought. They'd all grown up not knowing where the next meal was coming from. 'I've been working very hard because I want to do well, and there are some exams coming up soon. I've been overdoing it, that's all.'

'Will you be able to have a rest now?' Annie looked reassured.

'I've got two weeks off and I intend to sleep and sleep.' She laughed. 'And it's Mum's wedding next week, so we'll have a lovely party, won't we?'

Annie nodded, then turned to her mother. 'I'm sorry I said nasty things to you, but I was frightened.'

'That's all right, Annie.' Her mother paused. 'I should have noticed how tired Rose was getting, but I've been so wrapped up in the wedding, and hoping Wally would find another job.'

'Has he got anything yet?' Rose asked, noting her mother's worried face.

'I'm afraid not. Now, I think it's time we all went to bed, don't you?'

Annie took hold of Rose's hand and pulled her towards the stairs. 'You'll feel better in the morning,' she told her.

'Rose?'

'Yes, Mum?'

'You'll apologise to Captain Freeman when you see him. He looked a bit upset, and I wouldn't like him to think badly of us. He's a nice man.'

Bill paced up and down anxiously, stopping every so often to look at the clock. 'I was right, wasn't I? She isn't going to come.'

'The bus might be late,' John told him. 'Ah, here's another.'

They watched as its passengers alighted and Bill sighed

with relief when he saw Rose. She looked much better.

Grace hurried to open the door. Annie rushed in, threw her arms around John then hurled herself at Bill. 'You look happy today,' he said.

'I am because my Rosie's better.' Then she whispered, 'She's going to apologize for being rude. Mum told her to.' She giggled then turned and waved a notebook at Grace. 'I've done my lesson, Auntie Grace.'

'Let's go into the kitchen and have a look at it, shall we?'

Annie nodded, then said to John, 'She mustn't work too hard, today. She's still tired.'

Bill saw Rose's eyes roll with exasperation.

But Annie hadn't finished. 'I was wrong about Rosie not eating,' she told Bill 'because if she hadn't had enough food she'd have got thin, and she hasn't, has she?'

'I don't think so.'

Annie spun away from him, took her sister's arm and pulled it away from her side. 'Show him, Rosie. Look, Uncle Bill, she isn't thin, is she?'

He managed to keep a straight face, as he ran his gaze deliberately over her figure. God! She was beautiful. He felt his body stir in response.

'Well, Uncle Bill, what do you think?' Annie's voice cut through his thoughts. 'She isn't thin, is she?'

He shook his head. 'No, she isn't,' he managed.

The little girl smiled with relief, then hurried away with Grace.

John was busy polishing some imaginary spot off his spectacle lens. 'Bill told us you were exhausted last night.'

'Ah, yes.' Rose faced Bill with evident reluctance. 'I must apologize.'

She turned aside, but he wasn't going to let her get away with that feeble attempt. 'Go on, then, I'm waiting.'

'What for?'

'Your apology.'

'You've just had it,' she said sharply, her black eyes snapping.

'Not a very gracious one.'

'I'm not a very gracious person.'

He sighed theatrically. 'Ah, well, I suppose I must be grateful for small mercies.' He sat in an armchair and picked up a newspaper.

'Is he staying?' she demanded.

He glanced over the top of the paper. 'You won't know I'm here,' he told her, lifting the paper to hide his grin. He had been desperately worried about her yesterday, and it was a blessed relief to see her back to normal again. But if this tigress thought she could order him around, or get the better of him, he had a surprise in store for her.

Rose sat down and opened her books.

As he listened Bill was fascinated. It wasn't long before, clearly, she had forgotten he was in the room, and he realized she had a brilliant mind. University was the right place for her.

As the afternoon went by a feeling of unease crept over him. He wanted her more than he'd ever wanted anything in his life, but if he had any sense he would run for his life. Otherwise he would have to wait until she had finished her studies – maybe longer. He could see only heartache and frustration in front of him.

He glanced at the dark head bowed over the books,

and knew, with a clarity that shocked him, that he would wait for her, whatever the cost.

It was too late. He was hopelessly in love with her.

23

It was a perfect August day for a wedding, there wasn't a cloud in the sky and a soft breeze kept the heat at bay, but Rose couldn't seem to get into the swing of it. Wally was nice enough, and her mother seemed happy, but Rose couldn't understand why she wanted to saddle herself with another man. The first had made her pregnant then thrown her out on the street; the second had been a drunken brute. How could she trust another?

Marj came into the scullery, smiling. 'I've got some good news. Wally's found a job. The pay's a bit less than he was getting, but we'll manage.'

A burden fell off Rose's shoulders. At least she wouldn't have to worry about her family when she returned to university next term. This would be the start of her second year, and it was hard to believe that the time had passed so quickly.

When they were ready to leave for the church, Rose handed her mother a single red rose to carry. Annie had tied a large golden bow to it and left the ends trailing down. It looked pretty against the simple navy dress Marj was wearing.

A lot of the neighbours had come, Rose noticed, as she looked around the church. Her mother had insisted on a 'proper' wedding ceremony, and they had all made an effort to dress smartly. Flo had brought her young man with her, Nancy had grown quite pretty over the last year, and Will and Charlie were at that lanky stage. Only Bob was missing. And Bert and David, of course. Rose knew her mother still grieved for them.

When the ceremony was over, she had to admit that her mother and Wally seemed very happy. In fact, she had never seen her mother look so young and attractive.

As they made their way out of the church, she was astonished to see Grace, John, Bill and Harold standing at the back. Annie, of course, was beside herself with delight and chattered excitedly to them.

Later, when the bride and groom were having their photograph taken, Grace handed Rose a large tin. 'A wedding cake for your mother and her husband.'

'Mum!' Annie called. 'Auntie Grace has made you a cake.'

Rose pulled a face as she watched her sister scamper away to tell everyone the good news. 'Your brother has a lot to answer for,' she remarked to John. 'If he hadn't fixed her tongue we might have a bit of peace now and again.'

He laughed. 'Now, Rose, you know you wouldn't have it any other way.'

'You're right, I wouldn't,' she admitted. Then she gasped as the whirlwind returned, nearly knocking the cake tin out of her hands.

'Come on, we're going to have our picture took.' Annie tugged at her arm.

Wally strode over, a huge smile on his face. 'We'd like you all to join us.'

Grace gave Annie a loving look. 'If our child is a girl, I hope she's like Annie.'

'Are you expecting?' Rose asked, not sure she had heard correctly.

'Yes, and we're delighted. I'm four months now.'

After the photos had been taken, Marj and Wally insisted that Rose's friends joined their modest celebrations. They accepted with alacrity, which surprised Rose: Harold had never seemed the sociable type.

When they got back to the house, Rose spread their one and only tablecloth on the table and placed the cake in the middle. It had real icing and 'Congratulations' written across the top. She could see that her mother and Wally were delighted with the thoughtful gift.

Neighbours started to crowd in and, as if by magic, the table filled up with food. Mrs Jenks had brought a jelly and a blancmange and someone else a plate of sausage rolls; then cockles, shrimps, bread and butter appeared. Rose began to remember the many occasions when everyone had rallied round to help one of their own in trouble. When a baby was born, or illness struck, or a woman was badly beaten, someone turned up to offer help and support. Everyone here lived from hand to mouth, but they all pulled together – as they were doing now.

The food was demolished, the cake cut, and Wally got out his accordion. The noise was deafening and it was too much for Rose, so she wandered outside. She'd never forgotten the factory, and ever since those days noise had made her ears ring.

'Phew!' Bill grinned at her. 'That's better.'

'Mmm. Is the racket too much for you too?'

'Yes. I'm more used to the wide ocean and the quiet of a night-watch.'

'Is it peaceful?' Rose asked, trying to picture what it would be like to sail on the sea with no land in sight. Were the stars brighter, she wondered, when you didn't have to peer through London smoke to see them?

'Mostly, but there are times when the wind roars and mountainous waves toss the ship around like a twig . . . and there's nothing to compare with the noise of someone shooting at you.' He shook his head. 'That's like nothing else on earth.'

'How did you become a captain?'

He leaned against the wall of the house, silent for a few moments. Then he started to explain. 'My father has been in the navy since he was a lad, and I was sent to naval college, expecting to follow in his footsteps, but I didn't like it. I had an almighty row with my father, left, and went to Oxford to study architecture. He never forgave me.'

'But you joined up when the war started?'

'There wasn't any choice. Because of my background, I was called on immediately.'

'They made you a captain straight away?'

'Good Lord, no! I started as a gunnery officer, but at the battle of Jutland our captain was killed. As I was the only officer still alive I took command. They promoted me after that.'

He spoke calmly as if it was of no importance, but Rose could hardly begin to imagine the horrors he must have faced. She'd heard terrible stories about Jutland.

'When do you go back again?' she asked.

'I've left the navy.'

'Oh!' Rose was surprised. 'What are you going to do?'

'I haven't decided yet. When the war started I took

some hurried exams and qualified as an architect.' He straightened up and took her arm. 'Let's go for a walk.'

She tried to pull away, but he held her firmly. 'We're going to walk, I'm not about to molest you.'

'I don't like being touched.' Ever since the rape she had had an aversion to any man coming too close to her.

'You make that very obvious, but I'd never do anything to upset you.'

He gave her his gentle smile and she believed him – but, still, she didn't like being so close to him. It made her edgy.

It was a lovely evening. The sun had started to sink over the horizon and the heat had gone out of the day. As they walked in companionable silence, she started to relax. She had been making a fuss about nothing again; she really must stop being so proud and bloody-minded. And it was downright stupid to panic every time a man came near her. It was time she got over that.

After about half an hour, Rose realized where they were heading, and stopped abruptly. She hadn't been near that place since the attack.

'This is far enough.' She pulled away from Bill and started to walk back the way they had come.

He caught up with her in two easy strides. 'They won't miss us.'

'Maybe not, but I'm not going in there!' The words were out before she could stop them.

'Why?'

'I don't like that park.'

'But it isn't even dark yet, and you'll be quite safe with me.' Bill was clearly puzzled. 'Is it me you don't trust?'

'I trust *you*.' And she knew she spoke the truth.

'Something unpleasant happened to you in there, perhaps?'

'No.'

'Then what is it that frightens you?'

'It's none of your business – and I'm not frightened.'

He sighed, took her arm again, and they walked back to the party.

John collapsed into his chair. 'I'm exhausted. They certainly know how to throw a party.'

Grace smiled. 'You enjoyed every minute of it.'

'I did.' His eyes crinkled at the corners. 'Did you see Rose's face when she spotted us at the church? She didn't know we were coming.'

Bill laughed. 'And she wasn't too happy about it either, but Annie made up for that.'

'She's such a sweet child.' Grace sighed. 'She was so happy today because Wally has found another job, and Rose won't have to give her mother any more money.'

'I bet she still does,' John said.

Bill was puzzled.

Seeing his expression, John leaned forward to explain: 'To Rose, money is a commodity to be used, and has no value to her beyond providing the necessities in life. If you gave her a hundred pounds she wouldn't want it.'

'Why?'

'Because it would be more than she needed.' John laughed. 'That's hard to grasp, isn't it?'

'I still don't understand.'

Grace joined in the conversation. 'Although she has grown up in poverty, money for its own sake doesn't interest her. It's merely a tool to be used to feed, house

251

and clothe them, and I believe she would give anyone her last penny if she thought they needed it more than she did.'

'But she wants reforms – to see the slums knocked down,' Bill protested. 'Surely money will help to bring that about?'

'You're underestimating her intelligence and her understanding of the situation,' John remarked wryly. 'I've had long discussions with her on the subject, and she's convinced that no amount of money will bring about lasting change unless the people themselves want it.'

'Then how does she think it can be achieved?' Bill frowned.

'Through education.' Grace and John spoke together.

Bill sat back, deep in thought. Then he exhaled. 'My God, John, I've led a privileged life and have never really thought about these things, but I do believe she's right. The people we've been with today were enjoying themselves, making the best of a break from the usual worry and hardship, but I doubt they've ever made much effort to improve themselves.'

'Yes, but they're not content, merely resigned to their lot in life, and that is what Rose believes needs to be changed first – their attitude.'

'And did you notice the difference between her and the rest of them?' Grace added. 'She hates the place, and her discomfort is evident – she does not, and never will, accept that that is a fit way of life for anyone. If you can understand that, Bill, you might have an idea of what drives her.'

'She's a complex woman,' John told him, 'and underneath that aloof façade a fire is raging that she finds it difficult to control.'

'Good heavens, John,' Bill exclaimed, 'you make her sound terrifying.'

'She is, and the older she gets, the more formidable she becomes.' He gave his friend a sympathetic look. 'Don't get too fond of her, Bill.'

'Your warning comes too late.'

'I was afraid of that. What are you going to do?'

'I don't know. I'll have to sleep on it.'

But sleep was impossible. Images of Rose, smiling, then withdrawn, ran through his mind. And what had happened when they'd approached that scrubby little park? He was sure she'd been frightened of going in there, but why? He knew she'd had a tough life, but instead of grinding her down it had made her strong and determined. He was sure she wasn't as hard as she appeared on the surface. He'd seen the little gestures of tenderness towards her family and those who had helped her along the way, like Grace, John and Harold. He was positive that Rose Webster was capable of deep love.

Bill sighed and closed his eyes, willing himself to sleep. But how did you find the loving girl beneath the strong barriers she had erected around herself?

24

In October Rose was back at her studies, eager to start her second year. It had been good to see Angelina and Harriet again. Of course, she didn't have a lot in common with the two girls, who led very different lives from hers, but they got on well together. They tried to include her in their outings to the shops or the theatre, but Rose never went with them. She didn't have money to waste, and she didn't like frittering away her study time.

When she'd been unpacking this morning, the picture of Lady Gresham had fallen out of her Bible. Harriet had asked if she was a family member. Rose had said no, and quickly put it back in the book. However, the picture had reminded her that she hadn't been to see the old lady for some time, and she felt guilty.

She shook her head, dismissing the vexing subject from her mind, and settled down to read of how the Ancient Greeks had introduced the world's first democracy . . .

'Rose,' Harriet whispered, 'someone's left you a message.' She laid it on the open book, then left as quietly as she had arrived.

As soon as Rose saw the envelope, she knew who it was from. So they hadn't forgotten about her. She opened it.

My dearest Rose,

I am delighted to hear that you are doing extremely well with your studies. That makes me very proud. I know this because George has been keeping an eye on you, at my request.

I hope you will forgive this intrusion on your precious time, but you are constantly in my thoughts and prayers.

I don't suppose you have heard, but my grandson was killed in a motoring accident two months ago. Such a waste of a young life. I think the modern motor vehicle is an abomination, but the boy loved them. We are devastated. My son is taking it stoically, but I know he is grieving for his son.

I won't take up any more of your time, my dear, but this contact has brought me some comfort. You will always be welcome in my home.

With affection, Lavinia Gresham.

Loneliness and grief showed through every carefully penned word, and Rose felt ashamed of herself. It was a year since they had last met.

And Sir George, how must he be feeling? The loss of his son must be hard to bear. She remembered the only time she had ever met the boy: she hadn't liked him, but in the circumstances that was understandable. However, it was clear that his father and grandmother had loved him, and she was sorry he had died so young.

Rose had been touched by the letter, and it was on her mind all afternoon. As soon as lessons were finished for the day she went to Bloomsbury.

'Rose!' Lady Gresham rose to her feet, arms outstretched. 'I'm so happy to see you.'

'I got your letter,' she said. 'I'm sorry about your grandson.'

'Come and sit down, my dear.' She waited until her guest was seated, then turned to the footman still waiting in the doorway. 'We will have tea, if you please, Parsons. The blue china.'

'Certainly, my lady.' He left the room.

'Now, I want to hear all your news. How are you finding life at university?'

'It's hard work,' Rose told her honestly.

'Are you happy there?'

'Oh, yes! I still can't believe I've been given such a chance.' Rose spent some time telling her about the things they did and how she and the other girls had dealt with prejudice from the boys and some lecturers.

Rose was pleased to see Lady Gresham laugh: when she had arrived she had noticed how much older she looked.

When the tea arrived the china was so fine you could see the tea through it, and Rose couldn't help wondering why it didn't break as the hot liquid was poured into it. She was almost afraid to touch the fragile cup.

'Do you like it?' Lady Gresham asked, watching Rose examine it carefully.

'It's beautiful,' she remarked in awe. She had never seen anything so lovely.

'It was my grandmother's, and it's only brought out on special occasions.'

Rose looked up sharply. 'Am I intruding? Are you expecting someone else?'

'No, my dear, I thought you would appreciate something of such beauty.' She held out a plate of bread and butter. 'There's strawberry jam, and you must try a piece of Mrs Phipps's fruit cake – it is delicious.'

It certainly looked it, and Rose tucked into a hearty slice, but she noticed that Lady Gresham had only a cup of tea. 'You must eat,' she said. 'My little sister's always on at me because she thinks I don't eat properly.'

Lady Gresham took a thin slice of bread and butter. 'And is she right?'

'No.' Rose laughed. 'She's imagining things.'

'Tell me about your sister.'

By the time Rose had finished telling her about Annie, they were both crying with laughter.

'Oh, Rose.' Lady Gresham dabbed her eyes with a lace handkerchief. 'I would love to meet her. Would you bring her one day?'

'I couldn't do that,' Rose said, suddenly serious. 'She'd tell everyone.'

'Yes, of course. It was foolish of me to suggest it.'

Oh, damn! Rose thought. The old lady was lonely and now she had upset her. 'It isn't that.' She held up the delicate cup and pulled a face. 'I'd be scared to take my eyes off her.'

Lady Gresham brightened immediately.

Just then, the door swung open and Sir George strode into the room. He kissed his mother and turned to Rose. 'You two are having quite a party, if the laughter is anything to go by.'

Rose wasn't sure if he was cross or not until he smiled at her. She was shocked at the change in him. There was more than a sprinkling of grey hairs now, and deep shadows under his eyes. His son might have had many faults, but his father was grieving for him.

'I'm pleased to see you here,' he said. 'Thank you for coming.'

There wasn't the slightest doubt in Rose's mind that he meant it, which made her defensive. He had lost his son – would he try to make some claim on her? After all, neither Sir George nor his mother seemed ashamed that she had been born on the wrong side of the blanket.

'We will not interfere in your life, Rose,' Lady Gresham said softly, as if sensing her concern. 'All we ask is that you come to see us from time to time.'

She nodded. It was a reasonable request. She relaxed again, and looked up at Sir George – dark eyes meeting dark eyes. 'I'm sorry about your son.'

'Thank you.' He gave a faint smile. 'That is gracious of you, considering the way he treated you.'

'Just a young man having a lark.' There was no point, Rose thought, in holding a grudge against him now.

Sir George sat down and poured himself some tea. 'He had a reckless streak, I'm afraid, rather like myself at his age, but I grew up eventually.' He gazed at her and sighed. 'Not soon enough.'

'I'm sure your son would have turned into a fine man,' Rose said, hearing the pain in his voice.

He drank his tea and stood up. 'I'll stay for a couple of days, Mother.'

'Of course, dear.'

He gave them a courteous bow, then left the room.

Lady Gresham watched the door close behind him. 'This has hit him hard, and it also means the end of the Gresham line.'

'But he's still a relatively young man,' Rose protested. 'He could marry again and have other children.'

'He won't do that, even to produce an heir. He had a most unhappy marriage. After producing a son, his wife felt she had done her duty and refused to have more children. The kind of life she led after that was not . . . Well, she caused us much grief and shame.'

'I'm sorry,' Rose said. Was that why he had chased the maids? But it was none of her business. However, Lady Gresham had not finished.

'She was selfish and did not have a kind word for her husband, but she ruined the boy by leading him to believe that because he was from a titled family, he could do as he wished. George was never able to trust another woman.' She looked at Rose pointedly. 'The Greshams do not forgive easily when they have been wronged.'

That sounded familiar, Rose thought wryly. She seemed to have inherited a lot of the Gresham traits.

Soon after that, when she was about to leave, Sir George met her in the hall. 'Your company has done my mother good. Would you visit her again? When you have time, of course.'

'I can't make any promises, but I will try.' What else could she say? He had asked so humbly.

'Thank you, Rose.' Then he kissed her gently, turned away and walked up the elegant staircase.

She watched him. He looked like a man of sixty, yet he couldn't be much more than forty-five. He took each step as if it was an effort, and his body was slumped with dejection.

Rose didn't try to stop the stirring of pity within her.

Even their wealth and position could not protect them from heartache and tragedy. With a sigh she walked through the front door and heard the soft click as it closed behind her. She was going to have to be firm with them. She could not become a substitute for his lost son.

When Rose walked through the main door of the university, she saw Bill's tall figure leaning against a wall. She stopped in surprise, and he came over to her.

'There you are. I've been waiting for over an hour.'

'Really?' Her eyes flashed annoyance.

'Yes.' He slipped her hand through his arm and started towards the door. 'Come for a walk.'

'Wait a minute!' She dug in her heels. 'I don't want to go for a walk. And will you let go of me?' she hissed, casting a glance at a group of interested spectators, 'You're causing a scene.'

'Me?' he asked calmly. 'Are you sure you're accusing the right person?'

Infuriating man! She tugged at her hand, but his grip tightened.

'It's no good protesting, because you *are* coming for a walk with me, whether you like it or not.'

Determination was written all over his face, and she knew it would be useless to argue. 'All right!' she snapped. 'But only a little way.'

It was a pleasant evening and the street outside the university was crowded. Bill wandered along as if he had all the time in the world, but did not say a word.

'Where are we going?' she demanded. 'I've got work to do.'

'I only want half an hour of your time,' he said quietly. 'Is that too much to ask?'

Rose felt reproached. Why did anyone bother with her? All she did was snap at them – especially this man. She muttered an apology.

He bent his head. 'I didn't hear that?'

'Too bad. I'm not repeating it.'

He grinned and patted her hand. 'That's more like my Rose.'

'I am *not* your Rose!'

He started to whistle a popular song and kept walking. They had left the crowds and were now almost in Russell Square. If he didn't turn round soon she'd be back at Lady Gresham's. He was in a strange mood, she realized, and it was driving her mad, but at least he'd stopped whistling.

'Why did you come tonight?' she asked.

'I wanted to see you before I went away.'

'Oh.' Something like disappointment ran through her, but she dismissed it. This was ridiculous. She didn't care if Bill Freeman stayed or went. 'Where are you going?'

'I've got a job with a firm of architects in Cambridge.'

'That's nice.'

'Hmm.'

'When are you going?'

'Tomorrow.'

'Is it a good job?'

'Yes . . .'

'You don't sound very happy about it.'

'I'm ecstatic!'

'That's good. I hope you'll enjoy it.'

'I expect I shall.'

She stopped suddenly. 'Can we go back now?'

He glanced around then pulled her into a shaded doorway.

'What are you doing?' She was alarmed.

'Shush, don't be frightened. I'm not going to hurt you.'

Panic coursed through her. This was a deserted area, and he was a strong man. 'Let me go!' she quavered, and was disgusted by her cowardice.

'I've got to have something to remember you by.' He lowered his head and gently touched his lips to hers.

A sound of distress escaped her. 'Don't!'

He ran his hand over her hair as if he was trying to pacify an animal. 'Just a kiss, Rose, that's all.'

She didn't believe him. No man would stop at a kiss.

When his lips touched hers again, she froze. Then he murmured comforting words, and claimed her lips more firmly.

She felt the soft warmth of his mouth on hers; felt the gentleness, and remained still. This was nothing like the brutality of the rape, and some of her fear seeped out of her.

There wasn't anything threatening about Bill's embrace. He slipped his arms around her, holding her against him, but not too tightly. Eventually, after what seemed an age, he released her and stepped away.

She stared at him, bewildered and confused. 'Why did you do that?'

'Damned if I know. Come on, I'll take you back.'

Once in her room, Rose was relieved to find herself alone. Her emotions were in turmoil and it wasn't a feeling she was used to, or liked. When Bill had pulled her into that doorway, panic had ripped through her, but it was as if he had sensed her fear. Although he had insisted on kissing her, there hadn't been any force, just gentle persuasion. Her mind replayed the kiss and she smiled.

It hadn't been too bad . . . in fact, it had felt quite pleasant.

Rose sat cross-legged on her bed thoughtfully. Still, it was a good job he was going away because she didn't want him making a habit of it. She wasn't like Angelina and Harriet – she didn't have time for this silly romance business.

25

At the end of her first week back they were given the results of their exams. Rose couldn't wait for Sunday afternoon to tell John and Grace of her success. She was doubly pleased to find Harold with them.

'Don't keep us in suspense,' Grace said, as soon as she arrived with Annie.

'I got top marks,' Rose told them, unable to suppress a chuckle of delight. 'Harriet and Angelina passed as well. We put some of the boys to shame.'

'Well done, Rose! We knew you could do it.'

John and Harold were beaming with pleasure, and Rose knew that without their help she would not have got this far.

'She has justified all our faith in her, hasn't she, John?' Harold was clearly overjoyed.

'More than that – I'm so proud I could burst!'

'Don't do that, Uncle John.' Annie giggled. 'You'd make an awful mess.'

At that point, Grace went out, and returned carrying a tray with glasses, a bottle of sherry and some lemonade. 'This calls for a celebration.'

'Hold on.' Rose laughed. 'It's a bit soon to celebrate. I've still got to get through another two years.'

Harold dismissed her caution. 'You'll manage.' Then he started to laugh. 'I can't wait to see you out there with all the men. They're going to think an earthquake has hit.'

'And I won't be the only one,' Rose said.

'My Rosie's going to be the best, though,' Annie told them proudly.

'She certainly is.' Grace smiled affectionately at her, and handed her a glass of lemonade.

Annie watched intently as Grace passed round the drinks. 'Auntie Grace is getting big, like Mummy did,' she whispered.

'She's expecting a baby, Toots.'

Her face puckered. 'Won't she want to see us any more?'

'Of course I will, Annie.' Grace had heard the remark and came over to them. 'What makes you think I won't?'

Annie looked uncertainly at her. 'Well, Mummy didn't have time for us when the new baby came.'

'I'll always have time for you, sweetheart,' she assured her, and planted a kiss on her cheek. 'You know a lot more about babies than I do so I'll need your help.'

Annie's face cleared and she beamed.

'Right!' John stood up. 'Let's drink a toast to Rose and wish her success in the future. Hard work and determination have got her this far, and those qualities will take her through to graduation.'

'To Rose,' they all cried.

'I'd like to make a toast now.' Rose held up her glass. 'To Grace, John and Harold, I'd never have made it to university without your help and belief in me. Thank you.'

She took a sip of the sherry and decided she didn't like it.

Later on, when Harold had gone home and Annie was in the kitchen with Grace, Rose asked casually, 'Have you heard from Bill?'

'We had a letter from him yesterday.'

'Does he like his new job?'

'He's only been there a few days but he said it's very interesting.'

'Good.' Rose couldn't understand why she was asking these questions – she didn't care what he was doing.

John was silent for a moment. Then he said. 'When I write back, shall I tell him about your exams?'

She shrugged. 'If you like, but I don't suppose he'll be interested.'

'Hmm. I'll tell him anyway, shall I?'

'If you want to.'

They settled down to work, and as usual the time flew by. John drew her out, made her search hard for answers and reasons for her thinking. Nothing was ever set out in a rigid schedule for study: she was free to break off and argue any point with which she didn't agree – and argue was the right word, because sometimes they disagreed strongly. But as heated as their discussions became, they were always good-tempered, and it gave her a wonderful sense of freedom to vent her feelings and opinions.

At the end of the allotted two hours, John closed the books and sat back.

'Time to go, Rosie.' Annie had come into the room. 'Auntie Grace says I can see the baby as soon as it's born. I hope she doesn't keep having babies like Mummy did.'

'I don't think she will, Toots.'

★

Annie was still in a thoughtful mood when they walked into the scullery and found their mother flushed with excitement.

'I've had a letter from Bob. A sailor friend of his brought it back with him. He says he's happy in Australia. There's so much open space and a lot of opportunities for someone willing to work hard.' Then she looked sad. 'He says he won't be coming back, but he'll try to send us a message now and again. I'm glad he's found somewhere he likes.'

It took Rose some time to go to sleep that night. Things were changing. Her mother was married again and appeared happy; Flo was getting married next summer; Nancy was living and working at the orphanage; the others were growing up fast. She drifted, half awake, half asleep, and muttered when the figure of a tall sailor came striding towards her, a baby in his arms.

Rose became so engrossed in her studies that she was surprised to find it was nearly Christmas. Where had the term gone?

Angelina and Harriet had already left to go home for the holidays, and she was packing a bag to do the same, when there was a knock at the door.

'Come in,' she called, then wished she hadn't when Sir George walked in. 'Oh. It's you.'

'I've come to ask you a favour,' he announced, without preamble. 'Before you go home would you visit my mother?'

'I really don't have time.'

'Please, Rose, she would like to see you – just for an hour.' He picked up her Bible, which was on the bed, and began to turn the pages, pausing now and again to read the many passages she had underlined. 'You've read this right through.'

'I have,' she said curtly.

As she reached out to take it away from him, the photograph of his mother fell out. He picked it up and nodded to himself. 'You are remarkably like her. Have you seen the portrait of her when she was about your age?'

'She showed me a miniature – she even tried to give it to me but I wouldn't have it.'

'Ask her to show you the big painting next time you visit.'

Ah, Rose thought, we're back to that again. She continued packing her bag.

'I'll carry that for you.' Sir George reached out to lift it off the bed.

'I can carry it myself – and I'm not walking out of here with you!'

'Oh, yes,' he said drily, 'I'd forgotten – you're ashamed of me.'

Suddenly, she saw the funny side of it. 'That must be a new experience for you. Fancy a girl from the slums being ashamed to be seen with you, the great Sir George Gresham!'

'No, Rose,' he said quietly. 'I'm just an ordinary man who has made too many mistakes in his life. Mistakes he is sorry about and finds it is too late to put right.'

'Hmm.' He was behaving quite out of character. 'I'm afraid the humble act isn't fooling me.'

'Oh, damn,' he muttered. 'I thought it was quite an accomplished performance.'

Rose couldn't help smiling. 'Do you know? if you weren't such a bastard, I could almost like you.'

'You ought to watch your language.' He winced. 'If you're going to work as a solicitor you'll need to curb that colourful vocabulary.'

'Why?' she wanted to know.

'Because no one will employ you.'

Rose gave a satisfied smile. 'The people I intend to work for will.'

He stared at her for a few moments, then rubbed his temple wearily. 'I don't think I want to find out what you mean by that. I can make sure that you find a post with a prestigious law firm in the City.'

'You will do no such thing!' she blazed at him. 'I've already told you not to interfere in my life.'

He held his hands up in surrender. 'Forgive my presumption.'

'Oh, come on! This is me you're talking to, remember, not some gullible girl blinded by your aristocratic charm.'

He sat on her bed and folded his arms. 'Charm, Rose?'

'Get off my bed.'

Instead he made himself more comfortable. 'I don't understand you. You've a brilliant mind, I'm told, and are receiving a first-class education. You could climb the ladder of success and never look back.'

'I could,' she agreed, 'but that isn't what I intend to do with my education.'

'No, I suppose you've got it all mapped out, but I wish you'd let us help you.'

'You never give up, do you? We might have the same blood in our veins, but I will *never* . . .' she paused to let the word sink in ' . . . be able to think of you as anything but the man who treated my mother disgracefully. That will always be between us.'

He looked sad.

'Your mother told me that the Greshams do not forgive when they have been wronged,' Rose went on steadily. 'Well, in that way, I am a Gresham.'

'It's what I deserve,' he said. 'But my mother had no part in it so will you come and see her – as a friend?'

'Tell her I'll come after Christmas, before the new term begins.'

'Thank you. That will make her happy.'

He smiled and picked up her bag. 'What time's your bus to Bermondsey?' he asked.

'Any minute now.' Rose took the bag from him, ran out of her room and down the corridor.

'Happy Christmas, Rose,' Sir George called after her.

It was Boxing Day and Rose and her mother were just clearing up after dinner when John walked into the scullery.

'John! What are you doing here? Is Grace all right?' Rose was filled with anxiety.

'She's well.' He took her hands and squeezed them affectionately. 'And so is our son! He was a couple of weeks early and took us by surprise, but he's a healthy baby.'

'Oh, congratulations, I'm so happy for you both.' And Rose was: she knew how much they had wanted this baby.

'Can we see him? Can we see Auntie Grace?' Annie was pulling on John's sleeve, and bouncing around like a demented rabbit.

'That's why I'm here. Would you like to come tomorrow morning? Then you can stay and have lunch with us?'

'Oh, yes, please!' Annie bounded over to Rose. 'Is that all right, Rosie?'

'Of course.' She put her hand on her sister's shoulder to quell her.

The baby was much admired – out of politeness by Rose, who couldn't find anything to enthuse about in a newborn baby – and Grace was the picture of health. They stayed with her for half an hour and then, when the baby needed to be fed, the three of them went downstairs for lunch.

They left at about two o'clock, but when their bus arrived Rose made no move to get on to it. Annie watched it disappear into the distance.

'That was our bus, why did you let it go?' Annie stamped her feet and rubbed her cold hands together.

'Would you like to visit someone else?' Rose cursed herself as soon as the words were out.

Annie brightened. 'Yes, *please*, Rosie. I like meeting your friends. Where do they live?'

'Bloomsbury.' Rose made for the other bus stop.

The bus took them over London Bridge, on to Holborn, and then Russell Square. She could see that Annie was bubbling with curiosity as they arrived at the imposing house.

'I've never been here before,' Annie exclaimed. 'It's ever so posh.' She gasped when Rose walked up the steps and knocked on the door. 'Who lives in this big house?'

'You'll see.'

They were shown into the hall, and Annie nearly toppled over when she craned her neck to look up at the ornate ceiling. 'Rosie . . .?'

The drawing-room door opened and Sir George came towards them. He gave Rose a smile, then bent down to Annie, whose eyes were as wide as dinner plates. 'And who is this?' he asked.

'I'm Rose's sister,' she announced, returning his smile. 'My name's Annie.'

'Well, Annie, you must come and meet my mother.' He held out his hand. After only a moment's hesitation, Annie clasped it and allowed herself to be led away.

Rose rolled her eyes in exasperation. Her sister liked any man, even though she had continually warned her about them.

'Mother, this is Annie,' Sir George said.

Lady Gresham rose to her feet, a tall, impressive figure, despite her age. 'Welcome to my home.' Then she kissed the child. 'You must be cold. Come and sit by the fire. And you, my dear.' The look she gave Rose was one of undisguised affection.

Refreshments were called for and Rose was relieved to see it wasn't the paper-thin china they'd used the last time, but it was still lovely. Annie, however, was too excited to stay seated, and started to explore the room, looking intently at every exquisite ornament and the luxurious fabrics.

'Don't touch anything,' Rose warned nervously, as Annie's hand reached out towards a delicate shepherdess figurine.

The hand withdrew. 'I won't. You know I'm always good when you take me out.' Then she gave Lady

Gresham an appealing smile. 'You've got some very pretty things. I like the pictures ever so much, and,' she went to an alcove, 'this one looks like Rosie.'

Rose got up to have a look. Annie was right: it was remarkably like her. 'I didn't see this when I came before.'

'No, I've just had it brought into this room.'

After that they settled down to enjoy their tea. It was a pleasant hour, but Rose found it difficult to relax: Sir George had stayed, and Annie was chattering away, not at all intimidated by her surroundings. And, of course, she told the Greshams much more than Rose would have liked. But that serves me right for bringing her, she thought.

Later, when they left, she knew she would have to tell Annie who those people were. When the child paused for breath, Rose looked down at her. She was trotting along, her face alight with the wonder of it all, clutching a fine linen napkin the old lady had insisted she keep.

'You going to tell me who they are, Rosie?' Annie inquired.

Rose took a deep breath and started to explain, hoping she could persuade her sister to keep her mouth shut about the Greshams.

A forlorn hope, she suspected.

26

March 1921

For a moment Bill gazed up at the house, then jumped out of the car and hurried through the front door. His father was ill and had asked to see him, so he'd left his job and set off for Hampshire. That wasn't any hardship because he'd soon realized that he'd made a mistake in accepting the post – it was too far away from Rose.

He stopped in the hall briefly, then went upstairs. This was the first time he had seen his home in several years. It was large, ugly and full of memorabilia his father had collected during his years in the navy. Bill hated it.

'Ah, you're here at last,' his father grumbled, as Bill walked into his bedroom.

Bill looked at the frail, sick man, and felt sorry for him. 'I'd have come any time,' he told him. 'You had only to ask.'

'I know.' His father sighed. 'I was wrong to try to dictate to you what you should do with your life, but I loved the sea so much and I wanted my son to have the same pleasure.'

'Well, you had your wish,' Bill told him. 'The war came and left me with little choice in the matter.'

His father nodded. 'You distinguished yourself, and I'm proud of you.'

'But I didn't stay in the navy.'

'It doesn't matter.' His father lifted a shaking hand and grasped his son's. 'All I want is for you to be happy.'

Two days later, Bill's father died in his sleep. It was as if the reconciliation with his son had eased his mind, and he slipped away peacefully. Bill was sad that they had been separated for so long, but he took comfort from the healing of the rift between them. His father had had peace of mind at the end, he was sure.

When Bill started to wind up his father's affairs, he was staggered to find that he was now a wealthy man. He immediately put up the house for sale, and donated many of his father's possessions and medals to a naval museum. With that part of the business settled he sat down one evening to give his own future some thought.

He laid back his head, closed his eyes and took stock of his life. He could start up his own business as an architect. He had enough money to live on for some time, so a slow start wouldn't matter. He would never have a better opportunity than this to give it a try.

He opened his eyes and reached for the whisky bottle. He poured himself a small measure, then studied the golden liquid with deep concentration. That was the business side settled, but what about his personal life? Rose! He sipped the drink. It was impossible to think of a future without her. He was a fool, of course, because the chance of persuading her to marry him was remote.

Bill drained the glass and put it on the small table beside him. Common sense told him he should leave Rose alone, but he was too much in love to take any notice of that.

The house sold almost immediately, and then he started

to put his plans into action. The first thing he did was to look for business premises in London, and he had no sooner opened his office than the first commission came in. He was on his way, and could launch his pursuit of Rose.

He was considering how best to approach this when he received a letter from Grace and John. They started by wishing him every success in his new venture, but the last paragraph made him laugh: 'We would like you to be godfather to our son, and Rose will be godmother. She is taking a day off from her studies to do this for us. The christening will be on 28 April, and we hope you will accept.'

Bill picked up his pen. Of course he would.

'Uncle Bill!' Annie tore over to the tall man, who was talking to John and looking as unperturbed as ever.

Rose watched as he sank down so that Annie could throw her arms around his neck. Then he unwound himself and looked directly at Rose. He was wasting his time if he thought he was going to get another kiss! One had been quite enough. She held out her hand politely. 'Hello, Bill.'

He ignored the hand and kissed her cheek. 'Hello, Rose. As welcoming as ever, I see.'

A sharp reply hovered on the tip of her tongue, but she managed to stifle it. This was Grace and John's day: she was not about to spoil it for them.

Grace came over. 'Everyone's here so we can go in,' she told them, and handed the baby to Bill, who cradled him in his arms.

Rose couldn't help noticing how at ease he looked

holding the tiny baby, and something inside her jolted. He had filled out since she had last seen him, had lost that gaunt, troubled look. He was big and strong, but he looked right somehow with a child in his arms. He ought to marry and have children of his own – he'd make a wonderful father, she realized. She wondered why she felt so uncomfortable with the idea.

After the baby had been named Harold John William, he was handed to Rose. She took him with practised skill and looked down at him. He was gazing up at her trustingly, and she decided he was a nice baby.

'It suits you,' Bill murmured in her ear.

She clamped her teeth together and gave him a withering glance. She was *not* going to allow him to provoke her today.

They all went back to the house for refreshments and Rose busied herself helping Grace. Annie was in her element surrounded by all her favourite men. She was chattering away to Edward Trenchard, hanging on to Harold's hand, when suddenly she left them and came over to Rose. 'Rosie? Do you think that old lady would mind if I gave the napkin to little Harold?'

'I'm sure she wouldn't, Toots, but I've already given Grace a shawl from both of us.'

'I know, but I'd like to give him something of my own.' She pulled a brightly coloured parcel from her pocket. 'Look, I painted a special paper to wrap it in.'

Rose admired it, then said, 'In that case, you go and give it to Grace. I'm sure she will be pleased.' She marvelled that such an unselfish and loving child could have grown up in their harsh environment. It was as if the hunger and deprivation hadn't touched her. She knew that the napkin was a treasured possession, yet Annie was willing to give it away. Her little sister was special. But she had always known that, hadn't she?

'I'll tell the lady what I've done next time I see her.' Annie looked hopefully at her big sister. 'I liked her. You will take me to see her again, won't you?'

'Of course.'

Annie began to scamper off, then turned back. 'Do they know about your real daddy?'

'Grace, John and Harold do. You don't have to worry what you say.'

'I haven't told anyone. You sure it's all right to talk about it?'

Rose nodded – she knew what a struggle it must have been for Annie to keep a secret. 'Now, are you going to give Grace your present?'

Annie turned it over and over in her hands. 'Have you seen what Uncle Bill and the professor gave?'

'No.'

'Uncle Bill's is a baby's rattle, and the professor gave a cup, both *real silver*.'

Rose guessed at once what Annie was concerned about, so she sat down and drew the child close to her. 'Do you remember the Bible story I read to you about the widow who put the smallest coin in the collection when all the others were giving a lot more?'

'Yes,' Annie said. 'She gave everything she had, but the others still had plenty left because they were rich.'

'That's right. And what do you think the story means?'

Annie screwed up her face. 'It means that a gift doesn't have to cost a lot to be special?'

'Exactly. Some have given expensive presents because they could afford it, but ours are just as precious to Grace and John because they come with our love.'

Annie kissed her. 'Thank you, Rosie. You always explain things so I can understand.'

Bill watched the exchange between the sisters. From what he had been told, Rose had practically brought up the little girl from birth and she had certainly done a first class job. Annie was affectionate, polite, and altogether a delightful child; it was touching the way she always ran to Rose for advice and guidance. They were more like mother and daughter than sisters. What were they talking about so earnestly?

Annie came back to them with a parcel in her hands. Ah, Bill thought, so that's what it was all about.

'For the baby.' She handed the package to Grace and waited anxiously for it to be opened, hands behind her back.

'Why, thank you, sweetheart.' Grace opened it, trying not to tear the carefully painted paper. 'Oh, this is lovely,' she exclaimed.

Annie beamed. 'The lady gave it to me, but I want you to have it.'

Bill looked at the fine embroidery and frowned. It was a crest.

John took it from Grace and opened it up, examining it carefully. 'It's beautiful, Annie. Did you say someone gave it to you?'

'Rosie took me to see a nice lady and she told me I could keep it.' She gave a little self-conscious giggle. 'It was for when we had tea, but I didn't know how to use it. She showed me, but it was too nice to wipe my hands on.'

'Was it Lady Gresham you saw?' Grace asked.

Annie nodded and started to talk about the big house and all the lovely things she had seen, including the portrait. 'It looked ever so much like Rosie,' she told them all, 'and the house was big enough for ten families to live in.'

'Would you like to live in a house like that?' Bill asked, trying to contain his curiosity. Why would a portrait in some aristocratic woman's house look like Rose?

Annie bounced up and down. 'Don't be silly, Uncle Bill, we can't live in places like that – and I'd be frightened of breaking something. My sister couldn't take her eyes off me in case I did – but, of course, I'd never do anything to upset her.'

Annie had enjoyed her visit to a posh house, but Bill couldn't detect a thread of envy in her. Remarkable.

Then the child leaned forward. 'I met Rose's daddy. She asked me not to talk about it before, but she says it's all right now. She doesn't like him, but I thought he was nice.' Annie stood on tiptoe and was about to go into more detail when she stopped and listened. 'Baby's crying, Auntie Grace. Can I come with you?'

When they had left the room, Bill turned to John. 'What on earth was all that about? Rose's father is dead, surely?'

'No, that man wasn't her father, but it isn't my story to tell.'

'Don't worry, John.' Rose came and stood beside them. 'I'll explain. There's little point in trying to keep it secret

280

and, with Mum happily married again, I don't think I need to. Wally's been told about me.'

Bill saw the defiant tilt of her head and wondered what she was going to say.

'I'm a bastard,' she announced, without a hint of shame. 'My mother was seduced by the master of the house when she was in service, and was thrown out on to the street to fend for herself when she became pregnant.'

Bill wanted to take her into his arms and tell her it didn't matter – she was the girl he loved and nothing would change that – but the dark eyes blazed.

'I met my father recently, and I hate him, but his mother is a kind lady.' She smiled then and glanced at John. 'I took Annie to see her because she asked me to, and you should have seen that child's face when she saw all the lovely things. She was given the napkin as a reminder of her visit.'

'And now she has given it to us.'

'She loves you and Grace very much. It was her most treasured possession.'

'And therefore a most precious gift,' John said softly.

Rose nodded. 'Now I'll go and help with the clearing up.'

Bill tried to follow her but John stopped him. 'Let her go, Bill, she's said all she's going to.'

'Who is her father?' he asked, once the shock of her revelation had receded.

'Rose didn't mention his name, so I don't feel I can tell you, but he is someone of rank.'

Bill had already worked that out for himself. 'No

wonder she doesn't seem to belong in that dreadful street.'

'That's what we always thought, but I've come to the conclusion that we were wrong.'

'What do you mean?'

'Garrett Street is a part of her, always will be, and I believe that is the cause of her anger. She feels it isn't right for any human being to live like that, and she won't rest until she has done something about it.'

27

September 1922

Rose looked around the room. Everyone was here, and although Grace's house was much larger than theirs in Garrett Street, it was packed. Grace and John had insisted on throwing this party, and Harold was bursting with pride, as was her mother. Her own mood was of elation, mixed with disbelief. Against all the odds, she had been to university, and had graduated with honours. The last year had passed in a blur of study and determination, but it had been worth it.

'Congratulations, Rose.' Bill smiled down at her. 'What are you going to do now?'

'I've got plans, but I'm not telling anyone yet.' Excitement rushed through her. She couldn't wait to get started.

'Rose.' Harold was edging through the throng to reach her. 'I thought you were going to ask Angelina and Harriet to pop in tonight?'

'I did, but they have parties of their own to attend,' Rose told him.

'Of course – they would have. Will you be keeping in touch with them?'

'Harriet took my address, but I don't expect to hear from either of them again, really.'

'Why not?' Bill asked.

Rose gave him a studied look. 'After a shaky start the

three of us got on quite well together, and we were glad of each other's company at the university, but we never had much in common. Once they return to their own lives, our three years together will be forgotten.'

'That's a shame,' Bill remarked.

Rose picked up a small cake, then smiled at him. 'That's the way things go. It would be nice to see them again, but I'm a realist – our lives are just too different.'

The evening had been a great success and Rose was touched that her friends and family were so happy for her. Parts of the last three years had been a nightmare with family problems and lack of money, but most of it had been a joy. When she thought back on her childhood and how she had craved for books and a decent education, it had been nothing short of paradise.

'That was a wonderful party,' her mother said, as soon as they got home. 'Let's get the younger ones to bed and then we can have a nice cup of tea and a chat.'

The children were soon upstairs, and Marj had the tea ready. 'I expect it's going to seem strange being back here again,' her mother remarked. 'I know how you hate Garrett Street.'

Rose grimaced. 'I'll soon get used to it, I expect.'

'What are your plans, Rosie?' Marj asked, when they were settled at the table.

'I've got an idea, but I don't want to say any more before I've looked into it.'

Her mother nodded. 'I know you'll make a success of whatever you plan to do.'

'I hope so.'

★

First thing next morning Rose headed for a row of dingy shops at the top of Garrett Street, a cobbler's, a greengrocer's, a butcher's, a baker's and one other. She ran her hand over the roughly painted sign on the door, and as the grime came away the words 'Joshua Braithwaite, Solicitor' were just visible.

The inside wasn't much better, but that could soon be put right, she thought, undaunted.

'Can I help you, miss?' A scruffy man of about fifty got to his feet. His suit had seen better days, the shirt had never been ironed, and he had a beaten look in his eyes. In fact he looked as downtrodden as the area.

She treated him to her most brilliant smile. 'No, but I can help you.'

The look he gave her was startled. 'I doubt that, Miss . . .?'

'Rose Webster.' She grasped his hand and shook it. 'You need help, Mr Braithwaite. Please sit down and I'll explain.'

'I beg your pardon?'

Rose dusted off a chair and sat down, then waited patiently until he had sunk into his own. When he was settled she started her campaign. 'As I've said, you need help, and the best way to start is by employing me.'

That caught his attention. 'Employing – Miss Webster, my firm is on the point of closing for lack of clients. What makes you think I can afford to give you a job?'

She gave the room a detailed inspection, then turned back to Mr Braithwaite. 'You can't afford not to.'

'I don't think taking you on as an office girl would increase my trade, despite the appealing picture you would make.'

Rose flashed him another dazzling smile. 'I'm not an office girl, I'm going to be a solicitor.' She got the proof out of her bag and passed it to him.

'Hmm,' he muttered. 'Very impressive. But even if I could afford to employ someone else, it would be a man.'

'That is very short-sighted of you,' she declared. 'The women around here won't talk to a man, but they will come to someone who has grown up here.'

'Good Lord!' he exclaimed. 'You're not telling me you live here?'

'Garrett Street.'

He looked at her qualifications again. 'How did you manage to get into university?'

'Help from friends and hard work.'

'It couldn't have been easy for you,' he said, with more respect.

'It wasn't, and I want to put my education to good use.'

'So where do I come into this plan of yours?' He sat back, folded his arms and waited.

She noticed the alert gleam in his eyes, and knew that she had his attention. All she had to do now was sell him her vision. She chose her words carefully. 'The first thing we have to do is transform this place – open it up. Take that awful paper off the windows so everyone can see in.'

'That won't make any difference,' he objected. 'The people around here are too suspicious, as I've found out to my cost.'

She waved aside his objections. 'If they see one of their own inside, someone they know and trust, they'll come, even if it's only to find out what's going on.'

'Someone like you, you mean?'

'No, I'm a misfit here, always have been.'

'That I can believe,' he said drily. 'Who do you suggest?'

'My mother.'

He stood up. 'I think this nonsense has gone far enough. You're now suggesting I employ two of you.' He gave a grim laugh. 'I'm already living on the bread-line.'

Rose felt a flutter of panic – she was losing him. She gave him another confident smile. 'I can change that.'

He seemed bemused. 'I'm a fool to ask, but how do you propose to do that?'

'Offer an advice service as well as legal. Many people who live here can't read or write,' she explained. 'They struggle through life not knowing that help is available to them. We could tell them how to get this help, and fill in any forms for them.' She hesitated – he didn't look convinced.

'And how do they pay, or are you suggesting we offer this service *free*?'

'That's a lovely idea, but not practical.'

Mr Braithwaite gave a discouraging snort.

'We could charge, say, a shilling a time?'

He tipped his head back and laughed. 'And you think that will solve my financial worries?'

She wasn't going to let him beat her. 'It isn't much, I know, but the number of people wanting help will make up for that. Come on, Mr Braithwaite, think about it. You're not doing very well on your own, are you?'

He studied her speculatively for a while, then he said, 'Two shillings.'

'Absolutely not!'

'One and sixpence . . . and that is as low as I'm prepared to go.'

She had him! 'You drive a hard bargain.'

'Huh! You mean you do. Now, how do you propose I pay you and your mother?'

'We won't take much until business picks up.'

'I wish I had your confidence that this crazy scheme will work,' he shrugged, 'but what have I got to lose?'

'Exactly, Mr Braithwaite.'

'When can you start?'

'Right now.' Rose took off her coat, rolled up her sleeves, pulled a pinny out of her bag and put it on. 'I'll need a bucket of water to get that paper off the windows.'

'My God! What *have* I let myself in for?' He looked her up and down. 'You were so sure of yourself that you came prepared?'

'Of course. I'm not one to waste time.'

'What do you think, Mum?' Rose asked later that day, after she had finished the story.

'Are you sure I could do the job?'

'Of course. All you've got to do is sit within full view of passers-by, then talk to them when they come in.'

'Wally!' Marj called her husband into the scullery. 'Rose has found me a job.'

He came in and Rose had to explain all over again.

'I think that's a fine idea,' he said. 'Once word gets around I'm sure you'll have them queuing up at the door. It's just the thing this area needs.'

'I hope so. Mr Braithwaite is still sceptical about it, but I've given this a lot of thought.' For a moment Rose looked doubtful, then the determination came back into her face.

'It'll be a great success,' Wally encouraged her, 'and thanks for getting your mother the job.'

'I shouldn't get too excited,' Rose said. 'The pay won't be much to start with.'

'Oh, I don't mind that.' Her mother's face was alight with excitement. 'It'll give me something to do. I've missed not working since the war ended.'

'You'll have plenty to keep you busy – the place is in a shocking state. I've made a start, but there's a lot still to do.'

'I'll come with you tomorrow.' Her mother put the kettle on. 'We'll soon lick it into shape.'

'Annie!' Rose called, as she caught sight of her sister disappearing up the stairs. 'Would you do something for me?'

Annie's face peered around the door and broke into a delighted grin. 'Of course. What is it?'

Rose told her about the job, then said, 'I want a notice made so I can stick it in the window.' She wrote on a sheet of paper 'Advice Centre – no problem too small – Consultation fee 1/6d'. 'Do you think you can do that? I want "Advice Centre" in bright red letters.'

'I can do it, but I don't think I've got any paper big enough.'

'I've brought some home with me.' Rose unrolled a large sheet of cream paper.

Annie fingered it appreciatively. 'This will be fine. It'll take me a couple of days – I'll want to make a good job of it. Can't have you putting any old thing up, can we?'

How quickly Annie was growing up, Rose thought, as

she watched her sister go up the stairs. At eleven she was quietening down a bit, and although she was not academically brilliant, she was doing well enough at school. Her writing and English were good, and she had a real aptitude for art. She was sure her sister would do well in life, because she also had plenty of determination.

'I feel like a goldfish in a bowl,' Joshua Braithwaite complained, as he stared out of the sparkling window. 'No one's going to come in when they can be seen by all and sundry.'

'I've thought of that.' Rose opened the door of a room that had been used for storage, and revealed a sparsely furnished but clean space. 'And if we get more than one client at a time we can take them into the kitchen. So stop moaning, and tell me how you got on in court this morning.'

'I lost,' he grumbled.

She tutted. 'You'll have to do better than that. Why don't you let me help with the next case?'

'Good heavens, woman, you've only just been awarded your degree and you think you can do better than me! I've had thirty years' experience. Anyway, I didn't stand a chance today, the man was guilty.'

'I'm not suggesting I can do any better,' she said, placating him, 'but fresh ideas . . .'

'All right, you can work with me on the next one – if there is a next one,' he remarked despondently. 'I'm still waiting for this rush of clients you promised me.'

She winked at her mother and held out seven and sixpence. 'Put that in your cash box.'

He looked at it in disbelief. 'You've had five customers this morning?'

'Yes, and word's spreading. We're on our way, Mr Braithwaite.'

'Well, I'll be blowed. I never thought this idea of yours had a chance.'

'Why did you agree to it, then?'

'Because of your enthusiasm. I used to be like that a long time ago, but I've lost heart over the years. I've been on a continual downward slide, and when I ended up here,' he shrugged, 'well, it seemed like the end of the line and I stopped trying.'

'There's only one way you're going now,' she told him confidently, 'and that's up.'

'Do you know? I almost believe you.' Joshua Braithwaite laughed. 'I'd like you to call me Josh, Miss Webster. I shall enjoy working with you.'

'And I'm Rose. We're not going to earn a fortune, but we could make a real difference to some people's lives.'

Her employer didn't answer. He was gaping out of the window. 'Who the . . .?'

The tall, elegant lady getting out of the smart car was unmistakable – Lady Gresham. Rose opened the door for her.

'Thank you, my dear.'

'What are you doing here, Lady Gresham?' Rose was immediately suspicious. She hadn't seen either her or her son for some time.

'Business. I've come to see Mr Braithwaite.' Then she turned and looked at Marj. 'You must be Rose's mother.'

She gave a little curtsy – old habits dying hard. 'Yes, my lady.'

'You've done a fine job in bringing up your daughter. I regret you were treated so harshly, but I do not regret Rose being born.'

'Neither do I, my lady.'

Rose watched the scene through narrowed eyes. This meeting had been bound to happen sometime, but she could sense her mother's unease.

'Nevertheless,' Lady Gresham continued, 'I wish you had come to me on my return. I would not have allowed you to be turned out like that.'

'That would have been a waste of time, my lady,' Marj told her. 'I would never have been allowed to see you, and your son denied everything. It would have been my word against his.'

'And he would have been believed, not you.' Lady Gresham looked sad.

Marj nodded. 'This all happened a long time ago, when I was young and foolish and, as you can see, we've survived.'

Lady Gresham bowed her head in acknowledgement. 'But your life has been unnecessarily harsh, I think. Will you accept my sincere apologies at this late date?'

Marj gave a slight smile. 'I will, my lady. It was a long time ago and best forgotten now.'

'That is gracious of you.' Lady Gresham then turned to Rose. 'Now, introduce me to Mr Braithwaite.'

When that was done Josh said, 'Would you like a private room, Lady Gresham?'

'No, no, this is perfectly adequate.' She sat down and wasted no time in stating her business. 'I run two shelters for ex-servicemen. Many are destitute, and I want you to represent them in the fight for a better life. An organization called the British Legion has been founded for the purpose of helping struggling ex-servicemen. I suggest you contact them.'

Josh surged into life, and Rose guessed that some of his old spirit was returning. He had strong views on this matter, as she had discovered when talking to him.

'I would be delighted to take it on, Lady Gresham.'

'Good, good.' She handed him a piece of paper. 'My homes are at these addresses. As you can see, they are not in the most salubrious areas, but that is where the need is most urgent.' She glanced out of the window and gave a brief smile to the many curious faces peering in at her. 'I shall, of course, cover all your expenses, and I shall expect you to start at once.' She beckoned Rose. 'You do not object to this arrangement, my dear?'

When Rose glanced at Josh, his face was a picture in the art of pleading without saying a word. 'You're employing Mr Braithwaite, not me, and I'm pleased you're willing to try and help these poor men further. I firmly believe you've chosen the right man.' Rose held the old lady's gaze. 'As long as you don't try to engineer work for me.'

'I wouldn't dream of it. You've made it clear that I'm not to interfere in your life, and I won't. You want to succeed on your own, and I respect that.'

She stood up, leaning heavily on her ebony stick. 'Please find time to come and see me again, Rose, and bring your delightful sister with you again.'

Although the request was issued in a casual way, Rose did not miss the appeal in Lady Gresham's eyes. 'We shall come on Saturday afternoon, if that is convenient?'

'I shall look forward to it.' Then, with a gracious nod, she walked out, leaving a stunned silence behind her.

Marj let out a ragged sigh and sank on to her chair. 'She hasn't changed much!'

'My God, Rose, I feel shell-shocked after that encounter.' Josh laughed with delight. 'I've just been given the biggest chance of my career.'

'I told you you wouldn't lose by taking me on,' she joked.

'Er . . . I know it isn't any of my business, but I couldn't help noticing that you appear to know her.'

'She's my grandmother.' Rose was shocked at herself. It was the first time she had acknowledged Lady Gresham as such.

'But you said you grew up here?'

'I did.'

'Oh.'

'I can see your mind working, Josh,' Marj put in. 'I was expecting Rose before I married Webster, and I gave her his name, but she's Lady Gresham's granddaughter. I was in service and too innocent to refuse the advances of the master of the house, but I'm proud of my daughter.'

'I should think you are. She's unique. I spotted that as soon as she breezed into this office, and I wondered what the devil had hit me when she told me her crazy ideas.'

'They're not crazy,' Rose protested.

'I'm beginning to realize that. Now,' – he gathered papers together – 'I think I'll go and start talking to the men. It'll be a hard fight,' he said, with relish, 'but if they won't listen I'll make some damned big waves.'

'That will please Lady Gresham,' Rose remarked drily. 'She loves a good fight almost as much as I do.'

'I don't doubt it.' He grinned boyishly, straightened his tie and brushed down his jacket.

He looks ten years younger, Rose thought.

'Thanks,' he said earnestly. 'For the first time in many years I have something useful to do.'

When Josh had left Rose went and sat beside her mother. 'You didn't mind telling Josh about me?'

'No. After I'd spoken to Lady Gresham, I realized I'd been worrying too much about it. I was never able to forgive them, you see, but now I'm happily married, it doesn't matter any more.'

'I'm glad, because although I've managed to keep them at arm's length, I think they'll become a part of my life whether I like it or not.'

'Don't carry a grudge for me,' her mother told her, 'because I can see now that I wasn't blameless – and very foolish too. I think it's time to put it all behind us.'

'I agree. Now, I want to go to the council offices. Will you be all right on your own for a while?'

'You run along.'

28

April 1923

Bill pulled his collar up as a chilly wind whistled around his neck. Spring was reluctant to come this year. The open space in front of him was nothing yet, but in his mind's eye he could see the two houses he had designed for himself. His desire to have a home outside London had prompted him to find a suitable place, but when he had started to draw the plans, Rose had crept into his mind and taken over. He thought of it now as her home too. The longing to share his life with her was overwhelming.

He hadn't seen her since her graduation party, but he had kept in touch with her progress through John. She was earning herself quite a reputation as the women's champion – in and out of court.

'Nice spot you've got here, Mr Freeman.'

He dragged his thoughts away from Rose to the contractor he'd brought out here with him. Then he unrolled the plans. 'When can you start?'

'Next month is the earliest.' The man pondered the plans. 'Nice houses. This will be a good investment. Roehampton is an excellent area, and it's easy to get to London from here.'

Bill nodded. 'Let me know when you're ready.'

*

'Rosie? Can we go and see Auntie Grace? We haven't been for a long time.'

'It's only two weeks, Toots, and I've been very busy.'

Annie looked at her thoughtfully. 'Why do you call me that?'

'What? Toots?'

'Yes.'

'I don't know. I started calling you that when you were little. Don't you like it any more?'

She pulled a face. 'It sounds like a baby's name.'

'Oh, well, in that case I'll call you Annie because you're certainly not a baby.' Rose hesitated. 'Or would you rather Ann?'

'No, Annie's all right.' For a moment she had sounded rather grown-up. 'Can we go to Auntie Grace's?'

Rose put her papers back into the folder, and stood up. 'We'll go now, shall we?'

When she saw Bill there she was annoyed – he never came on a Sunday – but, of course, her sister was thrilled. 'I'm so glad we came today,' she cried, 'but I had a job getting Rosie away from her work.'

'You don't have to wait for me,' Rose told her. 'You're old enough to come on your own.'

'I know, but I like to come out with you – it's more fun.'

'How old are you now?' Bill asked.

'I'm twelve,' she told him proudly, 'and Rosie will be twenty-one this year.'

'My goodness,' Grace sighed, 'where have the years gone?'

'When's your birthday?' Bill wanted to know.

'March the sixth, and Rosie's is September the eighteenth.' Then she spun away from Bill. 'Uncle John, there's a lovely motor-car outside your house, is it yours?'

'It belongs to Bill,' John responded.

Rose glanced outside at the gleaming vehicle, then nearly burst out laughing when she saw what Annie was up to.

Her sister had sidled up to Bill with an appealing expression on her face. 'It's very pretty, Uncle Bill. Does it go fast?'

'It does, but I don't drive too fast because it can be dangerous, and I wouldn't like to frighten my passengers.'

Annie smiled up at him. 'Do you take lots of people out in it?'

Rose saw that Bill was fighting to keep a straight face. He lost the battle and chuckled. 'Would you like to go for a ride?'

Annie clapped her hands. 'Yes, please! Can we go now?'

'Tell you what, why don't we all go out? It's a warm afternoon and I know a lovely spot – we could have tea out instead of Grace getting it for us.'

There was immediate agreement and Rose found herself swept along in their enthusiasm. It would make a change and she needed a break from work.

Little Harold was soon ready and they all spilled out on to the pavement. Annie rushed to the front of the car and read the name. 'It's a Sunbeam,' she announced. 'I like that name.' Then she scrambled into the back of the car.

'Grace, you go in the back with Annie,' Bill suggested.

'I'll sit in the back too,' John said, settling his family comfortably. 'Then Rose can go in the front with you.'

During the journey, Rose couldn't help admiring the

car. The seats were cream leather, and there was a panel of gleaming wood with lots of dials on it. And as for the driver . . . well, he seemed to be working with hands and feet, but in a smooth, unhurried, efficient way. She glanced down to see how many pedals there were and felt a jolt as she saw Bill's leg muscles tighten as he worked one of the pedals. The modern fashion for men's trousers was too tight, she thought waspishly.

She gazed out of the window as they drove through Notting Hill. She hadn't wanted to sit in the front in the first place, and Bill took up such a lot of room.

'Look at that, Rosie!' Annie caught her attention.

Bill pulled over.

'What they doing, Uncle Bill?'

'Putting up new houses.'

Rose's irritation disappeared and she opened the car door. 'I want to have a look.'

Grace stayed in the car with young Harold, but the rest of them made their way across the road. Rose left them all behind in her eagerness to see what was going on. 'How many houses are you building?' she asked a workman.

'Ten.'

'What was here before?'

'Slums, but they was in a disgusting state. Nothing for it but to pull them down and start again.'

'Why are you working on a Sunday?' Rose fired another question at him.

'I'm not, miss. I've only popped along to sort out what needs doing tomorrow . . . Oh, hello, Mr Freeman, come to see how things are going?'

Rose spun round. 'These are yours?'

'No, but I designed them.'

She surveyed him with new respect, then grabbed his arm. 'Show me one that's nearly finished.'

Fifteen minutes later there wasn't a corner, cupboard or piece of plumbing she hadn't inspected, and she was thrilled with what she'd seen. 'You've done well,' she told him. 'Bathrooms, running water and electricity all laid on, and best of all a small garden for each house.'

Her intense gaze swept over the whole site. 'Set out beautifully, not back-to-back like the old ones.'

'I'm pleased you like – '

'Are they for rent?' Rose was too intent on asking questions to bother with anything else he might say.

'No, they're for sale.'

'Pity. They ought to be available for people to rent.'

'That isn't anything to do with me,' he explained patiently. 'I only designed them.'

'Of course.' She gave him a brilliant smile. 'Thank you for showing them to me. I'll just go and have another look.'

Bill and John caught hold of her before she disappeared, and urged her back to the car.

Rose spent the rest of the journey deep in thought, not noticing where they were going. She had forgotten Bill was an irritating man. Perhaps she had misjudged him – after all, he had designed some lovely houses.

'You know of any more being built like that?' she asked after a while.

'No, that was a commission I received when I first started my own business.'

'They're good.'

'Thank you.' He cast her a sideways glance of amusement.

'We need to clear the slums and replace them with houses like that.' She bubbled with enthusiasm.

'Rose, we're on a pleasant trip out,' John reprimanded gently.

'Sorry.' She turned and grinned at Grace and John. 'You know how desperate I am to improve housing conditions. But I promise I won't mention it again this afternoon.'

'Where are we going?' Annie asked, putting a stop to their conversation.

'Richmond Park,' Bill told her.

'Oh, that sounds nice. Is it much further?'

'We're almost there, sweetheart.' Then, a few minutes later, he drove through a pair of tall gates.

Rose loved it immediately, and Grace brought their attention to a group of animals.

'Oooh, what are they?' Annie cried.

Bill stopped the car. 'Deer,' he told her. 'Would you like to go and see them?'

Annie was already out of the car and heading towards the animals before Rose and Bill caught her up.

'Don't go too close,' Bill warned her. 'You might frighten them.'

'Are they dangerous?' Annie whispered.

'Not if you don't annoy them.'

'I won't do that. I never annoy anyone,' she told them confidently.

Rose caught Bill's eye and they exchanged a smile. Grace and John joined them and they all stood still to watch the deer munching the grass. Young Harold was wide-eyed at the sight.

'Look.' Annie tugged at Rose. 'One of the little ones is coming over.'

'If you keep very still it might come right up to you,' Bill told her.

Annie waited patiently and was rewarded when the deer came within three feet of them. 'I wish I had something to give it to eat,' she whispered.

'You mustn't feed them,' he said. 'They live on grass.'

'Is that all?' Annie sighed in disbelief, then gave a little jiggle of excitement. 'It's close enough to touch . . . Can I touch it, Uncle Bill?'

'Better not,' he told her quietly. 'They're wild animals, you see.'

'Isn't it a pretty colour? Oh, it's going away!' Annie's voice rang with disappointment.

'I think it's time for tea,' Bill said, and led them back to the car. When they were all settled again, he drove slowly through the park, giving them all a chance to admire the scenery.

'This is a beautiful place,' Rose murmured. 'Look at the trees, they're magnificent. I bet it's a glorious sight in the autumn.'

'It will be.' Bill glanced at her quickly. 'I'll bring you again, if you'd like to see it?'

'I'd like that,' she admitted.

They went out through another set of gates and Bill stopped on the brow of a hill. The Thames shimmered below them and curved its majestic way through lush countryside.

'I've seen pictures of this,' Rose breathed in awe, 'but it's more beautiful than any picture. You forget that places like this exist when you're surrounded by houses, streets and people, day after day.'

'I know what you mean,' Bill said. 'I grew up in Hampshire and I often long for peace and quiet and open spaces.'

'What river is that?' Annie asked John.

'The Thames.' He helped her on to a low wall so she could get a better look.

'You mean it's our river? Does it come all the way from London to here?'

'Yes – and I'm hungry!' He helped her down.

Bill took them into a small tea-room with blue and white checked tablecloths and cream china with little blue flowers decorating the edges.

'Oh, this is lovely.' Grace sat down with little Harold, who was now fast asleep.

Rose looked at the scene with a half-smile. Usually her mind was churning, but today she had managed to put aside all her worries and enjoy the occasion. She was among friends and there was nothing to do but be happy. It was a new experience for her, and she realized that she didn't know what it was like to have time to herself. And she didn't know what *fun* was. It was a poor reflection on the way she had lived her life.

'You're very quiet, Rosie,' Annie said. 'Aren't you enjoying yourself?'

'I'm having a lovely time, and I was just thinking about all the things I've never done.'

'Like what?' John asked.

Rose recited a list of the things she'd never seen in London. 'I'd forgotten that there's a world outside studying and working.'

Grace handed round the plate of quickly disappearing cakes. 'The last few years have been hard for you, but it's time to think about yourself now.'

Annie leaned across the table and caught hold of her sister's hand. 'If you're going out more would you take me to see the lovely pictures? I've always wanted to go to the big art galleries, but I didn't like to ask because you're always so busy.'

'First free day I've got we'll go to the National Gallery.' Rose smiled at her sister, her mind made up. It was all very well having her nose forever stuck in books, but it was time she started to broaden her outlook on life.

It was late afternoon when they got back to the car, and they drove slowly back through the park so they could see the deer again, then out through another set of gates.

'Look, there's some more houses being put up,' Annie told them.

Bill slowed as they went past, but didn't stop.

Rose could see only two. 'Someone's going to be lucky,' she murmured. 'This is a lovely spot. Where are we?'

'Roehampton,' was all he said, and picked up speed again.

Bill felt pleased with himself as he drove back into town. The trip had been a good idea: he'd found a way to get closer to Rose, and he had been able to show her a glimpse of *their* house. She also liked the others he had designed, and he hoped she was beginning to see him in a more favourable light. He had seen a softer side of her today, which was encouraging.

'You can drop us here,' Rose interrupted his thoughts. 'Don't go down Garrett Street.'

'You mustn't take your lovely car down there, Uncle Bill. There's lots of ruffians living here,' Annie chimed in.

Seeing that he was about to ignore the good advice, Rose touched his arm. 'This will do, Bill. We've got little Harold with us, remember?'

He pulled up outside her office, and watched the girls until they were out of sight. He felt sad to see them back in such squalid conditions after the beauty of the afternoon. He knew how much Rose hated the place, and her loyalty to her family showed the depth of her love. She tried to be hard, and in a lot of ways she was, but he suspected that she protected the gentle, loving side of her nature with anger.

Young Harold gave a tired grumble as Bill got back into the car. 'I'd better get you home,' he said.

After he had delivered the rest of his passengers safely, he went back to Kensington where he had a flat above his office.

For the first time since meeting Rose, he had hope for the future. She had been relaxed and happy today, and after seeing the new houses, her waspishness had disappeared. She had even smiled at him as if she meant it, which had given him a hint of what she might be like, if she ever stopped fighting.

29

The next morning Rose was at the council offices as soon as they opened. She was lucky and caught the chairman just as he was going into a meeting. When she called him, he glowered at her – he had already met her on numerous occasions. She ignored his ill-humour. She knew he considered her a nuisance, but she didn't give a damn.

'What are you doing about slum clearance?' she demanded, blocking his exit route.

He sighed. 'As I've told you before, Miss Webster, it takes time and we haven't got the money.'

'That's no excuse,' she said accusingly. 'I saw ten houses being built, but they were for sale, not rent.'

'Where were they?' he asked, looking as if he didn't care.

'Notting Hill.'

'Ah, yes, I know the ones. However, that is a private development and nothing to do with the council.'

He tried to move away, but she stepped in front of him again. 'I know that! But it does show there's some possibility for the run-down areas and it's your job to start doing something about it. And I don't mean private houses. Any built in Bermondsey should be for rent and given to the people who have always lived here, not for the privileged few who can afford to buy them.'

'Private ownership is considered the way forward.'

'And what about those who can only afford to rent?' she demanded, 'are you just going to forget about them?'

'Of course not.' He was clearly exasperated by now. 'And that development you saw is nothing to do with us – it's not in our borough.'

'I'm aware of that, but you should at least be looking into the idea of doing something here. You're going into a meeting, so bring the subject up, please.' She had added the 'please' reluctantly: these people needed a good kick up the backside – if you didn't keep on at them, they sat in their comfortable offices and didn't do a damned thing, except decide how much they could squeeze out of the residents of Bermondsey.

'The plight of the poor is always on our agenda,' he told her loftily, 'but we have a great many things to consider. Unemployment is rising at an alarming rate –'

'Then put them to work building new houses.' Rose knew from bitter experience that this was as far as she was going to get with this man today, so she gave a grim smile and softened her tone. 'I know it's a daunting task, but would you bring it up at the meeting today? There is little evidence of anything being done in the area.'

'We do what we can.'

'It isn't enough. I've seen how things could be improved, and as a representative of the people, it is your duty to explore all – '

'I'm well aware of my duty, Miss Webster, and you are making me late for my meeting.' He stepped past her and strode away.

It was a good thing he was too far away to hear what she called him.

The next item on her agenda was to call on Grace.

'Can you tell me where I can find Bill?' she asked, as soon as she arrived.

'Yes, I've got his office address somewhere.' Grace looked at some papers tucked behind the clock on the mantelpiece. 'Here it is.'

Rose took the printed card from her. 'Kensington? I'll have to catch the train and that's going to take what's left of the morning.' She gave a resigned shrug. 'I won't get much done today.' With that she sped out of the door and headed for the nearest station.

Very nice, Rose thought, as she studied the impressive brass plate with his name on it. She found his office on the second floor and marched in, expecting to see him there. Instead she found a young man of about nineteen, picking out the letters on a typewriter with two fingers.

'Is that the best you can do?' she asked, making him jump. 'It'll take you all day like that.'

'I know, but our typist is away ill.'

'How much have you got to do?' Rose went to the other side of the desk and peered over his shoulder.

'Two letters.'

'In that case . . .' She hoisted him out of the seat and sat down. 'Go and tell Mr Freeman I'm here and I'll do these for you.' She ripped his work out of the machine, put in fresh paper and started to type.

The boy gasped in admiration. 'You're much faster than our usual girl.'

'The WAAC trained me well. Now, go and get Mr Freeman, will you?'

One letter was expertly done and she was working on

the other when a voice said, 'Have you come to work for me, Rose?'

'Do you know her, Mr Freeman?' the boy asked, sounding flustered. 'She didn't give me her name.'

'She didn't have to,' Bill told him drily. 'I knew who it was the minute you said she'd taken over the office.'

Rose ignored them until the second letter was finished. She laid it on top of the first and stood up. 'I want to talk to you.'

'I'm with a client at the moment.'

'I'll wait' – she sat down again – 'but don't be too long.'

'Have you got any more typing to be done, Sam?' Bill asked the boy, with an amused expression on his face.

'Yes, Mr Freeman, there's that long report.'

'Give it to her. If you don't keep her busy while she's waiting she might just tear the place apart.' Then, with a chuckle, he went back into his office and closed the door.

'Bloody man!' Rose exploded, and glared at the door. 'He's talking about me as if I'm a wild animal!'

The door opened again. 'Sam?'

'Yes, sir.'

'Keep your ears covered. Her language is atrocious.' The door closed again.

The corners of her mouth twitched. Cheeky devil. She couldn't help noticing that the boy thought his boss might be right. 'Don't worry, Sam, I don't bite – often,' she told him. 'Nevertheless, you'd better give me the typing, because if he does keep me waiting too long, I might lose my temper.'

The boy tripped over the chair in his hurry to find the work and get out of her way.

She was on the last page when Bill came out of his office and saw his client to the door. She didn't look up until she had finished and, with a flourish, pulled the paper out of the machine. 'You shouldn't frighten your staff like that, Bill Freeman. Poor Sam really believes I'm dangerous.'

'You are. Have you looked in the mirror lately? You're stronger than a lot of men, and a look from your black eyes could stop anyone in their tracks.'

'I don't see any of this affecting you,' she replied, fighting a grin.

'Ah, but I'm different.'

'How?'

He tucked her hand through his arm, and led her towards the door. 'I'll tell you one day. Now, let's have some lunch and you can explain why you're here.'

As soon as they walked into the café, the food smelt wonderful. Bill found an empty table and handed her a menu. He insisted they eat first, and it wasn't until they had a cup of tea in front of them that he sat back. 'Right, what can I do for you?'

'I want to know all about those houses we looked at. What it cost to clear the site, lay the water-pipes and the electricity, and what you estimate the workforce will earn while they're being built.'

There was silence for a moment, then he asked, 'Anything else?'

'Yes, how much are they going to be sold for?'

He stirred another spoonful of sugar into his tea. 'It'll take a couple of days to get all that information together. I don't have it. I'm only the designer, not the contractor.'

'Oh.' Rose had assumed he'd know everything. 'In

that case I'll come back in two days.' She opened her purse to pay for her lunch.

'Don't you dare insult me by insisting you pay for your food,' he reprimanded her softly.

She looked up, surprised by the tone of quiet strength in his voice. 'I'm not trying to insult you, but I can't let you pay for me.'

'Why?'

'Because it isn't right when I've enough money of my own.'

He reached across the table and took her hand. 'It isn't a question of money, Rose. I'm pleased to see you and have enjoyed spending this time with you, so don't spoil it by arguing with me.'

Put like that, all she could say was 'Thank you.'

Rose walked outside while he paid the bill, and told herself sternly that she must learn to be more gracious.

'Who was that lady?' the boy asked, when Bill walked back into his office.

'Rose Webster. She's a lawyer.' He patted the boy on the shoulder. 'And she's not a lady – she has a vocabulary that would put the lowest deck-hand to shame.'

'She's very pretty,' he said, blushing fiercely.

'No, Sam, she isn't pretty . . . she's beautiful, and she isn't much older than you.'

He gaped in amazement. 'But she's so sure of herself.'

'She's had a tough life. It was a case of be strong or crumble, and she didn't intend to let *that* happen.'

'She was a bit frightening, but I liked her,' Sam told him.

'I like her too.' He walked into his office, shut the

door, and only just managed to stop himself giving a shout of triumph.

She had come to him. True, she had only wanted information, but it was a start.

Two days later he arrived at her office and handed her the information she had asked for. As she read it her brow creased.

'It's an expensive business,' he pointed out gently.

'So I see. Do you mind if I mention some of this to the council?'

'The costing for the development is no secret.'

His heart thudded as she looked up and smiled. He was glad she didn't do that too often because he wouldn't be able to stand it. It transformed her completely.

'Thanks, you've been a big help,' she said.

He sat on the edge of the desk and swung one leg casually. 'Have you taken Annie to the National Gallery yet?'

'I haven't had time.'

'Then make time.' He paused. 'Tell you what, I'll take you both tomorrow.'

'But I've got work to do.'

'Take a day off. You promised her,' he pointed out. 'I'll pick you up here at ten o'clock. We can drive around some of the sights, have lunch, and spend the afternoon looking at pictures.'

He watched her as she thought about it, and kept quiet: if he pushed too hard, she would refuse. One thing he had discovered about Rose was that she hated being told what to do.

'All right,' she said, suddenly, 'Annie would like it . . . and I would too.'

He was glad she had added the last bit. 'Good, I'll see you tomorrow.'

'Rosie! Hurry up, we mustn't be late.' Annie tore up the stairs to see what her sister was doing. 'I can't wait to show Uncle Bill our new coats.' She twirled in front of the old broken mirror. 'It's the best thing I've ever had.' Then her face went serious. 'You haven't spent all your money, have you?'

'No, they weren't expensive, and you know I never buy anything unless I can afford to pay for it. I'm earning more money now,' Rose added truthfully.

Her sister's face cleared. 'Won't Uncle Bill be proud of us!'

He was already waiting, and Annie danced up to show him her new coat. When Rose got there he was telling her sister how smart she looked.

'You won't be ashamed to take us out now, will you?' Annie said.

Bill stooped down to her. 'Sweetheart, I wouldn't be ashamed to be seen with you and your sister if you were dressed in rags.'

'Rosie used to be,' Annie told him, 'but she's never let me wear rags.'

'If you two have finished talking about me, perhaps we can go.'

Annie clasped her arms around Bill's neck and whispered, loudly enough for Rose to hear, 'She doesn't like anyone to know she's kind.'

'I'm aware of that, so we'd better keep it a secret.' He stood up and winked, which sent Annie into a fit of the giggles.

They drove along to Buckingham Palace and watched the soldiers on guard, then they had lunch at a proper restaurant, and after that they went to the National Gallery.

'Are you enjoying yourself?' Bill asked, as they gazed at the pictures.

Rose nodded. 'It was very kind of you to bring us.'

'I can hear a "but" in your tone,' he said. 'And I think you're worried about me paying again.'

'Yes, well . . .' Rose looked into his eyes and decided she'd better explain. 'Business has picked up tremendously and I'm earning a respectable wage now. I like to pay my own way.'

He took her hand. 'I know you do, but don't deprive me of the pleasure of taking you and Annie out today.'

She really was going to have to do something about her damned pride, Rose mused.

Annie was insisting she must see everything, so they walked until Rose's feet hurt and she found herself a seat. Having fun was a damned exhausting business, she decided, but she was enjoying herself. Bill was easy company, and knowledgeable on lots of subjects. Of course, that was hardly surprising: he had been to Oxford University so he must be clever.

Bill looked at his pocket watch. 'I think it's time we had tea.'

'There's lots more to see, but it's too much for one day,' Annie sighed regretfully, 'and I think Rosie's tired now.'

'I'll bring you again, and we can start from where we've left off,' Bill told her.

'Oh, yes, please.' Happy with that promise, Annie caught hold of Rose's hand and pulled her up. 'You hold her other hand, Uncle Bill, then she won't be so tired.'

Rose sighed inwardly. Her sister was incorrigible, but she didn't protest. Her temper was holding out quite well today, she thought. She hadn't snapped at him once.

After much discussion, they decided to have fish and chips instead of a proper tea, as they were all starving. It rounded off a happy day.

When they arrived home, they were both given a kiss, Annie on the cheek, and Rose on the lips, just a brief touch, but she didn't mind which was a bit of a puzzle: normally, she'd have been spitting mad at him for taking such a liberty.

By the time they walked into the scullery, Annie looked tired. She gave Rose a sleepy smile. 'Uncle Bill's very nice, isn't he? Do you like him?'

'Yes, I do.' And Rose knew that was the truth.

After a good night's sleep and lunch with the family, Rose and Annie set off to visit Grace and John.

'Oh, look, Uncle Bill's here,' Annie cried, as soon as she saw the car. Then she was off at full speed and erupted through the front door like a tornado.

Rose followed at her usual sedate pace, and found not only Bill but Harold too. 'Are you having a party, Grace?' she asked.

'It looks like it.' She hoisted her child over her shoulder. 'My goodness, he's getting heavy.'

Tea was a lively affair, and Rose was feeling surprisingly

tranquil. It had been a pleasant weekend: doing something apart from work had been good for her. She sighed contentedly. She was becoming quite placid, she thought, with a wry smile. That would never do in court.

30

June 1923

It was nearly ten months since Rose had burst into Joshua Braithwaite's practice and turned his life upside-down. During that time the local people had come to trust them and the business was growing. Josh was a changed man and took on worthy cases with enthusiasm, and won more often than not. As for Rose, she had been able to help quite a few women, but it was not enough: there were still too many out there suffering from injustice and abuse.

'There's someone to see you, Rose,' her mother said, poking her head around the office kitchen door. 'Better put the kettle on to boil. She's very distressed.'

'Show her in, Mum.'

When the woman slid through the door – and that was the only way Rose could describe it – she felt anger, quickly followed by pity. 'Please sit down,' she urged, not sure that the woman could remain on her feet for much longer. 'Would you like some tea?'

The woman nodded, then sat down with a thud. 'I shouldn't have come,' she murmured, 'but I'm at my wits' end.'

Rose motioned to her mother to stay, then put the cup in front of the woman, and smiled encouragingly. 'Will you tell me your name?'

'It's Ethel Grant . . .'

'And how can I help you, Ethel?' Rose studied her carefully as Ethel tried to make up her mind to speak of her troubles, though part of it was evident: she had been badly beaten.

'He's taken my kids away from me.' Ethel wrung her hands in anguish and tears flooded down her face. 'My little ones are frightened to death and – ' She started to sob uncontrollably.

Marj pulled up a chair and sat beside Ethel, holding her hand until she calmed down a little. 'Tell my daughter what's happened,' she suggested.

After another cup of tea and a little more coaxing, the story poured out. 'My hubby's a violent man when he's been at the drink, but just lately it's got worse. I can't do nothing to please him, and yesterday he near beat the life out of me, and I was scared and picked up a plate and hit him with it. I didn't hurt him none,' Ethel added hastily, 'but he chucked me out, and when I tried to take the little ones with me, he said I'd never see them again.' She began to wail once more.

Rose waited for a minute or two, then asked, gently, 'Do you mean he's going to divorce you?'

'Something like that – said he don't need me no more and he'd find himself a better woman.'

'Do you know if he's already got one?' By now Rose's blood was boiling. If she could have got hold of the man she would have thrashed him herself, but that wasn't the way to do it. It was time some of these brutes were taken to court to face their crimes.

Ethel leaned across the table and grabbed Rose's hand.

'He mustn't keep them! They're not safe with him – not without me to protect them.'

'Are you willing to take this to court? It will mean telling strangers how violent he is, and if he's committed adultery we can use that against him too. But it will be an ordeal for you.' Rose had had other cases like this, but none of the women had been willing to take things further. That had been frustrating because there had been little else she could do for them.

'Will it mean getting my kids back?'

'I can't promise that, but we'll have a bloody good try.'

Ethel looked up. There was a spark of defiance in her pale eyes. 'I'll do anything to get my babies away from him.'

That was what Rose had been longing to hear.

'How many have you got?' Marj asked.

'Six, and the youngest is only two.' Tears ran down her cheeks again.

'Where are you staying?' Rose prompted, trying to get more details.

'With my sister in Lambeth. She'd heard about you helping women, and told me to come and see you.' Ethel blew her nose. 'I didn't know if I should come because we ain't got much money, but I don't know where else to turn.'

'Don't worry about the money, Ethel.' Rose knew she would do this for nothing.

Once she had all the information she needed, she took Ethel to the hospital and, luckily, the first person she saw was Edward Trenchard. He came straight over to her. 'This is Ethel Grant,' she told him. 'Could you have someone examine her and give me a report of her injuries?'

'I'll do it myself.' Edward led the frightened woman away, and returned half an hour later with the written details she had asked for. 'Are you going to do something about this brutality?' he asked, clearly furious.

'Yes – at least, I'll have a damned good try.'

'You can call me as a witness, if you like.'

'Oh, Edward, that would be such a help.' Rose smiled at him in gratitude.

He patted her arm. 'You be careful. This could get nasty.'

The next few weeks were frantic for Rose, as the plight of Ethel and her children filled her life. She had pleaded, argued and even threatened, until at last she had a modest success. The youngest boy was allowed to live with his mother, but the father was flatly refusing to give up the others.

'You women ain't got no rights,' he'd bellowed at her, when she had confronted him.

After that she'd hired a private detective to watch him, and now had proof that he was committing adultery. With that and Edward's testimony she should be able to put forward a good case, and with a sympathetic judge they might stand a chance. She had hoped to save Ethel the ordeal of going to court, but now it was the only option left open to her.

Rose rested her head in her hands and closed her eyes.

'Tough case?' a voice asked.

She opened her eyes and saw that Bill had come into the office. She nodded.

'Can you spare a couple of hours? I've been told about another slum-clearance project, and they're having trouble getting the last family to move.'

Rose was on her feet and hurrying out of the door, her tiredness forgotten. 'Let's go.'

They were soon on their way and she sat back with a sigh of pleasure. What a useful thing a car was. 'Where is this new development?'

'Canning Town.'

'And the people who are refusing to move, have they been offered somewhere else to live?'

'Yes, the houses are a vast improvement on the ones they've been living in, and most of them have gone willingly enough but . . .'

'I know,' she sighed, 'there's always someone who doesn't want to move. I think they get frightened.'

Rose heard the shouting before they turned the corner, and was out of the car and running almost before it had stopped. 'What's going on here?' she demanded, elbowing her way through the crowd of men.

'Mind your own business,' one of the men growled belligerently.

'I'm a lawyer, and if you're threatening these people, then it *is* my business.' She planted herself in front of them, hands on hips. 'Now, who are you?'

'Bailiffs.' A man in a suit and a bowler hat stepped forward. 'We don't want trouble, but we've been given orders to get this family out today. They're holding up the work.'

This man seemed in charge and more approachable, Rose thought. She held out her hand. 'Can I see the eviction notice, please.'

He handed it to her and she studied it carefully, then gave it back. 'That's all in order. I'm Rose Webster,' she introduced herself, 'and if you would hold your men off for a while, I'll go in and talk to them. What's their name?'

'Perkins,' he said, 'and if you can persuade them to move, we'd be grateful. All our efforts have failed, but I'm reluctant to use force. There's children in there and I wouldn't like them to get hurt.'

With a nod, she walked up to the house and smiled reassuringly at the frightened faces looking out of the grimy window. 'Will you let me in?' she called. 'I want to talk to you.'

'We ain't opening the door to no one,' a man snarled.

'My name's Rose Webster, and I only want to talk to you.' She heard arguing going on inside and waited.

'You that lawyer from Garrett Street?' a woman called.

'That's right, Mrs Perkins.' There was more arguing. Then the door opened a crack, a hand came out and pulled her inside. The door slammed shut behind her.

The place was disgusting: the demolition work going on all around them had covered everything with a thick layer of brick dust, and the three children, in as bad a state as the house, were hanging on to their mother's skirt, their faces streaked with tearstains.

My God, Rose thought, they ought to be running out of here, eager to get into another place. Instead, they were holding on to the familiar, as if their lives depended on it.

'What you want?' the man demanded.

'Will you tell me why you won't move?'

'We've lived here all our lives. Why should we be

322

chucked out? We always pays our rent.' He stopped and looked at her suspiciously. 'We've heard about you. What you doing with that lot out there?'

'Persuading them not to come in here swinging hammers and pickaxes to break the door down.'

'They won't do that,' he sneered.

'Yes, they will, Mr Perkins.'

'Oh, we must go, Tom, please,' his wife begged. 'All our friends have gone – '

'Shut up, woman. I'm not leaving my home.'

Rose sighed in frustration. This was the kind of attitude that would delay a big slum-clearance operation in the future. 'Have you seen the houses they've offered you?'

'No, and I don't want to!'

'I have, Miss Webster. They're nice – much better than this dump.'

'What do you mean "dump"?'

Tom Perkins turned on his wife and the children howled in fear. Rose waded in and hauled the couple apart. Placing herself between them, she decided to get tough. The wife was willing to move, and it was only the man's stubbornness that was stopping them.

'Do you care for your wife and kids?' she asked him bluntly.

He was startled. 'Course I do.'

'Then why haven't you even been to have a look at the new place? Are you too scared to find out that you like it?' she challenged.

'I'm not scared of nothing,' he growled.

'Then go and see it.'

'How can I? If I leave, they'll be in 'ere like a shot.'

'Not if I stay with your wife and children.'

'Oh, please, Tom,' his wife implored. 'You can trust Miss Webster, you know what we was told about her. She grew up like us and look at her now – a famous lawyer.'

Rose smiled inwardly. 'Well?'

He was weakening and she moved in quickly, not giving him a chance to change his mind. 'I've got a friend outside. He'll take you in his car and bring you back. It won't take long.'

'Car, you say?'

Rose nodded. 'Let me out and I'll go and talk to him.'

'All right.'

'How's it going?' the bailiff asked, as she strode over to them.

'I've nearly persuaded them, but the man wants to look at the new place.' She turned to Bill. 'Would you drive Mr Perkins over there?'

'Of course,' he answered, without hesitation. 'I'll bring the car to the door.'

She clasped his hand in gratitude. 'Thanks.'

'Tell you what, miss, what if me and the lads go and have a bit of lunch? You might have sorted this out by then.'

She smiled at the bailiff. 'That's a good idea. If Mr Perkins sees you leave, it might relax him a little.'

'Come on, lads,' he called. 'Let's have a break and leave Miss Webster to see what she can do.'

They walked off through the rubble and she went back to the house.

'Where they going?' Mr Perkins asked.

'For something to eat while you have a look at the other house.'

'Blimey!' he exclaimed, rubbing a spot clean on the window so he could get a better view. 'That your fellow in that posh car?'

'Yes.' She pushed him out of the door. 'Don't keep him waiting.'

Rose watched Bill shake hands with him, always the perfect gentleman. The more she got to know him, the more she respected him. They drove away, Tom Perkins sitting proudly in the front passenger seat.

They were back within half an hour, and Tom Perkins came in looking quite different. 'Quite a toff, that man of yours, but not stuck-up nor nothing,' he said, with approval. 'Fought in the Great War, didn't he?'

'He was in the navy.'

'Jutland?'

'I believe so. What did you think of the house?' she asked, changing the subject. Time was running out.

'It's all right. Bill explained everything to me,' he told them importantly. 'Knows what he's talking about . . . He's an arch- arc- – '

'Architect,' Rose supplied.

'That's right. Anyway, I can see now it's much better than this.' He turned to his wife. 'It's got water what comes out of a tap in the kitchen, and a privy attached to the house.'

'I know, Tom. Can we go there?'

'Don't see why not. Bill says we'll be better off there.'

Rose saw the men coming back. 'Shall I get someone to help you move, Mr Perkins?'

'Thanks, miss.'

As she went out of the door, Mrs Perkins grabbed her hand. 'I don't know how to thank you.'

'Just be happy in your new home.' She left the squalid house and went over to the men. 'They've agreed to move.'

A cheer rang out from the workmen.

'But they will need some help.'

'We've got a cart ready, and we'll see they get everything over to the new place.' The bailiff looked at her with respect. 'Thank you, Miss Webster, you've saved us a deal of trouble today.'

Elated by the success of the afternoon, she went to Bill with a broad smile on her face. 'You really impressed Mr Perkins. "Bill explained everything to me,"' she mimicked, then burst out laughing. 'You're a real charmer, Mr Freeman. I think if you'd told him the moon was made of cheese, he'd have believed you.'

'I always thought it was,' he replied, straight-faced.

She giggled. 'Oh, this has lifted my spirits after the pressure of the last few weeks.'

'Feel like celebrating?' he asked, as he opened the car door for her. 'Come dancing with me tonight.'

'But I can't dance.'

'Time you learned, then.' He gave her a sideways smile.

Rose was in too good a mood to refuse. 'All right, but what shall I wear? I haven't got one of those new fancy dresses the girls are wearing these days.'

'Wear anything. You always look beautiful,' he said.

'Oh! I can't go.' She'd remembered something. 'I've promised to visit Lady Gresham tonight.'

He turned the car around. 'We'll go and see her now. I'm sure she'll understand.'

He drove straight to the house without her giving him any directions. 'How do you know where Lady Gresham lives?' she asked.

'John told me.'

'Oh.' She walked up the steps and he came with her. 'You don't have to come in with me, I won't be long.'

He ignored her and knocked on the door. He's good at that, she thought, as they were shown into the drawing room. He gets his own way without uttering a word.

'Rose! You're early.'

'That's my fault, Lady Gresham.' Bill stepped forward. 'I want to take Rose dancing, but she insists that she can't because she's visiting you tonight.'

'You must certainly go. I used to love dancing when I was a girl.' She made them sit down. 'What are you going to wear?'

'I've only got the navy blue frock.'

'No, no, my dear, that won't do at all.' Lady Gresham rang the bell and a servant appeared instantly. 'Ask Martha to get out my black crêpe-de-Chine.' She stood up. 'Come, my dear, let's see if it fits. We're much of a size,' she remarked.

The door opened before they reached it and Sir George strode in. 'George, entertain Mr Freeman while we sort out a dress for Rose. Her young man's taking her dancing and we can't have her wearing that severe dress she uses for her legal practice.'

Rose had only a moment to wish that everyone would stop referring to Bill as her young man, before she was hustled out of the room. She glanced back at him anxiously, but he looked as relaxed and unperturbed as usual. Does anything ruffle that man? she wondered.

The dress was exquisite. The delicate material flowed around her legs, the back was low, and the bodice shimmered with jet beads as the light caught them. It was also a perfect fit and Rose turned round to see it properly in the mirror. 'It's beautiful,' she exclaimed.

'I knew you'd like it.' Lady Gresham straightened the skirt. 'It's lovely on you and I'll never wear it again.' She looked down at Rose's shoes. 'We'll have to do something about those. These might fit.'

Rose took the soft black leather shoes, slipped them on and fastened the strap across the instep. They were perfect, and so comfortable.

'Good.' Lady Gresham looked as if she was enjoying herself. 'Now let's put this on.'

Rose watched in the mirror as a thin bandeau, sparkling with the same jet beads as the dress, was put over her short hair and adjusted until it was across her forehead. 'My goodness.' She viewed herself in the long mirror. 'Is that me?'

Lady Gresham nodded. 'Of course it is. Now, let us go and show Mr Freeman how charming you look.'

Rose knew that protest was useless. Over the last few years she had become very fond of her grandmother and she didn't want to upset her. It was only a dress, after all, and from what she had seen, the old lady's wardrobe was crammed with them.

The men got to their feet as they entered the room, and Rose realized with a shock that she was enjoying the attention and admiring looks. In fact, she felt quite feminine.

'Doesn't she look beautiful? Lady Gresham said.

There were murmurs of approval, and Rose received a kiss on the cheek from Sir George. 'Absolutely lovely,' he agreed.

Bill seemed lost for words.

'You will both stay for dinner,' Lady Gresham ordered. 'Then you can go straight to the dance. You are already smartly dressed, Mr Freeman, and have no need to change.'

During the meal the elderly lady seemed in her element, while Sir George was enjoying having another man to talk to. Rose noticed how well Bill fitted in with the Greshams: he was charming and his manners were impeccable.

'Mr Freeman?' Lady Gresham looked at him thoughtfully. 'You remind me of someone, and the name is familiar. Where is your home?'

'I live in London now, but I was brought up near Portsmouth.'

'Ah! I have it,' she declared triumphantly. 'I should have recognized you sooner, you are so like your father. How is the Admiral?'

'He died a little while ago,' Bill told her.

'Oh, I'm so sorry.'

Rose's mouth dropped open in surprise. Admiral?

'Did you know my father?' he asked casually.

'Indeed I did. I was quite tempted by the handsome devil when I was a girl.' Her dark eyes shone and she clapped her hands. 'This is perfect. The son of my first love has found my granddaughter.'

'Admiral Freeman?' Rose asked, when they were back in the car. 'Why didn't you tell me?'

'You never asked.'

Suddenly she began to shake with laughter.

'What is so funny?'

'Oh,' she gasped, 'I asked the son of an admiral to take Mr Perkins in his car.'

He chuckled. 'Don't worry, I kept all the windows open.'

The dance was at the Hammersmith Palais de Danse. Rose had heard of it, but never been inside. It was a warm evening so she hadn't brought a coat with her, and Bill led her straight into the hall. She gazed around in wonder. The place was crowded, but the thing that made the most impression on her was the music.

'Do you like jazz?' Bill asked, watching her face intently.

'Oh, yes.' She laughed up at him. 'It makes me feel as if I want to dance, even though I don't know how to.'

'I know what you mean.' He took her arm and led her towards a staircase. 'Let's have a drink first and then I'll teach you the steps.'

They took their glasses on to a balcony overlooking the dance floor, and Rose studied the throng downstairs, fascinated. Some of the dresses were outrageous, others stylish, but the one she was wearing was elegant, and she felt wonderful in it.

Later they went down to join the other dancers and Bill began to show her how to do the Jog Trot.

Rose watched the antics of the dancers all around her in amazement. 'I can't do that.'

'Of course you can. Just relax and move,' Bill encouraged her.

The music changed then and she was even more bewildered. 'What on earth is this called?'

'The Shimmy.' Bill demonstrated with great expertise, and grinned. 'Come on, Rose, forget everything and just move to the music.'

She found it difficult to unwind enough to join in, but soon the exciting jazz music got to her.

'That's perfect,' Bill shouted above the band. 'I knew you could do it.'

She was thoroughly enjoying herself, and an hour later he led her back to the balcony for another drink. She had never felt so happy and exhilarated. In fact, she felt like an ordinary young woman out to enjoy herself. What a lot she had been missing.

They sipped their lemonade and hung over the balcony watching the dancers.

'Look at that couple,' she said. 'I don't think they've got any bones in their bodies.'

Bill chuckled. 'They're very good. With a bit of practice you could do that.'

She looked at him in astonishment, then laughed so much she had to sit down.

The evening ended too soon. As they walked towards the car, Rose said, 'That was wonderful, thank you for bringing me.'

He stopped, turned her into his arms and kissed her firmly. It seemed to go on for a long time, but she wasn't frightened this time. Eventually he drew away. 'I shall be working in Scotland for a while,' he told her.

'How long will you be there?'

'I'm not sure.' He took her into his arms again and

the kiss was not so gentle this time. 'But I'll be back, you can be sure of that.'

31

Autumn arrived without a sign of Bill. Rose thrust away her disappointment. She was far too busy to be concerned about his continued absence, she told herself firmly.

Ethel's case was being heard, and she had much higher hopes of winning now. A new law, the Matrimonial Causes Act, had been passed, allowing women to sue for divorce on the grounds of adultery alone, and the husband could only have access to the children if he was a desirable influence. Well, Ethel's husband wasn't *that*.

But even with the new law, it did not prove an easy task: the legal system was still dominated by men and old prejudices were still strong. Her case was sound, though, and Rose presented it with confidence and determination. The evidence of the detective proved adultery beyond any doubt, and Edward Trenchard gave a description of Ethel's injuries. At the end of three often unpleasant days, Ethel was granted her divorce and the father was ordered to hand over the children at once.

It was a sweet victory, and Rose hoped it would serve as a precedent for similar cases in the future. It was widely reported in the newspapers, and heralded as a huge step forward for women. She also took satisfaction from the knowledge that, since 1920, women had been allowed to read for the Bar. It had crossed Rose's mind to do that, but she still felt she could achieve more in the job she was doing.

The next day, she worked late to catch up with some neglected paperwork and it was dark when she locked the office.

She was about to put the keys in her purse when something hit her and rough hands grabbed her arms. Every tiny detail of the rape rushed into her mind and, with a snarl of rage, she spun round.

It was not going to happen to her again.

Her eyes had become accustomed to the gloom and she could now see the outlines of two men. She clenched her fist and threw a punch at the nearest, putting all of her strength behind it. He screamed and covered his face with his hands, blood running through his fingers. 'You bitch!' he groaned. 'You've broken my nose.'

Rose ignored him. He wasn't going to cause her any more trouble. But before she had a chance to do the same to the other man, he caught her a stinging blow across the face, quickly followed by another.

Rose knew she couldn't expect any help. Whenever there was trouble, the people who lived here went in, shut their doors and kept out of the way. She was on her own.

However, she was not a young girl now: she was strong, and she used that to her advantage. Her blow made him stagger back and while he was stunned she took her chance: she seized his arms and forced them behind him. A quick look round told her that the other man had disappeared.

'Walk!' she ordered, and pushed him up the street towards the police station. When he tried to resist, she tightened her grip.

'Let go of me, you bitch!' he swore.

Rose had been too occupied to take any notice of who her assailants were, but now she recognized the voice of Ethel's ex-husband. She had known the man would be a bad loser. 'Keep moving or I'll break your arms,' she threatened.

The police station was about half a mile away, and her captive struggled and cursed every inch of the way, but she held him. The building was a welcome sight, though, and she hauled him through the door with a sigh of relief.

The sergeant on duty looked at her in amazement. 'What have you got there, miss?'

'She attacked me!' the now frightened man accused. 'Broke my mate's nose.'

Rose shoved him into a chair as two policemen came to her aid. 'Sit there and keep your mouth shut!' She introduced herself and explained what had happened.

'You want to make a complaint?' the sergeant asked.

'Of course I do. Why do you think I dragged him here?' she said impatiently. 'You lock him up and I'll prosecute him myself.'

'There's no need for that,' the man babbled. 'We wasn't going to hurt you, just wanted to teach you a lesson, that's all.'

She touched her bruised cheek and the rapidly growing lump on the back of her head. Who did he think he was trying to kid? 'So you thought an iron bar wouldn't hurt me, did you?'

'It wasn't an iron bar,' he protested loudly.

'Really? What was it, then?'

'Lump of wood,' he muttered.

Rose pointed to the form the sergeant was filling in.

'Put that down, and the fact that he has admitted attacking me with a weapon.'

'Bloody woman's too smart for her own good,' Grant snarled.

She gave a menacing smile. 'You've got that the wrong way round. I'm too smart for *your* good.'

'Do you know who the other one was?'

'Just look for a man with a broken nose,' she told the officer who had just joined them.

'What about you? Are you all right?' he asked, looking at a trickle of blood coming from the corner of her mouth.

'Yes, but you'd better get a doctor to have a look at him. I hit him a few times.'

The officer grinned. 'I've heard about you, Miss Webster. I'll bet they're sorry they tried to attack you.'

'What do you mean, "tried"? They damned near slit my skull open.' Rose didn't know what he was grinning at. She could see nothing funny about it.

'We'll have him in court at ten o'clock in the morning,' the officer told her, still struggling to keep a smile at bay.

'Good.' She turned to Grant. 'I'll see you in court – again.' Then she strode out of the police station.

She heard the officer chuckle and swore under her breath.

Rose crept into the house, trying not disturb anyone, but Annie must have been awake and waiting for her because she appeared almost immediately.

'You're late . . .' Then she caught sight of her sister's face. 'Oh, Rosie, you haven't been fighting again, have you?'

'You make it sound as if I'm always in a brawl.' Rose

put her hand to her head. She had a thumping headache.

'Sit down, and I'll make you a cup of tea. Then you can tell me who hit you.'

Rose was glad of the tea. The attack had been nasty – but it could have been worse. 'Ethel Grant's former husband and one of his mates thought they'd have a go at me, but I fought them off. One ran away with a broken nose, and Mr Grant is in a police cell.'

Annie looked anxious. 'Why did you have to choose such a dangerous job, Rosie?'

'It isn't dangerous, it's just that men aren't used to being dragged before the law to answer for their crimes.'

'But they haven't got any right to attack you.'

'I know.' Rose smiled at her sister, trying to allay her concern. 'You should have seen the other one run, and by the time word of this gets round, I don't think anyone will attack me again.'

Her sister giggled then. 'I bet they never thought you were so strong.'

'They've underestimated women for too long.' Rose stood up. 'Let's get some sleep.'

Ethel's ex-husband got a year, and the other man who had been found by police at a hospital received six months for his part in the attack. Rose left the court well pleased with the morning's work.

When she reached her office, she went into the back room where she could be alone and sat down. The attack had shaken her up more than she liked to admit. She had always been used to violence, but as a child she had escaped into books and study, shutting out her surroundings. She rubbed her temple. There was little

337

time for books now, and the nasty side of men's characters seemed to fill her life. She thought briefly of Bill and wished more men were like him.

Then she sat up and pounded the table with her fist. She was letting her emotions get in the way. It didn't take much effort to slam the door on her feelings, but she mentally turned the key for added security.

Bill walked into his office. He hadn't intended to be away for so long, but one job had led to another and he hadn't been able to leave Scotland. Later he took the stairs to his flat two at a time. It was good to be back. The journey had been long and tedious, but he hadn't minded because every mile had brought him closer to Rose.

At the thought of her, a spasm of anxiety ran through him. What if she'd found someone else while he had been away?

Without thinking about the lateness of the hour, he rushed out to his car. The traffic was light and he was soon knocking on John's door.

'Bill! When did you get back?'

'About an hour ago. Look, I'm sorry to call so late, but I'm not going to be able to sleep until I know how Rose is.'

As Grace and John told him what his dark-eyed stick of dynamite had been up to, he didn't know whether to laugh or cry. 'My God! She isn't safe to be out on her own. She needs someone to look after her.'

'It wouldn't do any good.' Grace sighed. 'I seriously doubt that she can be tamed. She has even joined the Labour Party, and is in the thick of the fight for reform.'

'I shouldn't have stayed so long,' Bill regretted. 'I was

just beginning to get through to her. When I took her dancing she was so happy and carefree.'

Grace looked at him sadly. 'I know you love her, Bill, but there's a demon inside her that controls her life. She is so involved in what she's doing that she has little time for anything else. She won't rest until she has done what she's set out to do.'

'And what exactly is that?'

'A better deal for women, and the destruction of places like Garrett Street,' John informed him.

He stood up, suddenly weary. 'I've just got to accept her as she is.'

There was quite a party going on when Bill pushed open the door of Rose's office and walked in.

'Uncle Bill!' Annie cried, seeing him immediately.

'Hello, sweetheart. My goodness, you've grown.' He stooped to be hugged.

'We're giving Rosie a twenty-first birthday party.' Her face took on a worried expression. 'She works too hard and needs cheering up. Have you brought her a present?'

'I've got something special for her.' He stood up and searched the crowded room. Everyone seemed to be here, all of Rose's family, the neighbours, many of whom he remembered from the wedding, Grace, John, Harold, Josh and even Lady Gresham.

When he saw Rose his heart contracted. She looked the same – and yet she didn't. The proud carriage and determined tilt of her head were still there, but as she turned to look at him, he saw something that almost tore him apart. There was a new toughness about her, and the effect of her battles showed: her eyes were cold and unyielding. The woman he saw in front of him had lost her softness, and in its place was ferocity. She was ready to do battle with anyone who opposed her.

Despair surged through him but it was quickly replaced with compassion and a steely determination. She needed some stability in her life and he was going to provide it.

'Hello.' She stood in front of him. 'John told me you were back.'

'Rose.' As he bent to kiss her she tried to move away, but he wouldn't allow her to and kissed her firmly on the lips, then gave her his present. It was something frivolous and he doubted that she'd ever had anything like it before. 'Happy birthday.'

'Scent?' Rose turned it over and over in her hands.

'Chanel No. 5, and it's the latest thing.' He took the bottle from her, opened it and held it out. 'Put some on your wrists, let it warm for a few seconds, then smell it.'

She did as instructed and her expression softened. 'Oh, that's lovely. Thank you.'

'Hmm. It certainly is.' He lifted her hand, smelt the perfume, then gently kissed her palm. Much to his delight she didn't pull away.

'I see you haven't changed,' she told him drily.

'No, and I'm not going to.' She walked away then and he mingled politely with everyone, but all the time he watched Rose.

'She needs your love, Mr Freeman.'

He turned and saw Lady Gresham standing next to him, her eyes fixed on Rose too.

'My granddaughter has suffered too many disappointments in her short life, and endured too many fights –

physical and mental. She is beginning to shut herself away from all feeling.' She glanced at him. 'That must not be allowed to happen.'

'I'll do what I can.'

'No, no.' The elderly lady shook her head vigorously. 'That's not good enough. I know you love her and you must make her yours. And don't take any of her nonsense – I am sure she cares for you, but will not admit to it. If she comes up against a will as strong as hers, she will respect and listen to you. She considers a loving nature weak, but you must show her that that is not the case.'

'You consider me man enough for such an arduous task?' he asked wryly.

'Yes. You have gentleness, patience and courage, and I believe you are the only man she will respect enough to marry. And she *must* marry before it's too late.' Lady Gresham kissed his cheek and walked out regally to her waiting car.

'You're a favourite.' Rose came over to him, and they watched Lady Gresham drive away.

'I like her. She has wisdom and a clear understanding of human nature.' He took Rose's hand and headed for the door.

'Where do you think you're taking me?' She wrenched her hand free.

'We're going for a ride,' he told her calmly, taking hold of her again.

'I can't leave my party. Everyone's gone to a lot of trouble.'

'Oh, you do care about other people, then?'

'Of course I do.' She gave him a penetrating look. 'What's the matter with you? You go away for months, then think you can sweep back and start ordering me about.'

'It's time somebody gave you a good talking-to.'

'Now just a minute – '

Before she could protest any more, he opened the door and pushed her out. 'Don't argue, Rose. You're coming for a short ride. I won't keep you long, but we need to talk.'

'We haven't got anything to talk – '

The look he gave her stopped the flow of words, and she sat silently beside him until he found a quiet spot by the river. He stopped the car, turned in his seat and took her face between his hands. 'I love you. Will you marry me?'

'*What?*' she exclaimed. 'Are you mad?'

The kiss he gave her was a mixture of love, hunger and frustration. 'Yes, I'm mad,' he told her huskily, as he pulled away. 'Loving you has made me like that, and the only cure is for you to marry me.'

'Don't be daft.' Rose gave him a disbelieving glance. 'I'm too busy for this nonsense and, anyway, I'm never going to marry.'

'Yes, you are. You've always been strong, but you're becoming hard now. Everyone's worried about you, and you no longer have time for the people who love you.' When she didn't speak, he drove the point home. 'Come on, tell me the last time you took Annie out? And when did you take the time to visit Grace, John, Harold and Lady Gresham?'

'I've been busy,' she muttered.

'That's no excuse. You're surrounded by people who care, but you shut yourself away, locking the doors against any kind of personal involvement. Obsession has taken over and it's driving you – '

'All right, I know,' she shouted. 'But how on earth is marrying you going to help.'

'Because I'll be there to give you something else in your life and, most important of all, I love you and care what happens to you,' he added quietly. 'I know you have fears, but I would never hurt you, and never force you to do anything you didn't want to.'

She laughed derisively. 'I can't imagine you wanting a loveless marriage.'

'I don't, and it won't be.' He ran his fingers gently down her cheek. 'You can trust me.'

'Maybe, but I don't want to marry you – or anyone else.'

'I'm not going to give up, so will you think about it?'

'This is a waste of time,' she said, clearly becoming agitated. 'I don't know what love is.'

'Yes, you do, but you've pushed it to the back of your mind and you refuse to let it surface. I've seen the love you've always had for Annie.'

'That's different. She's my sister and she's needed me.'

'And doesn't the fact that I need you mean anything to you?'

Rose sighed. 'I don't know what on earth you're going on about. I think your visit to Scotland has turned your head. Take me back to the party.'

'Not until you've promised to consider my proposal.'

'All right, I'll think about it. Now can we go?'

Bill started the car. It would be best to give her time to think things over. But he would give her one more jolt, he thought. 'I suppose I'd better go and ask your father for permission to marry you.'

She turned in her seat and glared at him. 'Don't you dare!'

He smiled to himself. At least that had woken her up.

32

The door opened and Josh swept in with a huge smile on his face. 'Rose, the day you came here changed my life. You're an angel.'

'I've never been called that before,' she said. 'Most people believe I came from the other place.'

'Then they're wrong. Our business is a success and we've been able to help a lot of people.'

What he was saying was true. But why didn't she feel better about herself? This uncomfortable, guilty feeling had been with her ever since Bill had made that ridiculous proposal three weeks ago. Since then, she had noticed that everyone was tiptoeing around her as if she was a bomb ready to explode.

'Don't look so unhappy.' He sat down. 'What's the matter?'

'Oh, nothing.' She dredged up a smile. The change in Josh was amazing. When she'd first met him he'd been shabby, downtrodden and beaten-looking. Now he was smartly dressed, lively and enthusiastic about life and work. 'Too much work, I expect. But never mind about me, what are you so pleased about?'

'The British Legion have asked me to act as their legal adviser.'

'That's wonderful. They're turning out to be a very useful organization.'

'Although I've only had a modest success in getting

increased compensation for some of the more badly injured, they're pleased I've managed to stir things up a bit. And guess who we've got on our side now?'

'No idea.'

'Bill Freeman. He's designing some homes for those who have difficulty getting about.'

'Oh?' Rose looked up quickly. This was news to her. 'Who's going to build them?'

'A private contractor.'

'I might have guessed,' she muttered.

'They'll be for rent, Rose. Don't condemn the scheme until you've heard the whole story.'

'I'm sorry.' Good heavens, what was the matter with her?

'You're too quick to judge,' he told her.

'I know what you're saying is true, but I get so frustrated. It's almost five years since the war ended, and improvement is so slow.'

'Change will only come gradually, but we're making our voice heard in a small way. That must help.'

Before she had time to answer, the door opened again and Bill strode in. Josh rushed up to him and shook his hand. 'Good to see you again. I've just been telling Rose about the new homes. Is there something I can do for you?'

'No, thank you. I've come to see Rose.'

'Right, I'll be off, then.' Josh paused at the door. 'Can you cheer her up? She's looking far too miserable for a young woman.'

'I'll see what I can do.' When Josh went out and closed the door Bill turned and smiled. 'Get your coat,' he ordered. 'I'm taking you out to dinner, and then to the

346

Hippodrome, for an evening of entertainment. And don't think about it, just do as you're told for a change.'

Rose looked at him uncertainly. Was he spoiling for a fight? No, she couldn't imagine him losing his temper enough for that. In fact, she doubted that he had one. But if she went out with him would she have to listen to another marriage proposal?

'This is just going to be a friendly night out. I'm not about to propose again, and I won't even touch you.'

He'd read her mind.

'Are you coming, or do I have to carry you to the car?'

He'd do it too, Rose thought. Oh, what the hell! She stood up, let him help her on with her coat, then marched to the door. His only comment was a silent lifting of one eyebrow.

Once they were on their way, she spoke. 'Josh told me – '

Bill stopped her firmly. 'We're not going to talk business tonight. We're going to have a good dinner, see a lively show, and enjoy ourselves.'

'I'm not dressed for one of your posh restaurants.'

'You look fine.' He gave her a sideways glance. 'You always do.'

'No, I don't! I look bloody awful.'

'Oh dear, we are in a bad mood,' he remarked mildly.

'*I'm* in a bad mood, not *we*,' she snapped. 'You seem the same as usual. Calm and infuriating as ever.' For some daft reason she felt close to tears, and she never cried. At least, not when anyone could see her.

Bill stopped the car. 'What's the matter, Rose?'

'You! You're what's wrong. I was all right until you came back with your silly proposal. I was doing all right until then . . .' Her voice wavered. 'Why don't you leave me alone?'

'Because I can't,' he said simply.

'Oh, that's right, you love me.' Her tone was scornful. 'How can anyone love a cold-hearted, stubborn woman like me?'

'You judge yourself too harshly. Your problem is that you care too much, but you won't admit it to yourself.'

The threat of tears had gone now, and she was feeling more in control. Was he right? She'd never thought of it like that before.

'Shall we get something to eat?' he asked quietly.

The restaurant he took her to was small, but the food was excellent. When she looked back on her childhood and remembered the almost constant hunger, she could hardly believe the difference in her life now.

'What are you looking so pensive about?' Bill's voice broke through her thoughts.

'I was just remembering what it was like when I was growing up.' She smiled, more relaxed now. 'Only today I was complaining that change was taking place too slowly, but my life has altered beyond belief. There's always food on the table at home, I can come into places like this, and afford to buy myself a new frock every year. All undreamed-of luxuries.'

'You've earned a better life.'

'I suppose you're right, but it's been a struggle. I seem to have been hammering on closed doors all my life, and some of them still won't open.'

'They will. Give it time.'

'I wish I had your faith. I've been trying to get my family out of Garrett Street, but Mum and Wally won't budge. Wally's afraid that if he loses his job, they'll fall into debt.'

'I understand his concern.'

Rose sighed. 'So do I, but I'd love to get Annie and the rest of them out of that place.'

'I know you would, and it will happen one day.' He gazed into her eyes. 'You could always marry me and let me deal with the problem.'

Rose surged to her feet, bristling with fury. 'You said you weren't going to mention that.'

He didn't speak while he paid for their dinner, or when he helped her on with her coat, or as they walked towards the car. For some reason, his silence was unnerving. It was only when they were driving towards the theatre, that he said, 'Have you taken Annie to the National Gallery again?'

'I haven't had time.' Rose was glad he'd changed the subject.

'I see. Then I'll take her next Saturday.'

'I'm not letting her go out on her own with a man.' She gasped as he braked fiercely and stopped the car.

He turned to face her and, for the first time ever, she saw anger blazing in his eyes. 'What are you implying?' He still spoke softly, but there was a steely note to his voice.

'Well, she's only a young girl – '

'My God, woman,' he growled, through clenched teeth, 'do you think I would interfere with a child?'

'Well, all men – '

'Don't say another word! I think you've insulted me enough.' He started the car again and spun it round in the road, making other drivers swerve, then headed back the way they had come.

Ignoring the mayhem he had just caused, he increased his speed. 'Little girls are not to my taste,' he told her tightly. 'I like big ones, and that shows what a bloody fool I am.'

Rose was shocked by his reaction. After all, she was only protecting her sister, and you couldn't be too careful – as she well knew. 'Bill – '

'Don't say another word, or I might forget I'm a gentleman and dump you in the gutter.'

She lapsed into silence, knowing by his tone that she had really done it this time. If she tried to explain, it would only make things worse. She usually liked a fight, but not with this man.

The car screeched to a halt outside her house. 'Get out,' he ordered, when she didn't move.

She did so, and watched him speed away. What had she done? Oh, come on, Rose, an inner voice taunted, you've insulted him in the worst possible way. He's a decent man, you blind fool. Why can't you learn to keep your mouth shut, and your suspicions to yourself?

She must have stood on the pavement for some time, because she suddenly realized it was raining and she was wet. She walked into the scullery to find Annie waiting for her.

'Uncle Bill was in a hurry, has he got to go away again?'

'I don't think so.' The last thing she wanted was her sister asking questions and putting two and two together.

'You stood out there a long time, and now you're all wet.' Annie touched her coat sleeve.

'Yes, that was silly of me.' Her laugh sounded forced

even to her own ears. She took off her coat and hung it by the fire, but she knew she wasn't fooling Annie. 'We had a row, and he was angry,' she admitted at last.

'Uncle Bill never gets angry.'

'Well, he did tonight. I insulted him.'

'Oh, Rosie, why did you do that? He's such a nice man and he loves you so much.'

'What makes you say that?'

'He watches you all the time.'

Rose dismissed the suggestion. 'That doesn't mean a thing.'

'You're very clever,' Annie told her, 'but you don't know much about people.'

'I haven't got the faintest idea what makes anyone tick and I wish I did, but I can't seem to trust anyone.'

'That's because you've been hurt,' Annie told her.

Rose looked up quickly. 'What do you know about that?'

'Well, Dad hit you, then those men attacked you after Ethel's case was finished . . .' She tailed off, and looked at her sister anxiously. 'And there was that time you came home hurt. You told us you'd fallen over, but I don't think that was true.'

'Oh, and why do you think I was lying?' Rose frowned.

Annie handed her a cloth to dry her hair. 'You were different after, and then you ran off to join the WAACs. I think you were miserable and just wanted to get away.'

'How do you know such things?' Rose asked. 'I thought I'd fooled everyone.'

'I watch people. I can tell if they're happy or not. You're quite good at pretending, but I know you.'

'You're right. I didn't fall over – a man attacked me. He hurt me bad.'

Annie's eyes filled with tears and she took her sister's hand. 'Uncle Bill wouldn't hurt you.'

'I know, Toots.' She used the old endearment without thinking. 'And I was wrong to insult him like I did – but you know me, I often speak without thinking first.'

'Are you going to tell him you're sorry?'

Rose nodded gloomily. This was becoming a habit. 'Yes. I'll have to.'

Bill eased his foot off the pedal as the fury evaporated. Where the devil was he? He'd been driving like a lunatic, not taking any notice of where he was going. What was that girl doing to him?

He stopped in front of a large house and took several deep breaths, relieved to feel his usual calm reasserting itself, but the fury was replaced with sadness. How could she accuse him of something so hideous? What hurt most was to understand that she believed all men were animals. What could have happened to her to convince her of such a thing? He knew she'd had a hard life, but Annie lived in the same environment and she was different. The little girl was loving, happy and trusting . . .

'Mr Freeman.'

He looked up in surprise and saw a man in footman's uniform standing by the car.

'Her ladyship saw you drive up and wondered if you would join her for a drink.'

Her ladyship? Bill glanced at the house again. Why on earth had he come here? It was miles out of his way. 'Yes, thank you.' He hauled himself out of the car and followed the man. He could do with some company.

'Mr Freeman.' Lady Gresham held out her hand. 'So good of you to visit.'

'I didn't intend to,' he admitted honestly. 'I've been driving around in a fury and didn't notice I'd come in this direction.'

'And who has been able to ruffle your calm façade?' she asked, with a knowing smile.

'Well . . .'

'Aha! It sounds as if you've had trouble with my granddaughter.'

He grimaced and took the large brandy the servant handed him.

'Sit down, Bill. I may call you that?'

'Of course.' He sat opposite her and stared into the fire.

'Would you like to talk about it?'

Feeling warm and comfortable, with the brandy burning a fiery path to his stomach, he explained what had happened.

'I know she was badly treated by her stepfather, but to have such a mistrust of all men seems excessive.' Lady Gresham gave him a penetrating stare. 'Do you know why that should be? Have you done something to make her doubt your integrity?'

'I don't think it's anything I've done.' Bill looked hopefully at the elderly lady. 'I was hoping you might have some idea.'

'Rose tells me little about her life, but one doesn't have to be a genius to know that it has been harsher than she will admit. I have learned more from her delightful sister.'

Bill gave a faint smile. 'She's a talkative child, much to Rose's dismay. And seemingly untouched by the squalid conditions in which they live.'

'I believe that is because Rose has protected her.' Lady Gresham smiled at Bill. 'I love my granddaughter, but I am aware of her faults.'

Bill took a large swallow of his drink, then put down the glass. 'I was horrified that the woman I love could think so little of me. Male pride, I suppose.'

'Pride is an affliction from which we all suffer,' she told him. 'What are you going to do now?'

'I don't know.' He sighed. And he didn't. He loved Rose desperately, but what was the use? Life with her would become a battleground, and he wasn't so sure now that he could handle that . . .

'May I give you some advice?'

'I would welcome it, Lady Gresham.'

'Don't go after her. Wait for her to come to you and apologize.'

He gave her a startled look. 'Do you think she will?'

'I'm sure of it. Rose has an abundance of Gresham pride, but she has called your honour into question and that will not sit easy with her. She will feel obliged to put that right.' Suddenly she smiled. 'She is fierce in court. She has only to fix someone with her dark eyes and they turn to jelly. In her opinion, injustice is something to be wiped out, and she has been unjust to you.' Lady Gresham gazed into space, then nodded. 'Yes, she *will* come to you.'

'She won't like doing it, though,' he remarked drily.

The door opened and Sir George strode in. 'Mr Freeman! What brings you here tonight?'

'Your daughter has been causing trouble again,' Lady Gresham informed her son.

'Never!' He lifted his hands in mock disbelief. 'Who has she been fighting with this time?'

'Me.' Bill was amazed by the Greshams' attitude. Rose was the product of Sir George's lusty youth, yet they spoke of her with pride and love.

Sir George chuckled, poured himself a drink and sat down. 'Did you ever hear what happened when I met her for the first time?'

The next hour was full of laughter, and Bill learned a great deal about the woman he loved. Yes, he still felt like that, and he knew nothing would ever change it.

As he took his leave, Lady Gresham whispered, 'Don't forget. Let her come to you.'

33

Two days after the argument, Rose's conscience was bothering her. It disturbed her sleep and work. *Why* hadn't she kept her mouth shut? All she'd had to do was say she would come with them. But no, she'd had to go and malign his character in the worst possible way. It made her feel sick to think of it. No wonder he'd been furious. He was never going to want to see her again, and for some reason, she didn't like that idea . . .

Rose massaged her temple. This damned headache wasn't helping, and she suspected it wouldn't go away until she'd faced Bill and apologized. A glance at the clock told her it was nearly five o'clock. She hauled herself to her feet. She had better get this over with or she wouldn't get any sleep again tonight. He was a gentleman and didn't deserve to be thought of as a child molester.

Her mouth set in a determined line. She grabbed her coat and hurried to the door. 'I'm going, Josh,' she called out. 'I'll see you tomorrow.'

The bus stop was crowded, and she knew it would be a long wait. She cursed silently. Why hadn't she done this earlier? By the time she reached Kensington, Bill would have packed up for the night. Then she remembered that he had a flat above his offices so he might be there. Now that her mind was made up she had to try to see him.

Two buses came at once and she was able to push her

way on to the second. The journey didn't take as long as she'd anticipated, and soon she was walking towards his office.

Bill was just coming out of the door, and Rose stopped, suddenly uncertain. He was with another woman. She only came up to his shoulder, but she was quite young and dressed in the latest fashion. Rose watched as she looked up at him and laughed. She wished she hadn't come. He obviously didn't care whether she apologized or not. He had already found himself someone else. Or had he always had this girlfriend, and just been amusing himself by proposing to her? Rose started to seethe.

She was about to walk back the way she'd come when he caught sight of her. 'Rose.' He strode towards her. 'What are you doing here? Is anything wrong?'

'No.' Rose saw the other woman walk towards them and said hurriedly, 'I came to apologize, but I can see you're busy.'

Just then a smart car pulled up and a chauffeur got out, bowing to the lady who was with Bill.

'Don't go away,' Bill ordered Rose, and went back to the woman. He shook her hand and waited until they'd driven off before he returned. 'Now, you were saying?' he asked.

'You didn't have to send her away,' Rose told him, a little more sharply than she should have done.

Bill searched her face intently, then smiled. 'Mrs Warrington and her husband have commissioned me to design a house for them. She came to see the plans today.'

'Oh.' Rose could have kicked herself – she'd jumped to conclusions again. She took a deep breath, anxious to get this over with. 'I've come to apologize. I should never have accused you of such a terrible thing.'

'No, you shouldn't. I would never do anything to hurt you or your sister, and I had hoped you trusted me.'

'I'm so sorry.' Rose dropped her gaze. 'What I said to you was unforgivable and I regret it. I wanted you to know that.' Without looking at him, she turned and started to walk away, but was stopped by a firm grip on her arm.

'I accept your apology, Rose, and forgive you.'

'You do?' Rose was surprised. She had not expected that. She regarded him with new respect.

'Are you hungry?' Bill asked.

She nodded. 'I haven't had much to eat today.'

'In that case' – he started to walk her up the road – 'I know a nice restaurant in the high street. You'll like the food there.'

Rose was lost for words, which was rare for her. She'd expected to be told never to come near him again. That hadn't happened, and he was even taking her out for dinner. Bill Freeman was a most unusual man.

They reached the restaurant in silence, but when they'd been shown to a table, Bill looked at her and said, 'I can recommend the rump steak. It melts in your mouth.'

Rose's stomach growled in anticipation. 'I'll have that, then.'

'Would you like some wine?' he asked, after he'd given the waiter their order.

Rose was about to refuse, but changed her mind. 'Thank you.'

'Red or white?' He raised a brow in query.

'I leave that to you. I don't know anything about these things.'

'Then we'll have red.'

Bill watched her right through the meal, hardly able to take his eyes off her long enough to eat. She was so lovely. Her hair shone with a blue tint under the bright lights. Her dress was plain and practical, but its dark navy was softened with a little white lace around the collar – not real lace, of course, the dress was too cheap for that, but she was still the most beautiful woman in the room. He was positive she was unaware of her stunning looks. One day he would get her into colours and fine materials, he decided.

At the end of the meal she folded her napkin and sat back. 'That was lovely. Thank you very much.'

'I'm pleased you enjoyed it.'

'I did.' Rose gazed out of the window at the nearly empty street. 'It looks late, I'd better get my bus.'

'I'll take you home.' Bill stood up and helped her with her coat.

'You don't need to do that,' she protested.

'Rose, it's nearly midnight. I'm not letting you go home alone.'

He was determined, and it seemed Rose recognized the quiet note of steel in his voice. She didn't argue with him, merely smiled and accepted.

The next day Rose was in quite a mellow mood, and she smiled to herself when she thought of their dinner last night. Bill had been charming and as gracious as ever, never once mentioning their argument. She had been dreading seeing him, but it had been a lovely evening. And the wine hadn't been too bad, either, after the second glass.

She put away the file she'd been working on. Her mother was only here three days a week now, and this was one of her days off. Rose thought she might as well join her at home. It was a long time since they'd been able to have a proper chat. 'I'm going home now, Josh.'

He looked up in surprise. 'It's only four o'clock. Are you feeling all right?'

'Never better. I've decided to knock off early for a change, and you ought to do the same, Josh, we hardly have any time to ourselves.'

'I agree, and I was going to talk to you about that.' Josh put his papers away too. 'Now that the practice is running smoothly we should take time off to spend with our friends.'

Rose realized she knew little about Josh's private life. She had always thought him a solitary man, but he had been taking extra care with his appearance just lately, and was really quite attractive. And there was something else; he looked happy.

'Have you got a special friend, Josh?' she asked.

He gave her a rather shy smile. 'Her name's Mary and I met her four weeks ago. Her husband was killed in the war and she was helping out at one of Lady Gresham's houses for veterans. We hit it off straight away, and I hope to persuade her to marry me.'

'Oh, I'm so pleased for you, Josh. I hope it all works out.' She kissed his cheek.

'Thanks, Rose.' Josh blushed a little at this unusual show of affection. 'Now, off you go and have a rest.'

As soon as she walked into the scullery, her mother poured her a cup of tea, and Annie was pleased to see her home so early. They were just settling down to talk when there was a rap on the door.

Annie was out of her seat in a flash to see who it was. She came back immediately, looking very serious. 'There's some policemen here.'

Rose's mother beat her to the door. 'What's happened? It must be serious to bring you down here.'

Rose edged past Marj, had a quick look at the scene and knew they were in trouble. There were two coppers on the doorstep with truncheons in their hands. A third was facing a jeering crowd in the road and smacking his truncheon against his leg.

With a growl of exasperation, she pushed past the policemen and faced the crowd. 'Go home!' she shouted. 'Haven't you got anything better to do?'

After a bit of disgruntled swearing, a few drifted away, but some stayed, the nastiest people in the street, but they didn't frighten Rose. 'Well? What are you hanging about for?'

'We're going to teach these coppers not to come down here,' a belligerent man called Stan snarled.

'What are you afraid of?' They shuffled uncomfortably. She knew every crime they had ever committed, and she used that knowledge now. 'Frightened they're going to find out what you've been up to?'

'We don't want no coppers down 'ere,' another man shouted.

Rose was now flanked by the three policemen. 'They've come to see me. They're not interested in you, so you'd better go home while you still can.'

Another round of foul language assailed her, but she didn't flinch. Her unwavering black-eyed gaze finally made them back down, and they started to leave, but as she turned to go into the house a stone caught her on the temple.

She spun round, ran towards a boy, caught him by the collar and shook him.

'Leave my kid alone,' Stan bellowed, and made a rush for her.

Still keeping a firm hold on the boy, she pushed the father away, making him stumble. 'If you dare to touch me, I'll have you and your son charged with assault. In fact, I think I'll do that anyway.'

The man was obviously alarmed by her threat. She had quite a reputation, and everyone in Garrett Street knew she didn't make idle threats.

'You don't have to do that – he didn't mean it for you, it was for one of them.' He pointed to the uniformed men, who were now standing behind her.

'That's worse.' Rose gave the boy a shove towards his father. 'I'll forget it this time, but you'd better push off before I change my mind.'

They did.

'You'd better all come inside,' Rose told the policemen. 'You'll be safer.'

Annie rushed to her. 'Are you all right? I saw that boy throw a brick at you.'

Rose put her hand to her temple, but there was only a small bump. 'I'm fine, and it was a stone, not a brick.'

Their mother had tea waiting for them, and Rose couldn't help grinning at the sight of three burly policemen filling the scullery, but she still didn't know why they were there. 'You'd better tell us what brings you to this dangerous neck of the woods,' she said, while they were all drinking their tea.

'Do you know a Charlie Webster?' the one with a stripe on his sleeve asked.

'That's my son. What's happened to him?' Marj was alarmed.

'Got himself into bad company, I'm afraid, and we've got him at the station. He's asking for his sister.'

Rose was already on her feet. 'I'll come straight away.'

'You'll get him out, won't you?' Marj looked imploringly at her daughter. 'He's not a bad kid.'

'I know. Try not to worry too much.' Rose paused at the door, then looked back at the men and grinned. 'You'd better come, too, so I can escort you to safety.'

With roars of laughter they walked up the street. Knots of people were standing at their doors, hurling abuse, but Rose was more than capable of doing the same.

They escorted her to the station then left to continue working their beat.

'Can I see my brother alone?' she asked the sergeant.

'Certainly, miss.' He took her to one of the cells.

'Oh, Rosie!' Charlie looked at her with a tearstained face.

She sat beside him on the hard bench. 'Tell me what this is all about.'

'It's that gang from Nelson Street. They met me from school and forced me to go with them to rob a shop. I didn't want to do it, but there was six of them and they

363

dragged me along.' He sniffed and gulped. 'They know you're my sister and they thought it would be funny to make me into a thief.'

Rose was appalled. Now her family were being picked on because of her. 'Did you steal anything?'

'No – honest. But when the police caught us the others shoved some things in my hands and told them I was the ring-leader. But I didn't do nothing.' He wrapped his arms around his body and rocked back and forth. 'And now I've been locked up.'

Rose slipped an arm around his shoulders. Her heart ached for her young brother. 'Don't be upset,' she told him. 'I'll get you out of here.'

When she explained to the sergeant what had happened, he nodded in agreement. 'That's how we see it, but we had to bring him in with the others. The Nelson Street gang are a bad lot and we know them well, but everybody's afraid to speak out against them.' He started to fill in a form. 'We'll release your brother into your care.'

'Thank you. Will he be charged?'

'No, he's only twelve and we're satisfied he's innocent.' Then he smiled. 'Would you like to see the others?'

'Yes, please, and all at once, if you don't mind.'

He showed her into a room and brought the six gang members to her. They laughed and jeered when they saw who was waiting for them.

'Hey, we're all right now,' the eldest sneered. 'The big lawyer's here.'

'You gonna defend us?' One of the others chortled as if it was a huge joke.

Rose looked from one to another in a leisurely way, a slight smile on her face. 'No, I'm going to prosecute you.'

There was a deathly silence as this unexpected news sank in. A couple even paled, such was her reputation.

The eldest boy recovered quickly. 'Don't take any notice of her,' he told his gang. 'You know everyone's too scared to talk against us.'

'Don't be too sure of that. I can be very persuasive, and I'm certain I can talk the shopkeeper and a few more into coming forward. And,' her gaze captured the eldest, 'I'm going to make you sorry you ever picked on one of my family.'

'It was a joke,' the youngest whimpered.

She treated this remark with the contempt it deserved, and turned to the policemen. 'You can put them back in the cells now.'

'Be our pleasure, Miss Webster.'

When she got back to the front desk, her brother was waiting for her. 'Come on, let's get you home,' she said.

'Just a minute!' The inspector hurried over to her. 'Are you serious about taking that gang on in court?'

'I never joke about such things.'

'Do you think you can make a case against them? Mention that lot and everyone closes their mouth in self-defence.'

'Not this time,' she told him. 'I'll get that shopkeeper to talk, and when he does, others will follow.' Then she walked out of the door.

For the first time she wished she was earning good money: then she would be able to get her family out of Garrett Street.

34

There was uproar in the court when the two eldest boys were sent to prison.

Bill watched Rose as she faced the angry crowd without a flicker of fear on her face. Lord, she had courage. All the time she had defended and fought for these people, they had regarded her as a heroine, but now some considered she had turned on her own. Not all, though, he was relieved to see. Some were cheering, almost drowning the jeers.

He left his seat and hurried to the door. She was going to need help when she came out, and he was damned if he'd let anything happen to her.

He needn't have worried. Rose had a policeman at either side of her, and she didn't look intimidated. 'What's all this racket?' she shouted. 'How many of you have had trouble with this gang?'

Bill held his breath as the noise died to a murmur.

'You know me, I've been working to help you, but there are some you *can't* help, however much you try.'

There were nods of agreement.

'Would any of you allow your family to be threatened?' She threw the question at them and waited. 'No, of course not, yet you think I should just sit back and see my brother hurt.'

'No, Rosie,' someone shouted from the back of the

crowd. 'That lot have got what was coming to them, and we'll all be better off without them.'

There was a chorus of approval now. Instead of running and hiding, she had faced her accusers and turned the tide with argument. Bill had always known she was something special, but today had shown him just how special – and he loved her even more. If that was possible.

Rose said something to the policemen, who nodded and walked away, then she saw him and came over grinning. 'Come to see the show?'

He looked at her in wonder: she was enjoying herself. 'You need someone to look after you.'

'I can look after myself.'

'But what about your family? You ought to get them out of Garrett Street.'

The smile vanished, replaced with a worried frown. 'Do you think I don't know that? Everywhere I turn I come up against a closed door. The landlords don't want anyone from Garrett Street – and many think I'm a trouble-maker. They price their accommodation out of our reach. Grace and John have offered to take Annie, but the stubborn miss won't leave everyone else.'

He tucked her hand through his arm. 'Let's go and get something to eat, see if we can find a solution.' He squeezed her hand. 'Aren't you going to say you're pleased to see me?'

'Well . . . yes, I am, actually.'

'Aha, progress!'

Later he drove out to Richmond Park again. 'I promised I'd bring you in the autumn.'

Bill stopped the car and they got out. The trees were a mass of orange, yellow, brown and gold, and the ground looked as if a multicoloured carpet had been spread on it. 'It's so peaceful after the court,' Rose murmured. 'I can't bear noise – not since I worked in a tin factory.'

'How old were you?'

'Eleven.'

The more Bill learned about Rose Webster, the more his respect for her grew. He could understand why she had grown up a fighter.

He turned her to face him and he brushed his lips over hers. 'Marry me, Rosie.'

'Why do you keep asking? I'd make a terrible wife.'

'That's a chance I'm willing to take.' His heart was beating uncomfortably hard – she hadn't refused him immediately this time.

'Then you must be mad. I'm hard, not affectionate, I hate kids and don't like being touched.' She grimaced. 'I'm also intolerant, stubborn and contrary-minded, and you should be running for your life.'

'You've left out a few,' he said. 'You're also loyal, caring, intelligent, and the most courageous woman I have ever met. And I love you with all my heart.'

'But I'm not sure I love you. I don't even know what the word means.'

'Tell me what you do feel for me.' He'd got her talking openly now and he wasn't going to let this chance slip away.

'Well, I like and respect you, you're kind, and honest. I feel I can talk to you.'

'Do you like being with me?'

'Yes, I do.' She laughed, then became pensive. 'But I

can't understand why you want to marry a woman who doesn't love you.'

'That will come.' She was actually considering it, he realized.

'It might not. I don't know if I could stand the physical side of marriage.'

She was silent again and he felt as if he was losing the advantage. He drew her into his arms and kissed her firmly. 'It won't be such an ordeal. You don't mind me touching you, do you?'

'I don't feel threatened by you.'

Why had she used that word? Bill knew about the beatings she'd received at home, and there had been the attack after Ethel's case, but was there more to it? He had to know – whatever it was.

'Tell me why you feel threatened by a man.' He watched her intently.

Rose lowered her head, deep in thought.

'Help me to understand, Rose,' he said.

Her head came up and the defiant gleam was back in her eyes. 'You'll never be able to understand how I feel about this, but you might as well know. Then we can forget about this whole silly business of you wanting to marry me.'

'Whatever you tell me, Rose, won't make any difference to my feelings for you.'

She gave a harsh laugh. 'This will. I was raped when I was fifteen.'

Bill felt as if he'd been hit, and for a few moments he was speechless. Why hadn't he guessed? It all added up: her dislike of being touched, her distrust of men . . . Oh, God. He groaned inside.

'Right, that's sorted *that* out. You can take me home now.'

The bitterness in Rose's voice jolted him back to life. She thought he was disgusted, but he wasn't: he was devastated that she should have suffered so much – and he wanted to marry her even more.

He reached out, caught her hands in his, then rested his forehead against hers. 'Rose, I love you so much. Will you marry me?'

She moved her head back to look him in the eyes. 'You still want to?'

'Yes.'

'I don't want kids yet.'

'I will be careful, until you change your mind – but you should know that I want children.'

'We could think about it in a year or so,' she conceded.

'Is that a promise?'

'You have my word.' Then she frowned. 'But it wouldn't work. I can't leave my family – they need me. Can I think about it?'

'No, Rose. I want your answer now. This is the last time I'm going to ask. If you refuse, I'll leave and never see you again.'

Mentally he crossed his fingers. He had probably sealed his fate with that ultimatum.

'I'd be sad not to see you again.'

'Then you know how to keep me.' He watched her expression carefully. That last unguarded remark gave him hope that she really did love him, even if she wasn't ready to admit it yet.

Her sigh was ragged. 'I won't give up my work.'

'I wouldn't ask you to. I know how important it is to you.' That had to be the last hurdle.

'I'll leave you if you start ordering me about.'

'I wouldn't dare!' he exclaimed.

The corners of her mouth twitched. 'All right, I'll marry you.'

He was elated, but he knew his problems were only just beginning. 'Thank you, my darling. You won't regret it.'

'When do you want to get married?' she asked.

'Christmas.'

'But that's only about six weeks away.' She spun away, and got back into the car.

'I know.' He followed, and started the engine before she could say anything else. He knew he must be crazy to make such a commitment on the terms she had set out. But he didn't have any choice: without her his life would be empty.

As they drove out of the park gates, Rose was wondering if she was in full control of her faculties. Whatever had possessed her to agree to marry him? She had decided long ago not to tie herself to a man, but the thought of never seeing him again had been painful, and she knew he had meant what he said. He would have walked out of her life and never come back. When had that begun to matter to her?

Her feelings had started to change on the night of the dance, and when he'd been in Scotland, she had missed him. Of course, she hadn't admitted it to herself at the time. She had just told him she didn't love him, but was that true? There must be some feeling deep inside her, or she would never have capitulated so easily.

And there was something else too. She had always been happy with her own company, but just lately she had wished she had someone to share her life with. Her mother was happy with Wally, and the children were growing up fast – even Annie didn't need her so much now. And she could see how happy Josh was with his Mary. It was quite a shock to realize that she was lonely.

Perhaps marrying wasn't such a crazy idea after all, she thought. And she would have to go a long way to find a man as kind, gentle and understanding as Bill.

Just then Bill pulled up outside a beautiful new house. 'We passed this the last time we came to Richmond,' she remarked, 'but it was just a building site then. Did you design it?'

'That's right. Would you like to see inside?'

'Oh, yes, please!'

He took a key out of his pocket, opened the door, and she peered in. 'Oh, it's furnished. Do you think the owner will mind us going into his house?'

'No, he won't mind at all. Come on.' He held open the door.

Half an hour later she was in raptures. 'It's beautiful, and you've thought of everything, loads of cupboards, and the bathroom . . .' Rose sighed wistfully. 'It must be lovely not to go to the public baths.'

'I'm glad you like it.'

'It's perfect.'

He held up another key. 'Do you want to see the one next door? It's almost identical to this, but three bedrooms instead of four.'

As they walked up the path, she gazed around in

wonder. 'They're not attached to each other. It looks strange after the rows of houses in London.'

'There's more space here,' he told her, as he unlocked the door.

'Yes, there is,' she said thoughtfully. 'Perhaps we should consider building on the outskirts of London.'

'I think it will be the only way to provide enough houses, but the government is slow to acknowledge this,' he remarked.

'I know – I've had enough arguments with the council about it.' She looked into the hallway, and smiled, her concern about slum clearance forgotten in the excitement of examining another house.

Rose wandered from room to room, with Bill following. That was another thing she liked about him – he knew when to keep quiet, and that was a rare quality.

At the last bedroom she stopped and gasped. 'Oh, how Annie would love this!' She rushed over to a small table and examined the notebooks, pencils and paints, all brand new. Then she laughed. 'She'd think she was in heaven.'

'So, you think she'll like her room?' he asked softly.

Rose spun round and searched his face, but he seemed serious. 'Would you repeat that?'

'Do you think Annie will like her room, then?'

He had been leaning casually against the windowsill, but now he pushed himself upright and came towards her. 'This house is for your family and the other one is ours.'

A lump formed in her throat. Her family would be safe!

Bill gathered her into his arms and held her until she

had got over the shock. 'Why didn't you tell me?' she mumbled, into his chest.

'The houses have been ready for some time, but I had to wait until you agreed to marry me.' He kissed her. 'I do have some pride, and I'd have hated to think you were marrying me to provide a home for your family.'

'I wouldn't have done that,' she protested, peeved that he should think she might only be out for what she could get. She had never been like that.

'I know you have high principles,' he assured her, 'but I couldn't take the chance. For my own peace of mind I had to be sure.'

She did understand – many women would have snapped him up for a decent home, without a pang of conscience. She looked at him earnestly. 'I could never do anything like that because I would lose my self-respect, which is very important to me.'

'I know.' He held her away from him and smiled. 'We'll move your family in tomorrow, shall we?'

Rose hugged him in a rare spontaneous show of affection. 'I can't wait to get them out of Garrett Street. Oh, but what about schools and Wally's job – '

'There's a very good school just down the road, and an excellent rail service into London. And as for Charlie and Will, the keepers at Richmond Park are looking for young boys to help with maintenance work. They might be able to get fixed up there.'

'They'd love that.'

'And if Wally can't find work locally, he can help me in the office.'

Rose felt as if her heart would burst with happiness. 'You've thought of everything.'

'I've tried,' he said simply. 'My biggest challenge has been getting you to like me enough to marry me.'

Her smile was cheeky. 'You're a persistent man, Bill Freeman, and you're growing in my estimation every minute.'

'Good!' The kiss he gave her this time was more passionate.

'You like doing that,' she gasped, as the embrace ended.

'I'd like to do a lot more,' he said.

She tipped her head to one side. 'Not until after the wedding.'

'God! I hope I don't die of frustration,' he moaned dramatically.

'It's only a few weeks.'

'You wouldn't consider making it the end of the month, I suppose?'

'You suppose right.' She grabbed his arm. 'Come on, let's go and tell Mum the good news.' She stopped suddenly.

'What is it?' he asked.

'I must have taken leave of my senses. I've been so excited about getting them out of London that I forgot to ask what the rent is. They won't be able to afford a place like this.' She gave him a tortured look. 'How much is it?'

'Nothing. If they'll pay the rates and electricity, I'll be happy.'

'You'll . . .?' Rose shook her head, trying to clear it. This was getting more confusing by the minute. 'Are you saying you *own* these?'

'Yes.'

She blew a strand of hair out of her eyes. She'd known he wasn't short of a bob or two, but this was a bit much to take in. 'Are you rich?'

'Not like the Greshams, but when my father died he left me some money and a large house, which I sold. I designed and had these built out of that money as an investment. What was left over went into my business, and that is doing well. We'll be comfortably off, you needn't worry about your family living here.'

'But you'd be able to make money from these,' she protested.

He spoke earnestly. 'I don't want to. All I want from life is to see you and your family settled and happy.'

Her eyes filled with tears again, and she brushed them away impatiently. What had she done to deserve a man like this? 'I'm becoming a real watering-can,' she complained.

'Don't be afraid to have feelings, my love. It isn't a sign of weakness.'

'I've always believed it was,' she told him honestly. 'If you have feelings, you can get hurt.'

When they walked into the scullery, the whole family was there, and Rose was troubled to see Will sporting a black eye. 'How did that happen?' she asked.

'I did it at work.'

'I want the truth.' She feared he had been picked on in revenge for what she had done to that gang.

'I did, honest. Some wooden boxes fell down and hit me.' He scowled. 'I hate that job. I've a good mind to go to sea like Bob did.'

'There's no need for that.' Rose gave Bill a nudge. 'Go on, tell them.'

He slipped an arm around her and smiled. 'I've asked Rose to marry me, and she's accepted.'

He didn't get any further because Annie hurled herself at him, nearly knocking him off-balance, then threw her arms around her sister.

'I knew you liked him,' she declared. 'Now Uncle Bill will be able to take care of you.'

He cleared his throat. 'I'd like to take care of you all, if you'd let me. I've got two houses in Roehampton, next to each other.' He smiled at Marj and Wally. 'One is for you and the children, the other for me and Rose.'

Wally looked concerned. 'What about the rent?'

They spent the next hour talking about it, drinking tea, and by the time everything was explained, Marj and Annie were crying with joy. Charlie and Will were enthusiastic about working in Richmond Park, and Rose couldn't believe all this was happening.

Had some of the closed doors started to spring open at last?

35

Christmas Day 1923. Her wedding day!

Rose sighed and laid back her head, luxuriating in the scented water. It felt as if a dozen elephants were stomping about inside her. With Bill's insistence that they marry at Christmas, it had been a terrible rush. He certainly hadn't given her time to change her mind – and anyway, how could she? Her family thought he was nothing short of an angel in disguise, and over the last few weeks she'd had to admit that she had never met anyone so completely unselfish. Everyone thought she was a very lucky girl – and she was, she kept telling herself. But one fact was inescapable: she was frightened of the step she was taking.

'Rose!' Grace called. 'It's time you were getting dressed.'

'All right. Just five more minutes.'

Rose closed her eyes, reluctant to move, and turned her mind back to the day they had all moved to Roehampton. What excitement there had been! When Annie had seen her room, she had thrown her arms around Bill and refused to let him go. Her mother and Wally had been speechless. The transformation in Rose's family had been remarkable. Her mother had never looked so happy and contented, Wally had managed to find a job in an office locally, and Charlie and Will were working at Richmond Park. They looked like different boys: their faces had filled out and they were always smiling and joking, loving every minute of their outdoor life, even in the freezing weather. Annie was going to a school where art was encouraged, and her talent was blossoming.

'Rose! If you don't come out soon I'm going to get John to break down the door,' Grace threatened.

'I'm coming.' Rose stepped out of the bath, dried herself quickly then put on her underclothes and a dressing-gown Grace had given her. They were getting married in London because all their friends were there, and Grace and John had put her up for the night, so she would be near the church.

'Thank goodness!' Grace exclaimed, when she opened the bathroom door. 'I thought we were going to have to drag you out. You're not having second thoughts, are you?'

'Of course I am,' Rose admitted. 'Didn't you?'

'No, but if you're going to back out, then for goodness' sake do it now. Don't let Bill get to the church before you tell him.'

'I wouldn't let him down,' Rose said, horrified at the idea that she might.

'I'm glad to hear it, because I've had doubts that you would go through with this. I know you've always been against marriage, but you don't have to be.' Grace smiled understandingly. 'The love between a man and a woman is wonderful if you've got the right man, and I'm certain you have.'

Rose nodded. 'I'm sure you're right, but I'm still a churning sea of worry and doubt.'

'You'll feel better when you get into your dress. Come on, you mustn't be late for the church.'

At the mention of the ceremony, her insides started to leap about again. 'I never wanted all this fuss,' she grumbled, allowing Grace to slip the frock over her head. Then her testiness faded as she gazed into the long mirror. It was the most beautiful thing she had ever had. The dropped waist was the latest fashion, and the hem came to just above her ankles. The lace veil was fastened, cap-like, to her head with a band of white flowers, and her shoes were delicate white satin. She couldn't stop smiling. How things had changed!

The door opened a crack and Annie peered in. 'Can I come in?' She opened the door just wide enough to slip through. She was in her lovely pink frock with flowers in her hair. Bill had insisted on paying for all this finery, and Rose had protested at first, happy to have a quiet wedding, but he wouldn't hear of it.

She took a deep breath. She was marrying a good man, for whom she had the highest respect. That was better than all this soppy love business.

'What a lovely frock.' Annie reached out to touch the lace. 'Uncle Bill's going to be so proud of you.'

Her insides gave another lurch at the thought of him waiting for her at the altar. Once she walked down the aisle her life would have changed for ever. She fought valiantly to push aside the anxiety. He was a passionate man, as the last few weeks had shown her, but he had held himself in check, respecting her wish to wait until the wedding night. Now it was nearly here and she was going to have to face her fears.

'There, you're ready now.' Grace stood back to get a full view of her. 'You look beautiful. Come downstairs and show John before he leaves to meet Bill at the church.'

John held her hands and grinned. 'What a vision.' He was about to say something else when there was a knock at the door.

'That will be Wally.' Grace hurried out of the room.

Rose couldn't believe her eyes when Sir George swept in, and she heard her mother draw breath sharply. 'I didn't invite him to the house, Mum,' she told her quietly.

'I knew he was going to be at the wedding,' Marj murmured, 'but I didn't realize what a shock it would be to see him.'

As her mother turned away, Rose faced her father, angry that he should barge in like this and upset her mother. 'What are you doing here?'

'I wanted to see you before you left for the church.' His gaze followed Marj as she walked over to Grace, then returned to Rose.

'Why?' she demanded. If he caused trouble today she'd kill him.

He didn't answer the question, but just stood gazing at her. 'I should be leading you down the aisle, not your stepfather.'

'Don't be ridiculous!' Rose gave an exasperated sigh.

'What's ridiculous about it?' He raised his voice. 'You're my daughter.'

'You've only been invited to the wedding because of your mother. And don't shout!'

'Will you two stop fighting?' John called them to order.

Sir George seemed to notice the room's other occupants for the first time. 'I apologize. It was very rude of me to walk into your house like this.'

'Why did you really come?' Rose demanded.

'My mother wants you to have this. She wore it on her wedding day.' He handed her a small velvet box.

When Rose saw the simple row of pearls with a diamond clasp, she shook her head. 'I can't.'

'Please accept it. You'll break her heart if you don't.'

'Take it, Rose.' Her mother had come up behind her. 'Lady Gresham wants you to have it.'

Rose turned and studied her mother's face, and was relieved to see that she was now composed and looking Sir George straight in the eyes. There was a card with the pearls. 'To my beloved granddaughter. Please accept this as a token of my love. I hope you will be as happy in your marriage as I was in mine.' At that moment Rose saw that she had been too harsh with the Greshams. They had shown her nothing but love and kindness, even Sir George in his strange way. She held out the necklace to him. 'Will you put it on for me?'

He stepped forward and fastened it around her neck, then stood back admiringly. 'They look perfect with the dress. Mother will be overjoyed,' he said. He looked at Marj and asked, 'May I speak to you privately?'

'You can say whatever you have to in front of *my* daughter.'

Rose slipped her hand through her mother's arm and felt her shaking slightly. She smiled down and squeezed her comfortingly. 'You don't have to talk to him if you don't want to, Mum.'

'It's time this was dealt with,' Marj said firmly. 'You owe me an apology, Sir George.'

He nodded, a gleam of respect in his eyes. 'I treated you disgracefully. I'm deeply ashamed and sorry for the suffering I've caused you. I know words can't right a dreadful wrong, but I hope you can find it in your heart to forgive me. I was wild and arrogant in my youth,' he added, with a grimace.

'In your youth?' Rose snorted.

'Now, don't fight again, you two,' Marj reprimanded her sharply, putting a stop to another quarrel erupting. 'You must give me time, Sir George, but this is a happy day, and you're welcome at the wedding of Rose and Bill.'

'That is gracious of you.'

Rose was proud of the way her mother had handled this awkward meeting with the man who had shamed her all those years ago.

'John!' Grace cried in alarm. 'Wally's here with the car. Bill will think we're not coming. We must all get to the church at once.'

As Rose walked down the aisle towards Bill, she thought how handsome and relieved he looked. She must have made the right responses, because the next thing she was aware of, they were signing the register. She was now Mrs Freeman.

They made their way outside to have photographs taken, and Rose couldn't for the life of her think how this had all come about. Had he cast some kind of a spell over her to make her change her long-held decision never to marry?

The reception was held in a local hotel, where they had a room to themselves. The buffet was excellent and the cake a masterpiece. Bill had insisted on paying for it all, knowing that the family couldn't afford such a spread. Her mother had felt it was her duty, but Bill's calm assurances had won her over.

Rose watched him as he mingled with the guests, talking and laughing. He was obviously happy, and so he ought to be, she thought. He had got his own way in everything without even raising his voice.

After the cake was cut, Wally got out his accordion and started to play. Bill led her on to the floor to dance and soon all the guests had joined them. Josh had brought Mary with him, and even Harold was beaming at everyone. Annie was dancing with all her favourite men, and Rose couldn't help comparing the laughing, happy girl with the sickly baby she had been. The change in her was tremendous, as it was with all her family. No one would ever believe they had grown up in Garrett Street.

'Will you honour me with a dance?' Sir George was standing in front of her. 'I promise I won't shout or argue with you.'

Rose held out her arms. It was time to forget the past.

Later, he took her over to his mother, who was sitting in state, surrounded by women. Rose suppressed a chuckle as she wondered what their guests thought about the Greshams being here. The family connection was obvious, but she didn't give a damn, and neither did Bill. He had insisted that they be invited and to hell with what anyone else thought.

Rose sat next to her grandmother. She had already thanked her for the pearls, but this was the first chance she'd had to talk to her properly. 'Are you enjoying yourself?' she asked.

'I am indeed, my dear. It's the best wedding I've ever attended.' Lady Gresham leaned forward to kiss her cheek. 'I'm proud to see my granddaughter marrying such a fine man, and honoured that you should have invited us.'

'I wanted you to come and so did Bill.'

Lady Gresham chuckled. 'That was brave of you. Our presence here is causing much speculation.'

'We don't care.' Rose kissed her grandmother's cheek.

'That,' said Sir George, standing tall and straight, 'is the greatest compliment you could have paid us.'

'Can we hope that you have accepted us at last?' her grandmother asked softly.

'I have – but that doesn't mean I'll let you interfere in my life,' she added.

'We wouldn't dare try!' Sir George laughed. 'And, anyway, you have a husband to look after you now.'

Rose felt all the old animosity drain away, and turned to the elderly lady. 'I will call you Grandmother from now on, but . . .' she looked up at Sir George ' . . . I'm not sure I'll be able to think of you as my father. Not yet, anyway.'

'That's no more than I deserve.' He sighed. 'I caused you and your mother great hardship. I will always regret that.'

Rose smiled at him warmly. 'It's all in the past now, and I think we should leave it there.'

'Thank you.' He looked quite overcome.

'Darling,' Bill was at her side, 'it's time we left our guests to party into the night.'

They slipped away without anyone noticing, much to Rose's relief. She'd had enough fuss for one day.

'Where are we going?' she asked, as he drove down the road.

'I want our first night together to be in our own home. Do you mind?'

'I would prefer it.'

'Good.' He reached across and touched her hands, which were clasped tightly in her lap. 'Don't worry, my love, I'm not going to rush you or force myself on you just because you are now my wife.'

She felt a little reassured. She had told Sir George that they should leave the past behind, and that was what she must do with the memory of the attack. It had happened long ago – in another life. Bill knew about it and it didn't worry him, so why should she let it concern her?

It was starting to snow again and Bill had to concentrate on the driving, so the rest of the journey continued in silence. Glad of a bit of peace, Rose closed her eyes.

When they reached the house it was snowing quite hard. Bill opened the front door quickly, but when she tried to step inside, he stopped her. 'I'm going to carry you over the threshold.'

'You can't!' she laughed. 'I'm much too heavy.'

He pretended to be hurt. 'Are you suggesting I'm a weakling?'

'No.' Rose couldn't contain her amusement.

'Then stop giggling, woman, and put your arms round my neck.'

He kicked the front door shut and carried her straight up to the bedroom. There was a fire burning in the grate and the whole house was lovely and warm.

He put her gently on her feet and kissed her long and passionately. She thought he had forgotten his promise not to rush her but she was wrong. 'Do you want to take a bath?' he asked, as he removed her headdress and veil.

'What about the hot water?'

'There's plenty. I've engaged a woman to do the house-work, and she came in today to see everything was ready for us.'

'A servant?' Rose's eyes opened wide.

'She'll come in twice a week to help, and don't look so shocked.' He grinned. 'We'll both be working and will have little time for polishing and cleaning.'

'Fancy having someone to help around the house.' Rose gave him a self-conscious kiss. 'You think of everything.'

'I try.' He urged her into the bathroom. 'Have your bath before I forget my promise and drag you off to bed immediately,' he teased.

Two baths in one day, Rose thought, as she sank into the hot water. How her life had changed, but such luxuries only made her more determined to rid London of places like Garrett Street. When she got back to work in the New Year, she would intensify her efforts to bring that about.

When she went back into the bedroom, there was no sign of Bill but she could hear him moving about downstairs. Glad of the chance to get into bed without him watching, she jumped in, and started. When she looked under the covers, she chuckled – there were four hot-water bottles.

She snuggled down and was soon drifting into sleep. This was unbelievable luxury.

Rose turned over and found herself up against a hard body.

'You're awake at last.' Bill pulled her close and kissed her gently.

'How long have I been asleep?'

'About two hours.'

'Oh, I'm sorry.'

'You're getting good at apologizing,' he told her, 'but you don't have to. You were tired.'

'I expect you are too,' she said, hopefully.

'Not a bit.' He rested on one elbow and gazed down at her. 'This marriage is going to be consummated tonight, my love. Any delay will only make you more apprehensive. Don't be afraid.'

She tried, she really did, but when he started running his hands over her body, she froze.

'It's all right,' he murmured gently. 'I won't hurt you.'

The trouble was, she didn't believe him.

'Let's have this nightdress off, it's getting in the way.' He sat up and eased it over her head. 'There, that's much better, isn't it?'

Was it? As flesh touched flesh, Rose realized that he wasn't wearing anything either, and there was a funny feeling low in her stomach.

The pain she had been expecting didn't come, and with a huge sigh of relief, she relaxed.

36

April 1925

Rose breathed in the spring air as she made her way to the station. It was more than a year since her marriage and she wouldn't have believed it possible that she could feel so content. When she looked back, which she did from time to time just to remind herself of how fortunate she was, it took her breath away to see how much their lives had changed.

Her mother and Wally were still happy together. Charlie and Will were both at the park and had made some friends. Flo had a decent council house, and seemed happy in her marriage; she had recently had a baby girl. Nancy was still at the orphanage and came home occasionally. They heard from Bob about twice a year, and Annie was leaving school at the end of term. Rose had tried to persuade her to go on to university, but Annie wanted time to think about it first.

Most importantly of all, Rose thought, she wasn't pregnant, which was nothing short of a miracle because Bill was a very physical man. He was also patient and had kept his promise: she was free to carry on her work without interference. And although he never hid the fact that he wanted children, he hadn't pestered her. She hoped he might forget about it.

The only fights she had now were for her clients and

with the council. She continually badgered them about clearing the slums, but they kept coming up with lame excuses. When she walked into her office, she found the girl they had employed in place of Marj waiting anxiously for her.

'Oh, Mrs Freeman, thank goodness you've arrived. Sir George Gresham sent a message asking you to go to his mother's house immediately.' Rose didn't wait to ask questions. Something serious must have happened.

As soon as she ran up the steps the door opened. 'Go straight upstairs,' the servant told her. 'Sir George is waiting for you in his mother's room.'

The curtains had been drawn but she could see Sir George by the bed, his head bowed. Without saying a word, she pulled up another chair, sat beside him and laid a hand on his arm. 'What is it?' she whispered.

He clasped her hand. 'Mother's had a stroke. A bad one, I'm afraid. The doctors say she won't last long.'

When she looked at her grandmother Rose's eyes filled with tears. She was so still and had the look of approaching death about her. Rose had seen it a few times, and her heart felt as if it would shatter. 'Can't they do something?'

He shook his head. 'All we can do is wait. Please stay.'

'Of course I will. May I use your telephone to cancel some appointments and let my family know where I am?'

Sir George nodded again, and she hurried down to his study. She would have to leave a message at Bill's office because her mother didn't have a telephone at home. Much to her relief, he picked the telephone up himself, so she explained what had happened.

'Oh, I'm so sorry, darling. Do you want me to come over?'

'There's no point. She doesn't know anyone.'

'Call if you need me,' Bill told her sympathetically. 'I'll stay in the flat tonight.'

'Thanks.' Rose put down the receiver and hurried back upstairs.

They waited into the night, never leaving the room for more than a couple of minutes at a time. Just before dawn, Lady Gresham opened her eyes, smiled at them both, sighed, then slipped peacefully away.

Rose was devastated. Her grandmother had always seemed so vital, so indestructible. Now she was gone, and she knew she would miss her dreadfully. She telephoned Bill with the news, and told him she would stay with her father for a couple of days. When she turned round, Sir George was standing behind her, a look of grief mingled with joy on his face. 'That's the first time you have ever referred to me as your father,' he told her.

'Well, you are,' Rose admitted. 'What's the use of denying it?' She knew he would be alone now, and if acknowledging him as her father gave him comfort, then that's what she would do.

He hugged her, his face wet with tears.

The funeral was a sad affair and Rose cried for the woman she had come to love. She clung to Bill's arm throughout the service and was grateful for his strong, steadying presence.

Back at the house when the will was read, she took little notice, not considering it had anything to do with her. Sir George inherited the bulk of the estate, which

391

was right and proper; a generous donation went to the British Legion, and a small bequest to Josh to allow him to continue with his work for ex-servicemen. However, Rose's attention was caught when she heard Bill's name mentioned.

'"I leave to William Jackson Freeman my sixty per cent share in the building firm of Grant Phillips."'

Rose's mouth dropped open. 'That's the firm who built our houses, isn't it? I didn't know Grandmother was involved in them.'

Bill looked stunned. 'Neither did I.'

Sir George smiled. 'She asked me what would be an appropriate gift for you, and we decided on the building firm. We bought a few more shares so you will have control in the business.'

'May we continue?' the solicitor asked.

They stopped talking and nodded.

'"To my beloved granddaughter I leave the blue tea service . . ."'

Rose smiled, remembering the first time they had drunk tea from it together. That was a lovely gift.

'" . . . the portrait of myself, the miniature in the gold frame, and five thousand pounds . . ."'

Rose would have fallen off the chair if Bill hadn't caught her.

The solicitor was still speaking. '" . . . to use to make one of her wishes come true."' He paused. 'There is one more small bequest. "To Annie Webster I leave the figurine of the shepherdess."'

He closed the file. 'That is the end of Lady Gresham's last will and testament.'

★

Rose and Bill were so shocked by Lady Gresham's will that they went outside and started to walk around the streets, trying to grasp what this meant to their lives.

'My God!' Bill gasped. 'This means I can design the homes *and* build them. But why did she leave it to me?'

Rose put her arm around her stunned husband. 'Grandmother did say that your father was her first love, so perhaps she did it for old times' sake.'

'Maybe.' He was silent for a few moments. 'But now I've had time to digest this, I think it's probably because I married you. You know what she's done, don't you?'

'I'm not sure,' Rose said. 'I can't seem to take it in.'

'She has set us up for life. You would never take anything from her when she was alive, so she has provided for you now.'

Rose tipped her head back and grinned. 'Sixty per cent means you'll be the boss. Do you like that idea?'

'Oh, yes, it's an exciting challenge.' He hugged her in delight, ignoring the curious stares of people in the street. 'What are you going to do with your money?'

'I'm going to set up a school for people who can't read or write,' she told him excitedly. 'I've always wanted to do something like that.'

Bill felt as if someone had just thrown a bucket of cold water over him. He stopped and turned her towards him. 'Rose, you're working yourself silly already. How are you going to find the time to do something like that?'

'Oh, I'll manage it.'

He saw the gleam in her eyes and sighed inwardly. As it was he hardly saw her. She was so involved in her work that she was growing away from him, and her family. Her passion for reform had become an obsession, and he was worried. He had known that this wouldn't be an easy marriage, but now he was starting to wonder if it stood a chance of surviving. Rose showed no sign of settling down and having the family he so badly wanted. He'd gambled everything on her becoming mellow in a happy relationship, but quite the opposite was happening.

They started walking again. What was the use of agonizing over it? he thought. He had enormous respect for what she was trying to do, and he loved her.

'You've gone very quiet. Don't you think it's a good idea?'

'Yes, I do, and I'm sure Lady Gresham would approve.' He stopped again. 'But what about us, Rose? We're wealthy now, and you don't need to drive yourself like you're doing. I was hoping that after we'd been married a year, you'd cut down on your work, or even give it up.'

'I can't do that,' she protested.

Bill turned and walked them back to his car. He wouldn't get anywhere with her today – he could see that she was already planning her school. He was going to have to find another way to make her ease up, or they would drift even further apart.

The next day Rose was up early. Sir George had lent her some money until her grandmother's estate was settled and she was eager to start on her school. The cobbler's next door to her office was empty and would be ideal for the purpose. The first thing she needed to do was see the owners and strike a good deal for it with them. Five thousand pounds was a lot of money, but there would be renovations to do, teachers to pay, and other expenses she hadn't even thought of yet.

'Morning, my darling.' Bill kissed her lingeringly. 'You were up early.'

'I've got a lot to do today.' She cast him a quick, embarrassed glance and felt herself colour as she remembered last night. He had never made love to her like that before. She had always known he was a passionate man but, good Lord . . .!

She pushed away the embarrassing memories. He had caught her at a vulnerable moment, that was all.

'I'll drive you, if you're ready,' he suggested, putting his coat on.

'Thanks.' She gulped her tea and grabbed her bag. 'You going into the building firm today?' she asked, as they got into the car.

'No, I'll give them a few hours to get used to the idea of a new chairman, then call a board meeting for tomorrow.'

He dropped her off at her office, and she set straight to work. By the end of the morning, and after a lot of haggling, she had persuaded the shop-owner to let her have it at a reduced rent. She had also engaged three unemployed ex-servicemen, two to do the decorating and one to see about advertising, which would have to be done mostly by word of mouth: the people she was trying to attract wouldn't be able to read. All she had to do now was find teachers.

'You got enough men?' Josh asked, when she stopped long enough for him to catch her. 'I know dozens who are desperate for work.'

'I don't need more at the moment, unless they're teachers or have had a good education.'

He shook his head sadly. 'Most of the poor devils

are labourers with little proper education.' He paused. 'Actually, there's one man who had a secondary-school education, but he's disabled. Lost a foot and his left arm in the battle of the Somme.'

'Send him along to see me,' she said. 'If he can teach others to read and write, he's got the job.'

'I'll go straight away.' Josh gave her a hug.

Rose pushed him off, laughing. 'Go and get the man and ask if there's anyone else.'

Later he returned with three men, all of whom had lost limbs. Her smile was warm as they stood there looking hopeful. 'Thank you for coming. Josh has told you what I require?'

'Yes, Mrs Freeman. I'm Peter,' one introduced himself, 'and this is Andy and that's Jim. We've all had a secondary education and would be grateful for something useful to do.'

Rose had only intended to offer one pound five shillings a week, but looking at these poor devils . . . What the hell! 'The hours will be from nine to six, Monday to Friday, and I will pay each of you two pounds a week.' She thought one man was going to cry, but he pulled himself together. 'Is that agreeable to you?'

'Yes, Mrs Freeman,' they said in unison.

'Good. I hope to be up and running within a week.' She went to her bag and handed them each two pounds. 'I'll pay you a week in advance.'

They were speechless with gratitude.

With the question of teachers settled, she took Josh with her to a shop and bought armfuls of books suitable for beginners, a few more advanced ones, pencils and notebooks. They stacked them in one of the back rooms, and went to put the kettle on.

A lot had been accomplished in a day.

'This is a good thing you're doing.' Josh sat down and rested his elbows on his knees. 'But I haven't asked you if you're going to charge for these lessons?'

'Certainly not!' Rose was horrified. 'My grandmother left me the money to spend as I wish, and if I'm careful it should last a long time. The education system is improving slowly, but this generation needs help.'

Josh sat up straight again. 'Can I send some of the ex-servicemen to you? They'd stand a better chance of getting a job if they could read and write.'

'They're exactly the people the school is aiming to help.'

'It was damned generous of Lady Gresham to leave me that money so I can carry on with *my* work,' Josh remarked. 'She also set up a trust fund so that the two houses can be kept open.'

'She's thought of everyone.'

'I expect she's watching us now to see we use the money wisely.' Josh chuckled.

'I don't doubt it.' Rose felt her throat tighten as she tried to visualize her grandmother looking down on them, urging them on. 'I'm going to call it the Lavinia School.'

'Sounds appropriate.' Josh yawned. 'And I've had enough for one day. See you tomorrow.'

Rose hadn't finished: her next stop was Harold's. Now that he'd finished his book, this was just the challenge he needed.

She would never have time to run this school herself.

Harold was pleased to see her, and jumped at the chance to teach again. They spent a long time in discussion, and when Rose looked at the clock, she gasped. 'Oh, Lord, I've missed my train to Roehampton – I'll have to stay at the flat tonight.'

'Do you want to telephone Bill?' Harold asked.

'No, he'll realize I couldn't get back.' Rose grabbed her coat and rushed to the door. 'If I don't hurry I'll miss the bus to Kensington, too.'

It was a long journey as some of the buses had been cancelled, and by the time Rose reached the flat it was nearly twelve o'clock. As she walked in the lights were on and there was a lovely smell of cooking.

'At last!' Bill didn't kiss her, which was unusual, but she was too tired to mention it.

'I expect you're hungry.'

'Ravenous, but what are you doing here?'

'Harold telephoned and told me you were staying at the flat tonight, so I came back.'

'You drove all the way back to London?' she asked, astonished. 'What on earth for?'

'I see little enough of you,' he told her sharply, 'and I'm not going to let you stay here without me.'

'It's only for one night.'

'Why didn't you let me know what you were doing?' he demanded.

'I was too busy, and I didn't know I was going to be so late.' What was the matter with him?

He turned away and started to dish up the meal.

★

Rose hardly remembered getting into bed and she must have been asleep as soon as she closed her eyes, but it wasn't a restful sleep. She was running down a long passage towards a door that was standing wide open, and then, just as she reached it, it slammed in her face. She awoke with a start and stared into the darkness, reliving the dream. She had an uneasy feeling that she had been the cause of the door closing.

She turned over and dismissed it. She was being silly, it had only been a dream.

The next morning Bill seemed to be his normal, affable self, and she was relieved. It was unlike him to be ratty.

'Is that a new suit?' she asked, seeing him dressed in a smart dark grey three-piece.

'Yes, what do you think? Do I look like the chairman?'

'Oh, of course, you've got your board meeting today.' Rose felt a surge of pride and love as she looked at her handsome husband. He wouldn't have any trouble at the meeting today: he had a quiet air of command, and knew how to handle himself in public. He was a good man and she was lucky to be married to him.

Everything was in full swing when Rose arrived at the office. At ten when they stopped for tea, her mind went back to Bill. He would handle the situation in his usual calm, authoritative way. She need not be concerned about him, she thought.

Then she plunged back into her work again.

37

Bill hesitated outside the boardroom, straightened to his full height, opened the door and strode in. His years of command in the navy hadn't been wasted, he realized, when he saw them all jump to their feet.

For the next two hours he listened, studied facts and figures, discussed the work being undertaken, then went into the financial position of the business. It was only when he had all the information that he understood what Lady Gresham had given him. This was a highly successful business and he was now a wealthy man.

After two hours he drove away elated. Everything had gone better than he had expected, and he had encountered no hostility. He started to whistle. He would arrange something special for himself and Rose. They hadn't had a holiday, so he would take her somewhere peaceful, she would like that.

After her grandmother's funeral, she had been different, more open and affectionate. Their lovemaking that night had been incredible – she had responded with passion, which she hardly ever did. He was never denied her body, she gave it willingly enough, but he wanted more: he wanted her love, and he wasn't getting it. She rarely made a spontaneous gesture of affection towards him, he always had to make the first move, and he longed for her to turn to him in the night.

He sighed. Apart from the day of the funeral when

she had been vulnerable, she never touched him. The rape had left scars, but he could handle that, so why was he fretting about it now? She had married him and he should be content.

But he wasn't! She was so absorbed in her work that she appeared to forget she had a husband who would worry if she didn't come home at night, and that was hard to take. If it hadn't been for Harold, he would never have known where she was last night. When she had eventually come in she had chatted away about the school as if that was all that mattered to her, and never once asked what he had been doing. She was taking him for granted, and that frightened him. He didn't want to lose her.

A week away from work would be a good idea. They needed time to be together, to talk, and discuss their future. Perhaps he would bring up the subject of children.

When he arrived at the shop Rose was turning into the school, she was disappearing up the stairs, giving orders. He waited until she came down, and caught her arm as she was about to walk past him.

'Oh, hello.' She gave him a distracted smile. 'I didn't see you there.'

'Are you coming home tonight, or staying at the flat?' he asked, as levelly as his irritation would allow.

'I don't know yet. It depends how the day goes.'

'That isn't good enough,' he told her sternly.

She sighed. 'What's the time now?'

'Four o'clock.'

'I'll come home, but I might be late.'

She tried to walk away, but he tightened his grip. 'How late?'

'I don't know. You can see how busy I am.'

'Be home by eight at the latest,' he told her quietly, 'or I shall be very angry.'

She laughed. 'You never get angry. Now, go away and let me get on.' She gave him a quick peck on the cheek and hurried off.

He walked out and closed the door behind him. He had always known she was obsessive, but she was getting worse. She seemed even more driven.

'Josh!' Rose called. 'If anyone wants me, I'll be at the council offices for about an hour.'

'Poor sods,' she heard him mutter, as she opened the door.

She glared at him. 'Don't be sorry for them, they need to be shaken until their teeth rattle.'

'And you're just the one to do it, Rose. Go to it.'

With nothing more than a grunt of agreement, she was out of the door and running up the street to catch the bus.

She caught the chairman and two councillors just as they were going into a meeting. She ignored their groans of despair and pitched into them. 'Is the question of slum clearance on your agenda for today?'

'It's always on our agenda,' the chairman told her drily. 'You never let us forget it.'

'Well, I can't see any evidence of you doing anything about it.'

'The cost . . .' one of the councillors muttered, but she stopped him with a ferocious stare.

'I've heard that one too many times. Now, if you'll just listen to me . . .'

The chairman looked at his pocket watch. 'We're late for our meeting.'

As they walked away she swore furiously under her breath. As far back as 1890 the Housing of the Working Classes Act had given local councils the power to close insanitary houses and build new ones with the proceeds of the local rates. Since then, there had been several acts along the same lines, the most recent last year. The Wheatley Act had increased the state subsidy for houses built for rent at a controlled level. Provision had also been made for the expansion of the building trades.

Rose made her way back to the office, deep in thought. Some progress had been made, but not enough.

'Harold!' she exclaimed in surprise, as she walked in. 'What are you doing here?'

'I came to see how you're getting on. I wondered if you'd like me to have a word with your new teachers, perhaps give them a few tips about teaching people to read.'

'Oh, would you? I'm sure they'd be grateful for your advice.' Rose was enthusiastic about his offer: she knew she needed all the help she could get.

Josh got to his feet. 'I'll go and fetch them, shall I?'

'Yes, please.' When he had gone she made a pot of tea for herself and Harold.

'How did your encounter go at the council offices?' he asked, the corners of his mouth twitching.

'The same as usual,' she grumbled. 'I don't know how to get through to them. They could find the money if they reviewed their budget and made some adjustments.'

'Hmm. Why don't you stand as a candidate in the next elections? They're only two months away.'

Rose stared at him in astonishment.

'Don't look at me like that,' he chided. 'You're just the person for the job. They need people with drive and ideas. A lot of them have been councillors for years and are set in their ways. I'd be willing to sponsor you.'

'Good heavens! Why – why didn't I think of that?' she stammered. 'But I wouldn't stand a chance.'

'Yes, you would. Everyone around here knows you and would vote for you. I'll get the papers for you to complete, shall I?' His eyes were shining with excitement.

'Yes, why not? It would be worth a try. Even if I don't get elected, I could stir things up a bit.' She grinned.

He patted her hand. 'Good girl. Now I'll go to the baker's and get some buns for our new teachers to eat with their tea.'

Rose arrived home just before eight, and Bill was pleased to see she had taken notice of what he had said. He took her in his arms and kissed her, but she seemed preoccupied.

'Hungry?' he asked.

'I had something before I caught the train. I think I'll go and have a bath.'

'Come and sit down for a while. I want to talk to you.' He had to speak with determination to gain her attention.

'All right,' she agreed. 'What do you want to talk about?'

He bit back a weary sigh. 'Don't you want to know how I got on today? Your grandmother's bequest is for your benefit too.'

'Oh!' Rose clapped her hand over her mouth. 'I'm so

404

sorry, I forgot about the board meeting. I've got such a lot on my mind. Tell me about it.'

When he had finished his story, she gave a grunt of satisfaction. 'I knew you'd be all right. You might be quiet, but there's an air of command about you.'

'Is that a compliment?' he asked quizzically.

'Of course it is. I know I don't have to concern myself with the business because you're more than capable of dealing with it.' She started to stand up, but he stopped her.

'I haven't finished yet.' He was going to have to be firm with her.

She sat down again and waited.

'I've arranged for us to take a holiday.'

'Holiday?' She didn't look pleased. 'What on earth for?'

'Rose,' he said patiently, 'we've been married for over a year and all we've done is work. We need a break.'

'I can't. I've got too much to do. When did you think we could possibly go away?'

'In two weeks' time. The weather's warming up and – '

'It's out of the question. Perhaps next year.'

He took her by the shoulders and turned her to face him. 'I want us to spend some time together without work always getting in the way. We need to talk about the future,' he told her earnestly.

Rose turned away impatiently. 'I can't go, especially now. There's the school to get going, I've got a court case coming up, and the local elections are only two months away.'

The word 'election' caught his attention. 'What are you talking about?'

'The borough council elections. I'm going to stand as a candidate.'

He surged to his feet and glared at her. 'How do you think you can fit that in? You're already working non-stop!'

'You said you didn't mind me working,' she retaliated.

'I was referring to your work as a solicitor, but ever since we married you've been taking on more and more. Damn it, Rose, I hardly ever see you now – what's it going to be like if you become a councillor?'

'But it's the only way,' she explained. 'If I get elected, they're going to have to listen to me.'

'And what about us?' he asked, controlling himself with difficulty. 'Do you ever give a thought to what I want out of life?'

She looked taken aback. 'Of course I do.'

'No, you don't. You've got everything you want from our marriage, and given me precious little.'

'Well, it was your idea, remember? And I never deny – '

'No, you don't. You give me your body because you feel it's your duty, that's all.'

'Well, isn't that what you wanted?' Rose looked puzzled.

For the first time in his life he was ready to explode with fury. 'There's more to it than that,' he grated, through clenched teeth. 'I want . . . need,' he corrected, 'some indication that you care for me, some response, but you lie in my arms like a rag doll.'

'I don't!'

'Most of the time you do,' he told her plainly. 'I can count on one hand the times you have shown any interest in our lovemaking. I want some affection, a family – '

Rose shot to her feet. 'I told you I didn't want children for a while.'

'You said a year or so. I've respected your wishes and been careful, but we should start thinking about it now.'

'Don't you dare make me pregnant!' she threatened. 'I'll never forgive you if you do.'

'And you believe I'd do that?' He felt as if she'd hit him. He hadn't thought she could distrust him like this. The blinkers were certainly being torn from his eyes. 'Don't you know that I would never put you in that position without your agreement?'

When she didn't answer, he swore fluently under his breath. 'Is that your opinion of me, after all this time? Don't you know me better than that?'

'Of course I do, but you're making a fuss about nothing,' she told him. 'I've explained that it isn't possible at the moment. What's the matter with you tonight? You've always been so reasonable and understanding.'

'Yes,' he said sadly, 'and that's my mistake. And as to what is the matter with me – well, you are shutting me out of your life and I don't like it.'

'Of course I'm not.'

He held his hand up. 'Don't deny it. When you have a minute or two to spare some time, think about it.'

'All right, I'll admit I've been preoccupied lately, but you're busy with your work too.' Rose made an impatient gesture with her hands. 'I don't know what on earth has got into you.'

'No, you don't, do you? And that is what's so sad.'

'Oh, this is silly.' She started to leave the room.

'Don't take me for granted,' he warned, with an edge of steel in his voice. 'There is a limit to my patience.'

38

The next few weeks disappeared in a flurry of activity. The school was open, and six ex-servicemen had come on the first day. Rose had knocked on every door in Garrett Street and persuaded two women and one man to come for lessons. The third of the original ex-servicemen, who was spreading the word, had found another four people. It was going to be a success, she was sure of it.

In a court case last week, a woman had been granted a divorce on the grounds of her husband's adultery, and given custody of the children because of the man's brutality. Things didn't change, Rose thought wearily. Thank God she didn't have a violent husband.

Rose massaged between her eyes. Another headache. They were becoming more frequent, and she knew that her punishing workload was part of the problem. But she suspected it was more due to Bill's coolness towards her, and she couldn't blame him. Since their argument about the holiday and starting a family, he had been distant with her. She had tried to involve him in the election campaign, but he had shown no interest at all.

'Rose,' Harold called cheerfully, 'time to get to the town hall. Hope you've got your speech ready.'

She tapped her head. 'It's all in here.'

'Come on, then.' He rubbed his hands in gleeful anticipation. 'Let's get things rolling.'

The place was packed and she recognized many of the

people sitting there. Harold had been right: they knew her, and wanted to hear what she had to say.

She was a good, confident speaker – a talent she hadn't known she possessed – and she handled the many interruptions with skill and humour. The audience liked that and applauded loudly when she had finished.

'Told you, didn't I?' Harold grinned. 'You've got another meeting at the church hall tonight, then one on Saturday afternoon.'

'This is hard work,' she complained, as her headache intensified.

'I never said it would be easy,' Harold reminded her.

'Oh, don't take any notice of me. It's just this damned bad head. If I can only get rid of it, I'll be back to normal.'

'Bring Bill along to some of the meetings,' Harold suggested. 'His presence might persuade some of the more affluent among them to vote for you.'

'He's very busy.'

Harold gave her a searching look. 'Don't shut him out, involve him in what you're doing. He'd be a strong man to have at your side.'

Sadness swept through Rose. Ever since they had married, he had been there, listening to her plans and calming her down when things got difficult. But that had been in the beginning – they hadn't had much time to talk just lately.

Harold caught hold of her chin and turned her face towards him. She squinted in pain. 'Why don't you go to the flat and get a couple of hours' sleep?'

'I think I'll have to.'

'Off you go, then. I'll just pop back and see that

everything's going all right at the school.' He marched up the road with a spring in his step.

On the bus her head was thumping so hard that she felt desperate to lie down in a dark room. It would be quiet at the flat: Bill wouldn't be there at this time of the day.

Strong hands were pulling her into a sitting position.

'Rose! What's the matter?'

She opened one eye, expecting the light to hurt, but there was only a dull ache now, so she opened the other . . . carefully.

Bill was looking down at her with a deep frown of concern.

'I had a bad head and had to sleep for a couple of hours,' she explained, and struggled to get out of bed.

He eased her back. 'Stay there and I'll make you some tea.'

'You don't have to,' she told him hastily. He didn't look too pleased to see her. 'My head's better now, and I've got to get to my next meeting.'

'Electioneering, are you?'

She nodded, worried by his grim expression. 'Would . . . would you like to come? It's quite fun,' she told him. She hated the tension between them.

'I've got a client to see this evening.'

'Oh, perhaps another time.' Her disappointment at his refusal, yet again, was crushing, but she had set out on this course of action and would see it through. Harold was right: becoming a councillor was the only way she was going to get anything done.

'You'd better stay here tonight,' he told her. 'It will

save you a train journey.' Then he walked towards the door with rolls of drawings tucked under his arm.

She couldn't let him go like that. 'Bill.'

He looked back.

It was time to be honest. 'I don't like us being angry with each other.'

'Neither do I.' He dropped the papers, stepped forward, took her into his arms and kissed her with more than a hint of desperation. Then he picked up his things again and strode out of the room.

Funny . . . her headache had vanished.

Her election address that evening was a roaring success, and she enjoyed every minute of the boisterous meeting, feeling brighter than she had all week. At one point she'd rolled up her sleeves, jumped off the platform and threatened one trouble-maker with instant destruction, much to the delight of the rest of the audience.

By the time it was over it was late, and she was glad she didn't have to go back to Roehampton. That afternoon Harold had bought himself a car, so he drove her to the flat. When she crawled into bed, she was exhausted. One day she would ease up, she promised herself.

Something woke her, and for a moment she couldn't think what it was. Then she felt Bill's warmth beside her and smiled into the darkness. She reached out and put on the light. It was time they started to talk to each other properly again.

He was lying with his hands beneath his head and an unreadable expression on his face. He wasn't going to make it easy for her.

'I'm sorry I'm so difficult to live with. Can you forgive me?'

He nodded.

'Thank you.' She went to turn out the light.

'Leave it on.'

'Why?'

'I want to look at you.'

'Oh.' Rose pulled a face.

She settled down again. He hadn't moved, which was unusual, because whenever they were in bed together he couldn't keep his hands off her. She glanced across at him. He was staring up at the ceiling. She couldn't stand his silence.

'Er . . . do you want . . .? You know . . .' God! She was becoming a gibbering idiot. Not long ago she had been arguing with confidence and fluency, but now she couldn't even string three words together.

'Say it, Rose.'

Why did she find this so difficult to talk about? They were man and wife, for heaven's sake! She took a deep breath. 'Do you want to make love?'

'There,' he smiled, 'that wasn't so hard, was it?'

'Don't make me angry with you again,' she snapped, rattled. She propped herself up on one elbow. 'You know I find it hard to talk about.'

He raised an eyebrow in query.

'Sex!' she shouted at him. 'There! Are you satisfied now?'

'Far from it,' he replied, with a glint of mischief in his eyes.

'What are you waiting for then?'

'I'm waiting for you to make love to me,' he told her calmly.

Rose looked at him suspiciously. 'What are you up to?'

'I'm tired of making the moves. It's time you learned to take the initiative.'

'Rag dolls don't know how to,' she threw at him, and regretted it when she saw him wince. Would she never learn to curb her sharp tongue? 'I'm sorry. I shouldn't have said that.'

'No, my love. *I* shouldn't have said that.'

She fiddled with the sheet. 'You had every right. I know I'm no good in that department.'

'That isn't true,' he told her seriously. 'It's just that you've got your emotions under such tight control that you can't relax enough to respond. On the odd occasion when you have let go you've been . . . well . . . All you need is a little gentle tuition.'

He winked and she laughed.

'I never knew you were a liar, Mr Freeman.'

'It's the truth.' He removed one hand to make a cross over his heart, then resumed his position again. 'Come on, I'm waiting.'

'What for?'

His sigh was dramatic. 'You to make love to me.'

'You're not serious, are you?' She was scandalized. 'Women don't carry on like that!'

'We are married, my innocent beauty, and it's quite proper for a woman to make love to her husband.'

Rose wasn't convinced, but she had already upset him enough, so perhaps . . .? 'I don't know what to do.'

'You do whatever you like.' He smiled encouragingly. 'The same things I do when I make love to you.'

She frowned. She'd always been happy with the way things were.

He removed his hands from behind his head and pulled her towards him. 'You can't touch me from over there, and I've decided to teach you the art of lovemaking.'

'Well, if learning this art means I've got to do everything, then you can forget it, mate.' She turned away. He'd never acted strange like this before.

'I'll guide you,' he coaxed.

Rose cast him a suspicious glance.

'Come on. It's easy, you sit astride me . . .'

'You're joking?' She was shocked.

He shook his head and continued to draw her forward.

She slipped one leg tentatively across his body, then stopped, sat up and folded her arms mutinously. 'I can't. I'm sorry, I just can't do that.'

He groaned and pulled her down in the bed, then rolled over until he was looking into her face. 'A man could die of frustration waiting for you to make your mind up.'

Bill stood at the back of the hall, praying that Rose wouldn't be elected, but he had a nasty feeling he was hoping in vain. Since their reconciliation he had attended a few of her meetings and had to admit that she was good. She spoke with conviction and fire, and the voters had come to believe she was their salvation.

Over the last few weeks she had tried to be more considerate and responsive, but he knew that she was wrapped up in her fight for justice. At least she had more or less handed over the running of the school to Harold. He sighed inwardly. Being married to Rose was like trying to ride out a force nine gale in a rowing boat, but he still loved her desperately – and knew he always would. And as much as he wanted her to lose this contest, when he'd listened to her impassioned speeches over the last few weeks, he had been proud of her.

Harold, Grace, John, Josh and Mary came up to him as soon as they saw him at the back.

'Our Rose is going to win,' Josh told him, smiling excitedly.

Harold was almost bursting with pride. 'Of course she is.'

John said nothing, but Grace squeezed Bill's arm and smiled up at him. 'Everything will be all right,' she told him. 'Rose has to get this out of her system. You've always known that, Bill.'

He gave a tight smile. 'I know, but it's more difficult than I anticipated. I always thought I had enough patience to cope but I'm not so sure now.'

Grace looked up at him sadly. 'Rose might not admit or show it, but she needs you, Bill. You and her family are the stabilizing forces in her life, and if she loses any part of that, I dread to think what will happen to her.'

John, who had been talking to Harold and Josh, turned to Bill. 'I always knew Rose was special, but I never dreamed that the scruffy girl of eleven who came to me for lessons would turn out like this.' He looked at her on the stage and shook his head in amazement. 'She's magnificent, isn't she, Bill?'

Bill nodded. That was something he had never denied. Rose was indeed *special*, but was she going to remain his?

A booming voice from the platform broke through his troubled thoughts.

The man was announcing the results, and Bill's heart sank as his hopes for a normal family life, and children, crumbled at his feet.

She had won.

39

December 1925

Rose tore into the house. 'I'm sorry I'm late.' Then she looked around at the festive decorations. 'Oh, this is lovely.'

'Where have you been?' Annie asked. 'You promised to come shopping and help decorate the tree.'

Rose saw the disappointment in her sister's face and felt awful. Then she glanced at Bill. He was angry, and had every right to be, she acknowledged. This was Christmas Eve and she had assured her family that she wouldn't work this afternoon – but something had come up and she couldn't ignore it. As the newly elected chairman of the council, she had called an extra meeting, much to everyone's annoyance, but swift action had been essential.

'We had to have a special meeting,' she started to explain. 'It's very ex – '

'We are not going to have any business talk,' Bill interrupted. 'Let's forget the rest of the world for a few days, shall we?'

There was a chorus of agreement from the family, so Rose kept quiet, although she was bursting to tell them the news. If that was the way they wanted it, she would keep it to herself. And perhaps it was for the best: there wasn't anything definite yet. But she would have loved to share this unexpected development with them.

'Perhaps we can have dinner now you've finally arrived,' her mother scolded. 'Everyone's starving waiting for you.'

'Why didn't you go ahead without me?' It looked as if they were all cross with her.

'Because it's Christmas Eve and we wanted to sit down together,' Annie explained, in a hurt voice. 'You're so busy these days, we hardly ever see you.'

She didn't miss the note of sadness in her sister's voice, or the look of censure on Bill's face. They would understand if they'd only let her explain, but she had clearly upset everyone, and they were not in the mood to listen to excuses, however good.

'Well, I'm here now, and I've got two days off.' She sat down at the table.

'Two?' Bill looked up sharply. 'I thought you were going to take four.'

Oh, Lord, more trouble. 'I can't.'

'What are you up to, my girl?' Her mother looked furious. 'You promised you'd forget work for a while and spend the holiday with us. We've got Grace, John, Harold, Josh, Mary and your father coming on the twenty-seventh. You must be here!'

Rose felt worse. She had even forgotten that. 'What time are they arriving?'

'Before lunch. And don't think you can slope off in the morning, because we know only too well that that will be the last we see of you,' Marj was evidently exasperated with her eldest daughter.

Annie glared at her mother. 'Don't shout at Rosie like that. She's doing her best.'

Rose looked down at the beautifully decorated table.

How could her sister continue to defend her when all she ever did these days was let everyone down? 'I'll stay at home that day.' It was the only concession she could make.

Annie smiled broadly, sat on the chair next to her sister and touched her hand. 'It'll be nice to have you here for a while.'

Rose looked at Annie's happy face, then round at everyone else. Her young sister was the only one who seemed to have forgiven her. Suddenly she felt ashamed of missing the shopping trip. 'Where did you go shopping?' she asked.

'Bill took us to Richmond. There were some lovely shops, you would have enjoyed it,' her sister said wistfully.

'I'm sure I would. Perhaps we can go in the New Year.'

'Don't make promises you can't or won't keep,' Bill told her pointedly.

Annie jumped to her defence again. 'She doesn't mean to forget, she's just got too much on her mind. Don't be angry with her, Bill. It's Christmas, so can't we forget it and be happy together?'

He nodded, then smiled for the first time. 'You're quite right, but don't take your eyes off her or she'll disappear again,' he teased.

'I won't.' Annie laughed and held on to her sister's arm.

The atmosphere lifted considerably and Rose felt herself relax. When did her sister drop 'Uncle'? I suppose she feels too grown-up for that now, she thought. The years were flying by. And they were right: she was working too hard. But she couldn't ease up yet.

It was a lively evening, with all the family in high

spirits, and Rose was pleased to see that the earlier unpleasantness had been forgotten. She gazed at each of her family in turn. What a difference in them since she had married Bill! The last person she studied was her husband, and saw with a shock that he had lost weight and looked very tired. Why hadn't she noticed before?

They put the last touches to the tree, and when she saw the parcels being put around it, she galloped upstairs: she hadn't wrapped her presents yet.

'You did find time to buy some presents, then,' Bill remarked drily, as he followed her into the room a couple of minutes later.

'Yes, I got them two weeks ago.' She hastily pushed his out of the way so he couldn't see it.

'Here, let me give you a hand.' He sorted through the modest gifts and frowned. 'You could have bought better things than this.'

'I couldn't afford to spend more.' Rose tied a lopsided bow, but it was good enough, she decided. Annie was the artistic one, not her.

'What do you mean?'

She looked up and found him frowning at her. Now what had she done?

'Why couldn't you afford to spend more? I give you a good allowance every week.'

'Oh, I couldn't use that. That's only for the house and food.'

He looked as if he couldn't believe what he was hearing. 'But that would never take all the money, surely?'

'Oh, no, you give me far too much. Anything I don't use is in the drawer over there. You can have it back, if you want.' Rose continued wrapping her presents.

Without saying a word, he walked over to the dressing-table, took a small cardboard box out of the drawer and opened it. 'My God!' he muttered. 'This is full of money. Why haven't you spent it?'

'I've been earning enough to pay my own way. That's yours.'

Bill sat next to her on the bed and took her hands. 'When will you realize that what we have we share? This money is for you to spend in any way you like.'

'But it's rather a lot, and I don't need it.'

He shook his head in disbelief. 'Rose, your grand-mother left us a thriving business. There's no need for you to scrimp and save. We are wealthy. You haven't taken the slightest notice of how we've prospered, have you?'

She shrugged.

'You really must try to leave Garrett Street behind. Those days are over,' he told her firmly.

'Not for the people who still live there,' she replied hotly. 'I see them, and dozens more like them, every day.'

'I know. But you are out of it now, and when I give you money, I want you to spend it on yourself or your family. Do you understand?'

Rose picked up the scarf she had bought at the market for her mother. What a blind fool she was. Her family had moved on, but she was still living in the past. In her daily life she confronted poverty all the time, and it still filled her mind. 'It's too late to get anything else. Do you think my presents aren't good enough?'

'No,' he assured her hastily. 'They'll love them because they come from you, but try to remember in future that you don't have to be careful with money any more.'

'I'll try.' She gave him a hesitant smile, but he didn't return it. Feeling the need to explain what had happened today, she tried again. 'I'm sorry I was late but something unexpected cropped up.'

His mouth set in a grim line. 'It always does.'

Her spirits sagged. He was still cross with her. 'I can explain.'

'I don't think anything can excuse you breaking your promises at this time of year. Your mother and Annie were bitterly disappointed.'

Rose watched him stand up and leave the room. I've got the best excuse in the world, she wanted to shout, but in the silence of the room, she lowered her head. She had wanted to share the exciting news, but what was the use? They didn't care.

She felt so alone.

Then she surged to her feet. What was the matter with her? She had always been alone. From the time she could talk, no one had understood her, except Annie perhaps. It had never bothered her before, so why should she fret about it now? She had set out to do something and she wouldn't rest until it was done. If she upset a few people on the way that was sad, but the demon driving her wouldn't let her give up.

She was just about to go downstairs, when Annie came tearing up.

'We're going to the midnight service,' she announced. 'Come on.'

Rose listened to the Christmas story being read in the beautiful language of the King James version of the Bible, and realized with sadness that she hadn't opened her own copy for some time.

Her thoughts wandered back to the day she had won it for being top of the school, and the many happy hours she had spent trying to grasp the meaning of the stories and Psalms. She must get it out again, because she had found great comfort in the words when her world had been in turmoil as a child. Perhaps it would help now, in this time of great change and tension in her life?

The next morning, as everyone was opening their presents, Bill laughed at their pleasure, and was pleased to see that Rose's gifts were received with equal enthusiasm. The leather case she had bought him would be useful, and he was pleased she had remembered to get something for everyone.

The floor was littered with paper and empty boxes and he smiled to himself, cherishing the moment. He loved this family, and he yearned for children of his own. After all, he wasn't getting any younger.

'Oh!' Rose gasped, and looked at him wide-eyed.

He went and stooped down in front of her. 'Do you like it?'

'It's beautiful, but it must have cost a fortune.'

He took the ruby and diamond ring out of the box and slipped it on to her left hand. Then he whispered in her ear, 'Happy second wedding anniversary, darling.'

Rose kissed his cheek, relieved that she'd had the sense to buy a special card for him. 'Thank you. I love it.'

He stood up and turned to face everyone. 'Rose and I have a special gift to hand out now,' he announced, taking an envelope out of his pocket and handing it to Marj and Wally.

'I don't understand what it means,' Marj said, after looking at the papers.

Wally seemed overcome, but eventually cleared his throat and spoke to his wife. 'Bill has given us the deeds to our house.'

'Does that mean it's ours?'

He nodded and Marj burst into tears. Then pandemonium broke out as they all surged around to thank them.

Rose was stunned at this act of selfless generosity. 'Why didn't you tell me?' she asked quietly.

'You're never around to talk to these days,' he told her, 'and when you do come home you're too tired to do anything but sleep.'

On the twenty-seventh, Grace, John, their son, Josh, Mary and Harold arrived with Rose's father. Sir George and Marj appeared at ease with each other now, the past forgotten, and he was happy to be included in the family. Rose couldn't help marvelling at the way her mother had forgiven him. Mary was proudly showing off a modest engagement ring, and Rose had never seen Josh look so happy. She was delighted that things were going so well for him.

After lunch they all sat around the fire and handed out more presents.

John stood up, looking very pleased with himself. 'I have an announcement to make. We are expecting another child in five months' time.'

After everyone had congratulated them, Rose's father

cleared his throat. 'And talking of children, I have a special gift for my daughter and her husband.' He handed Bill a large envelope tied with pink legal ribbon.

Intrigued, Rose watched Bill open it. When he didn't speak, she leaned forward to look at the papers, then she took them out of Bill's hand and jumped up. 'You can't do this!' she exploded.

'Yes, I can. You are my daughter and it's all legal. And there isn't a thing you can do about it.'

'What is it?' Harold was bursting with curiosity.

'I have made Rose my heir. The Gresham blood will continue through her, with my estate going to her eldest son.'

'Will you stop pacing up and down like an enraged lioness?' Bill demanded, when they were alone later that night.

Rose spun round. 'What the hell do you expect me to do? How dare he do this to me?'

'He's only made you his heir.'

'Only!' she raged. 'If we hadn't had visitors I'd have wrung his bloody neck.'

Bill sighed and looked up at the ceiling. 'You are his daughter, the only one left with Gresham blood. What he's done is right and sensible.'

'Don't you talk to me about what's right! I know you're on his side,' she shouted, completely out of control now. 'I bet you just loved that bit about our *eldest son* inheriting the estate. If the pair of you think you can put pressure on me . . .'

Bill stepped forward, but she stood her ground, too furious to curb her words.

'You're lucky I'm not a violent man,' he ground out, between clenched teeth. 'If you're accusing me of talking about our private life, then you're wrong. Our disagreement about having children is between us,' he continued. 'I have never discussed it with anyone else.'

'Huh!' She snorted.

'All right. Let's get this out into the open, shall we?' He gripped her arms. 'When we married you promised to have children in a year or so. Well, it's two years now, so tell me what you intend to do about it.'

'I don't want any!' she shouted. 'I've got too much to do to tie myself down to squalling brats.'

He looked at her for a few moments. 'Does this mean you'll never change your mind?'

'I don't think so. Bill, I'm just starting to get somewhere, but it might still take me years.'

'You can't leave Garrett Street, can you?' He stepped away from her and ran a hand tiredly over his eyes.

Rose started to pace again. 'I won't be able to let go of Garrett Street until I see it flattened. Do you know what it was like living with the dirt, vermin, violence, the life-sapping fight to find enough food, and the constant threat of being thrown into the street if you fell behind with the rent?' She shuddered. 'I hated that place, and I still do.'

'I saw it many times – '

'Yes,' she interrupted, before he could finish, 'but you could walk away, back to your comfortable, clean home. We couldn't escape the squalor, and neither can the poor buggers still living there.'

Rose held up her hand when he started to speak.

427

'Don't bother with meaningless words,' she growled. 'You wouldn't understand, not in a million years.'

'I never realized what a low opinion you had of me.' He spoke so quietly that the words were hardly audible. Then he walked over to the wardrobe, pulled out a couple of cases, threw them on to the bed and piled his clothes into them. 'A marriage without respect is dead. You want to be free of all family responsibilities, so from this moment you are.'

'Don't be silly!'

He didn't stop what he was doing. 'For the first time since I met you I'm being sensible. You are obsessed with your work, and I have been obsessed with you, making excuses for you all the time, but not any more. John told me once that you would destroy anyone who loved you, but I'm getting out before that happens to me.'

'John was talking rubbish, and so are you!'

Rose watched as he closed the cases. She had gone too far this time, she knew. 'I didn't mean to be nasty to you. I was angry.' It was feeble and she knew it.

'You always are, and I've come to the end of my patience.'

'Are you going to the flat?' She was frightened now. She'd never seen this shuttered expression on his face before.

'I've closed the office and no longer rent the flat.'

'Why didn't you tell me?'

'The changes I've made are because of increased business. Those premises are no longer adequate, and I would have told you if you'd been here long enough for us to talk.'

'Oh, we're back to that, are we?'

'You don't think it's a valid point?'

'This is ridiculous!' she shouted, as he walked towards the door.

He stopped and looked back over his shoulder. 'Rid yourself of whatever demon is driving you, Rose. Until you do that, you're never going to be happy.'

Bill drove towards London, and it wasn't until he arrived in the apartment on the top floor of Grant Phillips that he allowed himself to think.

Her accusations had hurt so much that the pain had been almost physical. He had relied on her softening once they were married, but that hadn't happened. He had watched her obsession gather strength and intensity over the last two years and shut his eyes to it, but he couldn't do that any longer. Her unreasonable fury at her father's action had stripped away the last of his illusions, and made him see how hopeless things were. And the most disturbing thing of all was that she had broken her word to him about having children. He had never believed she would do such a thing.

He poured himself a large whisky, and sank into a chair. He still loved her, but this was tearing him apart. Until she achieved her aims, nothing would stop her. She was like a runaway train, and the only thing he could do was get out of her way until she came to her senses – if she ever did.

He downed the whisky in one gulp. For a man who didn't believe in taking reckless chances, he had been incredibly stupid.

40

January 1926

Rose felt wretched and watched the cup of tea grow cold in front of her. She shouldn't be at home wasting her time like this, but Bill had been gone for a week now, and nothing seemed worthwhile any more.

'Where's Bill?' her mother asked, as she came into Rose's kitchen.

Rose shrugged. 'He's left me.' There wasn't any point denying it: her family were going to know sooner or later.

Her mother's expression was one of profound shock. 'Oh, you stupid girl. What have you done?'

'We had a blazing row after my father made that ludicrous announcement.'

'But why?'

'Bill wants children and I said no.'

Her mother shook her head in despair. 'I knew you'd agreed to wait for a while, but I didn't think you'd refused altogether.'

'I didn't when we married. I said we'd think about it in a year or so,' she admitted, but not without shame.

'So you led him to believe that you would eventually have children.'

'I suppose so, but I've told him now that I definitely don't want any.'

Marj thumped the table, making her daughter jump. 'You've broken your word! No wonder he's left you. That's unforgivable.'

'I can't have a baby,' Rose protested. 'There's too much to do.'

'What's happened to you?' her mother asked. 'Once upon a time if you made a promise nothing on earth would have made you break it. Now it seems to mean nothing to you.' Marj stood up and stormed out of the room.

'Oh, bugger!' Rose watched the bus disappear round the corner. It would be twenty minutes before another came. She needed to talk to someone and there was only one person to whom she could turn.

She set off across the park at a fast walk, and her flesh crept as she passed the bushes she had been dragged into. She made herself slow down and walk at a natural pace. With the kind of mood she was in, if anyone tried to assault her now, she would murder them.

Her temper was volatile without Bill's calm presence in her life. She missed him. She hardly ever went back to the house any more. Everything there reminded her of him, and her family were still angry with her. She wished her grandmother was alive: she could have poured out all her troubles to her. But Lady Gresham would probably have told her she had become a self-righteous bore, and she would be right.

Rose felt completely alone. It was only lately she had realized how much her family meant to her, and how much she had depended on Bill always being there when she needed him. But it was all her own fault, and she deserved to be abandoned. Grace and John had helped and guided her from the time she'd been thrown out of school at eleven years old, so it was natural for her to turn to them at this time of crisis.

She reached the house and knocked firmly.

'Look,' she said, when John opened the door, 'I know you're cross with me, but I need help and I don't know who else to turn to.'

He stepped aside. 'You'd better come in.'

Grace smiled when she walked into the front room. 'It's lovely to see you again, Rose. We'd begun to think you'd forgotten us.'

The greeting surprised her, but it was obviously sincere. 'I didn't think you wanted to see me again.'

'We're always pleased to see you,' John told her earnestly. 'Whatever problems you and Bill are having, you are still our friends.'

Rose felt a lump form in her throat. What a fool she was to have assumed that they wouldn't want her to visit. When was she ever going to learn not to think the worst of people? 'Thank you. I didn't think I had a friend left, except Harold, and he's too busy running the school for me. I don't think he even knows when I'm around.'

John laughed. 'I saw him the other day – he's having the time of his life.'

Rose smiled when she thought about the elderly man. 'I don't know what I would have done without him. He's running the school. Two of his pupils have already found jobs now they can read and write a bit.'

'He was here yesterday and he's overjoyed about their success,' Grace said.

When they were seated, John asked, 'How can we help you?'

Rose felt embarrassed. She was not used to baring her soul. 'I just need someone to talk to, John, and I thought of you – just like when I was a kid.'

John took off his spectacles, polished them, then sat back and waited.

She told him everything, pointing out her faults, especially her temper, and after several painful minutes she ground to a stop and looked at John with anguish. 'I've got worse, I'm afraid, without Bill to calm me down. Do you know if he's all right?'

'He's fine,' John told her.

'How's Annie?' Grace asked.

'All right, I think.' Rose felt her eyes cloud with tears. Lord, what a mess she was in.

John looked at her sharply. 'You think?'

'She hasn't spoken to me for weeks.' The friendly atmosphere had made her drop her guard and, to her shame, a tear trickled down her face.

Wiping her cheek with the back of her hand, she stood up. 'I'm sorry, I'm making an exhibition of myself.'

'No, you're not.' Grace was beside her, pushing her back into the chair.

'Aren't your family talking to you?' John asked gently.

'Oh, they're civil when they see me, but I don't go home very often now. I sleep at the office.'

'Well, you must,' Grace urged, taking hold of her hand. 'If they never see you, how can the breach be healed?'

★

Rose took Grace's advice and went home the following weekend, although she was uncertain how she would be received by her family. But Grace was right; if they never saw her, how could the breach be healed? She had never been on bad terms with her mother, and this was only adding to her distress.

'I'm in here, Mum,' Rose called, when she heard her mother's voice.

Marj came into Rose's comfortable front room. 'Why didn't you tell me you were coming? I'd have lit the fires for you.' She looked round hopefully. 'You on your own?'

'Yes,' Rose said sadly. 'I haven't seen or heard from Bill since Christmas. He's left for good.'

'Are you sorry?'

She turned on her mother, her fragile temper snapping. 'That's a stupid question to ask. Of course I'm sorry! I know you all think I've got a heart of stone, but that isn't true. I miss him and I'm a stupid fool . . .'

'Calm down,' her mother said.

Rose took a deep breath. 'I've been an idiot. I've lost him, and I've got to accept that. I wish I could take back the nasty words, but it's too late. I've just got to get on with my life as best I can.'

Her mother changed the subject. 'Your father came the other day.'

'What did he want?' Rose frowned, wondering why he was calling when she wasn't here.

'He said to tell you that he's back home again and would you go and see him.'

'Where's he been?' Rose wanted to know.

Marj sighed. 'He told you he was going to Scotland for New Year.'

Rose thought for a moment, then nodded. 'Oh, yes, I'd forgotten. I'll call in some time next week.'

'Make it earlier than that. He's a lonely man, Rose, and he loves you.'

She gave her mother a speculative glance. 'You sticking up for him now?'

Marj sighed. 'We've put aside all the past, as you know, and you'd have remembered that if you turned your attention away from work now and again.'

The reprimand stung because Rose knew her mother was right. Her desire for reform had become an obsession, and that wasn't healthy. What a fool she'd been.

'I'll go and see him the first chance I get.'

'Good. Don't make enemies of everyone. Sir George only did what he felt was right.'

'I know that now. For a supposedly intelligent woman, it's taken me a long time to acknowledge my faults and face them.'

'Are you facing them?' her mother asked quietly.

'I'm trying.'

'We'll see you for lunch tomorrow, then, shall we?'

'I'd like that.'

Fences were being mended. Her relationship with Grace and John was back to normal, and her brothers, who had just arrived, were acting as if nothing had happened. That left her father and Annie. If she could gain their forgiveness, perhaps life would have some meaning again.

Wally walked in, smiled and kissed her cheek. 'It's good to see you again. You shouldn't have stayed away so long, everyone's been worried about you. How are you managing?'

'I'm bearing up.' She tried to smile.

'Bill's been to see us a few times.'

'Where's he living?' she asked urgently.

Wally shook his head. 'Somewhere in London, but we don't know the address. If I knew where Bill was, I'd tell you. I believe you're both missing each other badly, and if you ask me, the pair of you need your heads banging together.'

'I'm sure we do,' she admitted.

Rose made up her mind, there and then, to try to put things right with her father and Annie. Bill was another matter, though. She couldn't go to him, but there was one place she could leave a message for him: Grant Phillips. It would have to be a letter, and that was unsatisfactory, but it was the only option she had. She *had* to make her peace with him, even if he never wanted to see her again. The thought of spending the rest of her life without him was agony, but Rose didn't think there was any choice. Bill wasn't going to forgive her this time.

The next day after breakfast Rose wandered out into the garden. The sky was clear, the sun had a touch of warmth in it and there were little clumps of snowdrops dotted about. Spring was not far away.

Part of her dream coming true was a distinct possibility now, but one success would be only the beginning, and she doubted she had the heart to continue fighting on her own.

Lost in thought, she bent down again to pull up a weed.

'Leave that, Rosie. It's a flower.'

She forced herself to look up at Annie, and was over-joyed to see her smiling at her. 'Is it?'

'Yes. Why did you stay away so long?' Annie asked.

'I didn't think you wanted to see me.'

'I was upset, but I didn't want you to go away too.' Annie looked at her imploringly. 'Are you going to tell him you're sorry?'

'Yes. I'll send him a letter because he doesn't want to see me.'

'Oh.' Annie looked down and kicked a pebble, then took Rose's hand. 'Lunch is ready.'

Rose went willingly, happy to be back with her family. It was a start.

Her father was delighted to see her and kissed her cheek when she arrived. She didn't waste any time. 'I'm sorry I was so rude to you at Christmas. It was unforgivable of me.'

'It was only what I expected – but I didn't want everything the Greshams have worked for to go to the government just because there isn't anyone to inherit.'

'You could have left it to any number of worthy causes,' she protested.

He swept a hand around the room. 'All this has been in Gresham hands for generations and I want it to remain that way. You are my daughter, but if you don't want it then it's only right that your children should inherit the estate.'

'You realize there might not be any children. Bill has left me.'

He patted her arm. 'Everything will turn out all right.'

'Don't patronize me.' She snorted, irritation rising in

spite of all her good intentions. 'If Bill divorces me, I'll never marry again.'

'I'm sure it won't come to that. Now, tell me truthfully, do you want him back?'

'Yes, but he isn't coming. He's had enough of me.' Rose dropped her head in a defeated gesture.

Sir George studied her thoughtfully. 'Lost your fire, have you?'

'Of course not,' she replied indignantly.

'Then stop feeling sorry for yourself and do something about it. Go and face him, or are you afraid to admit you were wrong?'

'I *was* wrong,' she shouted, 'and if I could find the bloody man, I'd tell him so.' She stopped when she realized they were facing each other like a couple of prize-fighters again, and he was grinning.

'What's so funny?' she demanded, glaring at him.

'That's more like my daughter, spitting fire.' He chuckled. 'I was worried for a moment.'

A smile tugged at the corners of her mouth. 'You're impossible, do you know that?'

His grin got broader. 'So are you.'

'Hmm. I must have inherited it from someone.'

They both roared with laughter.

'That's better,' her father remarked. 'Now go and tell that man of yours that you're sorry and miss him dreadfully.'

'There's a lawyer here to see you, Mr Freeman.'

'Oh.' Bill looked up from the report he was studying. 'Who is it?'

'Miss Webster, sir. She says it's urgent.'

438

He pulled his watch out of his pocket and flipped it open, more to give himself a chance to decide what to do than to check the time. What had brought her here? And why was she using her maiden name?

'Sir?' The secretary looked anxious. 'She was most insistent.'

'I have a meeting in ten minutes. Would you ask her to leave a message?' He smiled at the young woman who was looking rather apprehensive. 'She won't bite.'

She gave a nervous laugh. 'I'm not so sure. I've heard about her.'

He stood up. 'Where is she?'

'Downstairs, sir.'

When he got to Reception Rose had her back to him and was pacing up and down by the window. 'What can I do for you, Miss Webster?' he asked formally.

She spun round, and he was shocked to see how much weight she had lost. There were deep shadows under her eyes, and she looked . . . lost. He didn't know how else to describe it.

'What do you want, Rose?'

She glanced anxiously at the people coming and going. 'Can we go somewhere private?'

'I've only got five minutes. This will have to do.' God, he hated doing this to her, but he had set out on a course of action and he had to see it through. He knew he only had to hold on for a little longer and then it would be over, one way or the other.

'Very well.' Rose straightened up. 'I want to apologize. I know all those things I said to you are not true. I was angry and lashed out at the person nearest to me. You've never done anything to deserve being treated like that.

I deeply regret my unreasonable behaviour and I am thoroughly ashamed of myself. If you want to divorce me, I shall understand.'

Then she turned and strode out of the building.

He watched her hurry out with her head bowed. That worried him. He'd never seen her like that: her carriage was always proud and straight. And had that been a glimmer of tears he had seen as she'd walked away from him?

It took all of his self-control not to run after her.

'What a beautiful woman,' James, the firm's manager, remarked, gazing after the retreating figure of Rose. 'She looks familiar, who is she?'

'My wife.'

'Of course,' James exclaimed. 'I'd heard you were married to Sir George Gresham's ill – er, daughter. She's the image of him.'

Bill gave him an amused sideways glance. 'Illegitimate. You can say the word. She isn't ashamed of it, neither am I, and her father loves her. Though you'd never believe it if you saw them together – they fight as soon as they see each other.'

James chuckled. 'I can imagine, especially if she's inherited his fiery temper.'

'She has.'

'Good heavens, Bill, how do you manage her?'

'With difficulty,' he said drily. 'Now, is there any news about that contract we're interested in?'

'Yes. They've increased the area and there will now be room for forty houses.'

'When did this happen?'

'I got word yesterday when I had lunch with the minister in charge of the project.'

'When do they intend to start?'

'In two months.'

Bill tipped back his head and grinned at the ceiling, feeling rejuvenated. 'I want us to get that contract. What are the chances?'

'Nothing's confirmed but I believe it's as good as ours,' James assured him.

Bill took the stairs two at a time in elation.

Forty houses! These were going to be built for Rose.

41

April 1926

Rose massaged her temple as another headache threatened. She had had several since Bill left her four months ago. Was it really only that long? she thought, as the pain intensified. It seemed like a lifetime. She had filled every hour with work in an effort to get through the empty days, and at night she tossed restlessly until the bedclothes were in a tangle. Every time she won a case or made a dent in some injustice, the usual satisfaction wasn't there, and outside work she had nothing.

Rose needed to feel close to Bill, so she left the office and headed for their home.

An hour later she stepped through the door. His presence permeated every room in the house he had designed and built for them. It was all she had left of him now. The last few months had been agony: she had hoped all the time that Bill would come back to her, but he hadn't. She knew now that he never would and she felt like crying in despair every time she thought about life without him – without his love.

She walked into the drawing room and ran her hands over the back of his favourite chair, remembering the way he used to sit there reading or talking and laughing about something. Then she picked up the framed photograph of them after their wedding. As she looked at his smiling face, she started to cry. Great broken-hearted sobs racked her body. She'd had everything, but by her thoughtless, arrogant conduct she had lost it all. What a bloody fool.

'Rose.' Her mother had come in behind her. 'What's the matter?'

She put the photograph back on the shelf and blew her nose, but the tears wouldn't stop coming.

'Let's make you a nice cup of tea.' Her mother led her gently into the kitchen.

Rose knew there wasn't any cure for her distress: she was going to have to live with it for the rest of her life. Bill was the only man she'd ever loved, and there would never be another. She loved John, Harold and Josh, of course, as well as her family, but that was another kind of love. What she felt for Bill was different, the love of a woman for a man, and she'd thrown it away.

The tears flooded down her cheeks as she remembered the happy times they'd shared. The dances, the art galleries, the trips to Richmond Park, the laughter and his sense of humour . . .

'Want to talk about it?' her mother asked gently.

Rose shook her head. 'I can't. I need to be alone, Mum.'

'I understand.' Marj stood up. 'You staying?'

'No, I'm in court this afternoon.'

'Can't you cancel it?'

'I'm afraid not. If a case is scheduled for a certain time you have to be there.'

'Try to have a rest before you go back.' Her mother squeezed her shoulder and left.

Alone once more, Rose gazed into space. When she

recalled her visit to Bill, she moaned aloud. He had looked every inch the successful businessman, so strong and dependable. She had wanted to sink on to her knees and beg his forgiveness, but all she had managed was that stilted apology. He deserved better.

If only they'd had somewhere private to talk, she might have made a better job of it, but he'd only got five minutes, he'd said. That had hurt, but it had made her realize that that was exactly how she'd treated him. She'd never had enough time to be with him and talk properly.

He had loved her and she had taken from him, giving practically nothing in return. No man would put up with that indefinitely, not even one as patient and gentle as Bill. He had told her once that there was a limit to his patience, but she hadn't believed him – too wrapped up in her own activities to realize he was warning her. She had taken his love for granted, an unforgivable crime. She couldn't find a single thing to offer in her own defence.

Since that time she had gone about her business with determination, and never allowed herself to break down or let her feelings surface, but she couldn't do that any longer. She had lost him, and the realization was too terrible to bear. She started to sob again.

A hand clasped hers and she looked up to see Annie sitting beside her.

'Don't cry, Rosie. He still loves you.'

'I don't think so.' She blew her nose again and wiped her eyes. Normally, she wouldn't have let anyone see her like this, but she didn't care now. She'd had too much bloody pride all her life, and what was the good of that? 'Why aren't you at the shop?'

'Mum came and fetched me.'

'She shouldn't have done that. I'm all right.' Now she'd resorted to lying, Rose thought.

'It didn't matter, I'm leaving tomorrow, anyway,' Annie told her.

'Are you? What are you going to do? Are you going on to university?'

'No, I've got a job with a ladies' magazine.' She looked at her sister with concern. 'Do you want to be alone?'

Rose tried to smile. 'No, I'm glad you're here. Tell me about your new job.'

'Well, I expect I'll only be the tea-girl for a while, but they liked my drawings and said I wrote well.'

'That's wonderful, Annie.' This news lifted Rose's spirits.

'I'm really looking forward to starting.' Annie got up. 'Mum said you've got to go back this afternoon. Would you like me to get you something to eat?'

'I'm not hungry.'

'But you must eat,' Annie told her sternly. 'You don't look well.'

'All right. Just a sandwich or something.'

'We've got a pot of home-made soup at home. I'll go and get some for you.'

While Rose was waiting for her sister, she went into the bathroom and bathed her face with cold water. She was going to look a mess in court today, but she didn't care: the cry had done her good and seemed to have relieved some of her inner pressure. The deep sadness hadn't gone, of course, and she doubted that it ever would, but she felt more able to cope now. She had done her best to make peace with everyone she had offended, and that was all she could do.

'It's ready,' Annie called from the kitchen.

The soup was delicious. Rose hadn't realized how hungry she was, and her sister nodded approvingly as she polished off a second bowl.

They spent an hour talking about everyday things, and then, feeling much more herself, Rose picked up her bag to go back to work again.

Later that afternoon, Bill stood up, stretched, and turned to gaze thoughtfully out of the office window. The information he had been receiving from the family had told him that Rose was still driving herself. He picked up his coat and slipped it on. He didn't want to be on his own this evening: he would go and see Marj, Wally and the children. They were always pleased to see him and he hadn't been there for a few weeks.

When he arrived Annie met him. 'What's the matter?' he asked. It was unusual to see her anything but bubbly.

'Rose came home for a couple of hours today.'

He nodded, waiting for what she really wanted to say. 'Did she?'

Annie nodded. 'She was crying. I've never seen her cry like that before. In fact the only time I've ever seen her cry at all was after her first day in that awful tin factory.' She looked up at him. 'She promised me then that she'd never cry again, and I don't think she has until now.'

'I think everything's got too much for her,' Marj put in.

Bill felt as if he was being torn apart. Oh, God, he groaned inwardly, this was destroying them both, but he had had no choice. The course of action he'd embarked upon was distressing, but he couldn't see any other way. He wanted to rush straight to Rose, but he mustn't weaken now.

Marj poured him a cup of tea. 'Rose isn't an unkind person,' she said, 'but she's fought all her life and it's a habit with her now. She's always considered emotion a weakness, and it's hard for her to change. But if it hadn't been for her, I wouldn't have survived all those years in Garrett Street.'

'And I wouldn't be alive if she hadn't looked after me,' Annie told him.

'You don't have to remind me about how much she has done for you, I know she is strong, determined and kind,' Bill told them gently. 'But over the last couple of years the need to bring about change has taken her over. She has pushed aside everyone and everything else. She was impossible to live with, and my patience was finally exhausted. I did the only thing I could. We would have destroyed each other if I hadn't left,' he said softly.

'She's very unhappy,' Marj muttered.

'So am I, but one way or another this will soon be over, and we'll be able to get on with our lives.'

'I hope you're right.'

So did he! If he had misjudged her, he had caused them both a lot of suffering for nothing.

'Bill, what's going on?' Marj asked. 'What's Rose up to? And don't pretend you don't know because I'm sure you're keeping an eye on her.'

He toyed with the idea of telling her, but if Rose hadn't told her family, then he couldn't. They'd find out soon enough anyway.

Marj looked at him suspiciously. 'You've got the same look on your face as she has. You're both biding your time waiting for something to happen, aren't you? And don't try that innocent look with me, Bill Freeman, your eyes give you away.' She wagged a wooden spoon coated with flour at him. 'Rose may have lost her way for a while, but I know my daughter, and she'll come back fighting for what she wants – and that's you.'

He just sat there smiling and saw the moment when Marj finally realized what he'd been doing.

'That's what you've been banking on, isn't it?' There was a long pause. Then she shook her head. 'You've taken a terrible risk.'

'Bill came the other evening,' Annie told Rose, when she arrived for the weekend. 'I think he misses you. Why don't you go and see him again?'

'He wouldn't want to see me.' Rose sat down wearily.

'What's happened to you?' her mother demanded. 'I've *never* heard you admit defeat before. You've always fought for what you want.'

'I – '

'Don't make excuses. You're acting like a coward.'

'But he doesn't want me,' Rose protested.

'Then for heaven's sake *make* him want you.'

Her mother was right, Rose thought. She had never dodged a fight before. Why break the habit of a lifetime just because she was hurting more than she ever had?

'Just one more month,' she promised, her eyes flashing with determination. 'Then he won't know what's hit him.'

'That's more like it.' Marj looked at her speculatively.

'Er . . . why one more month? What's so special about that?'

Rose gave a tired smile. 'You'll see.'

42

Rose sat in the back office and rested her head in her hands. She was drained. One month had turned into two, with one delay after another, and she didn't know how much more she could take. It was the end of June and work should have started by now. Part of the plan had been put into operation, but the last part, the thing she most wanted, was still being resisted.

She gave a snort of disgust. The great reformer! How had she become conceited enough to think she could accomplish this? Who did she think she was?

'Rose!' Josh burst into the room just as a loud thud shook the building. 'They've started!'

Rose scrambled to her feet, shot through the door and ran the few yards to the top of Garrett Street. Then she ran past the workmen and the cheering groups of people, on and on, until she reached a rise in the ground where she would get a good view of the whole area. Gasping for breath, she turned and faced Garrett Street, derelict now as all the residents had been moved out a couple of months ago.

This was what she had worked so hard for and she wasn't going to miss a second of it. The racket was ear-splitting, but for once she didn't mind the noise as one wall came crashing down, then another and another. There was a shout from the workmen as rats ran for cover. Lord, how she and her mother had struggled to keep the vermin out of their house.

She stayed for ages, watching the army of men level each house. She had insisted on a huge workforce to get the job done quickly.

There was a crash as part of another house tumbled. It wasn't taking much to bring them down, she noted. They had probably been holding each other up, and when one prop was removed, the next building came down of its own accord.

Her thoughts drifted back to her childhood. All the pain, hardship, disappointment and struggle to survive were associated with this place.

Then, with a roar that shook the ground, the Websters' house collapsed in a cloud of dust.

'Bloody hell!' a man shouted. 'If these had been left much longer, they'd have come down on their own.'

Yes, Rose thought, killing the families packed into them. At least they were safe now, in their new council houses. As she looked at the piles of rubble, she felt the past drain out of her.

She had always believed that because she came from this dreadful place, all doors were closed to her unless she fought and struggled. But that hadn't been true. She remembered again the Bible verse, ' . . . behold, I have set before thee an open door, and no man can shut it: . . .'

Now she could understand what had happened. The door had never been closed, only pushed to, and the people she had met along the way had opened it with their love for her.

Her heart went out to Grace and John, who had helped

her continue with her studying. Then there was Harold: without his help she would never have gone to university. Josh had given her a job and become a firm friend. After a stormy start, her grandmother and father had given her love and understanding. And the day Bill had walked into her life had been the greatest blessing of all. He had swung the door wide open for her, but she had refused to walk through and leave her past behind.

She'd often wondered why she had married him, when she had always been adamant that she would never marry. She had capitulated so easily, and at the time it had been a mystery to her, but now she knew why: she loved him – always had – but she had been too blind and stubborn to recognize it.

There was another ear-splitting crash. Then, a quiet voice made her jump. 'Is it all over, Rose?'

It sounded like Bill, but was it?

She turned. He was standing just behind her, so tall and straight with the dust settling on the jacket of his dark business suit. He looked as weary as she felt, but she was faint with joy at the sight of him.

She wrapped her arms around him and let the tears of relief fall unchecked. 'Yes, it's all over.'

He held her close. 'Thank God!'

She reached up and kissed him. 'I love you.'

He smiled in his gentle way. 'I love you too. Can we go home now?'

'Yes, please. It's time we gave my father a grandson, don't you agree?'

'Not a moment to waste.'

Holding each other tightly, they walked through the rubble, but she no longer saw it.

She had stepped through the door and left Garrett Street at last.

AUTHOR'S NOTE

When the idea for this story came to me I knew I needed a strong character, someone with intelligence and determination. I thought immediately of my mother. She rarely spoke of her childhood, but I knew it had been tough. Born in London and the eldest of a large family, her mother had had great difficulty in feeding them and they were often hungry.

But my mother's hunger was not only for food. She had an insatiable appetite for knowledge. She was always in the public library and would bring home as many books as allowed. These would be devoured, returned, and her search would begin again for something she hadn't read, which would help her to understand what life was all about.

To the outside world she appeared tough, intolerant and hard, but anyone who knew her recognized this to be just a protective front. She could be hurt, upset, insecure and worried, just like anyone else, but was expert at hiding her feelings.

She was highly intelligent and loved school but, like Rose in this story, she was made to leave at eleven because they couldn't teach her any more. She won a copy of the Bible for coming top of the school and was given the opportunity to continue her education, but because of her circumstances it had not been possible. I know she regretted it all of her life.

Apart from that one incident, this is not the story of my mother's life, but of the fictional Rose Webster who has been endowed with my mother's strength, beauty, intelligence and forceful character.

My mother was not an easy person to know or understand, and it was only in the last few years of her life that I began to find out what she was really like. For the first time she started to talk to me about her life and her inner feelings, revealing a kind, caring woman. I am pleased to say that by the time she died at the age of ninety, we were friends.

My mother never did fulfil her full potential in life, but I made sure my fictional Rose did.

I hope you have laughed, cried, sympathized and even been exasperated with her at times. But I also hope you have found much to admire in her, and enjoyed following Rose's struggles as much as I have enjoyed writing about her.

B. M., 2002

The author's mother, 1923